She'd never been a big fan of cowboys, but this guy was seriously sexy.

His dark hair was mostly hidden by the hat, which shadowed his face, hiding the exact shade of the brown eyes currently locked on hers. He wore a crisp, blue T-shirt tucked into his jeans, filled to perfection by strong, muscled man.

Good gracious, he was gorgeous. And clearly not Tracy Jameson.

"Merry Atwater?" His voice matched his image perfectly, deep and smooth.

"That's me. Uh, where's Tracy?"

His lips curved in amusement. "Tracy Allan Jameson III, in the flesh. My granddaddy was Tracy, Dad calls himself Trace, I go by T.J."

She almost swallowed her tongue. "You're Tracy."

"Yes, ma'am, but please call me T.J."

Merry sucked in a breath. Summer camp had just gotten much hotter, in a completely new way.

ALSO BY RACHEL LACEY

Unleashed

FOR KEEPS

RACHEL LACEY

FOREVER

NEW YORK   BOSTON

Copyright © 2015 by Rachel Lacey
Excerpt from *Ever After* copyright © 2015 by Rachel Lacey

Forever
Hachette Book Group
1290 Avenue of the Americas
New York, NY 10104

www.HachetteBookGroup.com

Printed in the United States of America

First Edition: January 2015
10 9 8 7 6 5 4 3 2 1

OPM

Forever is an imprint of Grand Central Publishing.
The Forever name and logo are trademarks of Hachette Book Group, Inc.

The Hachette Speakers Bureau provides a wide range of authors for speaking events. To find out more, go to www.hachettespeakersbureau.com or call (866) 376-6591.

The publisher is not responsible for websites (or their content) that are not owned by the publisher.

To my own rescue boxer, Lacy.
You are one in a million.

ACKNOWLEDGMENTS

Huge thanks to my family for being so amazingly supportive. To my husband for always believing in me, and to my son, who proudly tells people that his mom writes books.

To my sister, Juliana, for being generally awesome, the best sister in the world, a wealth of knowledge on dog training and western riding, and also my most valuable beta reader. I can't imagine doing this without you.

To my agent, Sarah Younger, thank you for everything you do. You always have an answer to even the craziest question, and I am so happy to be a part of #TeamSarah. In short: you rock!

To my editor, Alex Logan, I am endlessly thankful for your help and guidance. And you get full credit for the title of this book, which I love! Many thanks to everyone else at Grand Central Publishing who lent their expertise and helped this book be the best it could be.

To my teacher and mentor, Lori Wilde, I can't put into words how much I appreciate everything you've done for me. You are an amazing teacher, author, and person, and I am so grateful to know you.

Thank you to my "critters," Annie Rains, Nancy LaPonzina, and Eleanor Tatum. Annie, when we put our heads together, magic happens! Thanks for helping me bring Merry and T.J. to life and for your invaluable critiques along the way.

Thank you to my #girlswritenight crew, Sidney Halston, Violet Henry, Tif Johnson, and Annie Rains. My writing nights are so much more fun, and productive, when you guys are around. Thank you for keeping me sane and giving me that extra push when I need it—love you guys!

Thank you to Will Goodwin and Violet Henry for answering my many medical questions, and to Violet for beta reading this manuscript for me. And thank you to Jennifer Oshnock for answering my questions about DSS and the process to become a foster parent.

Thank you to all the friends who've supported me along the way, and a special shout-out to the lovely ladies from Book Club aka "My book club can drink more than your book club." You ladies are the best!

And to my readers: thank you for taking a chance on me. I hope you enjoy reading my books as much as I love writing them. I am so grateful to you all!

FOR KEEPS

CHAPTER ONE

Merry Atwater was about to do something she hadn't done in almost a decade. She closed her eyes, clasped her hands together, and prayed. As in, to God. She had little faith the Big Guy was listening, but she was desperate.

When she opened her eyes, the numbers on the screen hadn't changed. Not that she expected God to alter Triangle Boxer Rescue's account balance, but He did perform miracles from time to time, didn't He? The truth was, the animal rescue she had poured her heart and soul into for the last six years was flat broke.

"What am I going to do?" She steepled her fingers and pressed them to her mouth.

Ralph, her six-year-old boxer, scooted closer on the couch. He plopped his head into her lap and gazed up at her with adoring brown eyes. Behind him, her foster puppies Chip and Salsa lay piled on top of each other. Collectively, they took up nearly the whole couch, but Merry didn't mind. She enjoyed having a couch full of happy dogs, especially knowing she had saved each one from an uncertain future at the shelter, guaranteeing them a happy ending through Triangle Boxer Rescue.

She'd founded TBR as a twenty-two-year-old fresh out of nursing school, eager to do more to help the dogs she'd come to love and depend on. Since then, she'd devoted as much of her time and hard-earned money as she could spare to saving abandoned and abused boxers in and around the small town of Dogwood, North Carolina.

She'd been successful too, at least at first. Several years ago, she'd begun receiving an anonymous donation of one thousand dollars a month from an unknown benefactor. She'd tried and failed to find out who was behind the mysterious donations, but at some point, she'd come to depend on them. Then six months ago, the donations had stopped. Now the rescue's bank account was drained, and she'd nearly maxed out her personal credit card trying to cover the difference.

She traced her fingers over the zigzag pattern on her pajama pants. It was nearly nine o'clock, and she was ready to call it a night. She had a twelve-hour shift ahead of her tomorrow and needed a good night's sleep.

A quiet knock sounded at her front door. Ralph lifted his head and let out a sleepy bark, while Chip and Salsa tumbled onto the floor in a tangle of puppy legs.

Merry sucked in a breath. Had God heard her prayer after all? Had someone arrived to miraculously bail Triangle Boxer Rescue out of financial ruin?

Not likely, but she'd always considered herself a glass-half-full kind of girl.

"Just a minute," she called as she herded the puppies behind the gate in the kitchen, then walked to the front door with Ralph at her side. She pressed her eye to the peephole, hesitant to open the door to an unexpected guest while in her pajamas.

A woman stood outside, dressed in a pink tank top and jean shorts. Wet tendrils of brown hair stuck to the sides of her face from the rain pouring beyond the safe shelter of Merry's porch. She looked vaguely familiar. A neighbor, maybe?

Merry pulled the door open. Ralph let out a powerful bark, eyes fixed on the bedraggled dog at the woman's side. It appeared to be some sort of Lab mix, with soggy amber fur and the kind of glazed eyes that Merry had seen too many times.

She gave Ralph a quick hand signal to keep him from greeting the unknown dog. He sat, tail wiggling against the hardwood floor.

"Hi," the woman said, extending a rain-drenched hand. "I'm Kelly Pointer. I live down the street." Kelly looked to the left, toward the cul-de-sac at the other end of the road.

Right. Merry had seen her before when she was out walking her dogs. She took Kelly's hand and shook. "Sure. Hi, Kelly. What can I do for you?"

"Well, I heard you rescue dogs." Kelly gestured to the dog at her feet. It stood, hunched, looking pathetic and miserable, and a heavy feeling settled in Merry's gut.

God hadn't sent an answer to her prayers. Instead, He'd added to her burden.

"Yes," she answered carefully. "I'm the director of Triangle Boxer Rescue."

She glanced pointedly at Ralph, still sitting politely at her side. He cocked his chestnut head, gazing up at their visitor with warm chocolate eyes that had melted many a heart.

"Well," Kelly said, "I found this stray. She's been wandering the neighborhood, and I was afraid she'd get hit by a car. I was hoping you could take her."

Merry looked at the stray. The rain-soaked Lab mix avoided her gaze, looking like she'd dart off into the watery darkness if given half a chance. "Have you called the Dogwood Shelter to see if anyone's looking for her?"

"Uh, no, I just brought her to you. I was hoping you could take her." Her neighbor extended a thin piece of white rope that had been fashioned into a makeshift collar and leash.

"Well, I don't exactly—" Merry gripped the rope, looking down at the pathetic dog on her front porch. This wasn't the first time someone had brought her a random dog, expecting her to take it because she worked in animal rescue, and it wouldn't be the last.

She'd always felt it a bit rude and presumptuous. It wasn't as if Kelly didn't have a home of her own where the dog could stay, warm and dry. Merry would have been happy to help her find the stray a home. But nope, she was apparently the designated receptacle for all unwanted dogs in the area, like it or not.

"Good luck with her. She seems sweet." Kelly tucked her hands into her pockets and turned to go.

"Thanks, but I'll probably have to bring her to the shelter in the morning."

Kelly's eyes rounded. "What? I thought maybe you could keep her, or something."

"I run a rescue, for boxers. This is not a boxer. I already have two fosters and a dog of my own. I really can't keep her." Merry said the words. She meant them too. Then she glanced down at the dog huddled on her front porch, and she knew she'd never follow through.

Kelly shrugged. "Well, that sucks. I hope she finds a home."

And with that, she walked off into the rainy night.

Merry looked at the dog who, for tonight at least, was hers. "So you're spending the night with us, huh?" The soggy Lab mix stared at the floor of Merry's porch, tail tucked between her legs. She reeked like wet, dirty dog.

Merry tied the rope around the railing. "Just a minute. I'll be right back, okay?"

She stepped inside and put Ralph behind the gate in the kitchen with her two nosy foster puppies. She couldn't introduce the new dog tonight, knowing nothing about her, and besides, she wasn't keeping her long enough for it to matter.

She'd have her scanned for a microchip, call the local shelters, and if all else failed, she'd look for another rescue to take her, because Merry couldn't keep her. She never kept more than three.

And in case God had forgotten, Merry was broke. She'd learned a long time ago that she couldn't save them all. It was a bitter lesson to swallow, but true, and important to remember, lest she drown in guilt over the ones who couldn't be saved.

She returned to the porch with a towel and gently rubbed as much rainwater as she could from the soggy stray. "Ready to come inside?"

The dog planted her feet, unwilling to enter the house. Merry shrugged, unfazed. She sat on the top step, staring out into the rainy June night, still warm and muggy despite the hour.

"Life's been pretty crappy to you lately, huh?" she said softly. "I know what that feels like. It's going to get better though. At least you have a dry bed waiting for you tonight, right?"

She kept talking, watching the rain fall beyond the protection of her front porch. Finally, the stray took a hesitant step toward her.

Merry reached out and stroked her chest, telling her what a good girl she was, patiently earning her trust. After a while, she stood and gave the rope a gentle tug. The dog followed her into the house.

The boxers in the kitchen barked and pranced, eager to make acquaintance with their visitor. Not yet. The dog at her side was tense, defensive. Terrified.

Merry sat with her while she adjusted to being in the house. She gave her food and water and took her outside to potty. Then she led the still-frightened stray to the crate she kept in the den for new dogs just getting settled.

It would do. For tonight.

* * *

T. J. Jameson leaned a hip against the counter and watched the pretty brunette's frown deepen. From the looks of it, his buddy David Johnson had just declined her credit card. David owned Dogwood Animal Hospital. T.J., on his way home after checking on a colicky horse out in Creedmoor, had stopped by to see if his friend might have a recommendation to replace the dog trainer who'd just bailed on him.

The brunette tossed back a curly lock of hair and rummaged inside her purse. She was dressed for suburbia in fitted jean shorts, a purple blouse, and sparkly flip-flops, with a brown dog at her feet. T.J. pictured her in Wranglers and cowboy boots, and he liked that image a whole lot better. Dressed like that, he'd really have a hard time taking his eyes off her.

She glanced over, and their eyes met. Hers were a bottomless hazel that sparkled with trouble.

She turned back to David. "Try this one," she said, handing over a blue credit card.

David swiped it through his card reader. "You've been paying for a lot of foster dogs with your personal card lately."

She shrugged. "This one's not technically a foster. I'm just keeping her for a day or two, to see if anyone shows up to claim her."

Behind him, the door chimed. T.J. glanced over his shoulder to see a teenager in baggy jeans and a T-shirt emblazoned with "#AWESOME" enter the waiting room, busily texting on his cell phone. A brown and white dog walked at his side, some kind of mixed breed. It lunged toward the one the brunette held, barking and snarling, straining against the end of its leash.

"Knock it off," the teenager said, pulling the dog toward the other end of the waiting room.

T.J.'s skin prickled. Clearly, that animal was not a suitable pet. It was only a matter of time before it bit someone. He ran a hand over his throat, feeling for the scars that had long faded.

He looked back at the brunette. She'd moved her dog out of sight behind the reception desk and was signing her receipt.

"Thanks, Dr. Johnson. I'll see you next week for the puppies' next round of vaccinations." She started for the door with the brown dog at her heels.

The teenager's mutt lunged again, and this time its leash pulled free. It bounded across the lobby toward the brunette and her dog.

Vicious barking shattered the air, setting T.J.'s adrenaline pumping. The brunette froze, and the dog behind her cowered against her legs. Easy bait.

His stomach soured at the thought of her at the dog's mercy, her blood staining that pretty purple blouse as she tried to defend herself. No. No way.

"Hey!" T.J. lunged in front of the runaway dog.

It stopped and snarled at him, teeth bared. T.J. felt the hair on his arms stand on end. He raised his arms as if he were corralling a wayward calf and took a step toward the animal.

The dog pinned its ears and growled.

"Brutus, no!" The teenager grabbed the end of the leash and hauled the dog, still growling, into an open exam room.

T.J.'s heart thumped against his ribs. The scars on his

neck stung, a vicious memory of the night he'd almost gotten his throat ripped out. He still heard the snarling barks, felt the teeth crushing his throat, and his own warm blood flowing over his skin.

"Holy shit."

He turned his head to see the brunette staring at him, her hazel eyes wide. His hand was on her shoulder before he knew what he was doing. "Are you okay?"

She nodded. "You are *so* lucky you didn't get bit just now."

Yeah, he knew that, knew it better than most. He pulled back, tucking his thumbs through his belt loops. "Better me than you."

"He wasn't really after me, he was after my dog, but I was ready for him." She opened her right hand to reveal a small, black spray canister.

T.J.'s eyebrows lifted. "Mace?"

"Citronella spray. It's kind of like mace for dogs, except it doesn't hurt them." She slid the can into her purse. "FYI, next time you might not want to wave your arms around in an aggressive dog's face. It's asking for trouble, but… thanks. Most people wouldn't bother to try. You're our hero."

She gave him a sweet smile, then strode out the front door, brown dog trotting along at her side.

T.J. stared, then snapped his mouth shut, feeling more confused than heroic. He turned to David, who still stood behind the reception desk, flipping through paperwork. "Who was that?"

David waggled his bushy eyebrows with a smile. "Merry Atwater. She's a nurse, so at least she could have patched you up if you'd needed it."

T.J. grunted. Good to know. "That kid with the vicious dog is a client of yours?"

"His father is, but he's out of town. Brutus isn't all bad,

but the family refuses to have him neutered, and he gets a little territorial around other dogs."

"Brutus? The dog's name is Brutus? That should be a warning right there." T.J. had never had a dog, never planned on getting one, but if he did, he'd find a reputable breeder and choose a dog with champion bloodlines and a solid temperament. He'd never understood why people took in dogs like that one, dogs of unknown heritage, with obvious behavioral problems.

He'd seen what happened when dogs like that got loose. He'd seen livestock attacked by packs of prowling dogs. Hell, he'd come within an inch of losing his own life to a couple of stray mutts. Dogs like Brutus were a serious problem.

"Brutus might need to be muzzled in the lobby area," David said. "I'll have a talk with them about it. So what brings you out my way?"

"Hoping you might be able to help me out."

David headed for the back room, motioning for T.J. to follow. "Oh yeah, how's that?"

"That dog trainer I hired for the summer camp bailed on me." He was seriously pissed about it too. He'd spent months getting everything in place, and now, with only a week to go, he was back at square one.

"So let the kids spend more time working with the horses," his friend said with a shrug.

"I could, but dogs are an important part of the camp, for Noah especially." And the whole point of the camp was to help his nephew. Noah had been diagnosed a few years ago as a child with high-functioning autism. He was a smart kid, bright as a hundred-watt bulb, but he struggled to communicate with his peers, which had led to problems at school.

T.J.'s sister Amy was a single mom fighting to make ends meet. She wouldn't accept money from him, no matter how hard he tried to help. Instead, this year he'd decided to establish a summer camp on his farm to help kids like his nephew, using his horses for equine therapy and incorporating a local dog trainer who'd bring several trained therapy dogs to work with the kids.

Noah communicated with dogs on a level he struggled to achieve with members of his own species. The camp absolutely couldn't happen without dogs.

"Well, here's an idea." David reached into a wire crate to check the IV port on a chocolate-colored cocker spaniel. "Merry Atwater, the lady who just left? She runs a boxer rescue, and I happen to remember one of her dogs is a certified therapy dog. Maybe she could help you out."

"Really?" T.J. thought back on the pretty brunette. He couldn't quite picture her getting her perfectly manicured hands dirty out on his farm.

David nodded. "She's good people. And between you and me, her rescue's in some financial trouble right now. If you offered her a donation in return for her help, I'm sure she'd be more than happy to be part of your camp."

"I don't know. She didn't really look like the farm type to me." The last thing he needed was some girly-girl running around on his farm, complaining about getting her expensive shoes dirty or breaking a fingernail.

But camp started next week, and at the moment, he had no other leads.

"She's tougher than she looks." David led the way back to the waiting room, where he pulled a business card from a pile in a drawer behind the reception desk. "Give her a call. See what she says."

* * *

Merry pursed her lips and tried to ignore the dog sulking in the crate at the far end of the kitchen. She'd called every shelter in the area to report her found, but so far, no owner had come forward. From the looks of her, the mutt probably hadn't had an owner in some time. Her fur was matted with burs and mud, her nails untrimmed, ribs protruding beneath her thick coat.

Merry couldn't bring herself to take her to the shelter, but she couldn't keep her either. She wasn't a boxer, for one thing. Not to mention, her tiny house was already at capacity with Ralph, Chip, and Salsa. And she was broke.

Couldn't forget that part.

Which led her back to the email on her screen. A woman named Tracy Jameson had emailed her, said she'd gotten Merry's name from her vet, David Johnson. She was looking for someone to help out with canine-assisted therapy at a summer camp she was running for local kids. In exchange, she'd write a check for a thousand dollars to Triangle Boxer Rescue.

Tempting. Very tempting.

Ralph was a therapy dog. Merry took him in once a week to visit the kids on the pediatric floor of Dogwood Hospital. He'd be great for the summer camp.

In fact, he'd love it a lot more than she would. To Merry, summer camp sounded dirty, sweaty, and exhausting. And while she did have some vacation time saved up at the hospital, she'd planned to spend it fund-raising for Triangle Boxer Rescue, not wilting in the summer heat on this woman's farm.

Still, a thousand dollars sounded pretty irresistible right now.

First things first, she had to figure out what to do with the stray dog in her kitchen. Merry approached the crate and eyed the nameless, hopeless dog. "So, I was thinking about putting up some flyers around the neighborhood. Want to come with me?"

The dog looked up, her brown eyes so sad, so empty, that Merry's heart broke. No matter what, this dog couldn't go to the shelter. She wouldn't last a week.

Merry opened the crate and coaxed the frightened dog out. She reached into the cabinet and pulled out a bag of training treats, then sat on the floor and praised and rewarded her for every shy wag of her tail.

Once No-Name had received a much-needed boost to her self-esteem, Merry clipped a leash onto her collar. She grabbed the pile of flyers she'd printed earlier, along with a stapler, and she was ready to go.

"You need a name," Merry told her. She named new fosters all the time, and yet, she couldn't bring herself to name this one.

The dog stood patiently beside her while she stapled flyers to lampposts up and down her street and around the neighborhood. It wasn't likely, but it was possible there was a family out there somewhere, looking for her and wanting her back.

No-Name stared straight ahead as they walked, making no eye contact with Merry, showing no emotion at all. Her tail hung limply behind her, which was a step up from tucked between her legs, but no amount of sweet talk from Merry could get it to wag again.

A high-pitched shriek was their only warning before a toddler barreled onto the sidewalk, arms outstretched. "Doggy! Doggy!"

Merry tightened her grip on No-Name's leash and tried to put herself between the dog and the runaway child, but it was too late. The little girl flung her arms around No-Name's neck with a squeal of glee.

"Violet!" A woman ran down the driveway after the wayward child. "Oh, my gosh."

Merry tensed, ready to intervene if necessary, but No-Name's tail wagged steadily. She looked calm. Happy even.

"Thank goodness your dog likes kids," the girl's mother said.

That was an understatement. Merry wouldn't have intentionally introduced such a new dog to anyone's child just yet, but now that it had happened, No-Name did indeed seem thrilled.

The little girl patted her roughly on the head, then ran off toward a pink tricycle outside the garage. Her mom waved and followed her up the driveway. No-Name gazed after the toddler, tail still wagging.

Merry hustled her home. As they walked in the front door, her cell phone rang. She glanced at the display. "Hey, Liv."

"Hi," Olivia said. "I got your message, and no, I can't take another dog right now. I nearly got evicted from my apartment when I was fostering those damn puppies."

"Oh, come on, please? This one's full grown. She's housebroken, and I haven't even heard her bark. She'd be easy."

"Nope, sorry." Olivia Bennett had never formally agreed to foster for Triangle Boxer Rescue. She was a friend of Cara Medlen, who'd moved to Massachusetts a few months ago, leaving Merry short a good foster home and a best friend, both of which roles Olivia had temporarily stepped in to fill.

"Know anyone looking for a dog? She's some kind of Lab mix, very shy, but well behaved."

"I'll ask around, but offhand... no."

"Okay, well, thanks anyway." Merry led the dog back into her kitchen. Since she'd received a clean bill of health at the vet, Merry had allowed her to make introductions with Ralph this morning, and it had gone well. No-Name had tucked her tail and bowed her head submissively when Ralph greeted her. It was a good start, but she wasn't ready to throw her somewhat less predictable foster puppies into the mix just yet.

Currently, they were asleep upstairs in her bedroom. If

No-Name stayed much longer, she'd think about introducing them all, but hopefully she'd be passing her along before that became necessary.

She opened her laptop to see if any of the Lab or all-breed rescues had responded. They hadn't, but the email from Tracy Jameson still waited in her in-box.

She didn't want to get involved in a summer camp, but maybe...

Maybe she could make it work to her advantage. She sent Tracy a quick reply, asking to meet with her to discuss things further, then closed her laptop to start preparing dinner for herself and the dogs.

The next day, she worked her usual twelve-hour shift at Dogwood Hospital. Exhausted, she grabbed a Cajun filet biscuit from the Bojangles drive-through and headed for Tracy's farm.

Like many towns in the area, Dogwood had experienced a burst of growth in the past decade due to its proximity to the Research Triangle Park, where many large pharmaceutical and other high-tech companies were located. Modern neighborhoods gradually gave way to rolling country roads that hadn't changed in generations.

She drove down one of these country roads past the rusted-out shell of a barn, a cornfield, and several miles of open farmland. Merry rolled her window down and breathed in the fresh air. She loved to drive through the country, see the horses and cows, smell the wheat and fresh earth. Actually rolling up her sleeves and getting dirty didn't sound as appealing, but if it would help the rescue, she'd take one for the team.

Tracy's farm was at the end of the road, a modest two-story, brick-front ranch house. Tracy had texted her a few minutes ago to say she was running late, so Merry pulled past the house and parked by the barn to finish her chicken biscuit. It melted in her mouth in buttery perfection. She washed it down with sweet tea and a sigh of contentment.

Behind the barn, two horses grazed in a lush green field, while a third lounged nearby beneath a shade tree. Merry's knowledge of horses was pretty much confined to the pages of *Black Beauty* (which had earned her a childhood nickname of Merrylegs), but these were obviously well cared for and absolutely gorgeous. Their brown coats glistened in the setting sun over sleek, well-muscled haunches.

She leaned back in her seat and settled in to watch them. The larger horse, a male, swooshed his tail to and fro, fly swatting for himself and the female beside him. Equine chivalry. Aww.

A few minutes later, a black Ford F350 pickup truck pulled into the driveway with a roar of its diesel engine and parked next to Merry's CR-V. She looked up, impressed. That was a badass truck for a chick.

Merry stepped out of her SUV, making sure she wasn't wearing any crumbs on her scrubs, and rounded the rear bumper just as the driver's door opened on the truck.

She saw the cowboy boots first, brown-stitched leather at least a man's size twelve. Her gaze traveled up a pair of jeans filled out by very muscular, very masculine legs. The man wearing them swung out of the cab and tipped his cowboy hat at her.

Well, well. It was her would-be hero from Dr. Johnson's office. What in the world was he doing here?

She'd never been a big fan of cowboys, but this guy was seriously sexy. His dark hair was mostly hidden by the hat, which shadowed his face, hiding the exact shade of the brown eyes currently locked on hers. He wore a crisp, blue T-shirt tucked into his jeans, filled to perfection by strong, muscled man.

He looked like he belonged on the cover of a magazine

for western wear. Good gracious, he was gorgeous. And clearly not Tracy Jameson.

"Merry Atwater?" His voice matched his image perfectly, deep and smooth.

"That's me. And you are?"

He extended a hand. "T. J. Jameson. Thanks for driving all the way out here. I figured you'd like to see the place before you made up your mind."

She took his hand and shook. "Uh, where's Tracy?"

His lips curved in amusement. "Tracy Allan Jameson III, in the flesh. My granddaddy was Tracy, Dad calls himself Trace, I go by T.J."

She almost swallowed her tongue. "You're Tracy."

"Yes, ma'am, but please call me T.J."

Merry sucked in a breath. So Tracy Jameson was a guy. And not just any guy, but a strappingly handsome cowboy oozing testosterone from every pore.

Summer camp had just gotten much hotter, in a completely new way.

CHAPTER TWO

T.J. rested his elbows on the top rung of the fence and gazed at his horses. He pointed to the handsome sorrel by the gate. "That's Tango, and the bay mare next to him is Twilight. They were both born and raised on my parents' farm. The palomino in back is Peaches. My nephew rides her."

He watched Merry for her reaction. His horses came from some of the finest stock in North Carolina. They were exquisite creatures, and if she was going to work here with him for the next month, he needed her to respect that. Her curly brown hair stirred with the breeze as she eyed Tango and Twilight. She wasn't dressed to impress today, in pink scrubs decorated with brightly colored unicorns and regulation rubber-soled shoes, but somehow she still managed to look classy.

"They're beautiful," she said.

So was she. He didn't go for the girly type, but he could admire a pretty lady. Merry's scrubs hid a delicate, yet curvy, frame, if the jean shorts she'd worn the other day were any indication. But her eyes really captured him, wide pools swimming with green and gold flecks, so warm, so full of life and emotion, that he lost his train of thought every time he looked into their hazel depths.

"You work with horses for a living?" she asked.

"I'm a large animal vet. I work with horses, cows, goats, all kinds of livestock."

"Well, I know nothing about livestock, but your horses are gorgeous."

"You ride?"

She sucked her bottom lip between her teeth and shook her head. "No. So what do you plan to do with them, for the kids? And where do I fit in?"

"A buddy of mine does some work with equine therapy, having the kids interact with the horses, guide them, ride them. Great for self-confidence and motor skills. We want them to leave their troubles at home for a few hours a day."

"So these are kids with developmental problems? Or physical disabilities?"

"A little of each. I've got four kids signed up. My eight-year-old nephew, Noah. He's autistic. We've got a boy with sensory processing disorder, a girl with cerebral palsy, and one with Down syndrome. They're all second and third graders."

"That's wonderful, and I'm guessing your nephew is the reason you're doing it. But it sounds like you've got your equine therapy camp. Why me? Why dogs?"

"Well, I only have two horses, for one." He looked out at the pasture. "Tango there's too feisty for the kids. That leaves Twilight and Peaches. But the dogs are a crucial part of the camp, for Noah especially. I've seen him come out of his shell with dogs the way he doesn't with people, or even horses."

She nodded. "Okay, I'll bite. You said you were interested in therapy dogs. I have one, Ralph, he's a six-year-old boxer. Absolutely fantastic. I take him to Dogwood Hospital with me once a week to work with the kids there."

"And you're certified in canine therapy?"

"I'm certified as Ralph's handler. I also run an animal rescue, and what I'd like to do is put together a group of foster dogs that are trustworthy with kids and let the kids help train them. Each child gets his or her own dog to train, teach basic obedience, bond with, and help get their dog ready for adoption."

T.J. shook his head. "That's not really what I had in mind. You mean, put the kids with shelter dogs?"

Merry raised her chin. "Shelter dogs that have been admitted into my rescue and passed a full behavioral assessment to make sure they're safe to work with kids. They'd be supervised by me at all times."

"I don't think..."

She cut him off. "I have two in my own home that would be perfect. They're five-month-old puppies, harmless but in need of plenty of obedience training. I have a couple of other dogs in mind too that might be great for the program. Ideally, you could foster one or two of them for me here at your farm during camp."

"What?" Somehow this conversation had run completely off course.

"You're asking me for a big-time commitment. I'll have to take time off from my job at the hospital. Surely you can help me out in return? It would be great if you could increase your donation to Triangle Boxer Rescue too."

"Whoa." He held his hands out in front of him. "I think we've got ourselves a misunderstanding. I'm looking for therapy dogs, not shelter dogs. And I don't have any kennels here to keep them."

She drummed her fingers against the fence and gazed at his horses. "I could get you crates, if you need them. The rescue pays for all medical care. You just provide food and water."

"Crates? You just put them in one of those wire cages in the backyard?"

Her nostrils flared. "Of course not. The dogs stay in your house. The crates are a training tool."

"In my house?" T.J. lifted his hat to run a hand through his hair. He'd grown up around dogs. They'd roamed the farm, been spoiled with scraps from the dinner table, and they'd slept in kennels behind the house. Dogs did not come inside.

And this conversation had gotten out of hand. He wasn't keeping Merry's shelter dogs for her, in or out of his house. The incident in David's waiting room yesterday had proven yet again how unpredictable that type of dog could be.

"Look, I'm not interested in keeping dogs here. And I'm really looking for a couple of therapy dogs to work with the kids, not shelter dogs. If you know someone who has another certified therapy dog that could come with you and Ralph, that would be perfect."

She crossed her arms over her chest. "Sorry, but one is all I've got."

They stared at each other for a beat of silence.

"Well, I appreciate you taking the time to come out here, but I think I'll keep looking and see if I can't find someone better suited for the camp."

She raised those hazel eyes to his, now flashing with anger. "You do that. Good luck with your summer camp."

And with that, she stalked off to her car, leaving him standing in a cloud of her dust.

* * *

Merry felt the steam pouring out of her ears. What an arrogant asshole. She'd liked Tracy Jameson a whole lot better when he'd been a girl. The nerve, turning his nose up at her foster dogs like she'd suggested his camp kids serve as bait in a dogfighting ring instead of sitting around petting a bunch of certified therapy dogs. Jerk. And she'd really needed his money too. Not to mention, she'd been counting on him to foster one of the camp dogs for her, freeing up a spot for No-Name in one of her other foster homes.

She punched the steering wheel and cranked the radio, tuned to her favorite Top Forty radio station. No country music in her car, thank you very much.

She fumed all the way to her little house at the end of Peachtree Lane. She'd given up the last precious hour of daylight with her dogs for that jerk. On the days she worked, she paid her neighbor's teenage daughter to let the dogs out for her, so at least they hadn't suffered for her wasted trip to T.J.'s farm.

Now she trudged into the house, exhausted and fired up at the same time. Ralph, Chip, and Salsa waited in the kitchen, squealing and dancing with glee. Their toenails clicked across the linoleum in a hectic tap dance until she sank down in their midst and let them cover her with slobbery kisses. When they'd finished, she put them out back, then went into the den where No-Name lay quietly in her crate.

She looked up at Merry with those heartbreakingly sad eyes. Her tail gave one shy thump against the bottom of the crate as Merry unlatched the door and let her out. "You're just pathetic, you know that?"

No-Name settled on the floor next to Merry with a bone-weary sigh.

"I thought I'd figured out a way to get you into a quieter foster home, but it didn't work out." She stroked her fingers through the dog's soft fur. "Since you're still here, it's time to make introductions, okay?"

No-Name and Ralph had met yesterday with no problems. Ralph was calm and well socialized and had always welcomed new fosters into the home. Chip and Salsa were too young to get territorial. They'd think No-Name was their new best friend.

No-Name herself was the wild card. She hadn't shown any aggression, but she was very antisocial and could easily become overwhelmed being introduced to three dogs at once, especially when two of them were hyperactive puppies.

Merry started by putting her on leash and taking her for a walk around the neighborhood. She gave the dog a chance to stretch her legs, relieve herself, and walk off as much tension as possible.

When they got back home, she fetched the other dogs from the backyard and put the baby gate across the doorway from the kitchen. Merry dropped the leash, but kept it clipped to No-Name's collar in case she needed to regain control quickly.

No-Name lifted her head and stared at the three faces on the other side of the gate. Chip and Salsa bounced against the gate in unbridled excitement. Ralph stood behind them, his nub wagging rapidly, ears pricked with friendly interest.

No-Name walked up and sniffed noses with Chip. Then Salsa pushed in, her brindle face smooshed against No-Name's shoulder. They postured and sniffed, reaching noses over the gate to check each other out. No-Name tucked her tail between her legs but made polite introductions.

Merry sat nearby, watching. This was good. She'd kept dogs separated in the past when she had two who didn't get along, playing musical crates, alternating who got to be out in the house, but this was much better. This gave her more time to find someone to take No-Name.

She left the gate up for a bit while the puppies calmed down. While they greeted, she pulled out her cell phone and sent a text message to her best friend. *Miss you. When are you coming for a visit?*

Cara texted right back. *Next month. Girl's night at Red Heels?*

Merry smiled. Many a night had been toasted by martinis at Red Heels. *I'm counting the days. You staying with me?*

That would be great. Thx.

I'll save a few foster dogs for you to take home, Merry typed.

Ha! Matt would kill me. I've already got three, plus Casper and Sadie.

Merry blew out a breath. Damn, she missed Cara.

She watched No-Name sniff Salsa's butt, then thumbed through her emails. Linda had sent a request to get her foster dog neutered. Trista's foster needed more heartworm medication. John's was still awaiting surgery to repair a torn ligament in his knee.

And the rescue's bank account had a whopping five dollars in it.

That was a problem. Not only did she need more funds for them and for future dogs, but also she hadn't exactly shared with Cara what a mess she was in, so she wanted to have it fixed before her visit next month. Merry had created Triangle Boxer Rescue, nurtured it, and watched it grow. Right now, her beloved rescue needed CPR, stat.

This was more than a financial crisis. If TBR went under, it would be a personal failure for Merry, the loss of the one thing in life she'd really gotten right. The prospect was both horrifying and humiliating. And the impact for the dogs would be even worse. For them, this was a matter of life and death.

With one eye still on the dogs, Merry scooted to the dining room table and opened her laptop. She sent emails to all her contacts at local pet stores and boutiques, inquiring about setting up fund-raising events. They always led to a few new adoption applications and modest donations. Plus they were fun.

A friend of hers with a local German Shepherd rescue had mentioned recent success with Facebook. Merry logged in to the page she'd created for Triangle Boxer Rescue. A hundred and thirty-two people had liked the page. That was a lot, wasn't it? Merry rarely found time to use social media, for herself or her rescue. She'd set up the page last year and done practically nothing with it.

What should she post?

After drumming her fingers against the keyboard for a solid minute, she attached a photo of Jake, the dog needing ACL surgery. She wrote, *Jake needs surgery to repair a torn ACL in his right rear leg. This is a painful injury and needs to be repaired before he goes on to his forever home. We need to raise $600 to pay for the surgery. Please visit our website and make a donation so that Jake can run again!*

She hit post, then sat back with a smile. Out of a hundred and thirty-two people, surely five or ten of them would be feeling generous.

Five minutes later, she got an email notification from Paypal that a donation had been received. "Yes!" She fist pumped the air.

The donation had come from Cara.

Merry scowled. Not that she didn't appreciate her friend's money—because she was grateful for every penny received—but Cara had given plenty to the rescue already. She needed fresh blood, a new source of funds to replace what she'd lost when her anonymous benefactor quit holding TBR's head above water.

Oh well. It had only been five minutes, after all.

So maybe she'd never had to figure out how to raise enough money on her own, with that anonymous money coming in every month. It didn't mean she couldn't learn now. She could do it. She had to.

The dogs had settled down. No-Name left the gate and curled up in the den by her crate. Merry decided to let her rest for now.

Merry had to work tomorrow, but then she was off for four days, and she'd get the dogs fully integrated while she was at home.

And, dammit, No-Name needed a name.

* * *

Merry arrived at Dogwood Hospital the next morning and rode the elevator to the third floor, the pediatric floor, where she'd spend the next twelve hours. She deposited her purse in her locker, then headed to the shift change debriefing led by the night shift charge nurse.

Luckily, it had been a quiet night, and the meeting was quick.

At the nurses' station, she scanned the board for her assignments. Charlene was the outgoing nurse on three of Merry's patients, which was lucky because she was a damn good nurse and meticulous with her notes.

Merry spied her halfway down the hall and hurried after her. "Morning, Charlene."

"Good morning." The other nurse smiled. "Who've you got?"

"Three-oh-five, three-oh-eight, and three-ten."

Charlene stilled, her hand extended toward the door to Room 305. "Brace yourself. Three-ten is a one-week-old with neonatal abstinence syndrome. He was admitted last night."

Merry felt a wave of cold wash over her skin. The babies got to her, every time. And the ones with drug withdrawals made her want to punch something, preferably the mother. "How bad?"

"Heroin withdrawal. Poor thing screamed most of the night. Mom's a junkie serving time for shoplifting. Social Services is overseeing the case."

Merry swallowed hard, then followed Charlene into Room 305.

Inside, four-year-old Tori slept peacefully, her face smooshed against a stuffed puppy wearing a pink tutu. From the recliner beside the bed, her mom gave Charlene and Merry a weary smile.

"Morning, Alice," Merry whispered.

Charlene briefed them on Tori's progress. A nasty stomach virus had landed her in the hospital with severe dehydration the night before last. She was scheduled to have her IV removed on Merry's next round, and if she continued taking fluids on her own, she should be discharged after lunch.

Doing her best not to disturb her, Merry checked Tori's vitals and her IV insertion site, then entered everything into her online medical record. Apparently exhausted, the girl slept through it all, even having her blood pressure taken. Merry waved to Alice as she and Charlene headed for the door.

Next up was Peter in Room 308, a little boy recovering from surgery to set a broken arm. He was awake and watching cartoons. Merry chatted with him about baseball while she checked him out, then continued to Room 310.

The only sound inside was the rhythmic beeping of the pulse ox monitor taped to Baby Jayden's foot as it recorded each precious beat of his heart. Merry walked quietly to the crib.

"He's finally asleep," Charlene whispered from behind her. Her phone beeped a page from the nurses' station, and she stepped out of the room to avoid disturbing Jayden.

Air whooshed from Merry's lungs at the sight of him lying there, in this sterile hospital room, alone. He lay on his back, swaddled snugly and wearing a blue-striped hat, his cheeks flushed bright pink. His chest rose and fell with rapid breaths.

Unbidden, her mind flashed on another baby, swaddled in a similar blanket, his face ashen gray. The pain, as always, slammed into her like a battering ram, and she pressed a fist against her mouth to fight past it.

Not making a sound, she choked back the memory and checked Jayden's IV. As she watched, he scrunched his face and let out a high-pitched mewl. His lower lip shook. So tiny, so innocent. He should never have to know the pain of heroin withdrawal.

"Shhh." Merry stroked a finger over his cheek, and he nuzzled against it, rooting for his next meal. She pulled her MedLink phone from the front pocket of her scrubs and called Jessie, her aide, to give him his next bottle. She ached to pick him up, snuggle him tight, but she didn't.

She'd cared for many infants here, but hadn't allowed herself to snuggle them, to hold them against her chest and breathe in their sweet scent. Not once.

And anyway, duty called. Her fourth patient for the day, an eight-year-old with a concussion, would be arriving soon from the ER. An intake could take an hour, easily, maybe longer.

Jessie entered with a bottle and lifted the tiny newborn into her arms. Merry felt the pressure in her chest ease to see him held, cradled, nurtured.

Without allowing herself a second glance, she headed down the hall to prepare for the intake of Noah Walton. She pulled up his online record. Eight years old. Concussion. Autistic. Mother was Amy Jameson.

Merry's brow furrowed. T.J. had an eight-year-old autistic

nephew named Noah. She scrolled to Amy's emergency contacts. Sure enough, T. J. Jameson was listed.

What were the chances he'd visit his nephew today?

"Shit," she murmured, and pinched at the headache brewing between her eyebrows.

* * *

T.J.'s boots ate the scuffed linoleum of the pediatric floor of Dogwood Hospital as he strode toward Room 311. Noah had fallen on the playground at school, hit his head, and lost consciousness. He'd been rushed to the hospital by ambulance.

That had been two hours ago, and T.J. was no doubt the last to arrive. As much as he hated not being here earlier for his nephew, these things were unavoidable in his profession. He'd been assisting with a complicated calving when Amy called. The calf was breach, which wasn't an uncommon occurrence, but potentially fatal for both cow and calf without assistance. In the end, the calf was born healthy, and its mother suffered no injuries during birth, which was the best possible outcome.

T.J. pushed through the door, his chest compressing painfully at the sight of Noah in a hospital bed, eyes closed, his face so pale, and bare of the glasses he usually wore. Amy sat to his left, clutching his hand in hers, her eyes red and puffy. His parents were on the couch along the wall, talking quietly.

All heads swiveled his way as he walked to his nephew's bedside. "How is he?"

"He has a concussion," Amy said. "They say he'll be okay. They just want to monitor him for a day or so. They were afraid he wouldn't be able to tell us how he was feeling, in case there were any complications."

"What happened? Where were his teachers?" T.J. reached down and covered his nephew's small hand in his. Noah's dad had taken off years ago, as soon as his son had shown the first signs of autism. No-good piece of scum. T.J. had taken it upon himself to make sure Noah never lacked for his father's absence.

"They didn't see him fall. One of the other kids saw him lying on the ground."

T.J. rubbed his neck. "That doesn't make sense. He never climbs on the playground."

Amy nodded. "I know. Apparently he did today."

"He'll be okay. He's a strong boy." Trace Jameson came to stand by the bed, tall and solid in a white button-down shirt with a bolo tie, jeans, and boots, the leather molded to his feet from years of wear.

The door opened again, and the nurse who stepped inside fired T.J. up in all the wrong ways. Merry Atwater. Well, how was that for an unfortunate coincidence?

She glanced at him as she walked to Noah's bed, looking not at all surprised to see him, or perhaps she just hid it well. "T.J.," she said with a polite nod, then turned to Amy. "Any change?"

Amy shook her head. "You two know each other?"

"We met yesterday," Merry said. She moved efficiently, checking Noah's IV, his pulse, and his blood pressure.

Today her scrubs were blue with colorful balloons all over them. Noah loved balloons. He willed his nephew to open his eyes and see them.

"Do you have livestock?" Amy asked.

Merry glanced at her. "No, why?"

"Oh, well, T.J.'s a large animal vet. I assumed that was how you met."

"Actually we were talking about the summer camp he's organizing."

Amy's eyes brightened, and she opened her mouth to continue the conversation.

"So, how is Noah?" T.J. interrupted. "Has he been unconscious since the fall?"

Merry shook her head. "He's asleep, not unconscious. He became agitated by all the activity down in the ER and wore himself out. He fell asleep after he was moved here to pediatrics."

Those eyes. Though her tone remained polite and friendly, her big hazel eyes gave him the inexplicable urge to apologize for turning her down yesterday. But that was ridiculous, because he didn't owe her an apology.

He just needed to find someone who could provide therapy dogs for his camp.

"So are you going to be helping with T.J.'s camp?" Amy asked, undeterred.

"No," Merry answered. "I'll be back in a little while to check on Noah. Press the button if you need me before then, okay?"

Amy nodded, and Merry left the room.

Once she was gone, his sister gave him a funny look. "What was that about?"

"I had her out to the farm to talk about helping with the camp, but it didn't work out. I heard she has a therapy dog, but she runs an animal rescue. She wanted to bring some of her shelter dogs out and have the kids help train them."

"Oh," Amy said. "That sounds perfect, actually. So what happened?"

"I don't want the kids hanging around with a bunch of untrained mutts from the shelter." That was an accident waiting to happen, a risk he wasn't willing to take.

"She works with kids all day. I can't imagine she'd do anything to endanger them. I think Noah would really love helping to train a dog."

"Dog?" The small voice came from the bed, where Noah squinted at them through heavy-lidded eyes.

"Hey, Bud. How's your head?" T.J. leaned against the bed. The mattress sagged next to him as his mom sat, reaching for her grandson's hand.

Noah shrugged, his eyes focused on the sunny yellow wall behind them.

"Hurts, huh?"

The boy nodded. He picked at the blanket tucked around him. He wasn't much of a talker, especially when he was upset. T.J. could respect that. He wasn't one to waste words himself, although it worried him when Noah withdrew within himself and quit speaking altogether.

"You know, I got a concussion when I was about your age," T.J. told him. "After I bugged him about it for weeks, your granddaddy finally let me ride King, and he tossed me like a sack of potatoes. Hit my head on the fence."

"That's right," Trace said, coming to stand by the bed. "Stubborn little boy, your uncle. Your momma too. Guess it runs in the family."

Noah ran a finger across his blanket. "Did it hurt?"

"So much I cried," T.J. told him.

Noah lay back against the pillow and looked away, still picking at the edge of the blanket.

EmmyLou reached around T.J. and bent over her grandson. "We're just so glad you're all right, sweetie. You rest that sweet noggin of yours and concentrate on getting better, okay?"

Noah nodded and closed his eyes. He thrived on routine and became agitated in new situations, so this had to be hard on him. The fact that he wasn't more upset about his surroundings spoke to how poorly he must feel.

While Noah slept, T.J. ushered Amy downstairs to the

cafeteria for a cup of coffee and a sandwich. She'd worked
the late shift at Finnegan's Pub last night and usually slept
most of the morning while Noah was at school.

"A concussion? It doesn't make any sense." She rubbed
her eyes and sipped gratefully from her coffee.

"I agree," T.J. said. Noah struggled with his coordination
and tended to avoid any sort of climbing or swinging activity
that made him feel out of balance. "Do you think some of
the other kids put him up to it?"

"No, why?"

"He mentioned something to me a few weeks ago about
a couple of the other boys in class. I got the feeling he was
trying to impress them, and call me cynical, but I'd hate to
think anyone was taking advantage of him."

Amy shook her head. "I don't think so. In fact, he's
actually made a friend from school who lives right in our
neighborhood."

"Really?" This was news. Noah didn't have friends. He
tended to be withdrawn and quiet in class because of his
autism. Still, while he struggled socially, he excelled aca-
demically and was holding his own in a mainstream second-
grade classroom at East Dogwood Elementary.

"Yeah. Anyway, I'll ask him more about it once he's
feeling better."

When they'd finished eating, T.J. stood and hugged his
sister. "It's okay. He's going to be fine."

She nodded. He wished there was more he could do to
help her. She'd shouldered the burden of Noah's upbringing
all on her own, and it hadn't been easy. She'd been his champion when he was diagnosed with Asperger's syndrome,
which was later classified as high-functioning autism. She
worked her butt off to keep a roof over their heads, put food
on their table, and afford the therapy he needed.

T.J. admired the hell out of her.

When they reentered the room, Merry sat in the chair by Noah's bed, looking at a picture book from his backpack. T.J. recognized it immediately because he'd given it to him: a Lego character encyclopedia. His nephew lived and breathed Legos and could build some of the most amazing and complex creations T.J. had ever seen, with or without an instruction manual.

"Lego super wrestler, he looks pretty intense. Do you have him?" Merry asked.

Noah nodded. His hands fluttered restlessly against his chest as she turned the page. Then his eyes brightened, and he pointed to something on the right-hand page.

"Aww, a Lego nurse." Merry pressed a hand to her heart. "She has brown hair just like me. Do you have her?"

Noah shook his head and shrugged, then flipped to another page.

"A ninja. A pharaoh. A zombie! Wow, they really do have a Lego for everything. Which one is your favorite?" she asked.

Noah reached for the book, but she closed her fingers over it with a warm smile.

"No, tell me without looking."

"Page fourteen, the cowboy," he answered without hesitation.

"Just like your uncle." Merry looked at T.J.

Something warm stirred in the air between them, tugging at his gut. He imagined how she might look on Twilight's back, galloping across the field behind his barn with that wild hair fanning out from under a cowboy hat. Goddamn, she'd look sexy on his horse.

Her eyes widened, as if she sensed the direction his imagination had taken.

T.J. looked away, and the connection was lost. Except later that afternoon, as he took Tango out for a ride, he could still feel the heat of those hazel eyes like a brand on his hide.

$\mathcal{C}$HAPTER THREE

$\mathcal{M}$erry sat on the edge of her bed and stared at the photo in her hands. Tyler smiled up at her from inside the glass, his sweet baby cheeks pink and full of life. His eyes, still that bright baby blue. She'd never gotten the chance to see if they'd turn hazel like hers or stay blue like his father's.

She brushed a finger over one of his brown, wispy curls, but felt only cold, hard glass. Her baby, her sweet Tyler. The scream rose up inside her like steam in a kettle brought to boil. She rolled onto the bed and pressed her face into the bedspread to keep it from escaping, because if she let it out, if she started screaming, she might never stop.

Ralph hopped up next to her and pressed his back against hers. Bless him. He always knew when she needed a shoulder to lean on. As the pain in her chest began to ease, she rolled to her side, and he burrowed against her, nubbin wiggling. He rested his face against her neck and breathed deeply. She rested a hand across his back and did the same. Sweet Ralph. He had a gift for easing people's burdens. He never failed to bring a smile to a sick child's face.

He was the most dependable man in her life, behind her

daddy, of course. But Ralph beat any man she'd ever dated. He was one of a kind, and she felt blessed every day that she'd been the one to pull him out of that dirty shelter four years ago. She'd saved him, and he'd returned the favor many times over.

With shaking fingers, she placed Tyler's photo onto her bedside table, cursing the God who hadn't saved him. Cursing herself for not having the ability to save him herself. How many others had she saved? But not the one who meant the most, not her own son. Her breath hitched, and Ralph nuzzled her neck, again bringing her back from the edge.

Baby Jayden had gotten to her today. It hurt her to her core to watch him suffer, to know his mother had caused his pain and now couldn't even be there to help see him through it. He'd lain alone too often today, sometimes held by the foster mother Social Services had assigned him, other times by various nurses and aides on the floor.

But not by his mother, and that gouged a hole in Merry's heart.

She slept that night with her arms around Ralph to keep the nightmares at bay. The memories of Tyler cold and gray and lifeless in his crib sometimes still left her screaming in a cold sweat in the dark hours of the night. She woke with Chip and Salsa sprawled across her legs, taking up every remaining inch of the bed.

No-Name slept in her bed on the floor. In the bedroom though, and that was progress. As early morning sun streamed through the window, Merry gazed at the brown mutt in the corner. She needed a name.

"Sandy?" she said aloud, eyeing her golden fur. The dog kept her back turned.

"Biscuit?" Nothing.

"Taffy?" The dog sighed.

"Amber?"

She raised her head and looked at Merry with big, brown eyes.

Merry pushed up on one elbow. "Amber? You like that?"

The dog's tail gave a shy wag.

"All right then. Amber it is. I'm still trying to find a home for you, you know, but you can stay here in the meantime. I promise you'll never be homeless again, okay?"

Another wag.

By now, Chip and Salsa were awake, both belly-up and gnawing on each other's tails with puppy squeals of delight. Merry knew better than to put her fingers in harm's way. Chip yelped as Salsa nipped too hard, and she turned to give her brother an apologetic kiss. They were teaching each other bite inhibition the old-fashioned way.

With a lazy yawn, Merry rolled out of bed. The clock on the dresser read eight thirty-two. Heaven. Today began her four days off. Wednesday, Thursday, Friday, Saturday. Her rest and recharge time to devote to herself and her dogs.

Sundays, Mondays, and Tuesdays she worked twelve-hour shifts at the hospital, with the occasional extra shift thrown in. She never turned down the opportunity to earn overtime. Overtime money always went straight to the dogs.

Today, she and Ralph would visit the pediatric floor to cheer up the kids. They usually visited on Fridays, but this Friday she was tied up with a fund-raising event at a local pet boutique. Hopefully it would bring in some much-needed funding.

Her Facebook plea had raised over a hundred dollars, all from her own volunteers, which defeated the whole purpose. Her volunteers were already giving their all. She needed money from the outside to keep Triangle Boxer Rescue afloat.

A bubble of panic rose in her throat, and she swallowed it down. She could still fix this. Surely there were people out there who would want to support her rescue. She just had to find them.

Still, she couldn't shake the queasy feeling in the pit of her stomach. If things got any worse, she wouldn't be able to pay her own bills, and what would she do then?

It wasn't going to happen. She'd find a new source of donations. Failure was not an option, not this time.

After breakfast, she took the dogs on a long walk, then got Ralph ready for his visit to the hospital. She groomed him, brushed his teeth, and trimmed his nails, then loaded him into the car.

They arrived at Dogwood Hospital just past eleven. Ralph looked dapper in his yellow vest announcing him as a therapy dog. His fawn coat shone under the fluorescent lighting, his head held high. He took such pride in his work. It was truly the highlight of his week.

Merry stopped at the nurses' station to say hello and get a list of patients to visit. Still in Room 311 was Noah Walton. She headed there first, remembering T.J. had mentioned Noah's special connection with dogs.

The boy lay on his side, sleeping, when she entered. His uncle sat at his bedside, his attention focused on the iPhone in his hand. Merry paused just inside the door, rooted to the spot as T.J. raised his head and looked at her.

Her insides heated right up. Today, he wore a plain black T-shirt tucked into jeans. She couldn't see his feet but suspected his trademark leather boots were in place. It was the damnedest thing. She'd never gone for the cowboy type before, but T. J. Jameson sure fired her up.

She'd be angling for a cowboy fling if he hadn't been such a jerk about her dogs because, if she wasn't mistaken, she saw the same level of interest reflected in his dark eyes.

Oh well. She turned her attention to the boy sleeping in the bed. "I'll come back later," she whispered.

T.J. shook his head. He tapped something onto his phone, then held it up for her to read. *He's not asleep. It's just how he copes when he doesn't feel like talking.*

She nodded and came to sit by the bed, Ralph at her side.

"That's a handsome dog," T.J. said. "What's his name?"

"This is Ralph."

On cue, Noah's eyes opened, then widened as he caught sight of the dog sitting beside his bed. Ralph cocked his head and stared up at the boy eagerly, his tail nubbin wiggling with anticipation.

"Ralph," Noah repeated, and the dog gave him a friendly doggy-smile.

"He's a boxer. He works here at the hospital once a week, visiting all the kids. Would you like to pet him?"

Noah sat up. He fidgeted with his blanket for a moment, then reached for Ralph.

"Go greet," Merry told him, and Ralph popped to his feet and approached the bed, tail a blur of happiness.

"Hi, Ralph," Noah said. He stuck his hand out, and Ralph pressed his face into it, licking his palm.

Noah smiled, the first time Merry had seen him smile. He swung his legs over the edge of the bed and cupped both hands around Ralph's face, looking at last like a carefree eight-year-old boy. "What a good dog."

"He likes you," Merry told him.

Noah beamed. He looked like a young Harry Potter in his round glasses, with his mop of straight brown hair. His boyish face lit with joy as he rubbed Ralph beneath his chin. In response, the dog leaned closer, his eyes closed in blissful appreciation.

Five minutes later, Ralph was belly-up in Noah's bed, and the boy was laughing. Laughing! It was a beautiful sound. Merry glimpsed a suspicious brightness in T.J.'s eyes as his nephew transformed into this happy-go-lucky child thanks to her dog.

Now she understood why dogs were such an important part of the camp. Maybe she was wrong to have pushed for so much in return. Maybe she should have just agreed to his terms and brought Ralph to work with the kids. He could have brought magic to that camp, to hell with the rest of it.

In that moment, as she watched Noah throw his arms around her dog's neck and squeeze him tight, if T.J. had asked her to reconsider, she would have said yes.

But of course, he didn't ask.

* * *

T.J. coughed to clear the painful tightening in his throat at the sight of his nephew playing with Merry's dog. This was why he'd decided to start a camp, to give Noah the chance to experience this kind of happiness, of normalcy, every day for a few precious weeks this summer.

The boy had been begging for a dog of his own for years. Unfortunately, with Amy's allergies, it could never happen.

Noah leaned forward, and Ralph nuzzled his neck. T.J. tensed, edging closer to the bed. One well-placed bite and his nephew would be fighting for his life.

Ralph turned his head to lay a sloppy kiss on Noah's cheek, and the boy laughed. T.J. forced himself to lean back in the chair and release his white-knuckled grip on the bed rail. He was overreacting. A well-bred dog with a solid pedigree and training like Ralph was unlikely to turn violent. His nephew was not in danger.

Noah whispered to Ralph in words only the dog could hear. Ralph listened closely, his stump of a tail wagging madly, eyes fixed on Noah's face.

"You have a way with dogs," Merry told him.

"I love them," he said, and clutched Ralph tighter.

Merry smiled, her eyes warm. She wore jeans today with a blue top that might go perfectly with a pair of boots. He cursed himself for allowing that image of her in cowgirl gear astride Twilight to invade his mind. It was pure fantasy. Merry Atwater was about as far from the girl of his dreams as a woman could be.

She sat patiently at Noah's bedside for much longer than he'd expected, laughing and bantering with the boy until he'd tired.

"Did you know it would take forty billion Legos to reach from the earth to the moon?" Noah asked Merry as he snuggled back against his sheets.

"That's a lot of Legos."

"There are over nine hundred and fifteen million different ways to combine six Lego bricks. I read that online," he said.

"You're a smart boy." Merry patted his hand.

"I'm going home this afternoon," he told her.

"That's great news. Be sure you tell your mom if your headache gets worse or if you see any funny lights behind your eyelids or anything like that, okay?"

Noah's hands slid restlessly over the blanket. "I missed the last day of school."

She stroked a hand over his hair. "Oh, honey, I'm sorry."

"Your mom said you could go by tomorrow to say goodbye to your teacher and get your stuff," T.J. told him.

"Okay." Noah's eyelids started to droop.

Merry said a quick good-bye and left, taking with her most of the light and energy from the room. Noah closed his eyes and lapsed back into his state of semi-sleep.

While his nephew rested, T.J. returned his attention to the task at hand: securing therapy dogs for his camp. He'd contacted every dog trainer and canine-assisted therapy organization he could find within fifty miles, and finally he'd had some interest.

A psychiatrist named John Wheeler had a therapy dog he used with some of his patients and wanted to hear more about T.J.'s camp. He emailed him back to schedule a meeting for the following afternoon.

Hopefully this one would pan out. He'd hoped to have several dogs on his property, but no one seemed to have more than one therapy dog, so he'd have to make do. As long as the dog was suitable. He'd had enough of mixed breed mutts to last a lifetime.

T.J. leaned back in the chair and rolled his shoulders. The straight-backed wooden chairs at Noah's bedside weren't made to sit in for any length of time. He'd volunteered to stay the morning while Amy got some much-needed rest before her next shift at Finnegan's.

While she was at work, Noah usually stayed with a sitter, a college student who spent several evenings a week doing homework on Amy's couch while Noah slept upstairs. Tonight Noah would be staying with his grandparents. Trace and EmmyLou had jumped at the chance to have him, and T.J. knew he'd be spoiled silly while at the same time getting the extra TLC he needed while he recovered from his concussion.

T.J. was headed there himself after he left the hospital. One of his dad's mares was due to foal any day now, and he'd asked T.J. to give her a once-over. This was Jewel's first pregnancy, and she'd been agitated lately, anxious over the impending birth.

The door opened, and Amy slipped into the room. She set her purse on the floor and sank into the chair opposite T.J. "How is he?"

"He just had a visit from a therapy dog, which cheered him up and wore him out."

Amy's eyes brightened. "Oh, how cool! I didn't know they had therapy dogs here."

"One of the nurses brings him in on her day off."

"Merry?"

He nodded.

Amy gave him an appraising look. "You like her, I can tell. You should seriously think about having her do the camp. What did you think of her dog?"

"Top notch. Noah really responded to him, but she's not right for the camp. She wanted to bring shelter dogs and have me keep them at the house."

She laughed. "She changed the rules. That's not allowed, right, little brother?"

He stood and reached for his hat. "Her rules don't work for me, that's all. I'm headed to Mom and Dad's to check on Jewel. I'll probably see you later when you drop Noah off."

"Okay. Thanks again for staying with him today."

"Any time." He headed out the door, opting for the stairs rather than the elevator to stretch his legs.

Outside, he inhaled deeply, breathing in the fresh, early summer air. T.J. had grown up on a farm and spent most of his time working outside with animals. Any time he spent too long inside a large building like Dogwood Hospital he started to feel claustrophobic, like the stale air wasn't properly feeding his lungs.

He set his hat on his head and started his truck, headed for his parents' ranch on the outskirts of town. Soon, the suburbs gave way to rolling green hills and sprawling farms. Cattle grazed on the left, while the large blue and white sign on the right announced Blue Sky Farm.

T.J. and Amy had grown up here, and the years lifted away every time he drove through its gates. He'd ridden these fields since he was a boy, been spilled into the grass more times than he could count. He'd gotten a concussion of his own right over by the pond when his father's prized stallion, King's Blue Sky, had tossed him into the fence.

He couldn't have asked for a better childhood or a more perfect place to grow up. He parked by the barn and waved at his mom, who was walking from the chicken coop with a basket of fresh eggs.

"You stayin' for supper?" she asked, shading her eyes with her left hand.

His stomach growled at the prospect of his mother's cooking. "Of course."

"I made spaghetti and meatballs. It's Noah's favorite."

"Sounds good. How's Jewel this afternoon?"

"Her bag's pretty full, could be the baby comes tonight. It's a full moon, you know."

T.J. smiled. His mom could be superstitious, but on this she was right. Nothing brought along a stubborn foal like a full moon. "I'll have a look at her."

"Your dad's in there now."

T.J. stepped inside the barn, greeted by a series of whinnies up and down the row of stalls as the animals caught sight of him. He'd birthed many of them, cared for all of them. His parents raised some of the finest foundation quarter horses in North Carolina.

Blue Sky Farm was currently home to two stallions, eleven broodmares, and an ever-changing number of weanlings and yearlings. Jewel's foal would be the fifth and last born this year. T.J. missed being a bigger part of things here, working daily with Blue Sky's many horses. Someday, when he had a wife and family of his own to help out, he hoped to grow his own herd.

His father stepped out of the office and tipped his hat. "Hey, T.J."

"Hi, Dad." T.J. unlatched Jewel's stall door and eyed the sorrel beauty inside. The mare raised her head and gazed at him with her warm doe-eyes, her coat gleaming in a shaft of afternoon sunlight as ruby red as her name indicated. She nickered, then sauntered over to check his palm for treats.

He fed her a carrot as he ran a palm over her swollen middle. Beneath his fingers, the foal gave a strong kick that caused Jewel to snort in discomfort.

"Big, strong baby in there, Miss Jewel. You done good, girl." He slid his hand over her rump, feeling along the base of her spine. Her ligaments were loose, soft, to allow the foal to pass through. He bent to check her bag of milk. As his mom indicated, she was full.

She snorted again, pawing at her bedding. Yep, tonight could very well be the night. His father had birthed many foals, but Jewel was a maiden mother, and a nervous one at that. Perhaps T.J. should stay the night, just in case. It gave him an excuse to have his mother's homemade biscuits and eggs for breakfast, at any rate.

"Can't wait to see this one," Trace commented from the doorway. With Jewel's exquisite coloring and fine lineage, combined with Blue's athleticism and soundness, the foal should be a showstopper, for sure.

"Going to be a beauty," he agreed.

While he was there, his dad asked him to check on another mare who'd cut herself in the pasture. By the time he'd finished in the barn, supper was ready and Noah sat at the table, staring into his empty bowl.

"Hey, Bud. How's the head feeling?" T.J. ruffled his hair gently on his way to the sink to wash up.

Noah shrugged. When he wanted to, the boy spoke just fine. The struggle was motivating him to. Unless the topic was Legos or dogs, he tended to stay locked inside his own head.

Noah picked at the frayed sleeves of his shirt, a nervous habit. He'd pick at his sleeves until they unraveled rather than engage in conversation.

T.J. would move heaven and earth to get his nephew talking, to help him overcome the social limitations of his autism. And the first step was finding a therapy dog for his camp.

* * *

Merry stared in horror at the gash on Salsa's shoulder. The puppy shook and cried, thrusting her head into Merry's lap for sympathy. This was a disaster. Not the cut itself, because she dealt with worse on a daily basis at work. But financially?

Oh, crap.

Salsa needed stitches and antibiotics.

"Oh, you poor clumsy puppy." She kissed the little dog's forehead and held her steady as she cleaned the wound with an antiseptic wipe, then wrapped a bandage around the injured shoulder. She and Chip had been wrestling in the backyard when Salsa turned a somersault, knocked over a ceramic flowerpot, and sliced herself open on one of the broken shards.

Amber watched from the patio, silent and stoic as usual, while Ralph and Chip crowded close, sniffing at their wounded comrade and making sympathetic sounds. Salsa, not being either silent or stoic, let out a series of high-pitched cries, milking her injury for all it was worth.

"All right, you. Lucky I already have the vet on speed dial."

Thirty minutes later, they were in Dr. Johnson's office. Salsa, little squealer that she was, was taken in back to be sedated and stitched while Merry sat in the waiting room and fretted. Not about Salsa. No, her accident-prone puppy would be fine.

But Merry didn't get paid until the end of the week. The rescue's credit card was still maxed out, and her personal card was dangerously close to the limit. She'd never been in this much financial trouble before, and it terrified her.

She swallowed over her fear and sent a text message to her supervisor, Diana, to see if there were any overtime opportunities coming up. She'd take any shift she could get.

Desperate, she accessed the rescue's Facebook page from her cell phone and typed out a quick plea for funds to help pay for Salsa's stitches. This was embarrassing, having to beg for help with each vet bill. She noticed three new postings on the page, from followers.

Intrigued, she clicked on the first one. A woman was inquiring about how to surrender her eight-year-old male boxer. He'd developed a heart condition, and she could no longer afford to care for him. Merry's temper spiked straight to red. She wanted to reach inside her phone and wrap her hands around that woman's throat.

The very *nerve*.

Later, when she'd calmed down, she would see if she could finagle a foster home for the soon-to-be-abandoned senior. As much as she wanted to help, available foster homes were as hard to come by as money for her vet bills at the moment. That poor dog. Old, sick, and unloved.

The next message was from someone advertising a litter of puppies for sale.

"Asshole," she blurted, then mumbled an apology when the woman next to her gave her a dirty look. *Oops.*

She deleted the inappropriate message and sent the offender a quick reminder about the purpose of Triangle Boxer Rescue and its Facebook page. Advertising the sale of any dog or puppy went explicitly against their mission.

Now thoroughly disgusted, she left Facebook and tapped her foot impatiently on the floor. Screw social media. Hopefully the adoption event at Perry's Pet Boutique on Friday would introduce her to some new potential volunteers and supporters.

A volunteer would be sketching caricatures of dogs and their families to benefit the rescue, and one of her foster families had put together a basket of doggy goodies for her to raffle off. She hoped to raise several hundred dollars by the end of the day.

It wasn't an answer to her long-term problem though. She needed a much bigger influx of money to replace what she'd lost and get Triangle Boxer Rescue safely afloat. How had she managed a rescue for six years without learning how to fund-raise? She was an embarrassment to her own cause.

The door opened, and Dr. Johnson came into the waiting room. "She's all patched up. It only took two stitches. You'll be able to remove them in about two weeks."

"Great." Merry followed him into the exam room and closed the door behind them. Yes, as a nurse, she was certainly capable of removing stitches, and anything that saved a vet bill was a win in her book.

"We gave her a mild sedative to keep her calm during the procedure, so she'll be a little woozy for a few hours."

Merry laughed, imagining her sweet, crazy puppy on drugs. "That should be fun."

Dr. Johnson smiled broadly. "She's a feisty one, that Salsa. Tell her no more gymnastics near breakable pottery."

"I'll do my best."

While she waited for the tech to bring Salsa out, she checked quickly to see if any donations had come in from her Facebook plea. They hadn't, but someone else had inquired about surrendering a dog. Damn social media to hell and back.

The door opened and Salsa stumbled into the room, her nub a blur of excitement, her eyes droopy and unfocused.

"Oh, look at you! You poor, adorable thing." Merry bent and scooped her up. At forty-five pounds, Salsa had nearly outgrown Merry's arms. In another month, she'd have to walk herself to the car, wounded or not.

They headed to the front desk, and Merry set her down as the vet tech rang up the damage. Salsa curled over her feet, uncharacteristically mellow following her ordeal.

"Your total for the exam, sedation, stitches, and antibiotics comes to two hundred thirty-five dollars."

Merry's stomach soured. "And that includes the rescue discount?"

"Yes, ma'am," he said. "And Dr. Johnson gives you an extra discount for being such a frequent customer."

Ha! That was sweet, if unfortunate.

Reluctantly, she handed over her personal card. She'd never hesitated to spend her own money when the situation demanded, but this month, she'd gotten way over her head. She flinched as he swiped the card.

The machine beeped. He frowned and swiped it again. The pit of Merry's stomach dropped to her feet.

"I'm sorry, ma'am, but your card's been declined."

Crap. "Uhh, Dr. Johnson sometimes lets me run a tab until I can make a payment. Can you just check with him?"

It was true. He'd let her run a tab a few times when the rescue's card was full. In fact, she already owed him over four hundred dollars. *Double crap.*

"Merry," Dr. Johnson came up behind the desk, his brow furrowed, "you can add today's bill to your tab, but I need you to start paying it down by the end of the week, and no more until your balance is cleared. I want to help, and you know how much I value what you do for these dogs, but times are tough here too. I have my own bills and employees to pay."

Her cheeks burned. "Of course. I'll make a payment by Friday, I promise, and thank you so much for your understanding."

She stumbled into the parking lot with Salsa and tucked the puppy into the backseat, then slumped into the front and rested her head against the steering wheel. Merry had grown up in a double-wide trailer. She and her dad had eaten spaghetti or baked beans most nights to make ends meet. As soon as she'd been old enough, she'd taken any job she could get to help pay the bills.

Times had been tight, but they'd always paid their way.

She wasn't about to change that now.

A thousand-dollar donation from T. J. Jameson would pay off the rescue's current debt, with a little left over to make it through the rest of the month.

Much as she loathed the prospect, it was time to get down on her knees and grovel for the chance to sweat her butt off at his summer camp.

CHAPTER FOUR

T.J. gave Tango a nudge with his heels and sat back as the horse galloped across the field, his gait smooth and supple as well-worn leather. Tango's chestnut mane billowed in the wind, and his hooves thumped rhythmically against the earth.

This was T.J.'s stress relief. He'd never been much of a drinker, and more often than not lately, he'd had no one to share his bed, so he turned to his horse when he needed to leave the world behind for a while.

They approached the stream at the far edge of his property, and Tango slowed to a walk. T.J. rolled his shoulders and leaned back in the saddle.

Jewel had indeed foaled last night, keeping him and his dad up most of the night. She'd been nervous, which had caused her labor to progress more slowly, but eventually she'd given birth to a beautiful filly. The filly had her mother's stunning chestnut coloration, which had earned her the nickname Ruby.

Tango walked along the edge of the stream, head down and relaxed. He snorted his satisfaction about the afternoon excursion.

T.J. tipped his head to the sky, a beautiful Carolina blue. An hour ago, he'd met with John Wheeler, the psychiatrist with a therapy dog. The man had shown up in a bow tie and polished loafers. His dog, some kind of terrier, cowered when T.J. bent to pet it. He might not know much about dogs, but he knew that was a bad sign.

Which meant he was back at square one, with camp starting in four days.

He rode Tango through the woods and around the property in a loop, coming in from the East. Twilight and Peaches whinnied loudly as they caught sight of him. Tango let out an answering call, his gait quickening.

T.J. lifted his hat to wipe his brow, then squinted at the silver SUV parked next to his truck. As he and Tango approached, he saw Merry Atwater leaning against the rear bumper, Ralph at her feet. She wore a green knit skirt and black top, her curls wild and loose about her shoulders.

Ralph stood at attention, his eyes riveted on the horse walking toward him. Probably he'd never seen a horse before. John Wheeler's dog had bolted when one of the horses approached the fence. He was curious to see Ralph's reaction.

The dog didn't move, never taking his eyes off Tango. T.J.'s mount was no more familiar with dogs than the dog was with a horse. Tango lowered his head and blew through his nostrils, an equine hello.

The hair along Ralph's spine rose, but still he didn't budge.

"It's okay," Merry said softly. "Go greet."

Cautiously, he extended his nose and sniffed at Tango. The horse snorted again, and Ralph jumped back, but just as quickly he sprang forward, fascinated by the beast before him.

"Merry." T.J. tipped his hat.

"T.J." She looked up at him, squinting against the sun, her eyes reflecting the mossy green tones of her skirt. Dangerously gorgeous.

"What brings you out this way?" he asked.

"Well, I just did a home visit not too far from here, and I thought I'd stop by and see if you'd found a dog trainer yet for your camp." She still leaned against the back of her SUV, one sandaled foot crossed over the other.

"Why? You interested?"

She shrugged. "I like your nephew, and he certainly seemed to hit it off with Ralph." She glanced down at the dog, currently sniffing noses with Tango. Ralph's tail stub wagged so fast it was a blur.

"Yeah, he did."

"Maybe I was a little too pushy the first time we spoke. If you're still looking, maybe you could give me a second chance."

Her demeanor was casual, but there was an edge to her tone. Merry Atwater didn't strike him as the type of girl who came asking for second chances. David Johnson had mentioned her rescue was hard up for money. Perhaps she was in worse shape than he'd realized.

"I'm listening," he said.

"Look, Ralph's amazing. You won't find a better dog to work with your kids. If you're still willing to honor the donation you promised on Monday, I'd be happy to bring him and be a part of your camp. I can promise he'll deliver the impact you're looking for."

"Just Ralph?"

She nodded. "If that's what you want, but will you at least hear me out on my reasoning for wanting to involve several foster dogs as well?"

"Still listening." He shifted in the saddle. Merry wasn't

what he'd had in mind, but he saw now that she and Ralph could carry out his vision. The foster dogs would be a harder sell.

"Did you know that Ralph was a shelter dog?" she asked.

"No." T.J. looked down at the dog before him. He looked to be a perfect specimen, gorgeous lines and flawless demeanor. Not his idea of a shelter mutt in the least.

"I rescued him when he was two years old, starved and neglected. When we bring a dog into rescue, they undergo a full behavioral test to check for any signs of aggression. Any dog that's to be around children is put under even more scrutiny. The dogs I have in mind for the program are all currently in foster homes. Two of them are five-month-old puppies.

"Imagine what it could do for the kids' self-esteem to help train them. It's a huge feeling of accomplishment to teach a dog a new command. I think that's as important to what you're trying to accomplish as having them interact with Ralph. Let them be a part of something bigger and even more rewarding."

T.J. sat for a moment, pondering her words. "That sounds great in theory, but I still think it's too risky to have shelter dogs around the kids."

"Stop thinking of them as shelter dogs. They're foster dogs now. They're all living in homes. They've been screened for any signs of aggression or other behavioral problems that could affect their ability to participate in camp."

"I don't know…"

She cocked her head. "I can arrange for you to meet all of the potential dogs ahead of time. No dog enters the program without your approval."

Dammit, he really hated having his opinion swayed, but she made a good argument for her cause.

"Why don't I bring a couple of dogs out to meet you and Noah and see what you think?"

He rubbed his neck. "Well, I guess that couldn't hurt."

"The two puppies I mentioned are my own fosters. They're adorable. The kids would love helping to train them."

That was probably true. "You have three dogs?"

"Four actually, but only Ralph is mine. The others are fosters. Three is my usual limit, but I've inherited a stray dog this week, and we're short on foster homes at the moment." She looked up with those big, bottomless eyes, and T.J.'s gut clenched.

"Oh, hell no. I'm not fostering a dog for you."

"Just one or two? It would be a logistical nightmare trying to get dogs from different foster homes out here every morning."

"I don't keep dogs in my house."

Merry didn't back down. "I have the perfect dog for you. He's two years old, completely housebroken, very well behaved. You'd hardly know he was here."

"No."

"Just let me bring him and the other dogs by and introduce them to you and Noah. See what you think."

T.J. swung down from the saddle to face her directly. "Bring them tomorrow, but I'm not making any promises."

Merry's chin lifted. "Okay."

"The trainer I had originally hired was going to bring an assistant with her. You're talking about bringing a lot of dogs out here. Do you have an assistant?" He needed another adult to make sure the children were fully supervised, and while he could probably beg his mom to come and help, if Merry wanted to bring her shelter dogs, then she needed to provide supervision for them as well.

These were kids with special needs, and he had to ensure

their safety on his farm. He also needed to secure their parents' confidence in his vision. Already it looked bad that his first trainer quit before camp started. He couldn't afford another mark against the credibility of Camp Blue Sky.

She crossed her arms over her chest. "If you agree to foster at least one of the dogs, I'll bring a second person with me to help out."

If he agreed to foster? Merry Atwater was too pushy for her own good. "No. If you want to bring foster dogs to my camp, you'll bring an assistant."

She stared at him for a beat of silence. "Fine."

"For now, we're agreed on you and Ralph participating in the camp, in exchange for a thousand-dollar donation to Triangle Boxer Rescue. I'll give you five hundred now, and five hundred upon the successful completion of the camp."

Something flickered in her eyes, something raw and desperate, and again he was struck by the uncomfortable feeling that she needed his money more than she was letting on.

But she blinked it away and nodded. "That sounds fair."

"All right then, I look forward to working with you and Ralph. I'll decide on the rest after I've met the other dogs."

Merry stuck out a hand. "You have a deal."

They shook, and he tried not to notice how soft and feminine her hand felt in his.

After she'd driven away, T.J. stood for a long time, stroking Tango's neck. He should feel relieved. He'd secured a well-qualified therapy dog for his camp. But he couldn't quite find his balance, and he suspected the spinning sensation was caused by a one-woman tornado named Merry Atwater.

* * *

Merry fist pumped the roof of the CR-V. Ralph cocked his head at her. "We've got this in the bag, don't you think?"

He panted happily in agreement.

Her impromptu meeting with T.J. had gone far better than anticipated. Her thousand-dollar donation was a done deal—or half of it was anyway—and she felt pretty sure he'd agree to use her foster dogs in his program as well.

He'd made a rookie mistake, agreeing to meet the dogs with Noah around. Her gut said the boy was going to fall in love, and what uncle could say no to a boy begging him to keep one? She was betting T.J. couldn't. He had a major soft spot for his nephew.

Still smiling, she pulled out her phone and dialed Olivia. "Hey, can I ask a huge favor?"

"Not if it involves taking in another dog," her friend answered.

"It involves a dog, but he doesn't have to stay with you."

"Okay," Olivia said.

"Could you go to Carla's house tomorrow, pick up Bosley, and bring him to T. J. Jameson's farm?"

"Sure, but why?"

"Because Carla's got a broken leg and can't drive, and I want T.J. to consider Bosley for his summer camp. Actually, I want him to foster him for me too. His nephew's going to be there, and I'm hoping he won't be able to say no in front of Noah."

Olivia laughed. "You sneaky bitch."

"All for the greater good. If he fosters Bosley, then I can place Amber with Carla."

"Sure, just let me know when and where to take him."

"I'll email you later." Merry decided not to mention the other half of her agreement yet, that if T.J. agreed to use her foster dogs, she'd bring a helper. She'd find a way to sweet-talk Olivia into it. Knowing Liv, she'd do it just for the chance to look at T.J. every morning.

He was definitely giving Merry hot flashes. If she'd thought him sexy before, he'd ratcheted right off the charts astride his horse. Perfection, both of them. A flawless team of man and beast.

She respected that and the way he treated his animals. He might not share her views on animal rescue, but he handled his horses with affection and respect and he cared for sick and injured livestock for a living, after all. She trusted that he'd take proper care of her dogs.

Her phone rang, and she snatched it from her purse, glancing at the display. "Hi, Dad."

"Hey, sweetie. Just checking to see if you're coming to The Watering Hole tomorrow night?"

"Definitely. Can't wait to hear you play." Her dad played the fiddle in a local bluegrass band. They performed most Fridays at The Watering Hole, which pretty much matched its name. It was a place for locals to come stomp their boots and drink a few beers after work.

"Great. We've got a couple of new tunes we'll be trying out. Bring someone to dance with."

"I'll see what I can do. See you tomorrow, Dad." Merry hung up the phone with a sigh. It seemed her recent slump had extended from financial matters into her dating life. She usually had several guys she could call to go dancing with her on a Friday night, but while she'd been busy worrying about her finances, they'd one by one moved into serious relationships.

And that really sucked. Wasn't she every man's fantasy? A girl who just wanted to have some fun, no commitments, no strings? Apparently not.

Well, no bother. She'd go to The Watering Hole tomorrow

night and meet someone new, dance the night away, and see where things went.

At home, she went through her evening routine with the dogs, feeding and playing and exercising. She really hoped she could get Amber into a quieter foster home soon. The poor girl needed some one-on-one attention. Being around Ralph and the puppies all the time was overwhelming for her. Merry suspected she needed peace and quiet for her personality to blossom.

Salsa whirled around the kitchen until Merry threatened her with crate rest to keep her from busting a stitch. Crazy pup. Ralph and Chip played tug on an old rope toy.

Amber lay in her usual spot in the corner, watching. Merry thought of the little girl who'd hugged her the other day. They'd encountered kids several times on their walks, and each time, Amber had perked up, looking eager to greet them.

What if she recommended Amber for T.J.'s camp? It was a little bit crazy, except it might not be crazy at all. Merry had already given her a full behavioral assessment, which she'd passed with flying colors. There didn't appear to be an ounce of aggression in her.

Still, camp could be overwhelming for a dog like Amber. On a hunch, Merry clipped her leash on and drove her to the local pet superstore.

She walked Amber up and down the aisles, dodging other shoppers and their dogs. Amber walked quietly at her side, shy but not fearful. A couple of older children asked if they could pet her, and Amber wagged enthusiastically while they fussed over her.

On the way home, Merry called her friend Julia, who ran a dog training center in nearby Raleigh. She arranged to drop Amber off the next morning for a full assessment around other dogs and children. The camp dogs would be working with kids with disabilities, and they needed to be absolutely bombproof.

Her gut said Amber would pass every test put her way. With her shy, quiet personality, she might be the perfect match for Noah. Camp might even be as therapeutic for Amber as it would be for him. It could be the start of something wonderful for both of them.

The next morning, Merry was up bright and early to prep for her adoption event at Perry's Pet Boutique. She'd be in the store from ten until four, with Chip and Salsa and several other foster dogs stopping by throughout the day.

By nine o'clock, she was on the road. She dropped Amber off at Julia's, then headed for the pet store with a backseat full of rambunctious puppies and a trunk full of goodies. Perry met her at the door and grabbed the leashes from her hand.

"Who are these two?" she asked, bending down for puppy kisses.

"Chip," she pointed to the fawn male, "and Salsa." Her brindle troublemaker.

"Well, isn't that just the cutest thing ever?" Perry brushed back her gray hair and straightened. "If you two don't get adopted today, I don't know what's what."

"We can hope. They're a bit rogue, but in a lovable way." Teenage hooligans was more like it. Their first family hadn't bothered with even the most basic obedience or manners, then dumped them in rescue when their behavior got out of hand.

Merry had gotten them somewhat civilized, but they were a long way from being considered well behaved. Case in point, Chip leaped up and planted his front feet on Perry, lunging for her face with overeager kisses.

"Ooh!" she laughed, stepping backward.

"Chip, off," Merry commanded with a tug on the leash to emphasize her point.

He jumped down and gave her a wounded look before sauntering after his sister in search of more trouble. Chip and Salsa were boxer mix puppies, probably boxadors—half boxer and half Lab. They'd be great dogs, but right now, with their bad manners and lack of purebred status, they were proving difficult to adopt.

Merry tied them behind the table Perry had set up for her. She set out a bowl of water and a blanket for them to lay on. Then she got to work setting up. She hung Triangle Boxer Rescue's banner, then arranged their goodie basket next to a bowl for raffle tickets, a separate canister for donations, pamphlets about the rescue, and a stack of volunteer and adoption applications.

Dana arrived to set up her caricature station. By the time everything was finished, Merry's adrenaline was pumping. She adored adoption events like this one, the chance to spend the day promoting her rescue, raising money, and hopefully adopting a few dogs as well.

"Oh, what cute puppies!" A woman approached the table, drawn by Chip and Salsa's sweet faces.

Merry smiled broadly. "Thank you. They're available for adoption if you're interested."

She spent the next two hours in happy mayhem as a steady stream of customers visited her table, leaving donations, entering the raffle, and having caricatures drawn of themselves and their dogs. Volunteers arrived with foster dogs, and Perry's Pet Boutique was filled with wiggling boxer butts.

By one o'clock, she had four fosters in the house, not counting her puppies, and a customer had brought in two of his own boxers to help celebrate.

Olivia breezed through the door, looking like a cover model with her shiny blond hair and petite figure draped in a pink cotton sundress. "Wow!"

Merry waved her over. "Hey, Liv. Come give me a hand."

"This place is a zoo. You must be raking it in."

Merry glanced at the donation jar, packed with singles and fives. "Well, there's probably close to a hundred dollars in there. We've had a couple of people fill out adoption applications too. One lady really fell in love with Trista's foster, Luke."

"Cool. Are you taking pictures to post on Facebook?" Olivia moved behind the table to greet Chip and Salsa.

"No. The only people who seem to visit our Facebook page are my own volunteers and people trying to surrender dogs."

Olivia looked up. "Be consistent, and you'll find an audience. Keep posting. And make sure your Facebook page is on all your promo stuff."

Merry shrugged. "I guess, but I seem to get a lot more interest from events like this."

A dog barked somewhere in the store. Chip's ears pricked. He lunged forward, and his leash came free from the table leg Merry had tied it to. He dashed off, darting into the crowd.

"Chip!" Merry ran after him.

Chip sideswiped someone's fawn boxer, who growled a warning. Luke, a TBR foster standing nearby, snapped at him. Chip darted for cover, but Luke and the visitor's boxer turned on each other.

Peaceful chatter was shattered by snarling, fighting dogs. Blood splattered the floor of Perry's Pet Boutique. Someone screamed.

Swearing under her breath, Merry bolted toward the melee.

$\mathscr{C}$HAPTER FIVE

$\mathscr{M}$erry managed to keep her chin up as she hustled out of Perry's Pet Boutique, but the effort cost her. Chip and Salsa, oblivious to her distress, yanked her this way and that as they sniffed their way to the car.

"Well, that was unfortunate," Olivia offered with a wry smile.

The fight had been easily broken up, but Luke suffered several puncture wounds, which meant more vet bills. Worse, Perry had ended the event early and suggested Triangle Boxer Rescue look elsewhere for their next fund-raiser.

It wasn't the end of the world but, combined with the ultimatum from Dr. Johnson and her shortage of funds and foster homes, it was a step in the wrong direction. And that pissed Merry off, big-time.

"This means we've really got to kick ass when we bring Amber and Bosley to T.J.'s later," she said. Julia had called earlier to report that Amber got two thumbs up for participating in the summer camp. She had remained calm and obedient through extensive behavioral testing.

Olivia nodded. "Failure is not an option. Got it. You said he's cute, right?"

" 'Cute' is not quite the right word. He's too, I don't know, masculine to be cute."

"That's not the guy version of 'she's got a great personality,' is it?"

Merry snorted. "Not even close. You'll see."

"Sweet. Okay, so I'll meet you there at five?"

Merry nodded as she loaded her troublesome pups into the backseat of the CR-V. She picked Amber up, then drove home and stood in her living room, twitchy with frustration and no way to let it out.

Her best friend Cara would go for a long jog. Her dad would spend some time with the punching bag. Merry had nothing but the overwhelming desire to scream until her throat was raw.

The dogs gave her a wide berth, sensing her fiery mood. They tousled in the kitchen while she fumed in the living room. Only Amber stayed nearby, watching quietly from her bed in the corner.

Finally, with a groan, Merry sank to the carpet and released a deep breath. She forced the anger back, bottled it, and screwed the lid on tight. She sat there until her pulse slowed, then looked at Amber. "I'm bringing you to meet a little boy and his uncle later today. Would you like to live on a farm?"

Amber's tail thumped the bed.

"So show them how charming you can be, okay?"

The dog rested her chin on her front paws. Sadness haunted those big, brown eyes. Merry ached to see her shed that sadness and romp happily in open fields, her tongue lolling out the side of her mouth, her eyes alive with joy.

She'd been unable to find a rescue to take Amber, so she'd listed her on Triangle Boxer Rescue's website as a courtesy posting. She didn't get many visitors looking for a Lab mix, but the rescue listing entitled her to post Amber on Petfinder .com, and anyone could find her there.

Like it or not, Amber was a TBR dog until she found her forever home, and as such, Merry was responsible for ensuring her happy ending.

Which started in approximately an hour, when she introduced her to T.J. and Noah.

* * *

T.J. took Noah's hand and guided him out the front door. The boy hadn't said a word since he had arrived an hour ago. He'd been resting at home since Wednesday, yet somehow he looked more exhausted than ever.

Maybe he should ask Merry to take a look at him while she was here.

Speaking of Merry, she was currently unloading a dog from the backseat of her SUV. She wore jean shorts and a pink top, and, even from a distance, she fired his pulse into overdrive.

The dog she'd brought today, unlike Ralph, appeared to be some kind of mutt. It was whiskey colored with a limp tail and world-weary stance. Also unlike Ralph, this was exactly what T.J. imagined a shelter dog to look like, exactly the kind of dog he didn't trust.

Exactly what he did *not* want for his summer camp.

He tightened his grip on Noah's hand. After thinking it over last night, he'd decided it would be best to stick to his original plan: Merry and Ralph only. Now he just had to come up with a viable reason why this dog couldn't participate in camp without upsetting his nephew.

Noah wiggled his hand out of T.J.'s. "Is this my dog for camp?"

And just like that, he was a normal, happy eight-year-old again.

"It's a dog Merry wants us to consider for the camp, but I have a feeling Ralph will be a better fit for you."

Noah was already walking toward Merry and the mutt. T.J. hustled after him.

Merry gave him a look that made all his nerves twitch, then turned her attention to Noah. "Hey, Noah. Is your head feeling better?"

The boy nodded, his eyes locked on the brown dog at her side. "I got a new Lego set yesterday. It's a garbage truck."

"That's exciting." She gave him a warm smile. "This is Amber. Would you like to say hi to her?"

He crouched down in front of the dog and held a hand toward her.

"Be careful," T.J. warned, staying close so he could yank his nephew away from potential danger.

"That's good, Noah. Just give her a minute to check you out. She's shy," Merry said.

Noah nodded as if this made perfect sense.

The dog leaned forward to sniff his hand, and her tail began to wag. She took a step closer to Noah. The boy rubbed her beneath her chin, and her tail wagged faster. Noah sat cross-legged in front of her and rubbed and petted while the dog seemed to sigh with contentment. She nuzzled his chin and curled up beside him with a paw on his knee.

"Wow," Merry said, looking awestruck. "This is exactly what I was hoping for."

"I like her," Noah said.

"And she likes you." She sat beside them. "What do you think, T.J.?"

He couldn't quite let go of the urge to pull his nephew to safety. "She seems nice, but she's too much of an unknown. I'd rather stick with Ralph."

Noah shook his head. "Ralph is Merry's dog. I want Amber to be *my* dog."

Merry smiled smugly, and T.J. realized belatedly he'd been set up. She'd known there was no way he could say no in front of his nephew. Well, shit.

He shoved his hands into the front pockets of his jeans. "You realize we're just talking about dogs to use in the camp, right? Amber or any other dog wouldn't be yours to keep."

"I know, Uncle T.J. I want her to be mine for the camp."

"Well, you just met her. Merry's got some other dogs for us to look at too, don't you, Merry?" He didn't want any of her foster dogs, but maybe he could find a compromise to keep Noah happy. Maybe one of her other dogs would be more like Ralph.

She nodded. "I do. My friend Olivia will be stopping by with another foster in a few minutes, and I could bring my puppies out tomorrow if you'd like to meet them too."

"All right. Let's meet them all before we make any decisions. I'm still not even sure I want to use foster dogs in the camp."

"I really want to help train a dog." Noah looked up, his youthful eyes so full of hope, gleaming with excitement over the ideas Merry had put in his head.

Dammit. "I'm considering it, but even so, I don't think this dog is a good match."

"Why not?" Noah was still petting Amber, looking completely smitten with the misfit mutt.

T.J. aimed a silent curse in Merry's direction. "For one thing, we don't know anything about Amber's background or heritage, do we, Merry?"

She stood to face him. "Well, she's a Lab mix, about four years old. No health problems, just a little shy. Except with Noah, it seems."

"I like her," Noah said again.

"She's a gentle soul," Merry said. "And she loves kids."

A red Toyota Prius turned into the driveway, and Merry glanced over her shoulder. "Here's Olivia now. Would you like to meet another dog, Noah?"

He scrambled to his feet, but stayed close to Amber's side. The dog sat next to him, her shoulder against his knee, panting in the humid North Carolina evening.

They watched as the Prius pulled to a stop and a leggy blonde hopped out. She fetched a white boxer from the backseat and approached their little group.

Amber's ears pricked, but she stayed at Noah's side instead of greeting the other dog.

"Hi," she said. "I'm Olivia, and this is Bosley."

Bosley wiggled with excitement, straining against his leash to greet them.

"Hey, Liv. Thanks for bringing him." Merry bent and held her arms out, and Bosley rushed over to lick her face.

"No problem," her friend answered.

Merry turned to T.J. "Bosley is two years old. He's a total sweetheart, very easygoing. Good with people and other dogs. Fully housetrained. Crate trained."

"I don't care if he's housetrained. He's not coming in my house. The camp will take place here on the farm."

Noah rocked from one foot to the other, his hands flapping restlessly at his sides. Then he placed a hand on Amber's head, and his body stilled, calmed by her touch. "But aren't we going to keep one during camp?"

T.J. shot Merry a look that should have made her hang her head in shame, but she lifted her chin, her eyes sparkling dangerously, daring him to defy his nephew. Behind her, Olivia smirked and gave an innocent shrug.

"Actually," Merry said, "it would really be a huge help if you could keep them both."

Oh, *hell* no.

"Can we, Uncle T.J.? Can we keep them both?" Noah was petting Bosley now, looking overjoyed with a dog on each side of him.

"They're both really easy dogs," Merry said. "Bosley's foster mom has a broken leg and wouldn't be able to drive him out here every morning, so it would make sense for him to stay at the farm. Plus, it would free up a spot in a foster home to be able to save another dog from the shelter. It's a win-win."

"For you, it is. What's in it for me?" he asked.

"Status as the coolest uncle ever?"

Noah nodded wisely, and T.J. knew he was sunk.

"You promised to bring an assistant if I use your foster dogs in the camp," he said.

She chewed her bottom lip. "Yes."

"Is this your helper?" He nodded toward Olivia.

The blonde's eyes widened. Clearly Merry hadn't clued her in on this part of the deal. Olivia looked even less suited to the farm than Merry in heeled sandals and a dress. What a joke.

"You could work your schedule at the café around camp, couldn't you, Liv?" Merry asked, having the good grace to look apologetic.

Olivia frowned. "And what's in it for *me*?"

Merry rolled her eyes. "Nobody wants to do a good deed out of the kindness of their heart?"

"I do plenty of good deeds," Olivia said with a wicked smile that made Merry snicker. T.J. scuffed a boot in the dirt and gazed over his shoulder at Tango, Twilight, and Peaches, grazing lazily in the pasture behind them.

"If you help with the camp, I'll come hold a sign with you the next time you're picketing that chicken processing plant. How's that?" Merry asked.

Picketing? He'd never seen the point. If you wanted to change something, go straight to the source. Sit down and talk man-to-man. Make a real change instead of wasting your time standing around holding a sign.

"Deal," Olivia said.

"Do you have any experience working with kids with special needs?" he asked.

She shrugged. "A lady I work with has a daughter with developmental delays. I babysit for her sometimes."

He shook his head, unconvinced.

"Olivia is extremely responsible and capable or I would never have brought her," Merry said. "I take my participation in your camp and the welfare of those kids very seriously."

He saw the look of indignant pride on her face. Truthfully, he had full confidence in Merry's abilities with the kids. And if she vouched for her friend, then he guessed he would have to trust her judgment on that too.

"All right then, you have a deal," he said, and like that, his fate was sealed.

Noah hooked an arm around each dog and looked up at him. He made eye contact with T.J., something he rarely did. Because of the dogs. "So we're keeping them both?"

He looked into his nephew's eyes, saw the gleam that Merry had put there. He couldn't be the person who took that away from him. "One. I'll keep one. Tell us more about Bosley."

"Bosley is a purebred boxer," Merry said. "He's an owner surrender. His family had to give him up due to financial hardship."

The noose around T.J.'s neck loosened. This dog hadn't come from the shelter. He was purebred, raised in a loving home, friendly, easygoing. Here was his chance to save face with his nephew. "Okay, I'll agree to have Bosley in the camp. I'll foster him, but only until the camp has ended. Then you take him back."

Merry nodded. "Only for the duration of the camp."

Noah fidgeted with his sleeve. "But what about Amber?"

"I can't keep two dogs. Merry will make sure that Amber finds a good home."

The boy flung his arms around the mutt's neck, and T.J. cringed. The dog leaned into him, her tail thumping against the red clay beneath her. "But I love Amber."

"She does seem to have a special bond with Noah," Merry said.

"She's...she's—" A mutt. A stray. Untrustworthy. "She's not right for the camp."

Merry crossed her arms over her chest. "She's exactly right for camp. She needs to be trained, and she happens to be great with kids."

"Bosley is the better choice." T.J. winced at the expression on his nephew's face. "I can only keep one, Noah."

"Then keep Amber. Please." Noah's pleading eyes poked at his weak spot, the part of him that would do anything to keep his nephew happy.

And this unkempt mutt seemed to fit the bill.

"Fine, I'll give her a try. A week. But if she so much as looks at anyone funny, she's going back." T.J. looked down at the mutt, and his stomach soured.

Merry nodded. "Deal. So Bosley and Amber are both in for camp, and you'll foster Amber. If you use my puppies as well, you'll have a dog for each child."

Noah squealed with glee.

T.J. looked down at the two dogs, the happy boxer and the miserable mutt who'd fallen in love with his nephew. This was not supposed to happen.

He always had a plan, and he always followed the plan. And yet somehow his well-laid plans had gone straight out the window the moment Merry Atwater waltzed into his life.

* * *

"This is fantastic. I can bring her over sometime this weekend. Does that work?" Merry managed not to gloat at her victory. It would have been perfect if he'd taken them both, but even agreeing to foster Amber and use her dogs in his camp was a huge deal.

"Yes." T.J. looked like a man who'd just swallowed a frog.

"I'm going to take this guy home. Great meeting you." Olivia waved before heading back to her car with Bosley.

Noah was practically bouncing up and down with excitement, the most animated Merry had ever seen him. It warmed the deepest parts of her heart to see him so happy, so *normal*. It was truly amazing to see such a socially awkward boy communicate so effortlessly with a little help from man's best friend.

"Noah, why don't you go into the barn and grab a couple of carrots for the horses? I'll meet you over there in a few minutes," T.J. said.

Noah gave Amber a hug, then ran off toward the barn, a streak of boyish energy.

"That was really amazing to see," she said.

Amber gazed after him with longing eyes. Her entire demeanor had changed since meeting Noah. Merry was so happy for her she could burst.

"Yeah." T.J. looked down at Amber.

"You owe me, you know." She grinned, pushing her luck.

His gaze locked onto her in an instant, those dark eyes blazing into hers from beneath the brim of his cowboy hat, making her sizzle in all the right places. "Oh yeah, and how do you figure that? Because the way I see it, you owe *me* mighty big for setting me up like that in front of Noah."

She threw her head back and laughed. "Finally figured that out, did you? I have a way of getting what I want, which is always in the best interest of my animals. And I do truly appreciate you taking Amber for me. You're making a huge difference for our rescue."

"Hmm." He tucked his thumbs through his belt loops, looking a bit deflated.

"Yeah." She'd gotten distracted staring at his hands, big calloused fingers toughened from years of manual labor. They'd probably feel sinfully fantastic on her skin.

Phew. Heat flushed through her cheeks, and she twisted Amber's leash around her palm.

"And how do I owe you, exactly?" He took a small step toward her, all strength and testosterone, the ultimate alpha male, and she went weak at the knees.

"Because I didn't tell Noah that Amber's available for adoption. That she doesn't have to be yours just for the camp. You could keep her. You'd be his hero."

"I'm already his hero."

Oh, boy. Had he taken another step closer, or had she? However it happened, they were standing way too close now. She had to tilt her head to meet his eyes. He was close enough that she could see the honeyed flecks in his irises and smell his scent, sweet like the oats he fed his horses, mixed with hay, and *man*.

Her heart thumped a steady rhythm against her ribs. T.J.'s gaze dipped to her mouth, and she licked her lips instinctively. He let out a rough, masculine sound, then turned on his heel.

"Call me about picking up the dog," he said.

Then he was gone, disappearing into the barn after Noah.

* * *

"You owe me one."

Merry snorted. "That seems to be the theme of my day."

Olivia narrowed her eyes. "Seriously, that was quite a setup with the camp thing. You nailed us both."

"Whatever. It's all for the greater good."

"Yeah, *your* greater good." Olivia took a long drink from her beer and rested her elbows on the bar. Around them, the hum of voices was offset by the clatter of glassware and the sound of a guitar being tuned.

Merry sat back, feeling chastised. "You and T.J. are getting stuff out of the deal too."

"Me least of all, but I'll do it anyway because I'm a good friend, and you're right, he is hot."

"Are you really upset about it?" When it came down to it, she didn't know Olivia all that well, and the last thing she wanted to do was alienate a friend. She was already short in that department.

"Nah, we're good." Olivia polished off her beer and slid it to the bartender. She had a new one in front of her in seconds. "Even if I don't stand a chance with the hot man."

"Why's that?" Merry gulped her own beer and felt it slide cold and crisp into her belly. Martinis were her usual poison, but on Friday nights she came here to The Watering Hole for a couple of beers and to hear her dad's band play.

"Because he already has his eye on you."

"You think?"

Olivia gave her the side eye. "Don't tell me you, of all people, didn't notice."

She felt a flush of warmth just remembering the way he'd looked at her earlier. "I noticed."

"Merry!"

She spun on her stool and bumped right into her dad.

Gerry Atwater slung an arm around her shoulders and squeezed. "Hey, sweetie, how are things? Any new dogs?"

She nodded. "A Lab mix, of all things. Found her a foster home today though. She's going to be well spoiled by an eight-year-old boy."

"Eight. That's a fun age." He smiled, his expression wistful, and Merry felt it slam into her like a fist to the gut. Tyler would have been eight this summer.

He and Noah might have been classmates. Maybe even friends.

Her throat swelled until she didn't trust herself to speak. She fiddled with her beer, but condensation made her fingers slick, and it skittered toward the edge of the bar.

Olivia grasped it with a steady hand, giving Merry an odd look. "I'm Olivia, by the way."

"Hi, Olivia. I'm Gerry Atwater, Merry's dad."

"Oh!" Olivia perked up. "You're playing in the band tonight, right? That's so cool. I played in a band in high school."

"Really, what did you play?"

"Electric guitar." Olivia strummed an air guitar.

His smile broadened. "Oh, neat. Do you still play?"

Olivia shook her head. "Not in years, but I love listening to live bands. Glad Merry convinced me to come with her tonight."

"I'll do my best not to disappoint." He chuckled. "Well, I've got to get ready. I'll stop by and see you ladies between sets, okay?"

Merry nodded. "Can't wait to hear those new songs, Dad. Break a leg up there."

"You shouldn't say that to an old geezer like me, might actually happen." With a goofy grin, he vanished into the crowd.

"Geezer, my ass." Merry shook her head with a smile.

Her dad was only forty-eight years old. He'd been barely out of high school when she was born. When Merry's good-for-nothing mother decided to hightail it out of town to pursue her dreams, Gerry had stuck it out on his own.

He'd put his own dreams on hold, working long hours at odd jobs to provide Merry a stable and loving home to grow up in. They'd pinched every penny, but they'd been happy.

"Your dad's so cool. Wish my dad played in a band." Olivia stared pensively into the amber depths of her beer.

"What does your dad do?"

"He's a lawyer. Both my parents are."

"Really? That's...shocking." Merry's lips twitched, then she laughed out loud.

Olivia gave her a dark look. "My dad's a defense attorney, and Mom works for the prosecutor's office. Most of my childhood was a big trial to decide which team I'd play for. Would I fight for justice like my mom or protect the innocent like my dad?"

Merry frowned. "But you didn't want to be a lawyer."

"Nope."

"Sorry, that sucks."

Olivia shrugged. "I wait tables at the Main Street Café. My parents are *so* proud."

Merry thought of her dad, who'd always been proud of her, no matter what she'd wanted out of life. It was sad that Olivia's parents hadn't been able to do the same. "Well, they should be. You're a kick-ass waitress, but more importantly, you're a good person. You care about how animals are treated. And you are a social media warrior extraordinaire. Halverson Foods hasn't known a moment of peace since you got wind they were abusing their chickens."

She smiled wryly. "Yes, Olivia Bennett, Facebook warrior. If only I could put that on my résumé."

"Seriously, what you're doing is important. People need

to know the truth about how animals are treated before they become our chicken nuggets and cheeseburgers. You're good at it. Take a compliment." Merry bumped her shoulder into Olivia's, and she smiled.

"Yes, I totally rock Facebook."

"You do. I really should schedule a time for you to give me a lesson."

Olivia's smile brightened. "Definitely. How have donations been lately?"

Merry sipped from her beer. "Well, we could always use more donations, but things have been a little slow this year."

She'd hidden the stark truth about her current financial crisis from everyone she knew, embarrassed that she'd let her rescue get into such dire straits. She'd be able to bail herself out this month with the donation from T.J., but she would have to spend every penny of it paying off vet tabs and the rescue's credit card.

What was she going to do next month? Because the expenses would keep coming, and there were always new dogs needing to be saved.

Olivia nodded. "I hear you. The economy's been tough on everyone. Well, we'll be seeing a lot of each other at camp. I'll help you work on your social media presence, okay?"

"Thanks. I'd appreciate that."

Her cell phone rang, buzzing against her hip while its cheerful ring tone was swallowed by the noise of the bar.

She slipped it out of her pocket and squinted at the screen.

T. J. Jameson.

What on earth did he need at eight thirty on a Friday night?

CHAPTER SIX

*M*erry stood on T.J.'s front porch at nine o'clock the following morning, feeling more than a little apprehensive about the deal she'd made. Amber stood beside her, blindly trusting in Merry to act in her best interest.

When T.J. called last night, he'd been looking for a way out. He'd wanted Merry to withdraw Amber from the program so that he could save face with his nephew. She'd refused on principle, but here, now, she felt guilty pushing the poor dog on a man who didn't want her.

Amber deserved better.

Still, she couldn't imagine T.J. actually mistreating her. At any rate, she was going to hang around this morning until she was one hundred percent comfortable leaving Amber.

The door swung open and T.J. stood there, filling the doorway with his solid presence. His T-shirt today was blue, tucked into his trademark jeans. His clean, earthy scent brought to mind fantasies of a romp in the hay, his skin on hers. And those boots.

She shook the image away as she met his gaze. "Morning, T.J."

"Merry." He looked down at the dog beside her, his expression unreadable.

"I have her things in the car, but I thought I'd bring her in first and let you guys get acquainted."

He nodded and stepped aside. A man of his word, even though he clearly wasn't happy about it. And she couldn't quite figure out why. He worshipped his horses, worked hands on with animals of all kind every day. Big, dirty farm animals. But dogs seemed to throw him off balance somehow, and it was more than having grown up with family dogs who didn't come inside the house.

"You're sure she's safe? No signs of aggression?" T.J. was staring at Amber, arms folded over his chest. Amber took one look at him and cowered behind Merry's legs.

"She's as submissive as they come," she answered.

T.J. reached a hand toward the dog, and she turned away from him, tail tucked.

First the dog at Dr. Johnson's, and now Amber. What was it about T.J. that made dogs so uncomfortable? She'd seen him on his horse the day she'd come begging for a place in his camp. They were like one together, in perfect harmony.

She studied T.J. for a moment, noticing his rigid stance and wary eyes. The repeated questions about aggression and biting.

Holy *shit*. T. J. Jameson was afraid of dogs.

She almost doubled over in laughter, except she was certain he wouldn't appreciate her being in on his little secret.

"Try sitting down," she suggested. "Look away from her. Give her a chance to get comfortable and let her approach you."

As it was, he towered over Amber, and his tension frightened her. Dogs couldn't truly smell fear, but they could sense it nonetheless. They were expert readers of body language, and a far better judge of character than most humans.

T.J. walked into the living room and sat obediently in a leather recliner. Merry sat across from him on the couch, beckoning Amber to follow her. She crossed the living room and lay at Merry's feet.

"So," she said, holding T.J.'s attention so that he'd stop staring at the dog, "she eats twice a day. I brought over a bag of food to get you started, with her portion size marked. I buy it at Dr. Johnson's. I bet he'll give you a discount when you need more."

He nodded. "And she's fully housetrained?"

"She hasn't had a single accident in the week she's been with me. She's crate trained as well. I crate her when I'm leaving her alone in the house, to help her feel safe. You can crate her at night if you like, but I've been letting her sleep in a dog bed in my room, and she hasn't gotten into any trouble."

He looked down at Amber, and she ducked her head behind Merry's ankles. This was a problem. She couldn't leave Amber here, feeling this uncomfortable around T.J.

To distract anxious man and beast, she made idle chatter, asking him more about the camp and his farm. He slid easily into his comfort zone. His posture relaxed, and his tone turned confident as he outlined all the details of the camp. He told her about his horses, how each of them had been born and raised on his parents' farm. His love and respect for them was unmistakable.

And she found herself wanting to show him that same love for dogs. It wasn't right for a man like T.J. to feel such discomfort, even fear, around them. She could fix it. She was certain of it.

"Why don't you come and sit next to me on the couch?" she suggested.

"What?" His head went up.

"For Amber. She's scared of you. We need to show her that you're a friend."

"Scared of me? Why?"

"You're a little intimidating to her. Come, sit." She patted the couch beside her.

T.J. stood and crossed the room. His body heat washed over her as he sat, keeping a careful distance between their bodies. She glanced up and lost herself in his whiskey eyes, his earthy scent, his dark hair tousled and spiky as if he'd run his fingers through it recently.

"This better?" he asked, his voice soft.

Much better. Her skin tingled with awareness at just how close he was and how much she wanted to get even closer. "Perfect," she said.

Amber watched them, her shoulder against Merry's leg. Then she leaned forward and sniffed T.J.'s boot.

"There's no reason for her to be afraid." He sounded bewildered. "I may not be crazy about having her here, but I'd never mistreat an animal."

"I know that, or I wouldn't have brought her here." Merry leaned down and stroked the dog under her chin. Amber's tail gave one shy thump against the hardwood floor. "Right, Amber? T.J.'s going to take good care of you."

She reached over and placed her right hand on his thigh to illustrate her point to the dog. T.J. was okay. He was a friend.

His well-worn jeans were soft beneath her fingers, and the warmth of his leg seeped through them onto her skin. He was all hard muscle beneath that layer of denim, and holy shit, she really should have thought this through.

She really should have touched his arm. His shoulder. Maybe just his boot.

Her hand was dangerously close to other, potentially

hard, parts of his anatomy, and by the fiery look in his eyes, he was just as aware of it as she was. *Good gracious.*

Resisting the urge to slide her hand a few inches north, she tore her gaze from T.J.'s and focused on the dog at her feet. "See, Amber? He's not so scary now, is he?"

"Scary's not the word I would use." T.J.'s voice was deeper, rougher, and holy mother of God, he sounded sexy.

She needed to take her hand off his leg. *Now.*

Amber crept forward and sniffed his hand. He gave her a little stroke under the chin, and she licked his palm.

Okay then. Merry yanked her hand to safety, but it was too late to extinguish the sexual tension crackling in the air.

* * *

T.J. stared at the dog at his feet, then shifted his gaze to the woman at his side. "Anything else I need to know?"

He was pretty confident he could take it from here, but he needed to keep her talking, because if he stood up right now, it was going to be embarrassing for both of them. He shifted his weight on the couch, adding a few much-needed inches between them.

"You can give her back to me at any point during the camp, no questions asked. It won't affect the rest of our deal."

"Well, that's downright considerate of you." He forced himself to look away from those bottomless hazel eyes, or he was never going to be able to get off the couch.

"I have my moments." She drummed her fingers on her thighs and stared at Amber. "I only want what's best for the dogs, you know."

"I know." He was getting that, loud and clear. And he respected it. He might not even hate having the dog here for a few weeks.

Amber seemed pretty harmless and well behaved. Besides, having her in his house gave T.J. extra time to get to know her and make sure she was trustworthy to be around Noah. He reached down and petted Amber, relieved when her tail swished against the floor, which also provided the distraction he needed from the vixen at his side.

Grateful, he stood. Amber stepped closer and sniffed his hand.

"She's starting to like you," Merry said as she pushed to her feet. "Why don't we take a little walk outside before I leave? You can walk her. Show me around the farm."

"Sure." He appreciated that she was taking the time to get him and Amber comfortable with each other before she left, although he suspected it was more for the dog's benefit than his. He took the leash she held toward him, and Amber moved obediently to his side.

Pretty hard to hate a dog so well behaved. Surely Amber wasn't going to tear his throat out, but then again, just a week ago she'd been a stray. Her behavior might be unpredictable.

Amber walked beside him as he led Merry out the front door and down to the barn. He expected she'd panic when she saw the horses, much like the shrink's dog had. Even Ralph had been frightened at first. He tightened his grip on the leash. Amber lifted her head and stared.

All three horses hung their heads over the fence and stared right back.

"Easy, Amber," Merry said, edging closer, clearly fearing the same outcome.

But the dog's ears pricked, and she began to jog, tugging T.J. toward the pasture. She marched right up to Twilight and sniffed noses with her, tail wagging.

"Whoa," Merry said. "If I didn't know better, I'd say Amber was a farm dog in her former life. See that?"

Yeah, he saw it. The dog loved horses, no doubt about it.

"I knew there was a reason I brought her to you. She's going to be so happy here." Merry sighed with contentment, resting her elbows on the fence.

T.J.'s gaze slid down to her ass, nicely displayed in a pair of jean cutoffs. And hell, her legs. Miles of smooth skin.

He squeezed his eyes shut. He really needed to get control of himself. He had to work with this woman five days a week for the next month, and it was going to be torture if he kept lusting after her this way.

There was no way he was getting involved with a bossy, troublemaking girly-girl, and that's all there was to it. He'd recently hit thirty, and it was more important than ever to look for a woman he wanted to spend his life with, a woman who wanted to live here with him, start a family, maybe get a few more horses.

Merry Atwater had heartbreak written all over her, from her red-painted fingernails to her purple, jewel-crusted flip-flops.

She stroked Twilight's forehead, and the mare thrust her face against her, eager for a good rubdown. Merry touched her reverently, as if she'd long wanted the chance to do just that. She reached up and scratched around Twilight's ears, and the mare head-bobbed her approval.

Watching Merry bond with his horse was doing nothing to ease his attraction to her. Just the opposite. He had to bite his tongue to keep from suggesting they take Tango and Twilight out for a ride. Damn stupid idea that would be.

While Merry rubbed Twilight, Amber stuck her head through the fence and made friends with Peaches, the little mare Noah rode.

Merry turned to him, her eyes soft and warm. "Looks like she's going to be right at home here, doesn't it?"

She smiled, and he felt it deep in his gut. Yep, it looked like both of them would be.

* * *

Merry woke Sunday morning to the buzzing of her alarm. Outside, the sky was still black. She smashed her face into the pillow, then reached for the bedside lamp and flipped the switch.

Sunday morning meant back to work. It was always a brutal adjustment after four days off, though truly she wouldn't change her schedule for anything. It suited her lifestyle perfectly.

Ralph, Chip, and Salsa wiggled closer, flopping against her for morning snuggles. Idly, she wondered how Amber was doing on her first morning with T.J. She briefly pictured them snuggled up in bed together, then giggled into her pillow.

Probably Amber had slept in her crate. Which was fine.

He'd promised to call if there were any problems, and he hadn't, so she assumed all was well. He might act tough, but he'd take good care of Amber. She'd seen enough of his heart to feel sure of it.

The next hour passed in a blur as she walked the dogs, showered, ate breakfast, and headed to Dogwood Hospital for her shift starting at seven. Sunday mornings were always a bit of a surprise, as many of her patients would have been discharged in the four days since she last saw them.

This morning, only one familiar face remained. Baby Jayden, still in heroin withdrawal. The baby would likely be in her care for weeks as they weaned him from his drug dependency, and that was assuming there were no complications in his recovery.

Merry stood in his room, hands pressed into the pockets of her scrubs. Sweet Jesus, he ripped at her heart in all the most vulnerable places. She reached out to touch him, and he looked up at her with big, brown eyes.

"Hey there." She smiled at him, aching to lift him up and hold him close. Instead, she busied herself checking his vitals. His withdrawal score this morning was a ten, a slight improvement over his scores from last week.

The door behind her opened, and Lavinia Thomas, his foster mom, stepped inside. She wore a cream-colored business suit that complemented her dark skin.

"Hey," she said as she joined Merry at Jayden's crib. "I just stopped in to spend a little while with him before work. How is he this morning?"

"About the same. He cried a lot overnight, but this time of morning seems to be his sweet time."

"Aww, my poor angel." Lavinia scooped him into her arms and cradled him against her chest. "Breaks my heart I can't take him home with me."

Merry swallowed over the lump in her throat. "He's responding well to the methadone. Hopefully he'll be home with you guys by the end of the month."

"Hear that, Jayden?" Lavinia adjusted the wires protruding from the infant's swaddle blanket and sat with him in the rocker. She rocked briskly back and forth, and his eyes soon began to droop.

"I'll check back in an hour or so. Will you still be here?" Merry asked.

"Probably not. I'll stop by the nurses' station on my way out."

Merry nodded, then slipped into the hall. Tears burned behind her eyes. *What the hell?* Jayden would be fine. His suffering was only temporary. He would go home with Lavinia and her husband, to be loved and cared for until... until what?

Until his junkie mother passed a urine test and asked for him back?

Merry knew as well as anyone that life didn't always deal

a fair hand when it came to parents. But she'd turned out okay, so hopefully Jayden would too.

Morning became afternoon. She handled one discharge and two new intakes, and through it all, Jayden screamed as his poor little body was wracked with the pain of withdrawal.

Something no infant should have to endure. She saw so much pain, so much suffering on a daily basis. It really tore her up to see a baby suffer from something so totally preventable, his pain one hundred percent caused by his mother's poor decisions.

Just past five o'clock, she went in to check on him. Jessie, her aide, had fed him a little while ago and said he'd finally fallen asleep. It was quiet inside his room but for the steady beeping of his heart monitor.

She bent over the crib to check his readouts. He lay with his eyes open, staring up at her.

"Oh, hey, sweetie." Merry reached down to stroke his cheek. He twitched.

"I'm just checking in to see how you're doing." She kept her tone soft and soothing.

Jayden's face twitched again.

And again.

She stilled, watching him more closely. That wasn't a facial twitch.

Jayden was having a seizure.

* * *

Merry didn't get off shift that night until eight, and she shuffled home, exhausted. Jayden's seizure had been heartbreaking to watch. A newborn seizure was much more subtle than older children or adults, but just as serious. Now he faced yet another hurdle in his recovery, another setback to overcome before he could go home.

She gathered Ralph in her arms and hugged him until the pain in her chest eased.

T.J.'s camp started tomorrow, but she hadn't been able to find anyone to cover her on such short notice, so she and her dogs wouldn't be joining Camp Blue Sky until Tuesday. The camp was four weeks long, running through mid-July. For the duration, she would work a half shift at the hospital on Mondays and Tuesdays, using vacation time to cover the difference. The rest of the week was her off time anyway.

That night, she ate, fed and walked her dogs, and fell into bed by nine thirty, bone tired and dead to the world. She'd slept restlessly the night before and needed a good night's sleep to power her way through tomorrow's twelve-hour shift.

She barely felt her head hit the pillow.

Her cell phone jolted her awake sometime later, singing happily from the bedside table.

She swore under her breath as she squinted at the clock. Eleven fifty-five.

Someone better have died to wake her up on a work night. She didn't recognize the number on the screen, but it was a local Dogwood exchange.

"Hello," she answered, her voice scratchy.

"Merry, it's T.J."

"T.J.?" Her half-asleep brain formed an image of him lying in bed, wearing nothing but his boxers, phone in hand. She smiled against her pillow.

"Amber's escaped. She ran into the woods behind my house, and I can't find her."

And just like that, she was wide awake.

* * *

T.J. felt completely incompetent, having to call Merry and tell her he'd lost her dog. She stood in his living room now, her hair a wild halo of curls, her face free of makeup, eyes still slightly unfocused after being jolted from sleep by his call.

She had on gray yoga pants and a pink tank top, braless, if the nipples pointing in his direction were any indication. So damn sexy he was getting a hard-on just looking at her.

"How long ago did she run off?" she asked, crossing her arms over her chest as if perhaps she'd just realized her lack of undergarments.

"'Bout an hour. I looked for her for a little while before I called you."

She nodded briskly, all business despite her sleep-rumpled appearance. "Okay. That's not long, she may still be nearby. Do you have a flashlight? What about hot dogs or something else really yummy and smelly? I brought dog cookies, but a hot dog would be better."

"I've got leftover fried chicken. And a flashlight."

"Perfect. Bring that. Is she wearing her collar?"

"No." He met her eyes, still waiting for the inevitable lecture for losing Amber, but so far she'd been very matter-of-fact. "She slipped out of it when I took her for a walk before bed."

"Okay. We'll bring it with us to put on her if we find her." She nibbled her bottom lip. "Wish I'd gotten her micro-chipped when I was at Dr. Johnson's on Wednesday. I always chip new dogs, but I was short on funds and hoping another rescue would take her."

T.J. rocked back on his heels. He'd lost the damn dog, and she was blaming herself? "Look, I'm sorry I let her get away from me."

She shook her head. "Amber was a stray. She's nervous. These things happen, more often than you would think, actually. Let's go find her, okay?"

Well, he certainly hadn't expected that. He'd been fully

braced for a lecture, but all right then. He walked to the fridge for the fried chicken, then pulled the high-powered flashlight he used on night calls from his vet bag.

Merry stood by the door, looking slightly forlorn. She followed him into the humid night, alive with the humming of insects and chirping frogs from the pond at the rear of his property.

"Trickier since she doesn't know her name," she mused as they walked toward the woods.

"Couldn't be much worse, I guess."

She snorted a laugh. "Oh, don't say that. It could always be worse. At least she's in good health and the weather's nice, right?"

"True." His boots crunched twigs, and he glanced back at Merry's pink flip-flops. Dammit, girly-girl. Did she not own closed-toed shoes? She couldn't have picked worse footwear for tromping through the woods in the dark.

They walked on, periodically calling for Amber. Merry took the bag of fried chicken from him, rustling the plastic and waving it through the air as they walked, hoping to entice Amber with its meaty, greasy scent.

That was his mom's fried chicken, and it did smell damn good. His stomach rumbled.

T.J. shone the flashlight around them, hoping Amber's eyes would reflect back at them in the darkness.

After fifteen minutes, they'd startled a couple of deer and a raccoon, but no sign of Amber. Merry tripped over a fallen log and swore, clutching at her right ankle.

"You okay?" he asked, shining the light on her.

"Stupid flip-flops." She rubbed at her ankle and took a limping step forward. "Next time I run out of my house in the middle of the night half dressed, remind me to at least put on sneakers."

"So you do own sneakers?"

She glared at him. "Of course I own sneakers."

He offered his elbow, but she pushed it away, limping on beside him.

"Make sure you wear them to camp."

She gave him a mock salute with her middle finger extended. "I'm not a total idiot."

T.J. swept the flashlight around them and caught a pair of eyes glowing from the darkness.

Merry sidled closer. "That is so creepy." She cleared her throat. "Amber?"

The eyes didn't move. It was hard to see what was behind them, but they looked about the right height for the missing dog.

"Here, girl," he said in his friendliest voice.

"Hungry?" Merry waved fried chicken in the animal's direction. "I hope I'm not enticing a bear with fried chicken right now."

"It's not a bear. Could be a coyote though."

"Oh, a coyote is so much better." Merry backed into him, her soft curls spilling over his arm. She smelled faintly fruity, like fresh berries. "Amber?"

The eyes moved toward them, slow and steady. Merry pressed against him, and he rested a hand on her shoulder. He should've brought his shotgun with them, on the off chance it was a coyote.

"Jesus Christ." She turned and grabbed onto his arm.

The animal picked up speed, loping toward them, two green eyes in a sea of darkness.

He pulled Merry closer against him. "Still got that can of doggy mace?"

CHAPTER SEVEN

$\mathcal{M}$erry resisted—barely—the urge to fling herself into T.J.'s arms. "It's in my car."

She never, *never*, left home without her citronella spray, and yet here she was, in the woods in the middle of the night with some friggin' creature running at her, empty-handed.

T.J. kept the flashlight leveled on the pair of glowing eyes still moving toward them, and to her great relief, Amber's honey-colored coat became visible through the trees.

"Amber!" Merry sank to her knees in relief, and the dog came and pressed her forehead against Merry's shoulder. "Oh, my goodness, sweetie, are you a sight for sore eyes."

Quickly, she snapped the collar around Amber's neck, then snugged it a little to keep her from slipping out of it again the next time T.J. walked her.

"You gave us quite a scare," T.J. said, sounding as relieved as she felt.

Amber's tail wagged.

Merry stroked her soft fur. "You don't want to be home-less anymore, do you?"

"There's a warm bed waiting for her at my house. She's not stupid."

"No, she's not." Merry fed her a bite of fried chicken. "Now if you don't mind, these woods are creepy at night. Let's go home, shall we?"

"Sounds good to me." T.J. led them through the trees until the lights from his house shone through.

Merry heaved an internal sigh of relief. Around them, the darkness vibrated with a chorus of creepy-crawly creatures she had no desire to identify. Probably she'd gained at least twenty mosquito bites to go with her sore ankle. Ick.

But they'd found Amber. Now that she was safely at her side, Merry could allow herself to realize how scared she'd been for the poor, lost mutt. She hated to think of Amber wandering these unfamiliar woods, frightened and alone.

T.J. led them inside the house, and Merry lingered self-consciously in the hallway. Here she was in his house, in the middle of the night, wearing nothing but a flimsy tank top and yoga pants. It felt way too cozy for a man she barely knew.

"Thanks for coming. Not sure she'd have come back without you." T.J. stood in the doorway to the living room, hands shoved into the pockets of his jeans.

Still fully dressed, right down to his boots.

Merry might as well have been standing there in her underwear.

"No problem." She crossed her arms under her breasts, mindful of the fact she didn't even have on a bra. *Jesus*.

T.J.'s gaze slid down, and her nipples hardened in response. Her skin flushed, and desire tugged low in her belly.

His expression heated until his eyes practically burned her.

She nibbled her bottom lip. "I should, uh, I should go."

"It's late," he said, his voice like gravel. It tickled all her sweet spots.

She stared at his hands, those big calloused fingers. Damn, but she wanted to feel them on her skin. Like, *now*.

"Really late." She took a step, but her feet accidentally carried her toward T.J., not the door.

He sucked in an audible breath, his eyes scorching hers. "I thought you were going."

"So did I." But fuck it. If she was going to be in his house in the middle of the night in her underwear, she might as well give him a kiss goodnight.

She'd never been known for her self-control, after all.

He watched her, not moving a muscle, as if he'd become rooted to the floor.

She put her palms on his biceps and pressed her lips to his. Just a quick kiss to test the waters, because they did have to work together for the next month.

His scent wrapped around her, filled her lungs, and stole her sanity. She lingered for a moment, her lips on his, so soft, so warm. Just enough to make her want more. So much more.

Her body pulsed with it.

She was about to pull back and tell him goodnight when his arms slid around her waist, securing her against the firm column of his body, and *oh God*, she was a goner.

"What was that?" he whispered against her lips.

She slid her hands up to encircle his neck. "A goodnight kiss."

"And why would you do something like that?" His voice vibrated through her.

"Because I wanted to." Their bodies were pressed together, and though he hadn't kissed her back, he wanted to. She felt the evidence pressed against her belly.

"Bad idea," he growled, his lips still touching hers, teasing, tempting.

"Oh yeah?" She could hardly breathe. Every nerve tingled with awareness, desperate for his touch, his kiss. *More.* More of everything.

Her heart throbbed in her chest.

T.J.'s eyes smoldered into hers, his pupils blown with lust.

His body vibrated with tension, his arms like steel bands around her. "Yeah."

"Then send me home." She wiggled in his arms, pressing into his erection, tempting him, willing him to kiss her back. Just for tonight.

She needed to be kissed. She needed to *feel*.

And he could make her...

His lips crushed hers, taking her so suddenly, so thoroughly, that she didn't have time to draw a breath. She heard herself groan, felt the desire inside her explode into something so completely out of control it almost frightened her.

Her back slammed into the wall, and her legs wrapped around his waist. His tongue plunged into her mouth, gliding against hers in a rhythm so perfect she shuddered in his arms. He lifted her hips, grinding himself against her until her eyes rolled back in her head, and...

Holy shit, holy shit.

She must have lost her mind. Her body burned, quaked, shook for him, and he felt so fucking good. He tasted like sin, sweet and sexy, like leather and cowboy boots, and...

Holy shit.

She needed more. She needed everything. She needed him buried deep inside her, groaning her name as he drove her over the edge, as he came inside her, and...

Holy shit.

This was completely out of control.

"Holy shit." The words came from T.J.'s lips, not her own, as he tore his mouth from hers and speared her with his gaze. He panted for breath, his body coiled against hers, so hard, so ready. She felt every inch of him still pressed between her legs, right where her body burned hottest for him. "What the hell was *that*?"

She laughed. "If you don't know, then you're more out of practice than I am."

He lifted her free of him and set her feet on the floor. She nearly melted in a puddle at his feet. Her knees shook as she locked them to hold herself up.

"Seriously." T.J. took a step back and raked a hand through his hair. "Bad idea."

She bit her lip. "Why?"

"Because we have to work together, for one thing."

"So what? I feel certain we could keep this chemistry going for at least a month." She grinned wickedly. "And after that, who cares?"

"Who cares?" His eyes narrowed. "That's your attitude toward relationships?"

She shrugged, cooling off rapidly under his searing scrutiny. "Why fight chemistry? The best way to burn it out is to let it happen."

He was looking at her like she'd just suggested he go jerk off in the shower. "Burn it out? That's what you want?"

"Well…"

"I'm thirty years old, Merry. I'm looking for someone to settle down and spend my life with, not a quick romp in the sack."

Okay, now she felt cheap, and she was pissed. "Seriously? One kiss, and you're talking about marriage?"

He shoved his hands into his pockets and shook his head. "You know what? I think it's time to say goodnight."

Oh, it was so far past time to say goodnight. Merry considered herself lucky she didn't feel his boot on her ass on the way out the door.

* * *

T.J. stroked Twilight's forelock. The mare nuzzled his pockets for carrots, plying him with wide, brown eyes and butter-soft lips until he complied.

The kids had just gone home after the first day of camp,

and it had gone well. Really well, all things considered. T.J. was pumped from seeing the excitement on the kids' faces while they had their first riding lesson. His Camp Blue Sky was going to make a difference.

Patrick O'Day, a longtime friend of the family, was overseeing the equine therapy. Pat ran Triple T Stables, just a few miles up the road from the Jamesons' Blue Sky Farm. At Triple T, he had been practicing equine therapy with disabled children for over twenty years.

Pat's daughters Madison and Savannah would be helping him here at Camp Blue Sky, providing extra assistance to the kids who needed help staying in the saddle. Today, they'd taken each child out one at a time on Twilight. Their riding lesson incorporated balance exercises and other activities that challenged their focus and coordination.

After lessons, grooming, and some fun and games in the barn, they'd had a picnic lunch before the kids were picked up.

Now only Noah remained. He sat on a stool in the corner, his unruly shock of brown hair tumbling over his glasses as he played a Lego video game on T.J.'s cell phone.

He hadn't spoken a word during camp this morning.

"You want to help me with Amber up at the house?" T.J. asked.

"Okay." He never looked up from the game.

"All right. I'm going to put Twilight in the pasture, then maybe we can take Amber for a walk."

Noah nodded. He had always struggled socially. T.J. hoped camp would help him develop more self-confidence around his peers, maybe even make a few new friends.

"Be right back," he told the boy, then walked Twilight out of the barn.

He led her to the pasture in back to join her buddies for the rest of the day. His horses had a good life here: green pasture to roam, plenty of shade trees, and a shelter to keep them dry when it rained. Often, during these balmy summer months, he left them out overnight as well. Let them be social and eat grass. Live like horses should.

He'd never understood keeping a horse in its stall unless weather or injury prevented them from going out. It wasn't natural for an animal that large to stand around in a square box all day, prevented from interacting with their own kind.

His horses had all been born and raised at Blue Sky Farm under his parents' loving hand. T.J. had helped deliver Tango, broke him to the saddle, trained him. The gelding had been his pride and joy for fourteen years now. He'd never known a horse with more spirit. Tango was perfection in every way.

Twilight had been intended as a broodmare, but ovarian cysts kept her from being bred. His parents had planned to sell her, but T.J. brought her here instead. He'd needed a companion for Tango, thought by now he'd have a wife to ride her. Twilight was healthy now, but someday she might require surgery, and T.J. wanted to make sure she received the best care when and if that time came.

Peaches had a similar story. Stricken with navicular disease, Peaches suffered chronic lameness in her front legs due to a degeneration of the navicular bone in her hooves. She would have been difficult to sell, hard to ensure a good home.

T.J. didn't hesitate to take her. Peaches had so much heart, and she enjoyed light riding. Noah rode her when he visited, and the mare loved every minute of it. Peaches was rock solid with kids, steady and even-tempered. As long as her legs didn't give her trouble, she'd be an invaluable asset to the camp.

In a few years, she might not be able to be ridden at all, but she'd have a home here with T.J. forever. He'd made that promise when he brought her here.

He slid the halter off over Twilight's ears. She gave him

a playful shove, then, with a whinny, she trotted over to join Tango and Peaches under the big oak tree along the fence.

Today had gone well. Tomorrow would be much busier once Merry and her dogs arrived. Just bringing her to mind filled him with a dizzying combination of lust and anger. On the one hand, he admired the hell out of what she did for her dogs and the kids she cared for at work.

But last night, she'd crossed a line. Hell, they both had. He couldn't even think about that kiss without getting turned on. Their chemistry was dangerous. Combustible. And off-limits.

He needed a wife, a life partner, someone to share this farm with.

He did not need a hot-headed, bed-hopping, free-spirited nurse who promised a few hot, sweaty nights during summer camp.

Not that he was opposed to a few nights of sweaty sex. Sweet Jesus he was getting hot just remembering the feel of her in his arms. But the truth of the matter was, Merry Atwater was not the type of girl he'd bring to church and brunch at his parents' house on Sundays, and there was no point dating someone he had no long-term potential with just because he wanted her in his bed.

Still, it was going to be a long damn month with her here on the farm every morning.

He blew out a breath and headed back to the barn, finding Noah exactly where he'd left him on the stool in the corner lost in his video game.

"Ready to go get Amber?" he asked.

Noah handed the phone over with a nod and fell into step beside him as they walked toward the house.

"You thirsty? Want a glass of lemonade?"

Another nod.

"It's just the powdered stuff, not homemade like your grandma makes."

Noah stepped through the front door and ran into the living room to fetch Amber from her crate. T.J. followed, unwilling to leave his nephew unattended with the stray, no matter how harmless she seemed.

Dogs could be unpredictable, just like people, especially the ones with troubled backgrounds.

Merry flitted through his mind again. Was there trouble in her past, something that made her shy away from serious relationships? Or was she just a fly-by-the-seat-of-her-pants type of girl?

Possibly a little bit of both.

"How 'bout that lemonade?" T.J. asked, herding dog and boy toward the kitchen.

Amber's tail wagged happily as she walked at Noah's side. She was young in years, according to Merry, but there was a world-weariness in her demeanor that made her appear almost elderly.

She never ran or jumped for joy. He'd never even seen her pick up a toy. Though, now that he thought about it, he hadn't remembered to buy her any.

"Maybe later we could go into town and buy Amber some toys. Would you like that?"

Noah nodded, his eyes bright. "I think she'll need lots."

"As many as you like." T.J. would promise his nephew the world if he'd just keep talking.

Noah was spending the rest of the day with him while Amy worked. He'd arranged for a colleague of his to handle emergency calls for him on camp mornings, and he didn't have any regularly scheduled appointments today.

That wouldn't be the norm though. Summers were busy. Lots of overheated animals, births, injuries. He'd be busy all right, especially cramming all his appointments into the afternoons.

T.J. opened the fridge and took out the pitcher of lemonade.

He poured a tall glass for himself, and one for Noah, and they sat at the kitchen table together. Amber curled up at the boy's feet.

"Did you have a good time at camp this morning?" T.J. gulped from his glass, parched.

"It will be more fun tomorrow with the dogs," Noah said softly.

"I bet it will be. Busier too."

T.J. kept talking, but he'd lost Noah. The boy's eyes had turned glassy and unfocused, as they often did. He sat with his knees drawn up, picking at the sleeves of his T-shirt. A string came loose, and he tugged, full concentration on the task.

T.J. itched to reach over and still his hands, stop him from the never-ending unraveling of his shirts.

Was it foolish to hope for a conversation over lemonade by the end of camp?

* * *

Merry took a deep breath and glanced over her shoulder at the three dogs piled into her backseat. Yesterday had been brutal. She'd powered through a twelve-hour shift on four hours of sleep, thanks to her late night rendezvous with T.J. And then Baby Jayden had suffered another seizure. She wanted so badly to make his suffering stop.

To make him just another normal, healthy two-week-old, snoozing away in his momma's arms. She punched a fist against the steering wheel.

From the backseat, three faces gazed at her in curious confusion.

"Right, okay, let's do this." She gathered her courage and stepped out of the car, stupidly relieved not to see T.J., still mortified over the way she'd left here Sunday night. Not only did she need to make it through today with her dignity intact, she needed her first day of camp to be great.

She needed T.J. to be glad he'd brought her in, to think of her as an asset to his camp, not something he'd settled for.

Olivia's Prius turned into the driveway. Right on time, thank goodness.

Merry turned to the backseat to unload her dogs. Ralph hopped out first, followed by a tangle of puppies as Chip and Salsa hit the earth. Immediately, they tried to yank Merry's right arm out of its socket as they explored their new surroundings.

Olivia walked over with Bosley, and they let the four dogs greet.

"Aw, how adorable, you accessorized her," Olivia said, eyeing Salsa's hot pink baby doll T-shirt.

"It's to keep her off her stitches," Merry told her. "But she looks so cute in it, I may have to keep dressing her up for camp."

"Totally. So what are we supposed to do?"

"Uhh…" Merry glanced at the house.

As if summoned by her look, T.J. opened the front door and stepped out. He placed his cowboy hat on his head as he walked their way.

God, he looked sexy.

Merry chewed her lip and averted her eyes, focusing instead on the dogs still tugging her this way and that. Salsa charged toward T.J., her nub a blur of excitement, yanking Merry several steps in his direction before she'd recovered her balance.

Except she might not ever really recover her balance around him. Not after she'd been stupid enough to kiss him.

"Merry," he said, his voice low and annoyingly formal. He nodded toward her, then turned to her friend. "Olivia. You ladies need anything to get ready?"

Merry sucked up her pride and met his eyes. "Just show us where you want us."

"I've got fans going in the barn if you want to work in there, out of the sun."

"That sounds great." Merry led her crew toward the barn, grateful she wouldn't have to stand outside in the burning sun all morning. T.J. had hung a blue banner over the barn's front entrance that said Camp Blue Sky.

Olivia followed with Bosley. "This guy's pretty sweet. I kept him last night so that I wouldn't have to go to Carla's before camp this morning. If you'd started me off with a dog like this, I might have kept fostering for you."

"Really? Want to keep him during camp?" Then she could get that senior male placed with Carla before he wound up at the shelter.

Olivia shrugged. "For the camp, I guess. But that's it."

"Deal." Merry grinned. Then she remembered the way Olivia had chastised her on Friday night. "And thank you, really."

"You're welcome. So what's the plan?"

Merry glanced around the barn. "I've got a dog for each kid, plus Ralph. I'm thinking I'll demonstrate with Ralph, then we'll go between the kids to help them practice with their dogs."

Olivia nodded. "Sounds good."

T.J. appeared in the doorway of the barn with Amber.

"Hey!" Merry grinned at the dog, who wagged her tail. She looked at T.J. "Can I use your hose to fill their water bowls?"

T.J. glanced down at the two large bowls she'd set out and nodded. He walked outside and returned a moment later with the hose, filling the bowls for her.

"Thanks."

"Welcome." He gave her a nonchalant smile that held not

even the tiniest trace of the desperate hunger he'd shown her the other night, when he'd pushed her up against the wall in his foyer and kissed the daylights out of her.

Well, she could play that game too. She gave him her coolest, most polite smile. "I guess the first thing we'll do when the kids get here is assign everyone a dog. Any initial thoughts on that?"

"We've got a girl with cerebral palsy who sits in a wheelchair. She might be better off with Bosley, since he seems calmer than the puppies. Wouldn't want her to get yanked out of her chair."

Merry nodded. "Agreed."

He frowned at Salsa. "Why's that puppy wearing clothes?"

"It's covering her stitches."

He eyed the shirt with distaste. "Well, Jules, the girl with Down syndrome, would probably like a dog dressed in pink."

"Okay."

"That leaves Parker, the boy with sensory processing disorder."

"He'll work with Chip. There, that was easy." She held the dogs in front of her, between her and T.J. A necessary buffer until she'd cooled off around him.

"Great. They should start arriving soon. I'm sure they'll be excited to work with the dogs, so we'll start with you guys, and I'll pull them out two at a time for their riding lessons."

A man strolled into the barn, dressed like T.J. in Wranglers, boots, and a cowboy hat. His belly strained the seams of his plaid shirt and lines creased his face. He might have been T.J.'s father, except she'd met Trace Jameson at the hospital, and this was not him.

"Pat O'Day," he said with a warm smile, extending a hand. "I give the kids their riding lessons."

She returned his smile as she shook his hand. "Merry Atwater. I'll be working with the dogs. This is my assistant, Olivia Bennett."

Two college-aged girls walked in with matching brown ponytails and big smiles.

Pat placed a hand on each of their shoulders. "These are my girls, Savannah and Madison. They're helping me with the equine therapy. They've been working at my camps for years."

They made introductions, then Pat went down the hall to start grooming Peaches and Twilight.

"We'd love to help out some with the dogs too, if you need an extra hand," Savannah said. She dropped to her knees to play with the puppies.

"That would be great," Merry told her.

"They're adorable." Madison rubbed Bosley, then went down the hall to help her dad get the horses ready.

Fifteen minutes later, the barn was full of children and dogs.

Jules clapped her hands with delight when Merry introduced her to Salsa. "So pretty! My dog is the prettiest. I *love* pink."

Bosley panted happily next to Lucy in her wheelchair. The sweet dog had been extra gentle with her, careful not to throw off her balance as she held his leash.

Noah and Amber sat together in the corner, away from the noise and chaos. Noah whispered in her ear, and Amber's tail thumped steadily against the dirt floor. Merry's heart squeezed. Oh, how she hoped they would be out here with the rest of the kids, interacting, before the end of camp.

Parker and Chip were the only match not made in heaven. Chip was his usual exuberant self, leaping and lunging, yanking on the poor boy's arms.

"Help!" he yelled. "He's too strong. Ahh!"

"Whoa." Merry passed Ralph's leash to Olivia and rushed to take Chip from Parker. "It's okay."

Parker crossed his arms over his chest. "I don't like him. He's not a nice dog."

Merry crouched down and hooked an arm around the puppy's shoulders. "He's very nice, I promise. He's just excited and forgot his manners."

"Bad dog. I want to go home." Parker ran out of the barn.

T.J. glared at Merry and turned to follow the boy. She shook her head. "Let me."

The look T.J. gave her told her how little he liked that idea, but he stayed in the barn as she jogged into the sunshine with Chip at her side. Behind her, she heard Olivia explaining the proper way to pet a dog to the remaining kids.

Bless her.

Parker stood in the driveway, kicking his sneaker against the gravel. "When will my mom be here? I want to go home."

"I could call her for you, if you want. But hear me out first."

"I don't like that dog." Parker eyed Chip much the way T.J. had looked at Amber the first time they met.

"I see that you're upset. There was a lot going on in the barn, a lot of noise and commotion. It's easy to get frustrated in a situation like that."

Parker stabbed the toe of his sneaker into the gravel. "I guess."

"Well, believe it or not, that's how Chip's feeling too. He's just a puppy. He doesn't know his manners yet. He got overwhelmed in there, and it made him act out."

Parker looked down at the puppy again. "Yeah, I feel like that a lot. That's why I have to go to therapy and do this stupid camp."

"Aw, it's not stupid." Merry gave him a wry smile. "You have an important job to do. You guys are going to help me train these dogs so that they can be adopted. We can't adopt out Chip while he's such a misbehaving little beast, can we?"

"Well," Parker kicked the gravel again, "I guess not. He really does need to learn his manners. He was not being nice to me in there."

"No," Merry agreed. "He wasn't."

The puppy sat and stared at them, head cocked.

"Bad dog," Parker told him again, his tone firm.

"He looks sorry, don't you think?" she asked.

"I guess."

"He's a lot calmer out here where it's quiet. I feel calmer too. How about you?" She had a basic knowledge of sensory processing disorder from work. It affected the kids' ability to interpret sensory input. External stimuli like noise, textures, and tastes could be overwhelming and cause the child to become agitated and upset.

"Yeah, it was kind of crazy in there," Parker agreed.

"So here's what I'm thinking. Let's give Chip a time-out for being naughty, and I'll take him through the first lesson. I'm going to let you work with Ralph. He's my dog, and he's pretty special. What do you think?"

"I guess." He scuffed harder in the gravel.

"Then when you feel ready, let me know, and you can try again with Chip. I really do need you to help me train him."

"Maybe."

Maybe wasn't good enough. For her own pride, not to mention the rest of her donation, Merry needed to make T.J. glad he'd hired her. She crossed her fingers behind her back, hoping like hell she could pull this off and redeem herself before the end of the morning.

CHAPTER EIGHT

This was exactly what T.J. had been afraid of. Not thirty minutes into the morning and already Parker had run out. By now, he would have asked Merry to call his mom. Yesterday, they'd made it until lunch, just an hour shy of the end of camp, before Parker had lost it and gone home. His mother had warned them it might happen, but it shouldn't happen every day.

And now Merry had gone after him, leaving the camp kids under the dubious direction of Olivia the waitress. Great. Just friggin' fantastic.

It was unbelievably important for the kids to have a good first experience with the dogs, for this to be rewarding and fun for them. For their parents to be impressed and satisfied with his camp. Merry and her gang were not off to a good start.

He walked over and stood near his nephew, watching Noah and Amber as they hid in the corner. Noah whispered something to the dog, and she rolled belly-up for him to stroke her tummy, tail swooshing through the dirt.

Olivia stood in front of the kids holding Ralph. "So who

wants to impress Merry when she comes back and show her how to tell your dog to sit?"

Lucy held up her hand. "I do."

"Me too, me too." Jules bounced on her heels. Salsa hopped beside her in her ridiculous pink shirt.

Olivia looked at Noah. "You too, Noah?"

The boy nodded eagerly.

"Okay then. Let's get started." She came around and gave each child a handful of treats, showing them how to keep their palm closed and hand up to keep the eager dogs from stealing an early reward.

Salsa, Bosley, and Amber sniffed and wagged excitedly at the promised bounty.

"Here's what you're going to do," Olivia said. "Take one cookie in your right hand, like this." She held up a cookie between her thumb and forefinger. Ralph's butt hit the dirt. Olivia laughed. "You're too good, Ralph. Stand up until I tell you."

She stepped back, and the dog stood to follow her. "Hold the cookie up and over your dog's head while you say 'sit.' When they look up at the cookie, they sit automatically. Like this."

She held a cookie over Ralph's nose while giving the command, and he sat. "Good boy!"

The kids clapped.

Olivia gave a little bow, grinning from ear to ear. "Thank you. Now your turn. One cookie, hold it up while saying 'sit' in a firm voice, and reward them with words and the cookie as soon as they sit, okay?"

Three heads nodded. T.J. rubbed a hand over his jaw. He knew for a fact Amber didn't know how to sit because he'd given her the command himself several times, with no luck. He didn't want Noah to be disappointed on his first day.

Lucy held a treat up and looked at Bosley. "Sit."

Bosley sat, and everyone clapped again.

"What a good boy! You are such a good boy." The girl stroked his neck, beaming with pride. As soon as Bosley stood, she repeated the trick.

In the corner, Noah stood. He looked down at Amber and held a treat. "Sit," he said in his tiny voice.

He moved the treat over her head exactly as Olivia had done, but Amber dodged backward to claim the cookie. Noah shook his head. "No, Amber."

She hung her head.

T.J. stepped closer, unsure whether to intervene.

"Uh oh," Jules said loudly. "Uh oh!"

He looked over to see Salsa with her front paws on the girl's leg, stealing the last of the cookies from her hand. Those puppies were a problem. He never should have agreed to them.

"Why don't we trade for a minute and let you practice with Ralph?" Olivia suggested.

Jules nodded. "Okay."

Olivia passed Ralph's leash and a fresh handful of cookies to the girl, and she had Ralph sitting within seconds.

Jules beamed with pride. "I did it. I did it!"

Everyone clapped for her. Jules clapped for herself, overjoyed.

T.J. smiled in spite of himself. That was pretty damn terrific.

"Me too," came a quiet voice from the corner.

Everyone turned to look at Noah. He faced Amber and said, in a clear, strong voice, "Sit."

He lifted the cookie over her head, and Amber sat.

Well, I'll be damned. T.J.'s throat tightened. "Wow, Noah. That was amazing."

Again the barn filled with applause.

Noah beamed. Amber's tail wagged. T.J. fought the urge to wrap the boy in a bear hug.

"Awesome!" Olivia came over and slapped a high five with Noah. "Way to go."

Parker stomped into the barn and stood staring. Merry came in behind him, leading Chip. She looked at T.J. and gave him a thumbs up.

Had she actually convinced the boy to stay?

"Okay, kids, are we ready to show Merry and Parker our new trick?" Olivia asked in her singsong voice.

"What trick?" Merry looked at her friend, brow wrinkled.

"Jules, why don't you go first," Olivia said.

"Goodie, I'm first." Jules held up a cookie. "Sit."

Ralph's butt hit the floor, along with Merry's jaw. T.J. swallowed a laugh.

"Yay!" Jules clapped as she fed Ralph the rest of her cookies.

"Okay, Lucy, your turn," Olivia said.

Lucy easily got Bosley to sit, producing another round of applause.

"Ready, Noah?" Olivia asked.

Merry's eyes widened. She shook her head at her friend, slashing her hand back and forth across her throat in the universal signal to stop.

Olivia winked and smiled.

Noah walked to the center of the barn with Amber at his side. He held up a cookie, lifting it over Amber's head. "Sit."

Amber took a step backward, and Merry bit her bottom lip.

"Sit," Noah repeated, unfazed. He again brought the cookie over Amber's head, and she sat.

"Holy—" Merry slapped a hand over her mouth.

Noah smiled proudly, and tears glistened in Merry's eyes. "Sweetie, that was amazing."

T.J. wrapped an arm around his small shoulders and squeezed. "Way to go, kiddo."

Because he understood what maybe no one else in the room other than Merry did. One, Amber, unlike the other dogs, hadn't known the command ahead of time, and two, it was pretty epic to see Noah communicating in front of this group of people.

Merry met his gaze across the room and smiled, her eyes still misty. She was so damn pretty, and not even all that girly-girl today in a yellow top, jean shorts, and sneakers, her hair pulled back in a simple ponytail. He hadn't let himself get close enough today to see if she still smelled like fresh berries.

It was in his best interest not to know what she smelled like or anything else about her, other than her ability to run this camp.

"You guys were busy while I was outside," she said. "I'm impressed."

Parker stomped his foot. "What about me? I thought I got to work with Ralph."

Jules held out his leash with her ever-present smile. "You can have him. I want my pretty Salsa back anyway."

"Thank you, Jules," Merry said. Olivia brought Salsa over to the girl and stood with them, helping to keep the puppy in line while Jules practiced the command with her.

"Sit," Parker said, and Ralph sat. The boy smiled, some of the tension leaking from his small shoulders.

T.J. felt his own shoulders relax a hair. Perhaps they'd survive the first day, after all.

"Uh oh." Jules's voice broke in on his thoughts.

He turned to see that Chip had tugged his leash free from the stall door Merry had tied him to and was humping Salsa for all the world to see.

* * *

Merry wiped sweat from her brow and kept her chin up under T.J.'s scrutinizing stare. She'd survived her first day of summer camp.

Barely.

"I think today went pretty well, all things considered," she said. The kids had been picked up a few minutes ago, and Olivia followed them out, needing to get ready for her shift at the café.

Merry was eager to follow her lead.

"There are a few things that need improvement," he said. "Those puppies are a problem."

She looked down at the troublemakers, uncharacteristically calm at her feet after their eventful morning. "I'll spend some extra time with them at home to work on their manners, and Olivia and I will stay close to Jules and Parker when they're working with them."

"And the other problem?"

Merry's cheeks heated. She could strangle Chip for humping Salsa in front of those kids. "He's starting to reach that age. I'm really sorry about that."

"Why hasn't he been neutered?"

Because I can't afford it. "He will be, very soon."

"See that he is. I don't want to have to explain to the kids' parents why they're learning about the birds and the bees at my summer camp."

"Right. No. It won't happen again, I promise." Merry hurried toward her CR-V with the dogs at her heels. She had to do better tomorrow. She had to get the rest of her donation.

Triangle Boxer Rescue's financial future depended on it.

She loaded the dogs into the backseat and cranked the engine, blasting the AC toward her overheated canines. They panted gratefully, tongues hanging from the sides of their mouths.

"You are in so much trouble," she told Chip.

He leaned forward to slurp her cheek.

"I mean it."

He kissed her again.

She backed up, risking a glance out the window to see that T.J. had walked over to the pasture to check on his horses. She wished she could see him ride again, that beautiful harmony of man and beast.

Stupidly, she wished she could ride with him. It had always been her forbidden dream. When she was little, she'd wanted to ride a horse so badly, yet she'd never dared ask. Her daddy would have put them into debt to pay for riding lessons if she'd asked. He'd have done anything for her, but money management wasn't really his thing.

Apparently not hers, either.

Shaking it off, she pulled out of the driveway and headed for home. A much-needed shower, a Diet Coke, and a sandwich, then she was off to work what remained of her shift.

Thankfully, tomorrow began her days off, because she was dead tired, physically and emotionally. This summer camp was both more rewarding, and more taxing, than she'd planned.

Already, she felt invested in the kids. The look of pride on Noah's face when he'd gotten Amber to sit. Sweet Jules, her face lit with joy every time she looked at Salsa. Merry wanted—needed—to see them all succeed by the end of camp. She'd do anything and everything she could to make sure that happened.

Lunch and a shower revived her. She lingered just long enough to make an appointment for Chip to be neutered on Friday. Luckily, she was able to get him in at a low-cost clinic she used for a lot of her fosters. One problem solved.

She left the exhausted dogs sleeping in the kitchen and hustled to the hospital in time to work the second half of her shift. She caught up with Debra, who had covered the morning for her. Together, they checked in on each small patient.

In Baby Jayden's room, Merry found an unfamiliar woman in a hospital gown cradling the infant in her arms.

Her long hair had been pulled back in a disheveled ponytail, which draped over her shoulder. Something silver protruded from beneath the baby's swaddle, connected to the arm of the wheelchair.

A handcuff.

Merry's back stiffened. Her eyes darted to the policeman against the back wall.

The woman looked up at Merry with red-rimmed eyes. "Hi, I'm Crystal. I'm Jayden's mom."

CHAPTER NINE

Merry lay the baby in his bassinet and busied herself checking his vitals to keep from staring at the woman in the wheelchair.

His mother.

The junkie who'd done this to him.

"His last score was an eleven," Debra said. She tapped the latest readouts into his electronic record while Merry checked his IV port.

Jayden twisted his face up and screamed, a high-pitched shriek that tore her heart fiber by fiber until it was nothing but a pulpy mess in her chest. Then his entire body grew rigid, his fists clenched against his chest.

"Shhh, baby," Merry murmured to him as she connected a fresh bag of IV fluids to the catheter in his right hand. She stroked his cheek, then reswaddled him and carried him back to Crystal.

"Is he going to be okay?" Crystal asked. She held Jayden against her chest, rocking him as best she could while hand-cuffed to the wheelchair.

"It's too soon to know if there will be any long-term damage," Merry said.

Crystal lowered her head. She held the baby closer, rocking and shushing, but nothing stopped his screaming.

Nothing ever did.

Debra walked to the door. "I'll have the aide come in and help you."

Crystal looked up, her pale cheeks streaked with tears. "I didn't mean for this to happen, you know."

"I'm sure you didn't." Merry noticed for the first time how young she was. Behind the rough-and-tough exterior, the girl probably wasn't much over eighteen. Not that youth gave her an excuse for her poor choices, but still Merry felt a twinge of sympathy for the girl shackled to the chair.

"I was in a really bad situation." Crystal ducked her head. "I used to keep myself numb. I didn't know I was pregnant. If I'd known…"

Merry took a step backward. "You don't have to explain yourself to me. Jessie will be right in to help get him settled."

Jayden's screams crawled beneath her skin and scratched at her nerves. She couldn't seem to draw enough air to fill her lungs.

"Can't you help me?" Crystal asked, still rocking him as he shrieked, red-faced and stiff in her arms.

"No," Merry said. "I can't."

And she bolted into the hall.

* * *

"Merry?"

She jumped, and her head smacked into a bridle hook. Jayden's screams still echoed in her head, raising goose bumps down her arms.

T.J. peered at her through a golden haze, and she tumbled right into the dirt at his feet.

"Hey, you okay?" His big, strong hands were on her arms, lifting her off the barn's earthen floor.

She shivered involuntarily as the last remnants of the nightmare slithered back into the darker recesses of her brain. Jayden's screams haunted her, day and night.

"Totally fine," she said, pulling free. The warmth of his fingers lingered on her arms, chasing away the last of the chill. "I just dozed off for a minute, and you startled me."

She reached down to brush dirt off her legs. Hopefully it was all dirt. Her nose wrinkled. *Way to make a great impression on the hot guy who semi-hates you. Just roll around in the dirt at his feet. That'll impress him.*

"Long night at the hospital?"

She nodded, not eager to rehash any of it. "It's been a long week, but I'm off for the next four days, so I'll bounce back."

He surveyed her, his lips compressed in a frown. "You look a little pale."

She rolled her eyes. "I am not. I'm just tired."

She turned on her heel and walked away, trying to maintain some shred of dignity. She'd left the dogs in an empty stall while she waited for T.J., which is how she'd ended up falling asleep and wallowing on the barn floor.

She probably had hay sticking out of her ponytail.

"Today went pretty well," he said behind her, his voice so low, so smooth, that it rubbed some of the friction out of her nerves.

"Yeah." She let her shoulders droop, releasing the tension in them. Her second day at camp hadn't gone badly at all. The dogs had mostly behaved. The kids practiced leash walking with Olivia while Merry spent one-on-one time with each of them.

She opened the stall door and clipped leashes onto her

dogs, keeping her back to T.J. "How's it going with Amber, has she caused any trouble?"

"No." He sounded closer now, close enough that his voice sent a whole new kind of shiver over her skin, the kind that left her hot, not cold. "She's been perfectly behaved."

"And you're being nice to her, right?" She said it jokingly as she turned toward him. Chip and Salsa ran forward to bounce against his legs, while Ralph stood beside her, wagging happily.

T.J. scowled at her, hands shoved into the front pockets of his Wranglers. "Jesus, Merry, I'm not a monster."

She threw her hands up. "I was kidding. But really, how does she seem when Noah's not around? Is she coming out of her shell at all?"

He looked down at his boots. "Well, she does have this little stuffed porcupine she likes to sleep with. And a duck."

Merry slapped a hand over her mouth. She had *not* sent toys over with Amber. T.J. had bought her stuffed animals to sleep with? "That's . . . that's adorable."

He scuffed his boot in the dirt. "Noah practically bought out the pet store when we went. That dog has more toys than she knows what to do with."

She grinned at him. "You big softie."

He grunted.

"Oh, it's okay. I won't tell." She breezed past him and out of the barn.

That night, she dreamed of Amber, snuggled up with her porcupine and her duck by T.J.'s bed, which was a massive improvement over Jayden's haunting screams.

* * *

T.J. stepped from the shower and wrapped himself in a towel. It was just past midnight, and he was dead on his feet. The afternoon and evening had been one emergency call after another. He'd finally gotten home twenty minutes ago, smelling like a cow's ass, too dirty even to eat before a shower.

Amber lay on the bath mat, waiting for him. She'd carried the porcupine in with her, and the duck. As he watched, she nuzzled the yellow stuffed animal, then licked it, like a mother dog grooming a puppy.

He shook his head and walked into the bedroom, where he shrugged into a clean pair of Wranglers and a worn T-shirt. Amber followed with the porcupine in her mouth. She set it in her dog bed, then went back for the duck.

He sat on the bed and watched her for a moment. "Are you a momma?"

She looked up at him and thumped her tail against the bed.

He slid down and crouched beside her. He lifted her right front leg to inspect her teats. Yep, she'd nursed a litter. Probably more than one.

"Hungry?" he asked.

His stomach was so empty it had started to devour itself, leaving him with a dull ache in his belly. He led the way downstairs. The soft shuffle of Amber's paws followed behind him.

He pulled a slab of roast beef from the fridge, cut a thick wedge, and slapped it between two slices of bread with a big squirt of mustard. He couldn't hold in the groan of appreciation as he took the first bite.

Amber curled up on the linoleum nearby, too polite even to beg.

"I really don't like mutts, you know," he told her.

She stared, her solemn expression betrayed by the steady thump of her tail against the floor.

"I don't know a thing about you. You could have been raised by wolves for all I know. You could be part coyote."

She rested her head on her front paws with a sigh.

"Well, fine, but only if you promise not to tell Merry." He dropped a chunk of roast beef into her bowl.

With a happy swish of her tail, Amber gobbled it up, then came to lay by his feet again.

T.J. stuffed himself on roast beef, then walked her outside. Just before one a.m., he stripped to his boxers and collapsed in bed, bone tired and dead to the world.

Sometime later, he jolted awake. A crack of thunder shook his bedroom, drowning out the howl of wind and the steady drumming of rain against the roof. He rolled over and stuffed an arm under the pillow.

North Carolina had some wild summer thunderstorms. He watched as a bolt of lightning streaked across the sky, followed by the resounding boom of thunder. His horses would have taken cover in their outdoor shelter, safe from the storm.

He'd always been awed by the power of the storm, the way it could light up the night and shake his house on its very foundation. Alas, tonight not even the majesty of Mother Nature could keep him awake. Desperately tired, he let his eyes drift shut. Sleep always came quickly for him, and he felt himself start to slide into its embrace.

A scuffling sound came from under the bed.

Instantly, he was awake. Alert. He heard it again, a scuffle, then a bump. What the hell? Something was under the bed.

Had a squirrel come in through the attic? Mice?

He peered over the edge of the bed, saw the empty dog bed, and groaned. Amber. He'd forgotten all about her. See, this was why dogs didn't come inside. Made them sissies afraid of a damn thunderstorm.

He swung out of bed and peered beneath it. Sure enough, there was an Amber-sized lump. "Hey, Amber. Come here, girl. Nothing to be afraid of, just a thunderstorm."

Lightning lit the room, revealing Amber huddled beneath the bed. T.J. reached his hand toward her. How the hell did you comfort a frightened dog? Merry would know.

He dropped to his stomach against the cool floorboards and reached for her. The next lightning bolt revealed two shiny rows of teeth gleaming back at him.

"Jesus Christ!" He yanked his hand back so fast he banged his head against the side of the bed. "Fuck."

The damn dog was snarling at him! Good-for-nothing mutt. T.J. rubbed at his temple as he glared at her from a safer distance. That's it, she was going back to Merry's house in the morning.

Amber scooted backward and watched him.

Why was her mouth open? Surely she wasn't still trying to bite him. He reached up and flipped on the lamp on his bedside table, then winced against the sudden onslaught of light. Beneath the bed, Amber panted as if it were a hundred degrees in his bedroom.

Slimy strands of drool dangled from her jowls, her eyes so wide he could see the whites all the way around. She hadn't snarled at him at all. She was just terrified of the storm.

Well, damn. "Come on, Amber. Buck up, woman. It's just a storm."

Amber stared back, her eyes glazed with terror.

"Being homeless must have been loads of fun for you, huh?" Exhausted, he sat on the floor and talked at her until the storm passed. Finally, she slunk toward him and climbed back into her bed.

T.J. collapsed against his pillow. He didn't even feel his eyes close before the alarm started beeping. Warm sunlight filled the room, stabbing into his weary eyes. Groaning, he rolled over. Beside the bed, Amber lay curled around her faux puppies.

It was hard to hate a dog who cuddled with stuffed animals.

T.J. swung out of bed. He visited the bathroom, then ambled downstairs to take her out. He'd never had a pet in the house before, was unaccustomed to having an animal underfoot.

It wasn't altogether unpleasant, although he certainly hoped he didn't have to talk her through any more thunderstorms. Still, he'd be glad when camp ended and Amber went on to whatever home Merry had planned for her. He wasn't sure how that worked, but she was a nice enough dog. Surely someone would want her.

A knock sounded at the front door. He glanced at the clock. It was ten past eight, a half hour earlier than the camp staff usually arrived. The kids didn't come until nine. And none of them regularly came up to the house before camp.

Amber slunk behind T.J. and tucked her tail between her legs. Some guard dog she was.

He strode to the front door and opened it without checking the peephole.

Merry stood there, dressed in a purple tank top and teal shorts, with several loose curls framing her face. The sight of her was like a dose of caffeine to his sleep-deprived brain.

"Hey," she said, looking uncharacteristically mellow. "Is it okay if I come in for a minute?"

He stepped back and opened the door wide. "Sure. Everything okay? Where are your dogs?"

"They're in the car with the AC running. Wasn't sure you'd want Chip and Salsa running loose in here."

He frowned, feeling somewhat like an ass. "You didn't have to leave them in the car."

She glanced up, brows furrowed, but then Amber trotted into the room, tail wagging, and Merry's face lit up. "Amber!" She bent and gathered the dog into her arms.

Amber licked her face eagerly. "T.J., she looks amazing. She's really blossoming here with you."

He shrugged. "We're doing okay."

"No, really, this is a huge change. She was overwhelmed at my house with Ralph and the puppies. It was too much for her. She likes it here." She paused. "She likes *you*."

The air between them heated. Merry sucked her bottom lip between her teeth and crossed her arms over her chest. Nope, she wasn't going to initiate things again, not after the way he'd treated her last time. Couldn't say he blamed her.

He could have handled that better, but he wasn't wrong. He and Merry weren't compatible romantically, no matter how hot she made him.

"Did you come by for something in particular?" he asked, before he lost his mind completely and crushed her against the wall again. Right now he was aching to do just that.

"I did." She looked away. "Some money went missing from my purse yesterday."

"What? How much money?"

"Five dollars. It's not a big deal, except…" She trailed off, still not meeting his eyes.

Why was she telling him this? Unless… "Are you suggesting someone from camp took money out of your purse?"

She nodded. "I can't be sure, of course, but I've been leaving it in the barn. I know I had a twenty and two fives in there yesterday morning. One of the fives is missing."

"Are you sure?" Because he had no fucking clue how much cash was in his wallet. Seemed a little OCD to keep such close track, and Merry didn't exactly strike him as that type.

"Yes. I went to the ATM on Tuesday to get cash to pay for a prescription for one of the fosters. When I got to the pharmacy, there wasn't enough."

"Don't you have a credit card?"

She rolled her eyes, and he remembered watching David decline her card last week. How much trouble was she in?

"That's beside the point. Someone took five dollars out of my purse. The only time I left it unattended was here in the barn. I'm not trying to start any trouble. I just thought you should know." She turned and stalked toward the front door.

Amber followed at her heels. Traitor.

"You're saying one of the kids took it?"

She shrugged. "I'd hate to think so, but kids these days, who knows? Like I said, I don't want to make any accusations. I just thought you'd want to know."

"You're sure you didn't spend it?"

She spun, hazel eyes snapping. "You think I'd be standing here if I wasn't sure?"

"You'll leave your purse here at the house from now on."

"Fine."

"And let me know if it happens again."

"You got it." She waved a hand over her shoulder and breezed out the front door, taking Amber with her.

T.J. stood there, watching her go. Had one of the kids stolen from her purse? It was a disturbing thought. He couldn't picture any of those kids for a thief. Sweet Jules, the girl with Down syndrome? Never. Lucy sat in a wheelchair. Parker? The boy had an attitude, but he was just a kid, and his mom drove a Mercedes. Surely he wasn't hard up for five dollars.

He'd be keeping a closer eye on them at any rate. There'd be no stealing on his farm, under his watch. And Merry Atwater? He'd be watching her closest of all.

* * *

This was embarrassing, having to wait around after camp to go up to the house with T.J. and get her purse. It almost felt like *she* was the one under suspicion.

Knowing T.J., that might be the case.

Merry narrowed her eyes at his back as she waited for him to finish fussing over his horse and turn her out to pasture with the others. He knelt beside Peaches, pressing and prodding her right front leg.

"Everything all right?" She leaned against a stall door and crossed one foot over the other.

T.J. stood, frowning. "She was lame during lessons this morning. I'll give her some bute and see how she does over the weekend, but I may need to give her a few days off from camp."

"Is she hurt?"

He shook his head. "She has navicular disease. It's degenerative. She has good days and bad. The bute will keep her pain-free for the weekend. It's a shame though, because she really loves carrying those kids for camp."

Yeah, Merry had noticed that too. Twilight looked bored walking in circles with the kids, but Peaches seemed to be having the time of her life. "That's terrible. What will you do when she can't work anymore?"

Her skin prickled with misgivings at the idea of this horse being sold in such a condition. Did horses still go to the glue factory?

T.J. looked at her, his dark eyes intense. "She's essentially already retired. I knew she had navicular when I bought her from my parents."

Merry's heart skipped a beat. "Oh."

Oh. T.J. had already rescued her. He'd taken a lame horse no one would want and given her a peaceful, happy life. That threw her view of him completely off kilter.

"She'll live out her days here on my farm, as long as I can keep her comfortable."

Merry came forward and stroked the mare's face. "You're a lucky girl, Peaches."

"Oh, she knows it." He looked so irrationally sexy she wanted to fling herself in his arms right there in the barn.

"So you know a thing or two about saving animals yourself."

He straightened. "Told you I'm not all that bad."

"Not half bad at all." Her heart was pounding now, every cell in her body begging him to kiss her.

That was the problem with chemistry. If you didn't give in to it, didn't let it start to burn itself out, it only grew stronger, until just standing within two feet of the man left her in danger of spontaneous combustion.

But hell, he'd set the ground rules. She stared straight into his eyes, daring him to kiss her, knowing he wouldn't. She might not be known for her self-control, but she could possess it when necessary, and there was no way in hell she was going to be humiliated by T. J. Jameson again.

Peaches thrust her head between them, and Merry distracted herself stroking the mare's soft forehead. She was a gorgeous creature with that golden face and flaxen mane and tail. Palomino had always been one of Merry's favorite horse colors.

"You like horses," he said.

"Sure. I've always liked them."

"So why don't you ride?" He stood near enough that her skin sizzled under his scrutiny, his scent mixed with the warm, earthy smell of the horse.

She kept her eyes on Peaches. "I've never been on a horse, if you can believe it."

T.J.'s head lifted, and she felt the intensity of his gaze. "Not even a pony ride when you were a kid?"

She shook her head, mortified when she felt the ache of tears pressing at the backs of her eyes.

"Why not?" His voice was lower, more intimate.

She felt heat gather on her face. No way. This was ridiculous. "I just never did."

"Want to?"

She threw her palms out in front of herself, backing away. "Nope. I'm good."

His lips curved in a wicked smile. "Yes, you do. You're a terrible liar."

"Really, no."

"I have an appointment to get to today, but stay after camp tomorrow. I'll give you a lesson on Tango."

She stared him straight in the eye. "That is such a bad idea."

He cocked his head, his eyes twinkling devilishly. "Scared?"

Terrified. "Not even a little bit."

"Okay then, wear jeans tomorrow. And boots, if you have them."

And with that, he unclipped Peaches from the cross ties and led her out into the sunshine to join her companions in the pasture.

CHAPTER TEN

Noah sat at the kitchen table, sliding his fingers back and forth over its smooth surface, lost in his own thoughts. T.J. sat across from him, ready to rip his hair out if he couldn't get a conversation started with his nephew soon.

"So your mom said you went over to Brendan's house yesterday. Did you have fun?"

"Yes." His brow furrowed as his fingers traced a swirl in the wood grain.

"You've been really quiet lately. Is something bothering you?" T.J. asked.

Noah shook his head, then got up and walked into the living room. Amber walked beside him.

"Hey, Noah, I'm just trying to help here. It's not polite to walk away while I'm talking to you."

"Sorry, Uncle T.J.," he said in his tiny voice. He stood by the couch, picking at the sleeves of his shirt until several new strings popped free, then busied himself unraveling them from the shirt completely.

T.J. watched, feeling wholly inadequate and ashamed of himself for intimidating the boy when he'd only meant to help. "No need to apologize. Just tell me what's bothering you."

Because even for Noah, this was unusual. It was Friday, the end of the first week of camp. Noah was more withdrawn than ever, and T.J. was at a total loss for what had gone wrong.

Noah and Amber were two peas in a pod, communicating with some secret language that no one else could hear, always touching, always together. At camp, he was mastering the tasks set forth by Merry with the dogs and Pat with the horses.

But he was talking less, and his autistic stimming—the repetitive arm movements and hand flapping—had increased to proportions T.J. hadn't seen since the boy was first diagnosed.

Why wasn't camp helping? Why was he getting worse?

"Talk to me," he said again.

Noah stared at his arm, fully intent on ripping a thread from the seam.

T.J. crossed the room and took the boy's hands in his. "Hey, stop that for a minute and talk to me. Did something happen? Is your head still bothering you from the fall? Has your new friend done something to upset you?"

Noah tugged free, flapping his hands wildly through the air until he turned and threw his arms around Amber.

T.J. raked a hand through his hair. "If you decide you want to talk, I'm always here, okay? I'm your uncle. I'm the guy you can tell things you're embarrassed to tell your mom, right? No judgment here."

Nothing.

"All right then, let's head down to the barn and see if anyone else is here yet."

"Okay." Noah scampered into the hallway to fetch Amber's leash. The dog ran after him and stood patiently while he clipped it to her collar. Amy had dropped him off early this morning to run errands, and T.J. had jumped at the chance to spend some extra time with him.

He just wanted to hang out with his nephew. Was that so much to ask?

T.J. took a deep breath and blew it out. He tamped down his frustration, throttling himself back before camp began. This was no way to begin a four-hour session with four kids, already feeling like he was ready to blow a gasket.

Noah yanked the front door open, then stood there with a huge smile on his face, the first smile T.J. had seen all morning. Merry stood in the doorway, looking like a vision in a gauzy yellow top and dark jeans.

"Morning, Noah. T.J." She ducked around the corner to leave her purse in the kitchen, then headed for the barn, hand in hand with Noah.

T.J. scowled as he followed them.

"Today we're going to work on teaching the dogs to lay down. How does that sound?" she asked.

"Good," Noah answered, then walked to his usual corner with Amber and sat.

"Why don't you stand over here with me today?" T.J. suggested. It was time for Noah to come out of the corner and join the group.

Noah shrugged, making no move to leave his usual spot.

At the other end of the aisle, Pat was already setting up. He waved.

Savannah, working next to her father, smiled at Noah. "Good morning."

He gave her a quick wave, his arm still wrapped around Amber.

Madison walked by on her way to the tack room and swiped him a high five.

Merry stood nearby, practicing commands with Salsa.

Ralph lay behind her, his leash discarded on the dirt floor. The best-behaved dog T.J. had ever met.

Currently, Ralph rested his head on his front paws, watching as Merry taught the puppy how to lay down on command. She held Salsa's leash in her right hand, a handful of treats in the left. The damn puppy wore a purple shirt today with rhinestones on the back.

"Okay, Salsa," Merry said. She palmed a cookie and pressed her index finger into the dirt. "Down."

Salsa slid down to her belly and thrust her snout into Merry's palm.

"Good girl! Oh, good Salsa." She lavished the puppy with praise and gave her the cookie. Salsa wiggled with joy.

T.J. had to hand it to her; she was good with those dogs. The kids too. They all adored her, even Parker, who was generally hard to please and often failed to listen when T.J. was directing him on grooming the horses.

"Ooooh, pretty Salsa!" Jules skipped into the barn, her brown eyes bright. She wore pigtails today, with a purple T-shirt and jeans.

Merry grinned at her. "Oh look, you guys match."

Jules looked down at her shirt, then clapped her hands with glee. "We do! So pretty. Salsa, you are the prettiest puppy ever."

Salsa looked overcome at the compliment. She bounced in circles around Jules, covering the girl with slobbery kisses. They were a match made in purple-jeweled heaven.

Parker dashed through the open door. "Where's Chip?"

"He had an appointment at the vet this morning, remember?" Merry said. "You get to work with Ralph today."

The little troublemaker was getting snipped, and not a moment too soon.

Parker nodded. "Oh right. Cool."

Merry handed him Ralph's leash with a warm smile. She

placed a hand on his arm and spoke to him softly. Parker listened, brow furrowed in concentration. He nodded periodically, then accepted a handful of dog cookies from Merry and began practicing with Ralph.

Merry stood close, watching and coaching as Parker asked the dog to sit, then practiced some leash manners. The grin he gave Merry left no doubt in T.J.'s mind that the boy was suffering from a preadolescent crush on his teacher.

If she realized it, she gave no indication.

By now, the rest of their group had arrived. Olivia led the group through basic exercises while Merry worked one-on-one with the kids, working on harder tasks and furthering the bond between the children and their dogs.

She was damn good at her job.

T.J., on the other hand, was failing miserably. While Pat, Madison, and Savannah gave lessons on Twilight, T.J. worked one-on-one with the kids to groom Peaches. She was too lame to be ridden today, but still thrilled to have the attention.

Jules flitted around like a happy butterfly, twirling with the curry comb until T.J. felt dizzy. Parker became frustrated when the mare didn't lift her hoof for him the first time he asked and stomped out of the barn.

He called his mom to come and pick him up early.

All the while, at the other end of the aisle, Merry worked her magic, somehow keeping dogs and kids in line without even breaking a sweat.

How the hell did she pull it off?

At noon, they all sat together at the shaded picnic tables behind the barn to eat lunch, then finished off the day by letting the dogs play in the sprinkler and feeding carrots to the horses.

By one, the kids were sweaty and exhausted when their parents came to claim them. The dogs lay in the cool shavings in the spare stall, stretched out flat and fast asleep.

Olivia tossed her blond ponytail and waved as she scurried toward her Prius. T.J. had to hand it to her, the girl worked hard, but as soon as the kids went home, she hit the road.

Merry usually lingered, helping him clean up, and hell, he couldn't pretend he minded. If he'd found her pretty before, seeing her hot and sweaty working in his barn was about the most gorgeous sight he'd ever seen.

She'd worn jeans today instead of shorts. She'd remembered about the riding lesson.

He couldn't quite figure where she stood with horses. She seemed to adore them, but there was a funny tension about her whenever he mentioned it. It was odd for a woman raised in North Carolina never to have even had a pony ride.

She stepped out of the stall where the dogs slept and brushed a brown curl from her face. "You know, those puppies weren't very reliable about sleeping through the night before camp started. This week? Not a peep."

"They're working hard."

"Yeah. So I'll just go get my purse..."

He crossed his arms over his chest and blocked her path. "Don't pretend you forgot."

She deflated like a ruptured balloon. "Look, I appreciate your offer to teach me to ride, but I have to pick Chip up at the vet soon, and Ralph and I still have to make our rounds at the hospital, so let's just call it a day, okay?"

"Nope. You love those horses, but there's something holding you back. I don't know what it is, but let's find out, shall we?"

Her chin went up. "There's nothing to find out. I've just never ridden before, and I'm not sure I want to start now."

"No time like the present." He walked outside.

All three horses lounged beneath the oak tree by the fence, grazing and swatting flies. Tango raised his head and whinnied, then trotted to the gate, hopeful for some attention after watching Twilight and Peaches work with the kids all morning.

T.J. unlatched the gate and slipped the gelding's leather halter over his ears. "You ready for some exercise?"

Tango tossed his head and snorted.

"We'll give the pretty lady a ride, then maybe I'll take you down to the stream to cool off."

Because T.J. was going to need as much cooling down as his horse after this lesson. Just thinking about Merry on his horse was turning him on. He didn't even want to contemplate his reasoning for wrangling her into a riding lesson. Clearly, he needed someone to knock some sense into his fool-headed brain.

She stood with her back against the wall, arms crossed over her chest while he led Tango into the barn. She looked at the gelding, her expression shuttered. "I can't believe I let you talk me into this."

Frankly, neither could he.

* * *

Merry stared at the horse and swallowed over the bolt of terror that had seized her by the throat. She loved horses. She trusted Tango, and T.J., for that matter. But the thought of getting up on the handsome red gelding was almost too much.

She'd wanted to ride so badly for so long that the idea of actually doing it left her mouth the consistency of sandpaper. What if it didn't live up to her expectations? What if she sucked at it? What if she fell on her ass and broke something? She absolutely could not afford a medical bill right now.

And somehow, in some stupid, ridiculous way, getting on that horse felt like letting her father down. As if it belittled the sacrifices he'd made in raising her to admit she'd wanted something so much and he couldn't afford to give it to her.

"I can practically hear you thinking," T.J. said. "Stop it."

"I should go check on the dogs."

"The dogs are fine. Come help me with Tango."

Good gracious. She was acting like such a baby that even T.J. could see she was being weird. This was so dumb. She'd let him lead her around on the damn horse, and then she'd go home.

End of story.

"First we're going to pick his feet," T.J. said.

"Right." She'd seen him show the kids how to do that with Twilight and Peaches.

"Like this, see?" He slid his hand down the back of Tango's leg, and the gelding lifted his hoof. T.J. propped it against his thigh and used a metal pick to scoop dirt out of the horse's hoof. "Be mindful of the frog, this part in the center. That's soft and sensitive. You want to scrape out the V-shaped part here."

He demonstrated, then handed the hoof pick to her. "Your turn."

She copied what she'd seen him do and soon held Tango's left front hoof in her hand. She bent and carefully scooped dirt. The pick snagged on something, then a rock popped out.

"See that?" T.J. said. "That's why we always pick the hooves before riding. Working with a rock like that in his hoof could make him lame."

"Gotcha."

Under T.J.'s guidance, she helped to groom Tango, then watched as he lifted the large western saddle onto his back. T.J. walked her through the process of tightening the cinch and putting the horse into his bridle.

Then the only thing left to do was ride him.

Great. Just that.

* * *

"Ready?" T.J. led Tango to the mounting block.

Merry stepped up, placed her left foot in the stirrup, and swung into the saddle. She gave a slight wiggle to center herself on Tango's back and smiled. It started as a small, tight smile, but quickly widened into a genuine grin that did funny things to various parts of his anatomy. He'd expected the rush of arousal, but not the funny sensation in his chest as if she'd literally taken his breath away.

"Okay, now what?" she asked, but the bite had gone out of her voice. That nervous edge she'd been sporting since he brought Tango into the barn vanished the moment she sat on his back.

Now it was T.J. who felt a nervous edge creeping into his tone. Because the sight of Merry on his horse was far more magnificent than he'd imagined. "Hold on to the horn here, for balance."

He guided her left hand onto the leather horn at the center of the saddle. Her fingers wrapped around its hard length and squeezed, and damned if his mind didn't nosedive straight into the gutter.

Merry's hazel eyes gleamed with excitement. She sat straight and tall in the saddle, her lean legs draped around Tango and anchored by the stirrups, her back stiff as a pole.

"You look like a natural up there," he said.

She shook her head, sending brown curls bouncing through the summer air. "I haven't done anything yet but sit here."

"First thing you need to do is relax."

She narrowed her eyes at him. "If I relax, I'll probably wind up in the dirt."

"He's going to bounce you around a lot, and the easiest way to ride is to relax and move with him. Stay loose here." He placed his hands on her hips, telling himself it was part of the lesson and not an excuse to touch her.

Merry sucked in a breath and glared at him.

He moved his hands to safer territory, stroking Tango's neck, before this exercise took a turn down a road neither one of them wanted to travel.

"Hold the reins like this in your right hand." He showed her. "Tango's mouth is very sensitive. You're going to want to keep the reins slack. Just lay them against his neck to turn him, left to go left, right to go right."

"Left, right, got it."

"To stop him, you're going to sit back in the saddle and say 'whoa.'"

"And pull back on the reins?" Merry's fingers tightened over the leather reins in her right hand.

"Nope. You won't need to."

She looked dubious. "If you say so."

"All right then, give him a nudge with your heels and let's get started."

Merry nudged Tango's sides, and the gelding started forward eagerly, bobbing his head in approval. Her body swayed to the rhythm of his gait, looking as natural as if she'd been doing this for years.

"Sure you've never been on a horse before?" he asked.

"Positive, and uh, why aren't you holding on to him?" She clutched the horn and gave him a slightly terrified look.

"Because you're not eight. Relax. Think of it like walking a dog."

She nodded, and the tension went out of her shoulders. Head up, she walked Tango in a circle around the ring, guiding him easily. Granted, most eight-year-olds could probably achieve the same thing on their first riding lesson, especially on that horse, but still he felt proud of her, conquering whatever it was she was conquering right now by riding his horse.

Her posture was still a little stiff, which was common in new riders. The more her body resisted Tango's movements, the more difficult it would be to sit in the saddle.

"Make sure you stay nice and loose in your hips," he said. "Just relax and let him move you."

Merry nodded. She kept her left hand on the horn, the reins held loosely in her right, and as he watched, her posture relaxed, and her hips began to sway with Tango's gait.

Beautiful.

"I haven't fallen off yet," she said over her shoulder.

"Not even close, sweetheart." He stood in the middle of the ring, thumbs shoved through his belt loops, watching Merry and Tango move together. Tango was alert but relaxed, ears pricked as he stepped them around the riding ring.

T.J. had her practice steering the horse left and right, starting and stopping, until she had gotten comfortable in the saddle. It was time to step things up a bit. "You ready for a jog?"

"Like trotting?"

He nodded. "Basically the same thing, a little slower and smoother on a western horse."

"Um, I think I'm good walking."

"Hey now, even the kids jogged on their first lesson."

Merry narrowed her eyes at him as Tango walked past. "No, they didn't. It wasn't until the third day of camp."

"Close enough. Just give him a little nudge with your heels and ask him to jog."

She tugged her bottom lip between her teeth, then nudged Tango into a jog. The gelding moved smooth as molasses, but even so, Merry quickly began to bounce and flail in the saddle, clutching the horn with both hands.

"Remember what I said, sit up straight and relax your body. Relax your back, your hips. Let yourself move with him."

She tipped dangerously to the left. "Help!"

"Whoa," T.J. called, and Tango drew himself to a halt just before Merry hit the dirt.

She gripped the horn and righted herself. "Yikes. I suck at this."

T.J. walked up to them and placed a hand on his horse's neck. Tango head butted him with affection. "On the contrary, you're doing really well. We're going to try again, and this time I want you to concentrate on moving with him. Pretend your butt is glued to the saddle and let your body do the rest."

"Easier said than done."

"When's the last time you tried a new sport that was easy on the first try? Go on now." He slapped Tango on the rump and sent them on their way.

Merry walked the length of the arena, then asked Tango to jog. She held on to the horn and bounced along, her ponytail flopping in the breeze.

"Remember, glue your butt to the saddle. Just absorb that movement through your hips." Why the hell was everything out of his mouth sounding dirty today? Maybe because his mind was still in the gutter. Goddamn but she looked gorgeous up there, even bouncing along like an amateur. He wanted her something fierce.

"I feel ridiculous," she panted, trying valiantly to keep her butt in the saddle.

"You're doing great. Keep your head up. Always look where you're going. You look down, you're picking out a spot to land."

Her chin went up. "Good to know."

She kept going, alternately jogging and walking on Tango until she'd somewhat found her stride on the horse's back. Her face glistened with sweat, but she smiled triumphantly. "Okay, that was pretty fun. Now I have a request of my own."

"Oh yeah, what's that?"

She looked at him, and he felt the heat in her eyes like a punch to the gut. "I want to watch you ride him. Show me how it's done."

CHAPTER ELEVEN

how you how it's done, huh?"

Merry wiped the sweat from her brow to keep from staring at him. "Yep."

"You want to watch me ride my horse?"

Well, now she was starting to feel foolish. But gracious, she really did want to see him ride. "Unless you're not in the mood to show off."

He chuckled, shaking his head at her.

She felt buzzed, high on adrenaline. She was breathless, sweaty, and probably going to be sore in some interesting places tomorrow, but horseback riding had been worth the wait. It was glorious and amazing to feel the powerful animal beneath her, to communicate and work together with him as he carried her.

"You ready to get off then?" T.J. asked.

She nodded, then looked down. "Uh, how do I do that exactly?"

"You're going to kick your feet out of the stirrups and swing your right leg over the saddle. Then slide down."

"Just slide down?" The ground looked pretty far away from where she was sitting.

"I'll catch you if you need catching." He tipped his hat back, looking totally ready to make good on his word.

I'll catch you if you need catching.

That sentence defined him perfectly, and for some stupid reason it made her want to swoon in his arms. It must be the horseback riding euphoria going to her head, because Merry Atwater did not need anyone to catch her. No thank you.

Except, as it turned out, she did.

She swung her leg over Tango's back, then hung there with her belly against the saddle, feeling ridiculous and terrified to let go, lest she land on her face under the horse. Then T.J.'s hands closed around her waist and lifted her free of Tango. He set her down as if she weighed nothing at all—which she greatly appreciated—then turned her to face him.

"You looked great up there, you know that?" His hands were still on her waist, and he looked so ridiculously handsome looking down at her from beneath his cowboy hat that she lost all control of herself and leaped into his arms.

"It was awesome." She clung to him for a moment, already feeling silly. She had so firmly resolved *not* to be impulsive around him anymore.

Horseback riding had seriously dangerous side effects.

She slid down him to get her feet back on the ground, and he let out a low, male sound, tightening his arms around her. Her pulse skittered into overdrive, shooting red-hot desire through her system.

"You are the craziest thing," he said, then his mouth was on hers, taking her in an all-consuming kiss.

She melted in his arms, kissing him until stars dotted her vision, tearing her mouth free before she passed out from oxygen deprivation. "Holy shit."

"That seems to be a common theme with us." His chest heaved beneath her fingers.

"We could try to keep ignoring it." She shrugged but made no attempt to pull free of his arms.

"But it's not going to go away, is it?"

She shook her head, remembering her words the first time they'd kissed. *Why fight chemistry? The best way to burn it out is to let it happen.*

And his reaction. Her body temperature cooled. "Unlikely. But even less likely? Us living happily ever after, so you know, why waste your time?"

A muscle in his jaw twitched. "I never said you were a waste of time."

She rolled her eyes and started to pull away.

"Dammit, Merry." Then he was kissing her again, and she was so far gone she couldn't even remember why it was a bad idea. All she felt was the magic of his mouth on hers, the need pulsing inside her, his hands on her butt, pressing her into him.

If there'd been a bed anywhere nearby, she'd have pulled him into it and surrendered blindly to what would have probably been blisteringly hot sex.

But they were standing in the middle of the riding ring with a mildly bored quarter horse watching them make out, the hot Carolina sun above them, even hotter earth beneath them. And she'd lost her damn mind.

She pulled her mouth from his and stepped backward out of his arms. No way was she having sex with T. J. Jameson because he wanted all the things she feared most: love, commitment, starting a family.

And somewhere deep inside, she was terrified that if she gave herself to him, if they surrendered to this all-consuming passion, she might forget the reason why those things didn't work for her.

Because T. J. Jameson meant more than sex. He was honorable and strong and dedicated. He championed his autistic nephew and took in a stray dog he feared because she'd asked him to. He'd make a fine husband and father.

And as she ran out of the arena without him, she realized she hadn't even gotten the chance to see him ride.

* * *

T.J. loped down to the creek at the back of his property on Tango, using the time alone on his horse to untangle what had just happened with Merry. The only thing he knew for sure was that he should have gone after her.

He hadn't.

She'd run, and he hadn't tried to stop her. Cowardly on both of their parts. The truth was, if she'd stayed, they'd probably be in his bed right now. And... *fuck*. Best not to think about it while on Tango's back or things could get mighty uncomfortable.

Tango waded into the stream where it widened at the bend. He bent his head and drank from the cool water, then pawed its clear depths, splashing them both.

"Thanks for the cold shower." T.J. lifted his hat to wipe his face. He wasn't complaining. The cool water felt good on his overheated skin.

The look in Merry's eyes just before she ran troubled him. She'd looked hurt, and if he'd been the one to hurt her, well, that made him feel like dirt. His daddy had raised him to always treat a woman right, and while he'd had a few cocky moments in his teens he wasn't terribly proud of, he'd never mistreated a woman.

Never felt he owed an apology. Until Merry.

She twisted him up, and turned him on, and pissed him off. One thing was for sure: the chemistry between them wasn't going away. The only question then was what were they going to do about it?

And damned if he knew the answer.

* * *

That night, Merry tossed and turned. Restless energy pulsed through her veins and twitched in her toes. There was no way she and T.J. could go back to pretending nothing had happened between them. Not after she'd flung herself in his arms, then run off like a coward after he kissed her.

Three weeks of camp remained. That was a hell of a long time to fight this chemistry without making things any more awkward than they already were.

She shoved her face into the pillow and exhaled into its feathery depths. Man problems of this magnitude weren't her forte. She didn't play games, didn't let messy emotions sneak in and make things complicated.

She didn't do complicated. Period.

Life was too short for complications.

She reached for her phone and groaned at the time. One forty-three. Tomorrow—or technically today—was Saturday, and she'd agreed to cover a shift for Tara so that the other nurse could spend the day with family in town for the weekend.

Much-needed overtime.

And the shift was going to kick her ass if she didn't get some sleep.

Five mostly sleepless hours later, she stepped onto the hospital's pediatric floor and began what promised to be a grueling shift. Saturdays were always busy, with extra visitors and patients cranky about spending the weekend in the hospital.

Her patients were all new, except for Baby Jayden. Hopefully in a few weeks he'd go home with his foster family and get the chance to be a normal baby, as normal as life could be for an infant with a rocky medical history and no family to call his own.

Merry tracked down his outgoing nurse, Nadya, and together they went into his room. He'd had another seizure on Friday, but nothing since. Maybe he was turning a corner in his recovery. Jayden usually slept during her first morning round, exhausted after a grueling night of screaming.

He was alone this morning. His mother, Crystal, had returned to jail on Thursday after receiving treatment for kidney stones.

He was better off without her. Wasn't he?

Nadya left the room, but Merry lingered. She stood by his crib and watched the baby as he slept, those pink cheeks and rosy lips that still quivered. She'd recognized the look on Crystal's face when she held Jayden.

Love.

Unfortunately, sometimes love wasn't enough.

Then again, who the hell was she to judge? At least Crystal's baby would survive. Merry had failed her own son so completely that Tyler had paid with his life.

Her tear splashed onto Jayden's cheek, and she swiped at it in annoyance.

Sometimes she missed Tyler so much it felt like her whole body might collapse, as if she'd grown hollow inside until there was nothing left but a shell. Someday, someone might accidentally squeeze too hard and crush her like an empty egg.

She pressed a hand over her mouth to keep from screaming, drawing ragged breaths until she'd gotten herself under control.

"Hang in there, Jayden," she whispered, then bolted from his room.

The rest of the morning passed in a blur. Too few hours of sleep, bolstered by untold cups of coffee, left her bleary-eyed and jittery from caffeine. She powered through on sheer adrenaline, relying on the energy reserve that had carried her through many longer shifts on less sleep. The job had to be done, and it had to be done well.

She'd finish her shift, then go home and collapse. Tonight she'd sleep like a stone.

She saw Jayden through more painful hours, endless screaming, and medicated sleep to help him rest. She cared for a girl recovering from a severe asthma attack, a boy who'd burned his fingers roasting marshmallows, and a toddler fighting an off-season case of the flu.

Her MedLink phone never stopped ringing, summoning her from room to room. Lunchtime came and went, and Merry had yet to sit down. She administered breathing treatments, changed bandages, and reassured frightened parents. By late afternoon, it looked like things might be slowing down.

And then Jayden had another seizure. This time, it took almost an hour for the doctors to get it under control. Dr. Lopez added a new label to his chart: seizure disorder.

Until his seizures could be managed, whether by medicine or naturally as his body detoxed from the heroin, he would have to remain in the hospital.

By seven thirty, Merry was in the elevator, headed for her car. Halfway to the first floor, the adrenaline crash hit. Her knees started to shake, and she leaned against the wall to brace herself.

She really should have taken the time to grab a sandwich before she left the hospital, but fatigue had robbed her of her appetite. She just wanted to get home, walk her dogs, and go to bed.

Sleep until her next shift. She'd pay the neighbor's daughter extra to come exercise her dogs tomorrow to make up for it.

She shuffled into the parking lot, rummaging in her purse for her keys. Her head swam, and spots danced in front of her eyes. Whoa. Okay, she should have stopped for food. She couldn't drive home like this.

There was a PowerBar in her glove compartment, wasn't there?

She'd eat it, revive herself, and make the ten-minute drive home before the sugar rush faded.

Where the hell had she parked that morning? She wandered around the parking lot for what felt like hours before she found the CR-V, then rubbed her eyes and stared.

T. J. Jameson leaned against the driver's door.

* * *

"What in the world?" Merry propped her hands on her hips and frowned.

He cocked his head and smiled, that annoyingly charming smile that melted her insides and made her whole body buzz. "I didn't quite like the way we left things yesterday."

She glared at him. "Why, because we didn't end up in your bed? Or wait, that's not what you wanted anyway. I can't remember."

And she was too damned tired to argue with him right now. Her hands shook. Her blood sugar was low, and she might just pass out at his feet if he didn't get out of her way.

He shook his head. "Whether or not I want you in my bed is entirely different from whether that's a good idea."

She pressed a hand to her forehead. "You think too much. Jesus."

"Don't you think we should have a conversation about this? While we're both clearheaded and calm."

"I am *not* clearheaded right now. It's been a really long day, and I just want to go home."

He pushed off from the car and stepped closer. "You okay?"

She put her fists against his chest and pushed. He didn't budge, but she almost knocked herself off her feet with the effort. "Move. Seriously."

He gripped her elbows and hauled her closer. "You're pale, and you're shaking. What's wrong?"

"I'm exhausted and seriously in need of food. So please, get out of my way." She shoved his chest again, with similar results.

"Should you be driving right now?" He tipped his head and peered at her from beneath the brim of his hat.

"I'm fine." Or she would be, as soon as he got out of her way and she ate the PowerBar waiting in her car.

"You don't look fine."

"Oh, my God." She shoved him again, and this time he released her and stepped aside. She tripped over her own damn feet and stumbled against the side of the CR-V.

"Merry—"

She threw a hand out to silence him. "Cut it out, macho man. I have a PowerBar in the car. That'll raise my blood sugar enough to get me home."

He twirled her keys around his index finger and shook his head. "I'm driving you home."

"How the hell did you get my keys?" She stared at her hands, dumbfounded.

"You're a little off your game right now. Quit being difficult and let me drive you home."

Her head was starting to buzz, and whoa—

She was in T.J.'s arms, wrapped up in his earthy scent, and wow, he was strong. She pressed her face against his chest and breathed him in.

"Dammit, woman." His voice was gruff. "I'm putting you in my truck."

She didn't protest, which was probably evidence enough of her current impairment. Instead, she wrapped her arms around his neck and let him carry her to his truck.

I'll catch you if you need catching, he'd said yesterday.

At least he was as good as his word.

CHAPTER TWELVE

T.J. set her in the passenger seat of his truck and tipped her chin up to see her face. "You okay? I'm going to drive you home."

She nodded, and her silence bothered him almost as much as the haunted look in her eyes.

He went around to the cooler he kept in the back of the truck and grabbed a bottle of water, a stick of beef jerky, and an apple. He rounded the truck and slid into the driver's seat, then tossed them into her lap.

She glanced up, eyes wide. "Where did that come from?"

"Back of the truck. I keep some essentials for when I work a long call and need to keep my strength up. Eat."

She picked at the beef jerky. "I've never eaten jerky before. Is it gross?"

"Chewy, salty. It's good protein." He backed out of the parking spot and headed for the nearest exit.

He would have asked how she made it through her shift in her current condition, but he already knew the answer. He'd been where she was, after running in crisis mode for several hours, then crashing hard when it was all over and the adrenaline stopped.

"You wanna talk about it?" he asked.

She took a bite of jerky and scrunched her face. "The jerky? It's okay."

"Jesus, Merry, don't be a smart-ass."

Her expression hardened. "It was a tough shift. I'm a nurse. It happens."

He turned left on Main Street. She wasn't just a nurse. She was a pediatric nurse, which meant she not only dealt with pain and suffering on a daily basis, but it was the pain and suffering of children.

"Where to?" he asked.

"Home," she said, then popped the last bite of jerky into her mouth.

"I figured, but where do you live?"

"Oh, right. 508 Peachtree Lane."

"Peachtree, is that off of Sturbridge Road?"

She nodded, guzzled half the bottle of water, then started in on the apple. The color slowly returned to her cheeks.

Good.

They drove for a minute in silence, then she turned to him. "So why were you waiting outside work for me?"

"I told you, I didn't like the way we left things yesterday."

"But I don't usually work on Saturdays, so how did you know where to find me?"

Aha. There was the Merry he knew. The food was doing its job.

He shrugged. "I called your cell a few times and you didn't answer, so I called the hospital and asked if you were on duty."

"Pretty desperate to see me, sounds like."

Ah, yes, even her sass was back. And yeah, he'd been feeling a little desperate. "Not so much desperate as thinking maybe we needed to have a conversation about where we stand."

"Whether I'm going to sleep with you."

That one hit below the belt. "I'm a little curious, aren't you?"

She shrugged. "You know, you were probably right the first time. Best not to complicate things. We do have to work together, after all."

"True."

"That's that, then. No more kissing." She wagged her finger at him.

"All right." But now that she'd said it, he wanted her to take it back. He wanted to kiss her. He wanted to lay her down in his bed and make love to her until they both forgot their names. He wanted to lose himself in her completely.

"Gee, so glad we had this conversation," she said, her tone artificially light. "Would I be pushing my luck if I asked to ride one of your horses again after camp next week?"

"Not at all. You're welcome to ride any time." He glanced over at her, her pale face surrounded by that wild mane of curls. Somewhere since the parking lot, they'd come free from the ponytail she'd worn when she left work.

"Thanks." She leaned her head against the headrest and closed her eyes. "And thanks for the ride, by the way. I was running pretty ragged back there."

"You're welcome." He slowed the truck for the turn from Sturbridge onto Peachtree. "Do you need a ride to work in the morning?"

She shook her head. "I'll call my dad or Liv to pick me up."

"It's no problem. I'll drop you off before I head over to my parents' for church."

"Church?" She flinched as if he'd offended her.

"You're not religious?"

"I work on Sundays."

He glanced at her. "That's not what I asked."

She looked away. "I'm nonpracticing at the moment."

"A nonpracticing what?"

"Methodist." That haunted look was back in her eyes.

"Wanna talk about it?"

She turned on him. "Let's save some time here. The answer to that question is always going to be no, okay? That's my house over there on the corner, the gray one with blue shutters."

He shrugged as he turned into her driveway. "Just trying to be friendly."

"Thanks again for the ride, and the jerky." She waved over her shoulder as she slid out of his truck.

"You're welcome. So I'll pick you up around six thirty?"

She nodded, then hurried up the walkway to her front door.

Frustrated, he pulled back onto Peachtree Lane.

When they met, he'd judged her for her girly attire and loose attitude toward relationships, but Merry Atwater was no floozy. She spent her life taking care of sick kids and abandoned dogs, and she'd held her own at camp. There was steel behind her brightly colored fingernails. And she had a big heart she tried very hard to keep under wraps.

Now he was left with the uncomfortable feeling that perhaps she was nothing like he'd originally thought. And he was a total idiot for not taking her up on her offer that night they first kissed.

* * *

Damn T.J. for forcing her hand. Now she'd gone and said there'd be no more kissing, which meant none of any of the other fun stuff kissing led to.

Which was for the best, really.

Sleeping with T.J. was asking for all sorts of trouble, and

besides, she really did need to work on her self-control. This was as good an exercise as any.

Groaning, Merry rolled over in bed and pressed her face against Ralph's soft fur. It was time to get up and get ready for her shift, and she was still bone tired. As badly as she'd needed it, sleep last night had been elusive. She'd been haunted by Jayden's screams, memories of his tiny body seizing and her pathetic attempts to calm him.

And when she'd finally quit hearing his screams, she'd fallen deep and dreamed of T.J. In her dreams, he'd been in bed with her, gloriously naked and thrusting inside her. She'd woken in a sweat, aching for him and totally unsatisfied.

All in all, a frustrating and less than restful night. She rolled out of bed and padded into the bathroom, then went downstairs to let the dogs out. She put Chip out first, since he was still recovering from being neutered and needed to take it easy, then kept him in the kitchen with her while Salsa and Ralph tumbled over each other across the backyard.

While the dogs romped, she poured herself a much-needed cup of coffee. For almost the first time she could remember, she was not looking forward to work today. She dreaded the heartbreak of seeing Jayden and hearing those bloodcurdling screams that might just haunt her dreams for the rest of her life.

Forty-five minutes later, she was showered and dressed, the dogs gated in the kitchen, as T.J. pulled into the driveway. Right on time.

Dependable T.J.

"You look about as tired as you did when I dropped you off last night," he said as she climbed into the cab of his truck.

"Gee, thanks, and good morning to you too." She glanced over at him, then wished she hadn't.

He was dressed for church in khaki slacks and a periwinkle blue button-down shirt, his cheeks clean shaven and carrying the faint minty scent of aftershave. And dear lord, he was handsome. She wanted to crawl into his lap, to breathe in his scent, to take up where they'd left off last night in her dreams.

"Didn't sleep well?" he asked.

"Nope." She clipped her seat belt, and he backed out of the driveway. "Thanks for the ride."

"No problem."

"You go to church with your parents every Sunday?"

He nodded. "Most weeks. Doesn't always work with my schedule, but I try."

"You're one of the good guys, aren't you?"

"Most of the time." He said it with an edge that sent shivers up and down her spine. Oh, she wanted to see him be bad. Really, really bad.

She clutched her purse closer and stared out the window.

T.J. cleared his throat. "So, you're not going to come out of work tonight looking like you did last night, are you?"

Smart man, changing the subject. "Nope. And I would have been fine last night. I had a PowerBar in my car that would have gotten me home."

He made a sound that said he disagreed.

Maybe he was right. She remembered the way she'd fallen into his arms and let him carry her to his truck. So maybe she'd been a bit pathetic last night. Maybe a small part of her had wanted to lean on him. To be carried for once, instead of carrying everything herself.

A little chivalry wasn't bad, once in a while. As long as she didn't make a habit of letting big, strong, devastatingly handsome cowboys carry her around because she was too weak to stand on her own two feet.

"Must be tough," he said. "Sick kids. I can't imagine some of the stuff you've seen."

She stared out the window. "You don't want to."

"I lost a foal night before last. He was breech, and the

mare had been laboring a while before they called me in. He was already gone when I got there, nothing I could do but help to get him out so that the mare would be okay."

"Aw, poor thing." She looked at T.J. "Was she sad? Do horses feel loss like that?"

"Yeah, she knew. She cleaned him up and nuzzled at him for a little while until I took him out."

"What did you do with him?"

"The owner and I dug a hole and buried him out behind the pasture."

"That was nice of you." She turned back to the window.

"Figured you know what that feels like."

She gasped as if he'd just sucker punched her to the gut, her skin prickling hot. She saw the dirt falling over Tyler's grave, the stares, heard the whispers from the other mourners, felt the raw grief that had almost swallowed her whole. "Who told you?"

She gripped the dashboard of the truck, her mouth sour. How in the world did he know about Tyler? Not even Cara knew.

"Told me what?" he asked. "Jesus, Merry, you look like you're about to be sick."

"I'm not . . . what? What were you talking about?"

He slammed on the brakes and veered onto the grassy edge of the road, then turned to face her, his eyes dark and intense. "I figured something happened to one of your patients yesterday, so I was trying to find some common ground, maybe get you to open up to me."

The breath whooshed from her lungs. He didn't know. He didn't know about Tyler.

"What did you think I was talking about?"

Oh, shit. "I . . . no, you're right. I did have a tough day with a patient yesterday."

He placed a big, warm hand over hers. "I'm sorry."

"This little baby, he's been through so much. It's hard to watch, that's all."

"A baby? Oh hell." He pulled her into his arms.

She burrowed against his chest and breathed in his scent until the nausea receded. Then she cleared her throat and sat up. "It's part of the job."

"You wouldn't be human if you didn't let it get to you sometimes." His fingers trailed over her cheek, and she almost flung herself into his arms again. What the hell was the matter with her?

"Oh, I'm definitely human." And his fingers were definitely still on her skin, as every one of her nerve cells could easily attest.

He moved his hand to the steering wheel and swung the truck back onto the road, and it took every ounce of her new-found self-control not to stop him.

* * *

T.J. aimed his truck for the open country roads outside Dogwood. He put the windows down and let the fresh, early morning air whip over his skin. He needed to get Merry out of his head before church, because right now his thoughts were definitely not appropriate to take inside God's house.

Then there was the small matter of whatever the hell had happened after he told her about burying the foal. She'd completely panicked, then covered with that story about the sick baby at work, but he'd accidentally touched on something else.

"Who told you?" she'd said. Her eyes held that glassy look of fear he'd seen in many a hurt or cornered animal.

Whatever it was, he didn't know, and it was none of his business. He needed to get his head on straight, because whether or not they succumbed to the chemistry that was burning them both up, she'd made it clear she wasn't interested in a long-term relationship. When camp ended, they would part ways.

There was no sense wasting time and energy on what he couldn't change. And anyway, Noah needed to be his top priority right now.

He drove until the sun blazed overhead, then turned his truck toward Sycamore United Methodist Church, where he joined Amy, Noah, his parents, and various other cousins and neighbors for Sunday service. After church, they all headed to Blue Sky Farm for EmmyLou's kick-ass brunch.

Per their Sunday tradition, Trace let T.J. know which horses needed checking on, and he headed to the barn while his mom got the food ready. "You want to come with me and give me a hand?" he asked Noah.

The boy nodded, then followed him toward the barn.

"So what did you think of the first week of camp?"

"It was fun." Noah sat cross-legged in a chair outside Jewel's stall, his hands moving restlessly at his sides. He bent his head and picked at a loose string on his shirtsleeve.

"Amber misses you when you go home." T.J. stepped inside the stall to check on Jewel and Ruby, her filly. At a week old, Ruby was already nibbling at her mother's hay. T.J. checked her out fully, feeling her legs, both to check for formation and to get her used to being handled.

Ruby tugged at his shirt playfully, then ran in a circle around the stall. Jewel came over and nudged him, checking his pockets for the carrots he always carried. He fed her one.

"So I was thinking maybe you could stay over one night this week, sort of a slumber party with Amber. What do you think?"

Noah peeked through the bars and nodded with a wide smile.

"Maybe we can order a pizza, watch a movie. What movie would you like?"

"*Air Bud*," Noah said.

"I haven't seen that one. What's it about?" T.J. held his breath, praying for an actual conversation with his nephew.

"A boy and a dog," he whispered, then went back to picking at his shirt.

"A boy and a dog, huh?" T.J. gave one last pat to the filly, then stepped out of the stall. "Sounds familiar."

He kept chatting as he checked on two other horses, with Noah mostly ignoring him, picking at his sleeves. He had a pile of strings in his lap by the time they were ready to head up to the house to eat.

Inside, no one was talking much as they all heaped their plates with muffins, biscuits, eggs, sausage, and grits. They ate until their bellies ached, lavishing EmmyLou with praise for her cooking, and then Trace and T.J. cleaned up the kitchen for her.

He found Amy in the hall and pulled her aside. "How are things? Has he talked about camp at all?"

She swiped a hand through her hair and shook her head. "Not much. He talks about Amber some. He's asked if I can get medicine for my allergies so that we could keep her."

"I'll talk to him about it."

"I think he has a little crush on Merry." Amy smiled.

T.J. chuckled. "Yeah, I noticed that too."

"That makes two of you," she said with a playful swat to his elbow.

"What?"

"Oh, come on. You go all starry-eyed every time someone mentions her name," she said.

"I do not."

"You should go for it. I think she'd be good for you. She might even lighten you up a little."

"Merry and I are looking for totally different things right now. And that's not what I wanted to talk about. I'm worried about Noah. He seems to be talking less instead of more. What's going on? Is something bothering him?"

Amy sighed, a deep, weary sigh that seemed to draw her in on herself. "It seems like it. He's been especially agitated and withdrawn lately, and I can't figure out why."

"You don't think it's camp, do you?"

"Oh, goodness no. The only time he smiles is when he's talking about camp. It's the highlight of his day."

"What then?"

Amy shook her head. "I can't figure it out. School's out for the summer, so it can't be anything there. We haven't made any changes at home recently, nothing to explain the way he's acting."

"I asked him if he'd like to sleep over one night this week. Maybe I can get something out of him then."

"That sounds great." Amy gave him a quick hug. "Let me know if he tells you anything, okay?"

"You know I will." He felt the weight of her worry. One way or another, he'd figure out what was bothering Noah. He'd find a way to help his nephew. And Amy too. He had to.

* * *

Merry stared at the spreadsheet, then rubbed her eyes. She was taking a sleeping pill tonight. Desperate times called for desperate measures. And she was desperately tired.

Today's shift had wiped her out. At least camp tomorrow meant only working the second half of her shift. Despite the heat and the sweat, she was enjoying working with the kids. They'd all made great progress with their dogs. Confidence was growing, bonds were forming.

Week one had been a success. Now she just needed to keep the momentum going into week two. She desperately needed the second half of her donation from T.J.

The rescue's bank account was again sitting on empty. She was right back where she'd started two weeks ago, the night Amber had been dumped on her doorstep. She'd spent the first five hundred from T.J., plus modest donations from the event at Perry's Pet Boutique and her pleas on Facebook.

How had she allowed herself to become so dependent on an anonymous benefactor? Stupid rookie mistake. The reality was, she needed to learn how to fund-raise on her own. It was ridiculous that she hadn't made more progress toward bailing TBR out. She needed to set up more adoption events, get more active on social media, and find new ways to bring in money.

She'd be flat out for the next two days with work after camp, but Wednesday afternoon when she got home, she was going to spend the afternoon at her computer and figure this thing out. No more messing around.

With a sigh, she shut down her laptop and took the dogs out. She went to the medicine cabinet and got one of the sleep aids she kept as a last resort. She hated taking them, hated feeling like she couldn't get to sleep on her own.

Just tonight. Eight hours of sleep, then a few hours on the farm to reset her system. Put a little salve over the rawness of Jayden's screams.

So for that night, she slept deep and dreamlessly, and she arrived at camp on Monday morning feeling refreshed and invigorated. It was amazing what a good night's sleep could do for a person.

By contrast, the kids were droopy and unfocused after a weekend off from camp.

"This puppy is impossible," Parker announced at nine fifteen, after working with Chip for a mere ten minutes. "I give up."

Chip hung his head, upset that he'd frustrated Parker,

not understanding that the boy's erratic yanking at the leash wasn't an invitation to play tug-of-war.

Merry spent the next ten minutes working with them, helping Parker lower his voice and calm his body so that Chip could focus on his own behavior. The more worked up Parker got, the more hyper Chip became.

Parker was able to get the puppy to sit, and with Merry's help, lay down. As a reward, she took them outside for a sprint across the field to let boy and dog blow off some much-needed energy. Savannah, who'd been sitting by the riding ring drinking a Diet Coke, joined them.

When they returned, Merry got everyone some cold water, then swapped dogs with Parker so that he could practice with Ralph for a little while. Chip and Parker were still a work in progress. She wanted to see them working in harmony before camp ended as her own personal milestone. She also needed Parker to stick it out so that he didn't give T.J. ammunition to withhold any of her donation.

"I see what he's doing wrong," Lucy said, after Parker had gone down the hall with Ralph. She pushed her wheelchair easily across the dirt floor of the barn, Bosley's leash looped through her right hand.

"Oh yeah?" Merry had been impressed with Lucy right away. The girl had a commanding presence and a calm, firm hand with the dogs.

"He's telling Chip different things with his words and his hands. See?" She reached for Chip's leash.

Merry handed it over and took Bosley from her, watching closely. The last thing she wanted was to see Lucy yanked out of her chair by the troublesome pup.

Lucy looked down at Chip and in a clear voice, she said, "Sit." With her left hand, she gave him the corresponding hand signal. Her right hand stayed in her lap, the muscles stiffened by her cerebral palsy.

Chip sat.

"Good boy!" She tossed him a cookie. "Down." Again, she gave the verbal and hand command simultaneously.

Chip slid to his belly on the cool, dirt floor.

"Good boy, Chip." She tossed him another cookie. "See? You're a good puppy."

"And you're a good puppy trainer. That was perfect, Lucy. Would you like to help me work with Chip later this morning?"

"Sure." Lucy smiled, her blue eyes bright. "I'm really enjoying camp. It's a lot more fun than I thought it was going to be."

"Oh yeah? I'm glad to hear it." Merry knelt beside Chip to give the puppy a hug. "What's been your favorite part so far, the dogs or the horses?"

"Definitely the dogs." Lucy paused and bit her lip. "I wasn't sure I'd be able to ride a horse, you know, with my legs. But it's actually been pretty fun."

"I saw you on Twilight on Friday. You looked great up there." Merry stood. "I had my very first riding lesson on Friday too. I was pretty terrified."

"Really? Your very first?" Lucy's eyed widened.

"Yep. My first time on a horse."

"Did you like it?"

"I did. I may even try it again."

"I bet you're good at it," Lucy said.

Merry winked. "Well, I didn't fall off."

T.J. walked up behind them and put a hand on the back of Lucy's chair. "You're not a real rider until you've fallen off at least twice, or that's what my daddy taught me."

Lucy cringed. "In that case, I don't want to be a real rider."

"Me either," Merry said.

"Don't worry." T.J. met her eyes for a moment, then looked down at Lucy. "I'm not planning to have any of you fall off on my watch. You want to keep riding past camp, be ready to hit the dirt at some point though. It's all part of the learning experience."

"If you say so." Lucy looked unconvinced.

"Pat's ready for you with Twilight," he told her.

"Okay." Lucy handed Chip's leash to Merry and wheeled down the hall toward the riding ring, throwing Merry an apprehensive glance over her shoulder.

"Gee, way to psych her up for her lesson," Merry said. "Get her paranoid about falling off."

He shrugged. "It happens. She'd be fine."

And with that, he turned and strolled out of the barn.

The rest of the morning passed uneventfully, but Merry couldn't stop thinking about Lucy and her natural gift with the dogs. Before camp ended, she was going to suggest to her parents that they consider looking into a service dog for her.

Lucy was smart, and motivated, and resentful when her physical limitations held her back. A service dog could increase her independence and provide her a sense of purpose as well.

It was worth looking into.

After the kids left, she went up to the house to grab her purse. She found Noah in the kitchen, filling a glass of lemonade. "Hey, Noah, great job with Amber today."

Noah froze, then bolted from the room, leaving a trail of lemonade droplets across the linoleum.

"Sorry if I startled you," she called over her shoulder as she left. "See you tomorrow."

She walked out to her car and started it to get the AC going, then went down to the barn to get the dogs. T.J. was in the pasture with the horses so she hustled Ralph and the puppies up the driveway to her car.

No need to invite trouble.

In the car, she checked her wallet as she did every day before she went home. It was silly; she couldn't really imagine any of those kids stealing from her, and they weren't likely to even see her purse up at the house.

She kept it in a back corner of the kitchen counter, where no one would notice it if they came into the house to use the bathroom during camp. Perfectly safe.

Her stomach plummeted as she counted the bills inside her wallet. Another five dollars was missing. She'd had a ten and two five-dollar bills in there this morning. One of the fives was gone.

This time, she was positive. Since the incident last week, she'd noted the amount in her purse before and after camp every day so that she could be certain in case they needed to bring an accusation against one of the kids.

Except none of the kids should have had access to her purse.

Then she remembered Noah in the kitchen, pouring lemonade. The way he'd run from her when she came in. *Oh, no*.

Was it possible that Noah had stolen from her? Why?

It made no sense. Noah was a good kid, a sweet kid. He was not a thief or a troublemaker.

But what if Merry wasn't the only one with financial problems? Maybe this was Noah's misguided attempt to help his mom. It couldn't be easy for Amy as the single parent of a special needs child. The last thing Merry wanted was to cause more trouble for her, or Noah.

She slid the wallet back into her purse with a heavy feeling in her gut. For now, she'd keep the information to herself. She needed to be sure before she said anything to T.J., because he certainly wouldn't take kindly to the idea.

If it turned out she was right, and she had to tell him his nephew had stolen from her, one thing was for sure: this would douse the flames between them once and for all.

CHAPTER THIRTEEN

Merry held her right hand in front of herself. "Stay."

She stepped backward away from Ralph, and he sat, watching her closely. After several long seconds, she bent and clapped her hands. "Okay, come! Good boy."

The dog bounded to her, wiggling with excitement, and she lavished him with praise while four little pairs of hands applauded his good behavior.

She turned toward the kids. "That's what we're going to be working on for the rest of the week: teaching them to stay. It's a harder command than anything we've done yet, and it's going to take a lot of practice. You guys ready?"

They all nodded.

"Okay, now that the demonstration is over, I'm going to take Parker and Lucy for their riding lesson," T.J. said. Pat and his girls were already waiting for them outside with Twilight and Peaches.

"Noah, you're up first with me," Merry said. "Jules, you're going to practice with Olivia while I work with Noah, and then we'll switch."

Merry put Chip and Bosley in the empty stall, then joined

Noah and Amber in their usual spot in the corner. "You guys ready?"

Noah nodded. Amber sat beside him, tongue lolling and tail wagging. She had truly blossomed in the three weeks since camp began. Farm life suited her perfectly, and she adored Noah. Unfortunately, although Noah returned her adoration, camp was not having the same effect on him.

While the other kids developed confidence and social skills, Noah stayed in the corner, withdrawn within himself. His eyes held a vaguely haunted look that Merry knew all too well. Something was troubling him.

It had been a week now since the incident in the kitchen when she suspected he had stolen from her, and she was ready to get some answers. Only a week of camp remained. She was running out of time.

"I'll let you in on a little secret that you might have already figured out," she told him.

Noah looked up, his blue eyes wide.

"Some of the dogs already know the commands we're learning in camp. Amber doesn't. Everything she's learned, you've taught her."

Noah smiled, and for a moment, the worry on his face lifted away. "I know."

"I figured. You're a smart kid." She tousled his mop of brown hair. "Ready? We're going to start small to help her learn."

Noah nodded.

"Okay, first I want you to come and stand here next to me."

He stood and scurried to her side.

"Now I want you to ask her to sit, and when she sits, praise her."

Noah raised his arm and gave Amber the hand signal to sit. She sat, and he grinned with pride, then gave her a cookie.

"That was great, Noah. Now I want to see you practice

with the hand and the verbal commands. It's important for her to learn to respond to both. Try it one more time."

Noah repeated the action, this time saying "Sit" in a strong, clear voice. Again, Amber sat, and again he rewarded her with kisses and cookies.

"Perfect." She patted his shoulder. "Great job."

It was a victory every time Noah used his words to communicate. Not only was he speaking, he was asserting himself. It was a great life skill to have.

"Now, while she's sitting, put your hand out in front of you like this." She showed him. "And tell her to stay. You're going to take a small step back, and if she stays, quickly go back to her and praise her. Make sense?"

Noah nodded. He raised his chin, squared his shoulders, then held out his right hand and said, "Stay."

He stepped back, and Amber watched. She leaned forward, stretching toward him, but Noah shook his head. Then he lunged back to her and fell to his knees, lavishing her with praise.

"That was fantastic! You guys are amazing. Let's keep practicing for a few minutes. When you're ready to release her from the stay, you'll say 'okay,' so say that right before you go back to her, okay?"

Noah nodded. They practiced together for another ten minutes. Sometimes Amber followed Noah, but often she stayed. She was a quick learner, and he was a good teacher. One advantage of using few words was that it gave each word he did use more weight.

When Noah spoke, Amber listened.

"You guys did great. You're really good with her, Noah. She trusts you, and that makes everything easier."

Noah beamed. He wrapped his arms around Amber's neck and squeezed, and her tail swished happily back and forth. Oh, how Merry hoped these two could stay together forever. She was going to lay a hell of a guilt trip on T.J. when camp ended.

In the meantime...

"I know my main job here is to help you guys with the dogs, but I want you to also think of me as someone you can trust. If you have anything on your mind that you want to talk about, I'm a great listener and a pretty good problem solver. I might be able to help."

Noah turned his face against Amber's fur.

"I just wanted you to know you can always talk to me. I know what it's like to be scared, and confused, and think no one will understand. Believe me, I've been there."

He peeked up at her but said nothing.

Merry was bluffing her way through this conversation. Truly, she had no idea what was bothering Noah. Amy seemed like a good mom, but as a nurse, Merry had seen plenty of kids come to harm by a parent's hand. It never hurt to have a solid ally outside the family.

"Anyway, just keep it in mind if you ever feel like talking. Here." She pulled a business card from her pocket and handed it to him. "You ever find yourself in a situation you don't like and aren't sure what to do? Just give me a call. I'll come, no questions asked. Okay?"

He took it and slipped it into his pocket with a shy nod.

"All right then, it's time for me to work with Jules and Salsa. You think about what we talked about and keep practicing that stay with Amber, okay?"

Merry led them back to the group, hoping against hope that she'd gotten through to him.

* * *

T.J. blew out a breath. Halfway through the third week of camp, the kids were all doing well for the most part. He was the one having a problem. He was frustrated, driven half-way out of his mind by the ongoing friction between him and Merry, Noah's increased moodiness, and having a dog underfoot every damn minute in his own house.

He was ready for camp to end. Ready to get his simple, orderly life back.

Except that he wasn't. He had a feeling nothing would be the same once they all left, once his farm was quiet and empty again.

He needed a nice long ride on Tango after camp today. They'd take a trail ride through the woods, let the peace and quiet reset both of their systems. Necessary stress relief.

Peaches was back in the ring today and thrilled to be carrying Lucy. Pat led her, while Savannah and Madison walked on either side. T.J. walked behind, leading Parker on Twilight. The boy seemed to find his center on a horse, calm and focused.

"All right, now," Pat said. "I want you to close your eyes and concentrate on feeling the horse move underneath you."

T.J. glanced up at Parker. The boy sat, eyes closed, both hands on the saddle horn, but his posture was relaxed. They walked a full length around the arena, while Pat had them focus on each part of their body individually, their legs, their shoulders, their arms, their necks. Then he asked them to open their eyes.

"Feels different when you can't see, doesn't it?" he asked.

"Kind of cool," Parker said.

Next, Pat had them extend their arms out to the side, learning to center their bodies over the saddle while increasing balance and muscle tone.

Both kids remained quiet and engaged. Confident. Everyone in camp had made great progress except Noah. Which frustrated the hell out of T.J.

He'd seen Merry spending extra time with him, and he wanted to know what they'd been talking about. So far, she hadn't volunteered anything, despite her promise to keep him in the loop where his nephew was concerned.

After lessons, the kids helped hose off Peaches and Twilight, then put them in the pasture to graze with Tango. T.J. had given Merry two more riding lessons last week. She was holding her own, still timid but solid in the saddle. Maybe he'd invite her to join him and Tango for a ride after camp, give Twilight a much-needed break from the monotony of lessons, and see if he could get any information out of her about Noah.

And of course, the chance to see Merry on his horse again. There was always that.

He found her in the barn with Ralph, the kids crowded around her.

"Your turn, Jules," she said.

T.J. stood in the doorway, watching.

Jules stepped up to Ralph. "Ralph, sit." Her voice was clear and strong.

"Stay," she said, holding out her right hand. She stepped backward, focused on the dog as she walked away from him. "Stay," she repeated before she turned her back, walked to the grain room, then turned and called Ralph to her.

He bounded to her, and she fed him a handful of treats, jumping with joy. "I did it! I did it! Ralph's such a good boy."

Merry looked at Jules with moist eyes. "That was absolutely perfect. Great concentration from both of you. Awesome. Come give me a high five, Jules."

The girl ran to her and slapped a high five, then Merry pulled her in for a hug. "I'm so proud of you."

Jules grinned. "I'm proud of me too."

T.J. couldn't fight his own smile. This was exactly what he'd envisioned when he'd created Camp Blue Sky. He waited until they'd finished their exercise and the kids had gone to fetch their lunch boxes, then stopped Merry. "I was thinking about taking a trail ride after the kids go home. You want to come?"

Her eyes widened. "What? Where?"

"Back behind the pasture, there are some nice trails. Tango and Twilight could use the exercise, and I wanted to talk to you about Noah."

Something flickered in her eyes, something guarded that made him even more eager to see what she and his nephew had been chatting about behind his back.

"You think I'm ready for a trail ride?" she asked.

"Sure. We'll go slow. Twilight's pretty bombproof out there."

"Well, okay. That sounds fun." She glanced down at her khaki shorts. "I think I have a pair of jeans in the car."

"Okay, let me know."

They sat at the picnic tables behind the barn to eat their lunches, then the kids played with the dogs until their parents arrived. After they'd gone home, T.J. headed up to the house for a cold drink while Merry settled the dogs in the spare stall.

She came in a few minutes later carrying a pair of jeans under her arm. "Just give me a minute to get ready."

"You get dressed, and I'll head down to the barn to get started with the horses. Help yourself to something cold from the fridge if you want."

She nodded, then went into the bathroom to change.

T.J. walked out to the pasture and put halters on all three horses. He led them in together and tucked Peaches in her stall with some of her favorite hay to keep her from feeling left out. The other two he tethered in the aisle.

He'd just finished grooming Tango when Merry walked in, backlit by the afternoon sun. It put fire in her brown curls and highlighted the way her jeans molded to her every curve.

He damn near dropped the hoof pick.

She walked up to Twilight and stroked her beneath her forelock. "You mind if I ride you this afternoon?"

The mare gave her a friendly shove.

"She's going to love it. She hasn't been on the trail in weeks. Amy's the only one who usually takes her out, besides the camp kids."

Merry kept her eyes on the horse. "This will be my first trail ride so go easy on me, okay?"

Twilight nuzzled her palms, checking for treats.

Fifteen minutes later, they were mounted and on their way. Merry looked at ease on Twilight, holding the horn with one hand for balance, the reins in the other. T.J. took the lead, guiding Tango down the worn trail toward the stream in back.

"Just keep the reins loose and let her follow. She's going to stick close to her buddy," he told her. Twilight fell in line behind Tango.

Peaches gave a mournful whinny from the barn.

"Aw, that's sad. She feels left out," Merry said.

"It's hard for them to be separated, but she'll be okay."

"Is she able to go on trail rides, with her bad legs?"

"Walking in a straight line down to the stream is actually easier for her than going in circles in the arena. Noah rides her out here with me sometimes." He turned Tango to the left, onto the worn path that led down to the stream. The gelding tossed his head and bunched his muscles, raring to go for a run. Often this was where he and T.J. let loose and galloped the rest of the way. Not today though. "Easy, boy," T.J. told him.

Tango snorted his frustration, but relaxed his posture to continue walking.

"Your horses have a charmed life, don't they?" Merry said from behind him.

"It's not bad, that's for sure. Same could be said about your dogs."

The beautiful sound of her laughter carried to him on the breeze. "That's true. They know it too."

They walked in silence for a few minutes. He listened to the call of the birds above, the hum of insects around them, the babble of the creek leading their way. As it always did, T.J. felt some of the stress leaking out of his muscles. He'd be lost without this place. The call of nature was strong in his blood.

"You okay back there?" he asked.

"Better than okay. This is awesome."

They reached the end of the tall grasses, and the trail widened to a lush green meadow sloping down to the stream ahead. T.J. slowed Tango so that Merry and Twilight could come up beside them.

"You've been talking to Noah a lot this week," he said.

She looked over, those hazel eyes piercing his. "He seems troubled lately. You know what that's about?"

He shook his head. "Hoping you might be able to tell me."

"He hasn't said much." She looked down at Twilight. "You think there might be anything going on at home?"

"Like what?" He shook his head. "Amy would have told me."

Merry shrugged. "We women like to keep our secrets sometimes, especially from an overprotective big brother."

"I'm her younger brother."

"Really? That's even sweeter, the overprotective little brother." She smiled. "I just wondered if she might be under any new stress lately that Noah might be picking up on. Money troubles, job troubles, anything like that."

"Not that I know of. She would tell me." At least, he hoped she would.

"Man troubles?"

Of this he was certain. "Amy hasn't dated in years."

"Well, I'm trying to earn his trust. I'll let you know if he tells me anything, I promise."

"Thanks. I appreciate that. It's really frustrating to see him going further inside himself while the other kids are all making such great progress."

"I know." Her voice was softer. "It's frustrating for me too."

They reached the stream, and both horses stepped into it, eager for a cool drink. Merry laughed with delight as Twilight stuck her nose in and drew a long gulp. Before long, both horses were pawing its surface, sending a shower of spring water over them.

"That feels awesome." She pushed a strand of hair from her face.

T.J. tore his eyes from her, because things were about to get really uncomfortable for him in this saddle if he kept staring at Merry, damp ringlets around her face, her yellow T-shirt wet and plastered to her chest. Instead, he focused on the line of storm clouds on the horizon.

"Better head back unless we want to get soaked," he said.

She looked at him with heat in her gaze. "I don't know, it might feel good."

Ah, hell. It'd be another cold shower for him tonight. Come to think of it, she might be right. Maybe a dousing from the heavens would cool them both off.

* * *

Merry was almost hoping they got wet because the sight of T.J. on his horse was turning her on big-time. Although T.J. on his horse sopping wet might be even sexier.

Phew.

It took them a few minutes to get the horses out of the stream. Apparently, splashing in its silvery depths was quite the popular attraction for them. She was enjoying it too, but T.J. wasn't wrong.

Those storm clouds were coming fast, mottling the western sky an ugly purple.

She fell in line behind him as the trail narrowed through heavier brush. Of course, now she was left with nothing to do but stare at his ass. As she had all the way down to the stream.

"Thanks for bringing me. It's kind of magical out here, isn't it?"

He turned and gave her a sharp look, one that sent funny tingles through her belly. "It's where I come to de-stress."

Come to think of it, she felt awfully de-stressed at the moment too. Wound tight with wanting him. But stress? Nope, she hadn't thought of Jayden or her financial troubles since they set out. It all seemed far away from the rhythmic thumping of the horses' hooves, the back-and-forth sway of Twilight beneath her, the faraway rumble of thunder chasing the happy chirping of the birds in the fields around them.

"I'd be out here every day if I were you." She imagined her dogs here with them, Ralph bobbing ahead of them on the trail, frolicking in nature the way he seldom got a chance to in their suburban home.

"I am, when I have the time."

Thunder rumbled again, closer this time. Twilight tossed her head, edging closer to Tango. "She's not going to freak out on me, is she?"

He shook his head. "Nah. The storm doesn't bother her."

A raindrop splashed her arm. Merry turned her face to the sky, letting the rain kiss her cheeks, cool and refreshing. She'd always been kind of infatuated with North Carolina's wicked summer thunderstorms.

It was Mother Nature's chance to show off her strength and prowess. They blew in fast and furious, soaked the ground with some much-needed rain, then hurried along, leaving behind freshly cooled air and sometimes even a rainbow.

Not that Merry wanted to play in lightning, but the lightning was still a ways off. This was just an outer band of rain that had reached them ahead of the storm.

T.J. glanced over his shoulder. "You okay back there?"

"Perfect." Actually, she was feeling a little giddy, like she wanted to throw her arms up and twirl around in the rain like a child, let it wash the day's sweat and grime from her skin.

By the time they reached the barn, it was coming down steadily, soaking through their clothes and the horses' coats. She helped T.J. take off their bridles and saddles and rub them down.

"Okay, let's get them out to the pasture before the thunder hits," he said.

"You're really going to turn them out in this?"

"It's just rain." He gave her an amused smile. "They've got a nice shelter out there that will keep them dry if they want it, but watch, they'll probably stand in the rain for a while. They like it. Can you lead Twilight for me?"

"Sure." She held the mare's lead line while T.J. got Peaches out of her stall. He led the way out of the barn with Tango and Peaches. Twilight followed right along. Merry probably could have taken the halter off her right there and it wouldn't have made a difference, but she led her to the pasture anyway.

She watched T.J. slip Tango's halter off, then Peaches'. It didn't look difficult. She unclipped the chin strap and slid the leather contraption off Twilight's face, freeing her to go graze in the rain with her friends.

T.J. turned toward her with that wickedly sexy grin of his. Water dripped from the brim of his hat and soaked the shoulders of his blue T-shirt, plastering it against his well-muscled chest. Her ears buzzed with the sound of the rain, splashing and splattering against the world around her.

Beautiful. She wanted to take a snapshot of the moment and imprint it in her brain to remember whenever she needed a pick-me-up to her day.

And then Mother Nature opened the floodgates. Rain dumped onto her so quickly, so forcefully, that she was drenched in seconds, soaked to the skin. Shocked, she stood there, rooted to the spot.

Then T.J.'s hands were on her, hot against her rain-chilled skin. They slid up her arms and down her back, and she fell against him. His mouth was on hers, kissing her with all the force of the storm raging around them. It consumed them, ignited them, made them wild.

She fisted her hands into his T-shirt and lost herself to the kiss. Then she was in his arms, her legs around his waist as the rain ran like a river over their heads and his mouth ignited an all-consuming need inside her.

Something hard pressed into her back, and she lifted her head to see that T.J. had carried her to the oak tree beside the pasture. He pushed her against its solid trunk, kissing her like a man possessed. The rain was less here, filtered by the canopy of branches and leaves above them. Merry sucked in a greedy breath of dry air as his lips roamed over her jaw and down her neck.

She felt his hard length pressing into her, driving her absolutely crazy. Her hips moved against him, and he groaned, deep and rough. He rocked his erection against her, and Merry saw stars.

Or maybe it was just the raindrops splashing in her eyes.

"Jesus Christ, Merry," he said finally, his voice strained.

"Don't fight it." She slid her hands beneath his shirt and raked her fingers over his bare skin. Hot. Taut. Firm. His muscles bunched beneath her touch.

Her hands roamed over his chest, through a smattering of coarse hair and across hard, muscled skin to the waistband of his jeans. His eyes closed, and his chest stilled. He held his breath as her fingers hovered over his fly.

He'd lost his hat somewhere, probably in the mud by the

pasture. *Oops.* Without it, he looked somewhat vulnerable, every nuance of his expression exposed to her gaze. She brushed her hand across the front of his jeans and watched the raw need flicker over his features. He swallowed hard, looking like a man on the verge of desperation.

She dipped her hand inside his waistband and gripped him. He was so hard, like red-hot steel in her hand. A rough groan tore from his chest, and he thrust himself into her hand. Her body clenched; that pulsing need low in her belly grew almost unbearable in its strength.

T.J.'s eyes opened, fiery hot and glazed with lust. He gripped her wrist and pushed her back, her hands finding their way to his neck. She clasped them together and held on. He kissed her again, until her head spun and her body trembled.

He stroked her through her jeans, and she gasped into his mouth.

"Don't stop," she whispered, desperate and overcome.

He did stop, but only to slip his hand inside her pants. His fingers reached her bare skin, and she cried out. His hot, rough skin was perfection. He moved in a perfect rhythm, and oh God, she was so close. Tension coiled inside her, and her hips bucked against him.

"Go ahead," he urged in that low, sexy voice. "I've got you."

He stroked his thumb over her center, and she came apart in his arms. Pleasure rained over her, mixed with the storm overhead. It was one of the most amazing moments of her life. She groaned as she rode out the orgasm, then collapsed in his arms.

T.J. was staring at her in wonder, his chocolate eyes so dark they looked almost black. "Goddamn, woman, you are about the sexiest thing I've ever seen."

"You're pretty damn sexy yourself." She smiled, her arms tight around him. "What do you say we go inside out of this rain?"

"I was kind of enjoying the rain," he whispered against her lips.

She shivered with delight. "Me too." She slid her hands around to his butt and cupped him. "But I don't feel anything in your back pockets."

"I always take my wallet out to ride."

"So you see the problem." She brought her mouth to his and kissed him.

He raised his head, gasping for air. "You're sure you want to do this?"

She nodded with a teasing smile. "Oh, honey, I wouldn't leave you in this state. It's not fair."

He drew back, his mouth pressed in a firm line. "That's not what I mean. We can still stop. We should stop."

"No, we shouldn't. We both want this. Why keep fighting it?" Her gut instinct was to reach inside his jeans and remind him why they should do this. Drive him out of his mind until he couldn't stop, until he lost control. That's what she would usually do.

But something told her that wouldn't work on T.J. She knew how to seduce a man below the belt. To work her magic using the head on his shoulders was a different ball game entirely.

"Maybe we should slow this down and think it through," he said.

She wound her arms around his neck and looked him straight in the eye. "We've done enough of that, don't you think? Please, T.J., take me to your bed."

He met her gaze. "You're sure?"

"I'm positive."

He crushed his mouth against hers one more time, then swept her off her feet and carried her through the pouring rain toward the house.

CHAPTER FOURTEEN

She looked up at T.J. with those big hazel eyes. Thunder crashed above them; rain poured over them. It dripped from her hair and hung in glistening drops on her lashes. And right there, with one look, she brought him to his knees.

She had no idea the power she had over him. No idea.

He carried her inside the front door. They were dripping wet and streaked with mud, a total mess. He kicked his boots off, tossed her sneakers beside them, then carried her upstairs, through the bedroom, into the bath. She slid to her feet on the green and white bath mat, her hands still locked behind his neck.

"What are we doing in here?" she asked, her lips teasing his.

"We're filthy, in case you didn't notice." He reached inside the shower and turned it on, letting the water get nice and hot.

She looked down at her mud-splashed yellow shirt, and the muddy puddle already gathering around them on the tile floor and laughed. "Oops."

"Consider this foreplay," he said and tugged off his shirt.

"I like your kind of foreplay." She trailed her fingers over his chest, tugging lightly at his chest hair, driving him absolutely crazy.

"Your turn."

She gripped her shirt, and he closed his fingers over hers, helping her lift it over her head. Beneath it, she wore a pale yellow bra with lacy flowers on the clasp between her breasts.

Sexy. So sexy.

He cupped her breasts in his hands. She grabbed his jeans, yanked him against her, and undid the button. The throbbing ache in his groin intensified. He was holding on to his control by a thread. "No touching."

She gripped him through the denim, and he pulsed in her hand. He swore roughly and pulled away. "I mean it, woman. Hands to yourself."

"That can be fun too." She gave him a wicked grin as she popped the clasp of her bra, allowing her breasts to spring free.

He reached for them, but she shook her head. "No touching, you made the rule."

He groaned. "Dammit."

Merry giggled. She shimmied out of her jeans, giving him a sexy little striptease that left her in nothing but skimpy yellow panties. T.J. went weak at the knees.

"Please..." He reached for her, but she batted his hand away with a playful laugh.

She hooked her thumbs through the strings at her hips and slowly, gloriously, slid her panties to the floor.

"My God, you are so beautiful." He just stood there for a moment soaking in the sight of her, all that smooth, creamy skin offset by the dark curls framing her face.

"Hurry up," she said and jumped into the shower.

He scrambled out of his pants and boxers and followed her. Here they were again, kissing as water poured over them, this time hot and steamy... and naked. He pinned her hands over her head, holding his body apart from hers by sheer force of will.

With his right hand, he grabbed the bar of soap and scrubbed it quickly over his arms and legs, not trusting Merry to behave if he released her. He brought the soap against her skin, and she bucked against him.

"Oh, my God," she panted. "You are evil."

She brought her hips against his, his erection against her hot, wet skin, and he was lost. He rocked against her belly as she gripped his ass, yanking him closer, and he was absolutely powerless to pull away.

"Condom," she gasped.

"In the bedroom." Which at that moment felt about a thousand miles away.

She made a sound of protest, her body still pressed tight against his.

"I told you not to touch."

She hooked a leg around his hip. "I should have warned you, self-control is not really my thing."

"Fuck, woman." He untangled their legs, then turned to shut off the water.

Merry was already halfway into his bedroom, a towel wrapped loosely around her shoulders.

She sat on the edge of the bed and beckoned him with a finger. Dear God, this woman was going to be the death of him.

He managed to walk—not run—to her, and when he reached her, she grabbed him and rolled him onto the bed. He landed flat on his back with Merry straddling him.

She bent her head and kissed him, her hair dripping onto his chest. She wiggled her hips, and his eyes rolled back in his head.

"Jesus, Merry, slow down, or I'm not going to last a minute once I get inside you."

Her fingers closed over his cock and squeezed. "Who says you have to?"

She stroked him, and it was so good, too good. He gritted

his teeth, then flipped them, bringing Merry onto the mattress beneath him.

Much better. He might not last, but he'd make sure that she didn't either.

* * *

One minute Merry was in control, the next she was flat on her back with T.J.'s big, strong body pinning her to the bed. He held her hands in his as he kissed his way from her mouth over her neck and down her belly.

Her body tingled in anticipation. She had to hand it to him, he was very attentive to her pleasure. Such a gentleman, even in bed. He used his mouth to drive her wild, until she was panting, begging for release.

He brought her so close, and then he pulled away.

She whimpered in frustration.

He rolled toward the bedside table and grabbed a condom. She snatched it from his hand and pushed him down on his back, straddling him. Much better.

He watched through eyes heavy with desire, burning with need. And so damn sexy, so handsome he took her breath away.

She ripped open the packet and rolled the condom over his impressive length. He lifted her hips, positioning her over him.

She sank onto him with a moan of pleasure. T.J.'s eyes closed, and his hands gripped her hips. He held her against him for a long moment as their bodies joined, and then she started to move.

She rode him hard, and he met her thrust for thrust, each movement bringing her closer to the edge. And then, with a cry, she went over. Her body clenched around him as the orgasm took hold. T.J. let out a rough sound, gripping her hips and thrusting into her, driving her higher and higher until with a groan, he followed her over.

She fell against his chest, sated and breathless, listening to the steady rhythm of his heart against her ear. "That was..." Great? Amazing? That, and more.

"Uh huh." His voice was low and gravelly, his arm slung protectively around her waist. She lifted her head to peek at his face, thrilled with the glazed look of satisfaction he wore.

They lay like that for a few minutes, skin to skin, while they caught their breath. Then he rolled her to her side and slid out of bed to get rid of the condom. He walked into the bathroom, then came back through the bedroom with their wet, dirty clothes in his arms.

"Be right back."

She closed her eyes and snuggled into his blanket. The bed smelled like him, warm and sweet like molasses. She pulled back the blanket and slid between the sheets, her face pressed to his pillow.

Sometime later, she heard his footsteps in the hall and dragged herself back to consciousness in time to see him come through the doorway, still buck naked, now carrying two glasses and a plate of something that looked gooey and delicious.

"Peach cobbler," he said. "My mom always sends me home with leftovers."

"Homemade peach cobbler?" Merry's mouth was already watering. She accepted the fork he held out and took a big bite. "Oh, my God, that is amazing."

He nodded as he set the plate on the bed between them and dug in.

Merry clutched the sheet against her and drank in the sight of him sitting there completely naked, eating cobbler without a care in the world. She wasn't complaining. The view was sublime. There wasn't an ounce of fat on his body, nor was he sculpted like the men she'd dated who spent too much time at the gym.

Nope, T.J. was lean and muscular from good old-fashioned life on the farm. He wrangled uncooperative live-stock and hoisted bales of hay to get the body she was now shamelessly ogling.

He handed her a glass of lemonade, and she gulped it down, parched. "Thanks."

"You're welcome." He scooted closer, and then they were kissing again.

He pushed her down and had his way with her, as slow and thorough as the first time had been fast and furious. By the time they'd finished, Merry was limp and panting. They dozed off together in his bed and woke to late afternoon sun streaming through the windows.

T.J.'s arm rested across her belly, their legs entwined. As she roused, his fingers trailed over her skin, stirring her emotions and a deep-seated restlessness within her.

"I should go check on the dogs soon. They've been in the barn a long time," she said.

T.J. grunted, and his fingers dipped lower. She swatted his hand away. "I mean it."

"You're talking about dogs at a time like this?" Unde-terred, he brought his hand between her legs and stroked her.

"It's late. I should go . . ." But her body arched against his hand. Wanting more. Needing his touch.

"It's four o'clock in the damn afternoon." He rolled against her, letting her feel how hard he was, how ready.

He kissed her, sliding his tongue against hers while his hands explored every inch of her body. He felt so good, tasted so good. Everything about him was right, so right it scared her.

She slid on top of him to work a little magic of her own. She needed to regain some control, get back on familiar ground because he was so damn chivalrous, so generous, it was almost too much. She couldn't ever let herself get comfortable with a man like T. J. Jameson.

He was forever, and she didn't want forever.

But she'd enjoy the hell out of this for however long it lasted. She slid down and took him in her mouth. He gripped the sheets and swore. She took him as close as he'd taken her earlier, then reached for the drawer and rolled a condom over him.

The next thing she knew, she was flat on her back, T.J. poised above her. He claimed her mouth with another heart-shattering kiss as he slid inside her. It was so good, so perfect. He thrust slow and steady until she was absolutely wild, then slid his thumb over the spot where their bodies joined and sent her flying.

They came together. He looked into her eyes as he found release, and she saw everything, his need, his pleasure, but more. She saw right into his soul. He'd opened himself to her completely. And as he collapsed against her to catch his breath, she felt the sudden inability to breathe.

That weird feeling in her chest had nothing to do with the unbridled affection she'd just seen in his eyes. No, definitely not.

She pushed him off her and went into the bathroom. She winced at her reflection in the mirror. Her hair was an ungodly mess. Maybe T.J. had merely been awestruck by the kinky mop on her head.

Yeah. Maybe.

When she came back out, he was just walking into the room with her clean clothes in his arms. He tossed them on the bed with a chuckle. "You're still worried about the damn dogs, aren't you?"

The dogs? She'd forgotten all about them, but they *had* been in the barn a long time. "You know me." She shrugged as she reached for her clothes. "Thanks."

He went into the closet and returned with a fresh pair of

Wranglers fastened low over his hips. She couldn't help but stare. She almost asked him to put on his hat and boots. He'd have looked like the cover of a romance novel.

"I suppose I should check on Amber. She's a little afraid of storms."

"Really?" There was something about the way he said it that warmed her heart. He was absolutely soft on Amber, not that he'd ever admit it.

"Yeah, she shakes and hides whenever it thunders."

"Aww, poor thing. Do you make her feel safe, tough guy?" She gave him a friendly jab, and he scowled at her.

"I rubbed her and stuff. Didn't seem to make a difference."

Merry's heart melted into a puddle at her feet at the thought of T.J. sitting with Amber during a storm, comforting her. "That's awfully nice of you."

"I'm a nice guy, what can I say."

They walked to the barn together and found the dogs fast asleep in the cool shavings, Chip, Salsa, and Ralph in a pile, Amber on her own in the corner.

They all leaped to their feet when the stall door slid open, and Merry shooed them out the door of the barn to do their business.

She kept a close eye on them to make sure no one ventured toward the road, but they all stayed in the field behind the barn, running and playing. Happy and carefree, the way dogs should be.

After a few minutes, she rounded them up and clipped on their leashes. She handed Amber's to T.J., then stood there, feeling awkward.

"So I'll see you in the morning then." He leaned in and gave her a kiss, as if it was the most natural thing in the world, as if their next meeting would be as a couple and not her reporting for work at his camp.

As if the entire world hadn't just shifted beneath her feet.

The puppies yanked on her arm, and she let them tug her free, let them drag her toward the car and away from T.J.

"Yep, tomorrow," she said, and ran for her car.

* * *

"I did a stupid thing," Merry lamented into the phone. "Why aren't you here? I really need a girls' night out at Red Heels."

"I'll make it up to you next week when I visit," Cara said. "But what did you do?"

"I slept with T.J." Merry curled her feet under her on the couch and gulped from the rum and Coke she'd poured.

"The hot cowboy running the camp?"

"That's the one." She gulped again.

"Why is that stupid?" Cara asked. "You're both single, consenting adults."

"Because…because we have to work together for another week and a half." She drained the glass and fixed herself another.

"So? Your relationships usually reach the month mark. Wait a minute. Is this more than sex? Is that what's got you freaked out?"

"No! No way. Just sex. *Really* great sex."

Cara laughed in her ear. "I think you're protesting a bit too much, Mer. Do you have feelings for him?"

"Stop it. No, but that's why we weren't going to do this. He's looking for someone to settle down with, and I'm not."

"He's a guy. I'm sure he's capable of having sex without wanting to marry you after."

Merry scowled. The rum was already going to her head. She took another sip. "Gee, thanks."

"You know what I mean. We girls are the ones who usually get all mushy after sex. In fact…"

"I am not mushy."

"Then why the post-sex freak-out?" Cara asked.

She stared into her glass. "I don't know."

"Oh, my God. You are...you're falling for him. Whoa. This is like, epic!"

"I am not," Merry said, but she sounded unconvincing, even to herself.

Cara squealed. "This is *so* Red Heels worthy. For this, I'd fly down tomorrow and go out with you. I'm totally serious."

"Cut it out. I like him a little, so what? It's not like I'm going to marry him or anything."

"Why not? I mean, not T.J. necessarily, but why are you so antimarriage?"

"I just don't think it's for me, that's all. Why can't a woman enjoy her own life? Why should I need a man to make me happy?"

"You don't *need* one, but...Is this because of your mom?"

Merry sighed. "Maybe partly. My dad raised me fine on his own, but marriage wasn't something I grew up seeing or wanting."

"So that's part of it, but it sounds like there's more to it than that."

Merry took another swallow of her drink. She missed Cara so much. Surely that was the reason she felt tears gathering behind her eyes. "I miss you. Can't you convince Matt to move back?"

"Aww, sweetie, I miss you too. And also...are you drunk? You sound funny."

"A little, maybe. I'm so pathetic without you that I'm drinking at home by myself." She sniffled as she drained her glass.

Cara was silent for a long moment. "Okay, let me rearrange a few things with Matt, and I'll come down for the weekend. Are you working?"

"Don't be silly. You'll be here the end of next week anyway, and a last-minute flight would be crazy expensive."

"Are you sure?" Cara asked.

"Positive, but thanks for being a good friend."

"Just returning the favor, my dear. So you never told me the rest of the reason."

"What?" Merry pinched at her brow.

"The reason you don't want a husband. A family."

"Oh, you know..."

"No, I don't," Cara said, sounding eerily serious. "But I always wondered."

"Really? You knew there was a reason?"

"Now you're freaking me out. What's going on?"

She pressed a hand to her chest. "I should have told you. I don't know why I never did."

"Told me what?"

Merry slid down the couch cushion and covered her eyes. Right now, she was bursting to tell Cara about Tyler. Why hadn't she ever confided in her best friend? And why had she gotten so drunk tonight? *Shit.* If only she could teleport Cara into her living room, she'd tell her now, but it was in no way a phone conversation, no matter how drunk she was. "I'm a little afraid I would suck as a mom, that's all. You can psychoanalyze me when you're here."

"Oh, Merry. You'll be the best mom! You are so warm, and loving, and generous. And you're great with kids. Just because your mom sucked doesn't mean you will."

She shook her head. "I really didn't mean to have this conversation tonight. We can talk more when you're here, I promise. I'm exhausted, and clearly I've had too much to drink."

"Okay then. Make sure you drink some water before you go to bed." Cara paused. "And call me back if you need me."

Merry hung up the phone with a sigh. Ralph came and nosed his way into her lap, comforting her as he did so well. But tonight it wasn't enough. The truth was, she wished she was still with T.J., wrapped safely in his arms.

CHAPTER FIFTEEN

*H*ere comes trouble.

T.J. watched from his bedroom window as Merry's CR-V turned into the driveway at quarter past eight, a half hour earlier than she usually arrived. He'd expected her early.

At least, he'd hoped.

He loped down the stairs with Amber at his heels, then frowned when he saw her start toward the barn with her dogs. He pulled open the front door. "Hell, Merry, they're all housetrained, right? Just bring them in."

She turned slowly to face him. The moment he looked into her eyes, he felt the air drain from his lungs. He simply couldn't draw breath.

She started walking toward him, and his pulse was already pounding. She was so damn gorgeous. He allowed his gaze to wander over her aqua top to the jean shorts that hugged every curve and revealed long, smooth legs, tanned from three weeks here on his farm.

He stood watching until she'd reached the doorway, then he yanked her inside and slammed it closed, unable to wait another moment before he pulled her into his arms and kissed her luscious, pink lips.

Merry let out a gasp of surprise. She dropped the leashes, and the dogs scampered off into his house, doing God knows what, but his arms were around her, and he was kissing her. It was like a light had come back on inside him, something that had been dark since she ran out of here yesterday afternoon.

She lifted her head, her eyes golden like honey in the morning light. "Good morning."

She gave him one of those little half-smiles, and he couldn't remember a single reason why he hadn't been kissing her every damn day since he met her. Not one.

"Mornin'."

"I thought we needed to have a little chat before the kids got here."

"You call this chatting?" He glanced down at her hands, currently gripping his ass.

She brought them to his chest and pushed him back. "Not quite."

He shoved his hands into his pockets and nodded. "Okay, I'm listening."

She stood there, adorably awkward. "I just figured we needed some, you know, ground rules."

He cocked his head and grinned at her. "You're not one of these women who overthinks everything now, are you? The way I see it, we've got this chemistry we can't fight, so let's just go with it for now and see what happens."

It was what she'd wanted in the first place, and he'd come around to her way of thinking, to an extent. Because the more time he spent with her, the more he wanted. And if their chemistry was still going strong when camp ended, he had no intention of letting her walk away.

She blew out a breath and nodded. "That works."

Salsa dashed across the room with one of his sneakers in her mouth. Chip ran after her, leashes dragging across the floor. Merry blanched. "Salsa, drop it!"

The puppy froze, then dropped the sneaker with a shamed look. She wore a multicolored shirt today, like a misbehaving clown puppy. T.J. grabbed his sneaker and inspected it for damage, but other than a little puppy drool, it appeared unharmed.

"I'm sorry." Merry clutched Salsa's leash, looking as ashamed as the puppy. "I should have left them in the barn."

He shook his head. "It's all right."

"I should head down anyway."

"You've still got ten minutes." He grabbed her and pulled her up against him again. "I've got appointments all afternoon, but I was thinking maybe we could get dinner later."

"Dinner?" Her eyes rounded. "Oh okay. Sure."

He fought back a niggle of annoyance at her reaction. Had she thought they'd just sleep together once and leave it at that? Had she really been planning to go straight to the barn, or was she going to drop the dogs off, then come up and see him at the house?

It wasn't worth fighting about, either way. Instead, he slid his arms around her and kissed her. A much better use of their last ten minutes alone.

Except he and Merry never just kissed. Within minutes, she was in his arms, her legs wrapped around his hips, and he was hard as steel and frustrated as hell. He kissed her until they were both oxygen starved, then lowered her to the floor with a groan of regret.

Merry's eyes had regained their playful sparkle. She tugged at the waist of her shorts to give him a glimpse of pink lace. "For later," she said with a wink.

"Jesus, woman." He yanked her up against him for one last kiss. He was going to need yet another cold shower before he followed her to the barn, and even so, it was going to be torture looking at her all morning, thinking about that pink lace and how many hours he had to wait until he could take it off her.

* * *

Merry's phone rang as she walked toward the barn. She didn't need to check the screen to know it would be Cara.

"Just making sure you're okay this morning," her friend said.

Merry rolled her eyes—at herself, not at Cara. "I'm totally fine. I don't know what was the matter with me last night."

Cara laughed. "Well, we all have those moments."

"I wish I could chat, but camp starts in a few minutes."

"Okay, but promise you'll call if you need me?"

"Promise."

Merry walked toward the barn feeling uncharacteristically out of sorts. She'd never felt awkward with a guy the morning after they had sex. Not until T.J. She hadn't had any idea what to expect from him this morning, but he seemed to have gotten on board with her no-strings, surrender-to-the-chemistry plan.

So that was great. Awesome. Exactly what she'd wanted. Except, for some reason, it didn't feel like what she wanted. T.J. had thrown her off balance almost from the moment they met, and now she had no idea what to do with him.

But surrendering to the chemistry and hoping it burned itself out by the end of camp seemed as good a plan as any.

Amy was in the barn with Noah, and they waved as she approached.

Merry waved back. "Good morning. T.J. should be right down with Amber."

"We're a little early this morning." Amy gave her a funny look.

Merry felt her cheeks flush. Was it obvious she'd been in the house kissing T.J.? Was her lipstick smeared? She should have checked herself in the mirror before walking into the barn, but she hadn't really expected anyone to be here yet.

"Noah, why don't you take these carrots to the horses?" Amy passed him a bag of carrots, and he scampered out of the barn.

"Everything okay?" Merry asked. She couldn't imagine why Amy would care, but she didn't exactly want to have the conversation either.

Amy's eyes sparkled. "Are you and my brother…?"

Crap. "Yes. Is it a problem?"

Amy grinned. "Not at all. I was kind of hoping it might happen."

Really? "It's just a casual thing. We're not exactly spreading it around, if you don't mind keeping it quiet."

Amy twisted her fingers over her mouth to indicate her lips were sealed. "Not that it's any of my business, but my brother's a really great guy. He's pretty picky about who he dates too. You're his first non-farm type; that must say something about you."

Yeah, it said that chemistry had overridden common sense. Merry busied herself settling the dogs in the spare stall, unsure how to respond.

"I'm not trying to be nosy," Amy said behind her. "I actually stopped by to talk about Noah."

Merry turned to face her. "Has something happened?"

"Yes, but I don't know what." Amy's brown eyes were troubled. "He's not himself lately. I think…I think he lied to me the other night."

"Really?" Merry gestured to the plastic chairs at the end

of the hall. Amy sat in the closest chair, and Merry sat opposite her.

"I caught him using my laptop without permission. When I asked him what he was doing, he said he was playing Lego games, but he was acting so guilty that I pulled up the browser history after he was in bed. He'd been on Apple's website looking at iPads. I mean, why would he lie about that?"

Merry thought of the money missing from her purse. It was on the tip of her tongue to mention it to Amy, but something held her back. She had no proof Noah had taken it, and she would never forgive herself if she unfairly accused the boy. "Maybe he wants to buy you one for your birthday?"

"My birthday's in February, and I have a laptop already. I don't need an iPad. I've never even mentioned one."

Merry looked down at her hands. "He's seemed troubled to me lately, like something's bothering him."

"I know." There was anguish in Amy's voice. "That's why I wanted to talk to you. To see if he'd said anything to you, or if maybe you could talk to him for me."

"I have," Merry confessed. "I've tried everything I could think of to get him to open up to me. Is there anything going on at home he might be worried about? Money troubles? A new boyfriend? Anything you can think of?"

Amy laughed bitterly. "Money's always a struggle, but he has everything he needs. Boyfriend? Not lately. Nothing's changed, Merry. I've dedicated my whole life to keeping things steady for him. He hates change."

Merry twisted her fingers. "I'm sorry."

"I thought things were looking up, you know? He has this new friend, Brendan. His first real friend. I thought it was going to be a major breakthrough for both of us."

"Could his friend be the problem?"

Amy shook her head. "Brendan's at my house almost

every afternoon. He's the sweetest boy. In fact, I suspect he's somewhere on the autism spectrum like Noah. They sit and play with Legos and do math workbooks together."

"That sounds adorable."

Amy's eyes warmed. "It is. I'm so thrilled for him."

"He should be happy."

"He should." Amy nodded. "But he's not."

"No."

"I trust you, Merry. You seem like a good person and a good friend to Noah. If he tells you something, anything, promise you'll tell me."

Merry looked her in the eye and nodded. "I promise."

* * *

T.J. opened his door at seven o'clock that night to find Merry on his doorstep holding a pizza box and a six-pack of beer. She'd changed since that morning, wearing snug black pants that reached just past her knees and a blue sleeveless top that revealed just enough cleavage to distract him.

But the biggest distraction was wondering if she still wore the pink lace panties he'd glimpsed that morning. Because he'd been thinking about them all day.

"Hungry?" She thrust the pizza box at him, then leaned in for a kiss.

"Starved." He tossed it onto the coffee table and yanked her into his arms. The beer hit the couch with a thump.

He kissed her long and hard, then she pulled free and dropped onto the couch. "You like baseball?"

"Baseball?" He repeated like an idiot.

She nodded. "My dad's from Kentucky, near Ohio, so he raised me a Red's fan. They're playing the Padres tonight."

"Sure." He handed the remote control to her. He preferred football to baseball, but he certainly wasn't going to complain if she wanted to eat pizza, drink beer, and watch sports.

"I ordered a supreme. You're not picky, are you?" She flipped open the box to reveal a pizza laden with a variety of meat and vegetables.

"Not picky at all." He went into the kitchen for plates, then loaded up a couple of slices and snagged a beer.

She turned on the game, then grabbed her own pizza and beer. "Except when it comes to women."

He took a bite and stared at her. "What?"

"Amy said you were picky about who you dated."

He choked. "You talked to my sister about us?"

She shrugged. "She brought it up, not me."

"Oh." He chewed through the rest of the slice.

"I asked her not to mention it to anyone." Merry kept her eyes on the TV.

"Why?"

"In case...you know." She shrugged again.

He set his plate on the coffee table and turned her toward him. "In case what?"

Those gorgeous eyes widened. "I don't know! We had sex yesterday, can't we leave it at that?"

"The hell we can. You're here tonight, and I hope you will be again tomorrow. Where I come from, that's called dating."

She looked away. "You can call it whatever you want as long as we're on the same page about what we're doing. You made it very clear that you want to get married and have a family, and I...I don't. It wouldn't be smart to forget that."

He sat back against the couch. "No, it wouldn't."

"So I vote we enjoy the hell out of this chemistry until camp's over and then go our separate ways before things have a chance to get messy."

That made total sense, and yet he didn't like it one bit.

"Do we really have to decide that right now? Why not take things a day at a time and see what happens?"

"T.J., I can't give you the things you want out of life. We already know how it's going to end for us. I'd much rather have a couple of awesome weeks with you and part ways friends than stick around until things go sour and we wind up hating each other."

He took a long pull from his beer. This conversation was pissing him off big-time. "Why?"

Her eyes widened. "Why what?"

"Why don't you want a family?" It made no sense. She was warm and caring, and she adored kids. Nothing about her made a damn bit of sense.

She drew back. "I just don't think I'm cut out for it, that's all."

Her bottom lip quivered, and his anger faded away. He'd done it again, poked at the wound she tried so hard to hide. Merry Atwater was not the carefree party girl she pretended to be. Someone or something had made her close herself off to the idea of love.

He was foolish enough to hope he could change her mind. "Anything you want to talk about?"

She glared at him. "I think you already know the answer to that question."

"Never hurts to ask."

"Look, I don't like messy breakups. I like being able to call up a guy I used to date and see if he wants to go dancing on a Friday night."

"You do that a lot?" Because he really disliked the idea of her dancing with another man, let alone a guy she'd slept with.

"Go dancing on a Friday night? Almost every week. Call up an old boyfriend? Not that often." She winked. "And never when I'm dating someone else."

"Good to know. Because whatever you want to call this, if you're sharing my bed, you aren't dancing with any other men."

"You're not the jealous type, are you?" She slid closer and draped an arm over his lap.

His brain promptly quit functioning. "Uh…"

"Because you've got nothing to worry about." She slid her fingers up his thigh. "I was hoping *you'd* take me dancing tomorrow night."

"Dancing?" He stared at her hand, silently begging her to slide those fingers a few inches north. His dick hardened in anticipation.

"My dad plays at The Watering Hole on Friday nights. It's bluegrass, I bet you'd like it. Lots of great beer on tap. Totally casual."

"That doesn't sound so bad."

"You'll have fun, I promise." She lifted her hand from his leg to snag another slice of pizza, leaving him aching for her touch.

"All right then." T.J. couldn't actually remember the last time he'd gone to a bar or taken a woman dancing. He spent most of his nights working or riding. No wonder it had been so long since he'd had a woman in his bed.

"Oh, come on. He was safe!" She shouted at the TV, leaning forward just enough to give him a glimpse of the pink lace he'd been fantasizing about all day.

Hallelujah.

They polished off most of the pizza and beer by the time the Red's lost, 4-5, to the Padres.

"Son of a bitch." Merry clicked the TV off with a scowl.

T.J. gripped her waist and slid her onto his lap. That was better. She scooted closer, wiggling her hips against his, and he damn near lost his mind. "You make me absolutely crazy."

She bent her head to his. "Likewise."

And then she kissed him.

Everything he'd been holding back since that morning surged to life as her tongue tangled with his. He'd been waiting all day for the chance to touch her like this, to feel that lace beneath his fingers.

Merry's hands wandered beneath his shirt, stroking fire over his skin. He unclasped her pants, revealing the pink lace beneath. He touched her, and she gasped, arching against him. He'd intended to take things slow, but here, now, he couldn't wait.

His own need was overpowering, but even more erotic was the look on her face as he teased her through her panties, the way her hips thrust against him, her groan of pleasure when he slid his hand beneath the lace.

He couldn't resist the satisfaction of watching her lose control. Sweet Jesus, it was beautiful. He stroked her with his fingers, completely overtaken by the look of abandon on her face. Her eyes closed, and she cried out as she found release, grinding her hips against his.

Holy shit, the only thing more powerful than his own orgasm was watching hers. His dick throbbed, aching for her. He rocked against her, feeling her pleasure, letting it fuel his own need.

He felt greedy as he slid her pants over her hips, helping her as she shimmied them to the floor. She grasped her panties as if to yank them off, and he stopped her. Hell, no. He was not finished with the lace.

"Hurry, T.J.," she whispered. She yanked off her blue top, leaving her in a matching pink bra and panty set.

Christ. He hadn't counted on even more pink lace. He trailed his fingers over the contour of her bra.

She slid a hand inside the waistband of his jeans, gripped him, and squeezed.

And he forgot all about the lace. He thrust into her hand, momentarily overcome by his own need. Her fingers were like heaven, gripping and stroking, urging him toward release.

He fumbled with her panties, but she pushed his hand away. "How about I keep these on, since you like them so much, and let's focus on you for a little while."

She unzipped his jeans and took him in her hands.

He gripped the couch and fought for control. "Jesus, Merry, I can't—"

"Relax, Cowboy. I've got you." She winked, then lowered her head.

He almost lost it just from the feel of her breath on his dick. Then she closed her lips over him. He swore, trying to hold back, fighting for control and losing to the thrill of her tongue swirling over him, her fingers stroking him closer and closer to the edge.

He buried his fingers in her hair and surrendered. His whole body tightened as his world narrowed to the sensation of her mouth on him. It was magic. It was...

Abruptly, she lifted her head, leaving nothing but cold air where her lips had been. He groaned in frustration.

"Your phone's ringing. Turn it off." She thrust her hand into his pocket and pulled out his iPhone.

"What?" Through the haze of arousal, he heard his phone ringing, saw the name on his screen. Fred Lamboutin, a farmer out in Creedmoor. "Shit."

He flung his head back against the couch.

"Turn it off," she whispered, trailing her fingers down his cock.

He shuddered. *Fuck.* "I have to take this, Merry. It's a client. He doesn't call after hours unless it's an emergency."

She glanced down at his dick. "This is an emergency too."

Damn right it was. *Fuck.* He slid her out of his lap, zipped his pants, and answered the call.

Merry sat on the couch, looking pouty, wearing nothing but the pink lace bra and panties that would fuel his romantic fantasies for possibly the rest of his life.

"T.J., sorry to bother you this late, man, but I've got a cow in labor. Calf's not coming, so I examined her. Uterus is twisted."

"I'll be there in fifteen minutes," T.J. told him. "Keep her on her feet until I get there."

He hung up the phone and looked at Merry. "I have to go. I have a cow in labor with a twisted uterus. If I don't get there quickly, she and the calf could both die."

Merry sobered. She, more than anyone, understood the urgency of an animal in distress.

"Will you wait here for me? Stay the night?" he asked.

She shook her head. "I can't. I'm sorry, my dogs . . ."

He nodded. There was no time to argue. Hopefully by the time he got to Fred's farm, he would have recovered enough composure to do his job.

*C*HAPTER SIXTEEN

*M*erry watched from the doorway of the barn as the kids sat around the picnic tables, eating lunch beneath the shade of the big oak tree where she and T.J. had shared that incredible rain-soaked kiss only two days ago.

It felt like a lifetime.

Since Wednesday, she'd become hopelessly tangled up with him, so much so that she had done her rounds with Ralph at the hospital a day early so that she could spend the rest of the afternoon here at the farm with him and Noah, then she was bringing T.J. with her to The Watering Hole tonight to see her dad play.

That felt like a lot more than casual sex, but she was loving every minute. So what if she enjoyed his company? Hopefully the fact that she genuinely liked him would make it easier to walk away on friendly terms.

At the picnic table, Jules chattered a mile a minute about how her parents were taking her to see the Fourth of July fireworks tomorrow night for the very first time. Lucy listened and smiled in between bites of her peanut butter and jelly sandwich. Parker ignored the girls, bouncing in his seat as he maneuvered an action figure around in his potato chips. Across from him, Noah sat quietly, eating grapes.

He'd be having his real lunch in a little while with Merry and T.J. when they took the horses for a picnic trail ride down to the stream. She couldn't wait. T.J. had even given Peaches the day off from lessons so that her legs would be sound enough for the ride.

Merry was hoping the extra time with Noah would give her a chance to find out why he was stealing from her purse and lying to his mother. This was a child who never disobeyed, never misbehaved. Whatever had happened was something he didn't feel comfortable talking to his mother or uncle about. That left Merry.

She was determined to gain his confidence and help him before his problem got any worse. Because lying and stealing never led to anything good.

T.J. came up beside her. "I peeked inside the picnic basket Amy dropped off. I saw homemade blueberry bread."

"Mmm. That sounds heavenly. She really didn't need to cook for us though."

"She loves baking, and when I mentioned taking Noah for a picnic this afternoon, she insisted on providing the food." He shrugged. "Which is probably best, since I'm not much of a cook."

"You don't have to cook for a picnic. Sandwiches, fruit, drinks. Not that I'm complaining about the homemade blueberry bread." But she was feeling rather inadequate that T.J.'s sister had provided their picnic. Merry was entirely unsuited for domesticity. Her idea of a home-cooked meal was a TV dinner.

"I never complain when someone gives me food."

"Good point. I was thinking Ralph and Amber could come along with us."

He looked down at her. "Really?"

"They both mind well off leash. I think they'd enjoy it."

"I don't know." His brow furrowed. While he'd loosened up around the dogs in camp, he was still distrustful of them in general. She wanted to fix that too, before camp ended.

"It will be fun. Trust me." She patted his arm.

"If you lose one, I'm going to say I told you so."

"I won't lose one."

Not one of the dogs anyway. But the stubborn cowboy and his troubled nephew? That was a different question entirely.

* * *

Merry gripped the saddle horn and watched them run. Ralph darted in and out of the brush, ears flying in the breeze. Amber trotted behind him, tongue lolling, tail up.

In front of Merry, Noah rode Peaches. T.J. and Tango led the way. She tipped her face toward the sun and breathed in the fresh air. It really was infectious. She still hated being sweaty and dirty, but wow, the warm scent of earth and wildflowers, the rhythmic gait of the horse beneath her, the soft clop of hooves against the earth. She could see how it got inside a person and refused to leave.

"Everyone okay back there?" T.J. called over his shoulder.

"Perfect," she answered.

"Noah?"

"Good," he answered in a small voice.

The boy looked solid as an oak in that saddle. His uncle had obviously taught him well, and camp had improved on his already admirable horsemanship skills.

The path widened, and Merry nudged Twilight up beside Peaches. The mares nickered to each other. "You think you'll work with horses when you grow up, like your uncle and your granddad?"

Noah shook his head. "I'm going to be a mathematician and have a lot of dogs."

"Oh, I like that plan. Maybe you'll foster a few for me."

He nodded. "I want to save all the good dogs like Amber from the shelter."

"You and me both, kiddo."

Noah looked over at her and smiled, and Merry felt an uncomfortable pinch in her heart.

"Promise you'll stay in touch after camp's over, okay? You can come play with my dogs any time."

"Okay."

T.J. rode ahead of them, silent through the conversation, but now he turned to give Merry a deep and searching look that made her stomach quiver. She hoped she could stay in touch with Noah, hoped she'd see him blossom past this socially awkward stage and come into his own, hoped maybe her dogs could help with that.

And she still hadn't given up on the idea of T.J. keeping Amber. She hadn't mentioned it to him yet. He wasn't ready, but she'd broach the subject before camp ended. It would be so perfect for all three of them. Amber could keep her happy farm life, Noah could keep the dog he'd bonded so deeply with, and T.J., well, he'd be taking a step past his fear and distrust of shelter dogs.

They reached the clearing by the stream. Ralph leaped in and hopped around like a frog. Amber stood at the edge of the water and watched, then dipped her head to lap from its silvery surface. The horses followed them in for a splash and a drink.

T.J. led Tango back onto the grass and dismounted. He looped the horse's reins over a nearby tree and took their supplies from his saddlebags. Merry followed with Twilight. T.J. helped her and Noah off their horses and left all three in the shade of the tree, happily munching grass.

Merry busied herself spreading out the blanket and arranging their picnic. Amy had sent chicken salad sandwiches, blueberry bread, fruit salad, cookies, and lemonade. Merry decided she needed to stay friends with her too, because wow, that all looked and smelled amazing.

Noah sat beside her. She handed him a plate, and he filled it quietly. He helped himself to a big slice of blueberry bread, then carefully picked all the blueberries out of the fruit salad and lined them up on his plate.

Merry smiled as she watched.

"Look up there by the tree line," T.J. said as he dropped down beside his nephew. "See that red-tailed hawk? Wonder what he's hunting."

Noah fiddled with the blueberries on his plate.

Merry bit into her sandwich. Poor T.J. He seemed to have an especially hard time communicating with Noah, no matter how hard he tried. Maybe he just tried *too* hard.

"Think it's a mouse?" T.J. asked. "Could be a mole, or a lizard even."

Noah popped a blueberry into his mouth. Amy had mentioned once that round foods were his favorite. No doubt why she'd included blueberries and cookies in their picnic.

After they'd eaten, T.J. went to tend to the horses, and Noah followed the dogs into the stream. Merry curled her feet underneath her and watched them. Ralph hopped and splashed while Amber lay at the water's edge to cool herself.

Noah rolled his cargo pants up and fastened them at his knees, then waded out to the middle of the stream. He bent and searched beneath rocks, looking for whatever little boys loved. Bugs? Fish? Frogs?

Merry shuddered. Pretty much anything that lurked beneath the slimy rocks at the bottom of a stream ought to be left alone as far as she was concerned. But this was a prime opportunity to bond with Noah so she rolled up her jeans and followed him in.

"What are you looking for?" she asked. The water rippled around her legs, making her toes seem to wiggle like snakes. Snakes! There weren't any snakes in streams like this, were there?

She cringed, curling her toes under her feet.

Noah grabbed at something and held it up proudly, a little lobster-like creature that wriggled and pinched its claws in her direction.

"Holy sh—" Merry clapped a hand over her mouth. There were things like *that* in the stream? That might be worse than a snake.

"It's a crawfish," Noah said. "It won't hurt you."

Ralph stuck his fool face at the thing, and it pinched at him. He jumped back just in time, then bounced in the water and tried to sniff it again.

"Not too smart, Ralph," she said.

Noah put the crawfish back in the water, and it scampered away. Merry's toes cringed.

"There are fifty-two different colors of Legos," Noah said.

Merry smiled. She'd noticed he often recited Lego facts when he was trying to start a conversation. "You know a lot about Legos."

"I have two thousand, eight hundred and fifty-three, counting the ones at my house and here at Uncle T.J.'s."

"That sounds like quite a collection. You and Amber did great today with that stay. I had a feeling she'd outlast all the other dogs." She gave Noah a friendly nudge, and he beamed.

"She's smart."

"So are you. What do you think of the other kids in camp?"

He shrugged.

"Your mom was telling me about your new friend, Brendan."

Noah stooped to peek beneath another rock.

"My best friend when I was your age was a girl named Britney. She and I hung out after school almost every day. She lived right down the street, just like you and Brendan."

Noah nodded. "We play Legos a lot."

"I had a lot of Legos when I was a kid too. My favorite thing was to see how tall I could stack them before they fell down."

"A hundred and fifty-three," Noah said.

"What?"

"A hundred and fifty-three bricks. That's my tallest."

"Oh," she said. "I can't remember mine, but that sounds pretty tall."

He nodded and turned over another rock. Merry said a silent prayer that he didn't uncover another creepy-crawly stream dweller.

"One time, Britney and I snuck out of her backyard and went down the street to these big cement pipes we'd seen there for construction work. We played in there for hours until my mom came to get me, and Britney's mom realized she had no idea where we were. We both got grounded for a week."

"A whole week?" Noah looked up with wide eyes.

"Yep. You and Brendan ever break the rules when you're together?"

He shook his head emphatically while flipping over another rock. He lunged after something, and Merry winced. Whatever it was got away, but Noah kept his back to her.

"I had another friend when I was about your age, Tabitha. She liked to break the rules, and she was always trying to get me to do things I didn't want to do. I didn't want her to stop liking me either, so sometimes I did them."

"That's not a nice friend," Noah said.

"No, but it's hard to see that while you're still friends with them. Being a kid is really tough, Noah. It's not an easy gig. And kids can be mean. Sometimes it's hard to talk to your parents or your family about it. I can't ground you, right? And I give pretty good advice."

He stared at her for a long beat in silence, and she held her breath.

"Will Amber live with you after camp?" he asked.

"Until she finds her forever home."

He swiped his hands against his pants. "I wish she could be mine, for keeps."

Oh, Noah. "I wish that too."

He turned away and poked underneath another rock. Her feet were tingling by this point, terrified of a creepy creature shooting out from under one of those rocks and biting them. She stuck it out another minute in case he had anything else to say, then sloshed her way to the shore.

"He out there catching crawfish?" T.J. asked.

She nodded.

He tugged her around behind the horses and gave her a quick kiss. She melted like butter in his arms. "He talks a lot with you."

"I work with kids. They tend to like me." She saw the frustration on his face. It was killing him that he couldn't get his nephew to open up to him, and she hated it for him.

She kissed him back, then pulled from his arms before Noah caught them canoodling. "You're coming with me to The Watering Hole tonight, right?"

He nodded. "I've got to drop him off around supper time."

"And I've got to get the dogs home. Want to come over after you drop Noah off?"

Heat flared in his eyes. "Love to."

"All right then."

"Please tell me you're wearing those pink lace panties again." The look on his face reminded her of how they'd left things last night.

Yep, she owed him one. Or two.

"Sorry," she said, and his face fell. "These are green." She leaned forward to whisper in his ear. "And really, really skimpy."

He sucked in a breath. "Green is my new favorite color."

"I bet it is." She winked. "Did the calf make it?"

He nodded. "It was close, but he pulled through."

"Glad to hear it. I'll make it up to you tonight." She gave him a playful smile and pulled away to pack up the remains of their picnic.

T.J. snagged a cookie and walked off toward the stream. He stuffed the cookie into his mouth, then kicked off his boots, rolled up his jeans, and joined his nephew in the water. Ralph, who had been poking his nose underwater to see what creatures Noah was hunting for, hopped with joy, splashing them both.

Noah giggled, and T.J. looked like he'd just won the lottery.

Merry concentrated on her task to keep from just sitting and watching them. When she glanced up, they each held crawfish, wielding them at each other in a mock shellfish battle. She fumbled in her back pocket for her phone and snapped a picture to capture the moment.

She'd just finished filling Tango's saddlebags when they joined her, both wet and smiling.

"Is that a boy thing?" she asked. "Crawfish wars?"

"Must be." T.J. threw an arm over Noah's shoulders and squeezed.

They rode back to the farm together in good spirits. The dogs trotted beside them, tongues out and heads down, exhausted. They'd be ready for a good nap after this.

While T.J. and Noah tended to the horses, Merry tucked Amber and Ralph into the extra stall with fresh water and adjusted the fan that blew over them. They both plopped down in the clean shavings, stretched out, and closed their eyes.

She took Chip and Salsa out for a quick romp and potty break, then put them back in with the others just in time to follow T.J. and Noah to the house.

While they went upstairs to shower and change, she settled on the couch and thumbed through messages on her phone. Anything to keep from thinking about T.J. upstairs, naked and sudsy in the shower. She wished she could have joined him, and not just for naughty reasons. She was sweaty, and dirty, and who knew what was on her feet after wading around in that stream.

Crawfish poop? *Yuck.*

She shook away the thought. They'd be dropping Noah off at his mom's in a couple of hours, then heading to Merry's house. She'd shower then. Maybe she'd even invite T.J. to join her.

The boys came downstairs, and they spent the rest of the afternoon playing board games. Merry got her butt whupped at Ticket to Ride by Noah and Monopoly by T.J. Both were fiercely competitive and strategic thinkers. Fly-by-the-seat-of-her-pants Merry didn't stand a chance.

"Geez, you could have at least let me win one," she whined as they were putting the games away. Noah sent her a sweet smile that belied his ruthless winning streak.

T.J. scoffed. "Let you win? We Jamesons never *let* anyone win. Makes you appreciate it that much more when you do win."

"Uh huh." She shook her head, fairly certain her dad had let her win on many an occasion, and she'd turned out just fine.

She loaded all four dogs into her car—Amber would stay

at her house while she and T.J. were out tonight—and followed T.J. as he drove Noah to Amy's.

He pulled up in front of a brick-front apartment building in an older, working-class part of town. If idyllic Dogwood had a ghetto, this was it, and Merry hated that this was where Noah had to grow up. At least he had his uncle's farm to roam whenever he wanted.

Noah jumped out of the truck and came around to her window. "Can I take Amber down to Brendan's house, just for a minute?"

"That should be okay. What did your uncle say?"

"He said it was fine if you didn't mind."

Merry nodded. "Don't take her inside though, okay? Do you want me to come with you?"

He shook his head. "I'll ring the bell, and Brendan will come out."

She got out of the car and helped retrieve Amber from the back without freeing the rest of the pack. "Bring her right back. These guys are all exhausted. They're on their way to my house to sleep for the rest of the evening."

"I will." He took the leash and started down the street with Amber, looking so confident and proud that an ache rose in Merry's throat.

T.J. stood on the sidewalk, watching. "They look good together."

She looked up into his dark eyes. "You ever think about keeping her?"

He rocked back on his heels, and a muscle ticked in his cheek. "Dammit, Merry—"

She threw her hands out. "Forget I said it." She hadn't meant to. She'd known it was too soon.

"You just can't stop pushing, can you? Look, you'll get your donation, and I've fostered her without complaint, but a deal's a deal. You take her back after camp's over."

Well, that stung. "It was just a question. You seemed like you were getting fond of her, and it's the closest Noah will ever come to having a dog of his own."

"Don't put that guilt on me. Amy has allergies or she'd have gotten him a dog years ago."

"But you don't. Amber adores you, your farm, and your nephew. Why not keep her?"

He took a step closer, his eyes narrowed. "Maybe for the same reason you're tossing me out as soon as camp's over. You don't do long term with men, and I don't make long-term commitments with a dog."

Merry stepped back against the hot bricks of the apartment building and crossed her arms over her chest. "Well, tell me how you really feel."

He shook his head and stared at her, like he had no idea what to say. Neither did she. She didn't want to fight with him. She didn't even really want to think about giving him up once camp was over. She just wanted to take him home, have her way with him, and go to The Watering Hole later to dance and drink beer together.

Why did this have to be so complicated? She'd never had trouble keeping things light with a guy before. But her feelings were hurt now, and there was no taking it back. She blinked past the sting of tears.

"You know, I should probably take my dogs and go home. You wait for Noah and Amber. I'll see you Monday at camp."

He moved to block her. "Seriously? You're going to walk away?"

"I just—"

Tires squealed down the street, followed by a thump and a scream that stopped her heart cold in her chest. T.J. was already running, sprinting down the street, and she followed. Her legs felt like rubber, her heart pounding.

Three houses down, Noah lay in the street, his shirt stained with blood.

Oh God. *Noah…*

The calm veneer she wore during emergencies at work failed her as she raced toward him. Her chest simply refused to draw air. *Noah.* She'd stabilize him, patch him up, and keep him calm until the EMTs got here.

She was trained for this. Her hands shook, and she clenched them into fists.

And then she was in front of him. She fell to her knees, and Noah looked up at her, his face streaked with tears. An anguished wail tore from his throat.

"It's okay, sweetie. Where are you hurt?"

Two fat tears slid over his cheeks. "Not me. Amber…"

Merry looked down, realizing for the first time that Noah was crouched, not crumpled, over the prone form of Amber.

The dog lay without moving, her golden fur streaked red with blood.

CHAPTER SEVENTEEN

T.J.'s knees went limp with relief. Noah was okay. He knelt beside the boy and gently checked him over to make sure it was true, then scooped him into his arms and squeezed the daylights out of him. He felt like he'd aged ten years since the horrifying sound of the car's impact.

The car, a white Nissan, had stopped a little ways down the road. He needed to check on the driver and find out what the hell had happened.

"Amber—" Noah sobbed, wiggling out of his arms.

T.J. looked down at the dog. She lay motionless on the asphalt, eyes wide and glassy. Blood ran from an open fracture on her right front leg. Her breathing was quick and irregular as her body went into shock.

Merry crouched at Amber's side, speaking softly to her, one hand on the dog's shoulder to keep her from trying to stand up.

"What were you doing in the road?" T.J. asked as he brought Noah to the curb and sat him down.

His nephew rocked back and forth, arms clasped around himself, staring wide-eyed at the dog in the road.

Jesus.

An elderly woman walked up to them, tears streaming down her face. "He just came out of nowhere! Oh, my heavens. Are you okay?"

"He's fine, ma'am. Were you driving the car that hit the dog?"

"Dog?" She looked over and blanched. "Oh, dear. I did hit something. I knew it. Oh—"

She was shaking so badly that T.J. eased her down on the curb next to Noah. "Are you all right?"

"I'm fine, just shook up." Her voice wavered. "The dog... is it dead?"

"No, ma'am."

She put an arm around Noah. "I was driving along, and all of a sudden he was right there in front of me, running like the devil was at his heels. I thought I'd hit you—" She squeezed Noah as more tears ran from her eyes.

The boy pulled away, arms flapping at his sides. He stared at Amber with wide, unfocused eyes.

T.J. needed to get Amy down here to get him. Noah didn't need to sit around and watch this. The truth was, the dog could die at any moment. T.J. had no idea how serious her internal injuries were or whether she'd sustained head trauma.

"Stay put, both of you." He walked into the street and crouched beside Merry.

"Her right front leg's broken, and she may have internal injuries. She's going into shock." Merry spoke in the calm, even tone of a nurse, but her eyes gleamed with anguish.

"I'm a vet, remember? I can handle this." He bent over Amber. There were no external signs of injury other than the busted leg, but her insides might tell a different story. He felt first along her spine and found no obvious fractures, then gently probed her abdomen.

Amber yelped and struggled, but Merry held her gently. Her abdomen was firm, possibly from internal bleeding.

"We need to get her to the vet. You go call David. Then bring me something I can use to splint this leg, drumsticks, a ruler, anything like that. I'll need disinfectant and a cloth to wrap it with, and something firm to move her on, an ironing board, cardboard, whatever you can get your hands on. Go quickly. And send Amy down here to get Noah."

Merry nodded and raced up the street toward Amy's apartment building.

Noah sat on the curb, still rocking, eyes wide behind his glasses. Beside him, the elderly woman looked similarly stricken, one hand pressed against her chest, visibly shaking.

Amy burst from the building and ran toward them. She grabbed Noah and clutched him to her chest. "Oh, my God, baby. Are you sure you're okay?"

She glanced at Amber and winced, then turned to the woman sitting on the curb. She spoke to her quietly. The woman nodded, then reached for her purse and followed Amy and Noah in the direction of their apartment.

A few minutes later, Merry came out, her arms laden with supplies. She sat next to him, spreading out clean cloths, an ace bandage, a bottle of hydrogen peroxide, a plastic ruler, and a wooden spoon. "What can I do to help?"

"Did you call David?"

She nodded. "He'll be waiting for us, and Liv is on her way to get the other dogs out of my car and drive them home."

"Okay, let's clean and splint this leg first. You hold her head for me." Wounded animals could become aggressive, no matter how docile they normally were. While Merry held her, he poured peroxide over the wound and dabbed at it with a washcloth. Amber whined, but made no attempt to bite either of them.

Next, he took the ruler and the spoon and positioned them on either side of the fracture. He wound the ace bandage around her leg, securing them in place. As makeshift splints went, this one was top notch.

One of Amy's neighbors ran up with an unassembled cardboard box, laid flat. "Amy called me. Will this work?" she asked.

"That'll do just fine. Thank you." He took it and laid it on the ground behind the dog, then turned to Merry. "On the count of three, we're going to slide her onto the cardboard."

She nodded and moved her arms under Amber's front end, putting herself in the danger zone if the dog lashed out as she was moved. T.J. slid his palms under Amber's haunches. "One, two, three."

They lifted and slid her onto the cardboard. Again Amber yelped. He eyed his truck, then Merry's SUV. "Put your dogs in the truck. We'll drive her in the CR-V."

Merry didn't stop to question, just ran to get the three dogs from her car. She hauled them toward the truck—each one straining toward Amber—and boosted them inside one by one. T.J. flinched, praying no harm came to the interior of the F350, but the backseat of a pickup truck was no place for a dog with possible internal or spinal injuries. They could lay her flat in the back of the CR-V.

When Merry returned, they lifted the cardboard between them. It sagged beneath Amber's weight as they carried her to the CR-V. Merry had already put the backseats down, and they slid the cardboard into the open space.

"I'll ride beside her," she said, already climbing in.

He sensed it was pointless to argue so he slid behind the wheel, pushed the seat back, and drove as fast as he safely could toward Dogwood Animal Hospital. He worried about the emotional toll for Noah if she didn't make it, but as he glanced in the rearview mirror at the blood-streaked dog, his stomach clenched.

He didn't want Amber to die either.

* * *

Merry paced in the exam room until T.J. pulled her into his arms. "Poor Noah. If she dies, he's going to hold himself responsible."

"I never should have agreed to let him walk her down there alone." His voice sounded gruff.

She leaned into him. "But he looked so proud."

The door opened, and Dr. Johnson came in.

Merry's heart jumped into her throat. She'd lost fosters before. It was part of the job. She'd cried for each of them because she loved them all, but for Noah's sake, if not her own, she couldn't lose this one.

"I have good news," Dr. Johnson said.

She sagged in T.J.'s arms. "Oh, thank goodness."

Dr. Johnson gave them a second look, as if just noticing the way T.J. held her. His eyebrows raised. "She'll need surgery to repair the fracture in her right front leg. I've scheduled it for first thing tomorrow morning. Other than that, I see only bumps and bruises. No significant internal bleeding, no sign of head trauma."

"That's . . . wow. That's amazing," Merry said.

"She's in shock. We've started her on IV fluids and pain medication and splinted her leg for the night. She'll rest tonight to get her strength up for surgery tomorrow."

Merry swallowed over a new kind of fear. Surgery would be another thousand or so dollars that she didn't have. This pit she was in just kept getting deeper. Every time she managed to claw herself partway up, the bottom fell out all over again.

But Amber was going to be okay.

The money would come. Extra shifts had been hard to come by this month, but it was summertime. Lots of people took vacations in the summer, and Merry would cover for everyone she could. She'd get more events scheduled. She'd find a way to fix this.

Her father hadn't raised a quitter. She wasn't going down without a fight.

* * *

T.J. hadn't been dancing in too many years to count. He'd been gifted with two left feet, a Jameson family legacy. Therefore, it was utterly ridiculous that he'd been the one who insisted they come to The Watering Hole tonight.

Something in Merry had dimmed since Amber's accident. The light in her eyes had lost a few watts, and he had a hunch a night out might charge it back up. Of course, he had a few other ideas that might cheer her up later, but going out and socializing was a big part of Merry, so he hadn't wanted her to stay home just because she was worried about the dog.

Amber was going to be fine. Her camp days were over, but she'd make a full recovery. Noah was still upset, but hopefully the good news about Amber would help. He'd been so agitated that Amy had put him to bed early.

T.J. pulled open the heavy wooden door to The Watering Hole, and bluegrass music spilled into the night. He preferred country, but bluegrass wasn't bad, and he was curious to hear Merry's father play.

She stepped through ahead of him and headed straight for the bar. Her mood was still somewhat subdued, although she seemed to loosen up a bit after she settled herself on a bar stool and ordered a Blue Moon.

She'd showered and changed after they finally made it to her house, and now she smelled like fresh honeysuckle, which was almost as distracting as the cleavage peeking out of her lacy pink tank top. He sat beside her and ordered a Yuengling.

"Hell of a day," he said.

She nodded. "Glad I have tomorrow off. I may sleep all day."

"Or do something in bed anyway."

She gave him a sly look. "Or something."

Her eyes sparkled, and he felt himself getting aroused just staring into their hazel depths. This woman had a crazy hold over him with nothing more than a look and a wink.

The bartender slapped two cold beers in front of them, and T.J. felt his own tension slipping away. He didn't get out often and hadn't been to a bar with a woman in far too long. It wasn't a bad way to end a long week.

Merry took a long drink from her beer, then licked the froth from her upper lip. "Did Noah say anything to you about what happened?"

"Hmm?" His brain had shorted out watching her tongue dart over her lip. "No, he hasn't said a word."

"I hate that he was the one walking her when it happened." Her brow creased. "He must feel so guilty about it. I should go talk to him tomorrow."

"I'll talk to him." He said it without thinking, then saw the way she drew back. "I mean, maybe you could come with me."

Dammit, why were they constantly stepping on each other's toes? Neither of them had mentioned the argument they'd had right before the accident, which he was thankful for. He didn't see any way out of their opposing views on Amber's future.

"There's my dad." She gestured to a tall, lean man with

dark hair standing near the stage. He wore jeans and a plaid shirt and held a fiddle under his right arm.

T.J. sent silent thanks for the subject change. "You going to introduce us?"

"He'll be over in a few minutes to say hi." She stared into her beer, still with an uncharacteristically brooding look on her face.

"You know Amber's going to be fine, right?" he asked.

She nodded. "She's lucky."

"Then what's bothering you?"

She looked up at him, her eyes bright with pain. Then the lens slid over them that she kept in place, holding him and everyone else at bay. "Sorry, the day just got to me, that's all. Thanks for dragging me out here. I promise I'll be more fun once I get a couple of beers in me."

"I don't care if you're fun. Feel whatever you're feeling."

She scoffed, then downed the rest of her beer and smiled. "Have you forgotten my name? It means 'cheerful and lively.'"

"How'd you wind up with that, anyway?"

"I was born on Christmas Eve. My parents were feeling, well, merry I guess." She winked. "Want to guess my middle name?"

He narrowed his eyes at her. "Don't even tell me it's Christmas."

She snorted. "Thankfully not. It's Joy."

"Joy's a normal name." Then he said them together in his head. "Oh."

"Right. Merry Joy Atwater. I had no choice but to grow up happy."

"Merry Joy." He looked over at her father, still standing beside the stage tuning his fiddle. "Were they hippies or something?"

"Teenagers right out of high school. Sadly, the happiness

faded for my mom around the time the Christmas decorations were put away. She couldn't handle the responsibility so she took off."

"Damn. That's rough."

She shrugged. "I obviously don't remember her so it's probably better that she left before she had a chance to disappoint me."

"And your dad? He obviously stuck around."

She smiled again, a genuine smile full of warmth and emotion. "My dad is amazing. He raised me on his own, and he did a pretty good job if I do say so myself."

"He sure did." Yeah, her dad must be a pretty all right guy, to have stepped up and raised a daughter when he was barely more than a child himself. "That must have been tough for him."

"Oh, it was." She paused to smile at the bartender as he replaced her beer. "Thank you."

He watched her drink from it, wondering if growing up motherless had anything to do with her lack of desire to start a family of her own.

As if he'd sensed their conversation, her dad looked over and spotted them, then crossed the room and rested a hand on Merry's shoulder. "Hey, sweetie. Who's this? New boyfriend?" He turned to T.J. with a friendly smile.

He stuck out his hand. "T. J. Jameson."

"He runs the camp I'm working at," Merry said.

"Oh, that's right. What a great thing you're doing! I'm Gerry Atwater, by the way. Merry's dad, if she didn't already tell you."

"She pointed you out earlier, said you'd be over to say hi," T.J. said.

Gerry nodded, still smiling. "She comes out most Fridays to see me play. Pretty good daughter, if you ask me."

She laughed. "I'm a damn good daughter."

"So how's camp going?" Gerry asked.

"Great. The kids are all doing really well." He didn't point out that his own nephew was the one exception to that statement. "Merry's been a big asset. She's really gifted with the kids, and the dogs."

"That she is." Gerry nodded proudly in agreement. "You're lucky to have her."

"All right, all right." She elbowed her dad playfully. "Isn't it almost time for you to play? Go break a leg, Dad."

"She says that every week. I keep telling her I'm getting too old for that kind of talk. Might actually happen." His eyes twinkled in amusement.

T.J. took an immediate liking to the man. "Looking forward to hearing you play."

"Hope you like it. Great meeting you." He waved and headed back toward the stage, where the rest of the band had begun to assemble.

"I can see why he named you Merry Joy," he said.

She nodded. "He's a happy man, and he raised a happy daughter."

Overall that might be true, but he'd seen glimpses of something darker. Like a fool, he wanted to dig deeper, to know more than she'd ever want to share.

They sat at the bar and polished off a few more beers, and when the band took the stage, he got up and danced with her. Or, at least, he gave it his best effort. He moved his feet to the beat while she danced in his arms.

It was almost midnight by the time they made it back to her place, and he was damn near dying to get her upstairs and out of her clothes. Naturally the dogs had other ideas. They were ecstatic to finally have her home—with a visitor no less—and leaped and howled around the kitchen in delight.

Merry let them out back, then pushed him against the wall and kissed him senseless. "You're staying, right?"

He didn't need to hear that invitation twice. "Hell, yeah."

"Good." She slid her hands down to pinch his ass, then tugged free. "I just need a few minutes with the dogs, then I'm all yours."

Damn dogs. His jeans were so tight he could barely walk, but he made it to the couch. Tonight was the first time he'd been inside Merry's house. It seemed to suit her, small and homey with warm walls the color of terra-cotta and white lacy curtains.

He sat there, trying and failing to think about anything other than how much he wanted the woman in the other room. He wanted to make love to her until the sun rose, until they'd forgotten their names and all the troubles they faced.

Until they'd forgotten why this relationship would only last as long as his camp.

And then she fell into his arms, and he forgot it all.

* * *

Merry woke to the warm caress of the sun. It streamed through the windows, bathing her and T.J. in its amber rays. He lay beside her, naked and asleep, half covered by the sheet, looking gloriously handsome in her bed. She ogled his abs and the one big, muscled leg that had come uncovered during the night.

He'd kept her up pretty late screwing her brains out, and she'd loved every minute. She'd give him a few more minutes to sleep and recharge, then she'd see how he felt about morning sex. Something told her he'd be in favor.

She rolled over with a happy sigh, feeling relaxed and peaceful. Then she looked down and saw the three sad faces gazing up at her from their dog beds on the floor. Oh yeah, they were pretty pissed at her for kicking them out of bed so she could enjoy some grown-up time with T.J.

She stifled a laugh. They'd get over it. But if he slept over many more times, he'd learn to sleep amid a tangle of dogs, because she couldn't kick them out forever.

T.J. stirred behind her, and she rolled over on top of him.

"Good morning," she said between kisses.

"Sure is." He slid an arm around her, pulling her closer.

The sheet had become tangled between them, but she felt him through it, already hard and ready for her. She rocked against him, and he groaned.

God, he was gorgeous. Her body ached for him as red-hot desire washed all residual sleepiness from her brain. She moved against him, keeping the barrier of the sheet between them so that they didn't rush. There was something special about morning sex, something more intimate about seeing a man when he was still groggy and rumpled from sleep.

T.J.'s eyes were closed now, but he most definitely was not asleep. He was hard as steel beneath her, his hands gripping her ass as he moved her rhythmically against him, and oh sweet Jesus she was so close. Her body clenched in anticipation.

"Wait," she gasped. She'd meant for this to go slow.

He squinted up at her with a smug smile. "Already? Jesus, you're easy."

"Slow down. I want to wait for you."

"Oh, baby, nothing gets me hot faster than watching you come." He slid her forward so that the head of his penis pressed against her through the sheet. He brought his hand between them and stroked her as his cock nudged, teasing, pushing against her until she came apart with one of the fiercest orgasms of her life.

She bucked against him, half crazed with pleasure.

"Goddamn." His voice was hoarse, strained. "You slay me, woman, you know that?"

She was still on top of him, feeling him pulse against her, his arousal fueled by her pleasure. "Now, T.J., please."

She tugged at the sheet, but he closed a hand over hers. "Not so fast. You said you wanted to take this slow."

"But you..."

"I can wait," he said as he flipped her easily beneath him, then proceeded to kiss and caress every inch of her until she was on fire for him all over again.

Finally, he grabbed a condom he'd placed on the nightstand and covered himself. She gasped as he slid inside, holding still for a glorious moment as their bodies came together as he always did. But his control broke easily this time. He thrust into her hard and fast until another orgasm gripped her, and with a groan, he joined her.

He poured himself into her, then withdrew with a muttered curse. He looked up at her, those gorgeous brown eyes drawn in concern. But she knew. She already knew, because she'd felt it too.

The condom had broken.

*C*HAPTER EIGHTEEN

T.J. looked into Merry's panic-stricken eyes. "I'm sorry."

His head spun. However many years he'd been having sex, he'd always used a condom and never had one fail. He wanted kids, but he wanted them with a woman who wanted to have his children, preferably his wife. And Merry wasn't looking thrilled at the prospect.

"It's okay," she said finally. "I'm on the pill."

Relief surged through him, and he flopped back against the pillow. "Really?"

She nodded. "I like to have a backup plan in case, you know."

"Good. That's good." His heart rate gradually returned to normal. He leaned over to give her a kiss, then went into the bathroom to get rid of the busted condom.

When he came back, Merry was up and dressed. She brushed past him on her way into the bathroom. Three dogs stared at him from beside the bed.

He scowled at them. He'd almost forgotten they were there. It felt a little voyeuristic to think of them down there watching while he and Merry went at it in bed. As soon as he made the mistake of looking at them, the two puppies were up and lunging at him.

"Whoa!" He pushed them away and grabbed for his pants before he suffered permanent damage.

Chip grabbed one pant leg, while Salsa took the other, growling and tugging. Damn puppies.

He managed to wrestle his jeans free and get them up and buttoned by the time Merry came out of the bathroom.

"Come on, pups." She herded them toward the stairs, keeping her back to him.

He caught up to her at the back door and turned her toward him. She kept her eyes on the floor, her back stiff.

"What's wrong?" he asked.

She tugged free and went into the kitchen to start a pot of coffee. "Nothing. You've never seen me in the morning before. I'm a zombie until I get some coffee."

"You didn't seem too zombie-like a few minutes ago."

She gave him a half-smile. "Well, that's good to know."

"Seriously, we're okay, right? I'm clean if that's what you're worried about. I've never even had unprotected sex."

"Really? Never?"

"Never."

She looked skeptical. "Not even when you were a horny teenager?"

"Not even." And never really thought much about it either, until now. Now that she'd put the notion in his head, all he could think about was how it might feel to be inside her, surrounded by her hot, wet heat without that barrier of latex. His dick hardened.

"Well, I guess you're a gentleman through and through then." She patted his shoulder and turned to the cupboard to fetch two coffee mugs.

He didn't feel like a gentleman at the moment, but he'd work on it. He watched as she poured the coffee, then got out cream and sugar. She handed him a mug decorated with frolicking boxers.

"Thanks." He added some sugar and took a sip. Not bad. He took a few more swallows, letting the caffeine permeate his system.

She opened the pantry and pulled out a container of blueberry mini-muffins. "Sorry, it's all I have."

He grabbed one. "Looks better than what's in my pantry." He popped a bite of muffin in his mouth and chewed.

Merry crossed her arms over her chest and studied her shoes. Awkward. But why?

"I have to go out in a bit and run some errands," she said. "And I want to check on Amber. She should be going into surgery soon. Will you go see Noah today?"

"Planning to. Hoping you'll come with me."

"Maybe you should talk to him first." She turned away and went to get the dogs from the backyard.

They blew into the kitchen like a hurricane. He lifted his coffee mug on reflex, getting it out of harm's way. It was different with Amber. She tiptoed around the house so quietly he almost forgot she was there. These three? Total mayhem.

Merry fed them, then turned to T.J. with apologetic eyes. "I, uh, hate to run you out, but…"

"Errands?" He set his empty coffee mug on the counter.

She was such a bad liar. She just wanted him out of the house. Either she was still freaked out about the condom thing or she just didn't do the morning after very well.

Either way, it was time for T.J. to hit the road. "All right then. I'll call you in a little while when there's news on Amber. And maybe we can ride over and see Noah this afternoon?"

"Maybe." Her tension was palpable now.

He was getting a very uncomfortable feeling about this. "You going to see the fireworks tonight?"

"What?"

"It's the Fourth of July, you know."

She stared at him blankly. "I completely forgot."

"Been a few years since I've gone downtown to see the fireworks. Want to go?"

"We'll see."

"I'll call you." He leaned in for a good-bye kiss, then headed for the door. He was going to see her later today whether she liked it or not, because she was worrying him the way she was acting right now.

He found his truck parked a few houses down where Amy had dropped it off last night on her way into work. He climbed in and glanced at the backseat, grateful not to see any obvious signs of damage from the three dogs who'd occupied it during yesterday's emergency.

He cranked the engine and let it idle while he dialed David for an update on Amber.

"She's stable. Pretty bruised up, but lucky it's nothing more than that. I'll get started on the surgery to pin her leg in an hour or so."

"Thanks, David. Call me when you get out, okay?"

His friend chuckled. "Will do. I hear you're fostering this one. Merry can be pretty persuasive when she wants to be."

"No kidding." He watched as she came down the driveway and hopped into her SUV.

So she really did have an errand to run. Maybe he was wrong about her reaction, but no, she'd been acting weird since the condom broke. She was upset, and he felt like an ass for leaving her to deal with it alone, although he'd be damned if he knew what the alternative was. "I've got to run. Call when you can."

"Will do."

The CR-V backed out of the driveway and turned right, away from town. He didn't make a conscious decision to follow her. He just pulled in behind her, figuring he was hard to miss in his big-ass truck.

Merry followed Peachtree Lane to the end, then turned onto Route 221. She drove to the outskirts of town, then made a sharp right.

T.J.'s blood ran cold. She'd just pulled into the Dogwood Community Cemetery.

* * *

Merry saw the truck turn into the lot and forced back the tears that had already pooled in her eyes. He shouldn't be here. She'd realized peripherally that he was behind her on the road, but, shit, she had obviously not been thinking clearly.

And there was nothing she could do about it now.

He parked and got out of the truck, coming toward her with those dark eyes locked on her like lasers burning into her soul. She wrapped her arms around herself and lifted her chin. "Go away, T.J. I need to be alone right now."

He put his hands up. "I don't mean to intrude. Just trying to figure out what's going on here."

What's going on here? That was a good question. Hysteria bubbled up inside her, harder and stronger than she'd felt in years, and she couldn't hold it in, couldn't hold it back.

Not this time.

"Please," she whispered, not sure what she was asking.

T.J. came toward her, but she shook her head. She turned and walked down the path to her left, between rows of headstones, until she reached the one she sought. She tumbled to the ground at Tyler's grave and let go of the tears threatening to drown her.

Except they wouldn't come. The pain filled her so completely that nothing could escape. T.J.'s arms came around her, pulling her up against the solid wall of his chest. She fisted her hands in his T-shirt and held on until the wave of grief had passed.

"Whose baby is this?" he asked, but when she looked up, she saw that he already knew.

"Mine," she whispered, and felt her soul crack at that one simple word.

"Jesus, Merry." His arms tightened around her. "I'm sorry. So sorry."

"I miss him." So much she wasn't sure how she was ever supposed to make peace with it. She pressed her face against his chest.

"What happened?"

He'd read the dates on the tombstone. He knew her son had lived only two months. That wasn't supposed to happen. It was wrong, so horribly wrong.

"I was a single mom in nursing school. Between classes and clinicals and studying, I was barely holding my head above water. That night, I came home, and I just fell asleep, and I slept..." The guilt closed over her, crushing her until she could barely draw breath. "Tyler never slept through the night. Never."

She shuddered, and T.J.'s arms tightened around her.

"When I woke up the next morning, he was gone. Cold. He'd been dead for hours. If only I'd gotten up to check on him..." Her voice broke, but her eyes stayed dry.

She was too broken even to cry.

"Oh God, Merry. Don't do that to yourself. SIDS. It was SIDS?"

"That's what they said eventually."

"And before that?"

She squeezed her eyes shut. "I was a strung-out nursing student who'd gotten pregnant by accident. I was in over my head, and they knew it. The police came and asked questions. They took pictures and samples from his crib to see if I'd done anything to him. But they couldn't find anything so..."

T.J. hauled her up to look in her eyes. "They have to do that. If you'd been a suburban housewife, they'd have done the same. But you didn't cause his death."

She wrenched free to face the tiny grave where her baby lay. "I was so tired. Maybe he cried for me, and I didn't hear him. I was so busy going to school, learning how to save other people's kids, but I couldn't even save my own son."

* * *

T.J. kept one arm firmly around Merry's waist. Below them, Tango carefully picked his way along the trail. After leaving the cemetery, Merry had been emotionally spent yet buzzing with tension.

He'd followed her home, then brought her here to the place that always calmed him when nothing else could, hoping it would do the same for her. But even to have her on Twilight's back seemed too far away, so he'd put her in front of him on Tango.

They rode in silence broken only by the steady clop of the horse's hooves, the hum of insects, and the trickle of the stream. Nature's beautiful harmony.

He'd brought her to the stream before, but today he'd take her further, show her his inner sanctum. She leaned back in the saddle so that she rested against his chest, his arm still looped securely around her waist.

It felt right having her here with him, on his horse, in his arms. Everything about her felt right. He'd prejudged her that first afternoon in David's lobby, thinking her a girly-girl who had no business in his world, but he'd been wrong. She'd held her own here on his farm, with his horses, his nephew. With him.

He didn't want to let her go. Not today. Not at the end of camp. Maybe not ever.

Tango sloshed along the water's edge, head down and relaxed. He knew where they were headed without needing any guidance from T.J. They came here often, but this would be the first time T.J. had brought anyone with him.

At the back of his property, the stream narrowed, growing deeper and more swift. It continued on into county conservation land. He encountered the occasional hiker and even more occasional illegal hunter, but largely the area was untouched by the human hand.

Tango carried them along the stream's sandy bank and through a stand of trees to the hidden pool he considered his own. On its left, a rocky outcrop rose up, obscuring it from view. Its right-hand shore was sandy and strewn with pebbles. And directly across from them, a waterfall kept it full and clean.

"Wow," Merry said.

"Mm hmm." T.J. dismounted, then lifted her down. He opened the saddlebag and spread out a blanket for her.

While Merry took in their surroundings, he loosened the cinch and removed the saddle from Tango's back. He slipped the gelding's bridle over his ears and replaced it with a halter, which he clipped onto the line he'd fashioned here years ago.

Merry stood with her pants rolled up in water to her knees, staring at the waterfall. He walked up behind her and slid his arms around her, pulling her against him.

"It's beautiful," she said.

"I come here when I need to unwind. It's peaceful."

Her breath hitched, and he turned her to face him. She looked up, her face streaked with tears.

"Thank you," he said, "for telling me about Tyler. For sharing him with me."

"You didn't leave me much of a choice." She went for her trademark half-smile, but it collapsed, and she pressed her face to his shoulder as the dam broke. She sobbed until she was breathless, her fingers clutched into his shirt. He held her, one arm securing her to him while the other stroked her hair, offering what comfort he could.

Now he understood why she didn't want to settle down. Why she claimed not to want kids when she spent her life working with them, helping them, healing them. She blamed herself for her son's death, held herself responsible for something only God himself could have prevented.

He felt an overwhelming need to take away that pain, that guilt. How? He had no idea. But if she'd let him, he'd keep trying until he figured it out.

* * *

Merry stripped to her bra and panties and dove in headfirst. Yeah, the pond was probably filled with snakes and crawfish and whatever the hell else lurked beneath the slimy rocks along the bottom, but she was feeling reckless.

A restless need inside her pulled her in and wouldn't let go until she'd submerged herself in it and swum to its center, shivering against the chill of the water.

"Are you coming or what?" she called to T.J., who stood on the bank, watching.

Coming, apparently. He stripped to his boxers and swam after her.

She turned and swam to the waterfall, letting it splash over her until she no longer felt the sting of tears on her cheeks. T.J. came up beside her, floating next to her as the water splashed on their heads and over their shoulders.

He slipped his hand in hers and laced their fingers together. They drifted together from the waterfall to the center of the pond. Overhead, a couple of blackbirds raced across the sky.

Floating there in the water, she felt like she was flying with them. It was a heady feeling. Out of nowhere, she laughed. T.J.'s fingers tightened over hers.

Something bumped her leg. A snake? T.J.'s foot? She stifled a scream. "What was that?"

He turned to her with a serious face. "I suppose now's a bad time to tell you this pond's infested with snapping turtles."

"What?" She flailed, flinging herself into his arms, which only submerged them both. She surfaced with a scream, frantically pulling her legs upward to get her toes out of harm's way.

And T.J. was laughing.

"What's so funny? You'd better get me out of here in one piece!"

He shook his head and splashed her. "I'm kidding. There's only one snapper in here, far as I know, but he's a big one."

She paddled for shore. "That's supposed to make me feel better?"

He grabbed her ankle, and she screamed again. Dear God, if a turtle grabbed her toe, she might never recover from the horror.

"I'm just teasing. There aren't any snappers in here. I'd have told you before you jumped in if there were."

Well, now he was in for it. He'd let go of her ankle but hadn't moved out of harm's way, so she kicked a deluge of water in his face, then made a beeline for shore. She sloshed over slippery pebbles to safety, then turned to glare at him, arms crossed over her chest.

T.J. was still laughing. The arrogant jerk.

She stalked to the blanket he'd laid out and sat, dripping wet and shivering. "I'll probably never swim again, thanks to you."

He came out of the water and lay on the blanket beside her, one arm over his eyes as he laughed himself silly.

She curled her arms over her knees. Swimming in the pond had been a stupid idea. Now she and her underwear were soaking wet, with no towels in sight. She glared down at T.J.

He peeked at her from beneath his arm, then laughed harder. Her lips twitched. This was *not* funny. She sighed, which turned into a giggle. Then she flopped down next to him and laughed until her sides hurt and her eyes watered.

The sun was warm on her skin. She lay next to T.J. and watched it slant through the branches of the trees across the pond, beginning its afternoon descent. Her energy went with it. It had been a hell of a day. A hell of a last two days.

"Amber should have had her surgery by now," she said. "I forgot to call."

"I talked to David earlier. He said Amber's surgery went well. She'll be ready to come home tomorrow."

"That's awesome news." She huffed out a sigh of relief, semi-angry at herself for having all but forgotten about the poor dog in the rest of the day's drama.

"It is," T.J. agreed.

Exhausted, she rolled to her side, rested her arm across his stomach, and closed her eyes.

She woke to the sound of a horse snorting, followed by a splash. She opened her eyes to see T.J. asleep beside her, flat on his back, her arm still draped over his abs. In front of them, Tango stood in the water, splashing around like a child in a wading pool.

She felt unburdened by the fact that T.J. knew about Tyler, grateful to him for bringing her here and helping to lift her spirits. He knew more about her than any man ever had. They might bicker constantly and never agree on dogs in the house, but when it came right down to it, he was a hell of a guy.

After today, she'd never forget that.

She watched him as he slept, the steady rise and fall of his chest, the strong, angular square of his jaw. The afternoon sun cast an orange glow and deep shadows over his profile, illuminating a funny set of lines on his throat.

They almost looked like teeth marks.

She leaned closer. Scars. His throat was mottled with scars, so smooth and faded they were almost invisible. Holy shit.

He peeked at her through one half-opened eye, then tugged her on top of him.

She sat up, straddling him. "Your turn to spill your deepest, darkest secrets."

One corner of his mouth quirked. "I'm fresh out of secrets."

"Tell me about the scars on your neck." She reached down and traced a finger over them.

He flinched. "You won't like it."

"Try me."

"I was working late on the farm one night, on my way in from fixing a busted fence post in the back pasture."

"At your place?" she asked.

"My parents'. I was eighteen, in college. Couple of stray dogs came out of the woods. They were stalking one of the new foals. I tried to shoo them off, and they turned on me, had me on the ground before I knew what was happening, damn near ripped my throat out."

She sucked in a breath. "Oh, my God. How did you stop them?"

"I didn't. My dad saw it happening and came running with his shotgun. He fired a shot, and they took off." He held her gaze, his dark eyes steady.

"I'm sorry that happened to you, T.J. You're lucky you survived."

"Don't I know it." His brow creased. "You're not going

to tell me I shouldn't have waved my arms around in their faces, that I was asking for trouble?"

She smacked him on the shoulder. "Stop it."

This story made his jumping between her and that dog at the vet's office the day they met all the more brave. No wonder he was afraid of dogs, especially strays.

She bent her head and kissed his throat. "I hate that you had to go through that and what it did to your opinion of the canine species."

"I don't hate dogs."

"They scare you."

He frowned. "I'm not afraid of them. I just don't trust them."

She lifted her head to meet his eyes with a smile. "Oh, honey, I've been onto your secret for a while now. I just didn't know why you were afraid. Now I do."

He scowled at her. "Seriously, I am not afraid of dogs."

"It's okay, you're still my favorite big, strong, badass cowboy."

"You're being ridiculous."

She shook her head. He'd grown hard beneath her as she straddled him, which was highly distracting. "No I'm not, but I'm determined to get you past it before the end of camp."

His scowl deepened. "Will you stop with this end of camp crap?"

Ah, arguing again. What they did best. To hell with it. She bent her head and kissed him to shut him up. Igniting chemistry straight out of the stratosphere? Yeah, they did that even better.

Within minutes, he was fumbling for his jeans. He sheathed himself in a condom and took her out of her mind right there on a blanket by the pond for the world to see. Or at least, his horse.

When they'd finished, lying in each other's arms sated

and breathless, she looked into his eyes. He'd been honest with her, now she owed him the rest of the truth. "About this morning..."

He rolled toward her, his eyes warm and earnest. "If you got pregnant, I wouldn't be sorry."

Her heart thumped painfully. Jesus, he blew her mind. "Well, I would. But that's what I wanted to tell you. I... when I got pregnant with Tyler, I was on the pill."

He stared at her for a beat of silence. "Then I mean what I just said even more."

"Stop it." She put a hand on his chest. "Look, I panicked, but I've had a chance to think about it now. I was a teenager when I got pregnant, an irresponsible kid in nursing school who probably—definitely—was no good at remembering to take the pill on time, or even every day."

"Okay," he said.

"But I'm responsible about it now, and I'm supposed to get my period in a few days anyway, so we shouldn't have anything to worry about."

And damn him, he almost looked disappointed.

Feeling all kinds of weird things she did not want to be feeling, she stood up and started rummaging for her clothes. He followed suit, then went to get Tango tacked up and ready for the ride home.

It was past lunchtime, and she'd barely eaten today. Her stomach felt like it might start clawing its way out of her if she didn't put something in it soon. "I need to get home and check on the dogs, but do you want to get something to eat after?"

He gave her a look heavy with things unspoken, so heavy that she had to look away. "Sure. Amy's working at Finnegan's tonight. Maybe we could stop by and see if she's been able to get anything out of Noah about the accident yesterday."

"Perfect." She rolled up the blanket and tucked it into Tango's saddlebag.

"Still up for those fireworks tonight?"

Fireworks? They were going off in her chest right now just looking at him. "Okay. And maybe we could check on Amber too."

T.J. nodded.

"I'm glad her surgery went well." She sighed. "Now if only I had the money to pay for it."

"Oh, I'm sure David would work out a payment plan for you."

She gave a sarcastic laugh. "Are you kidding? He's had me on a payment plan for years. Problem is, I seem to have maxed out my revolving credit line."

"Ah." He gave her a searching look. "How about I cover it and call it the rest of my donation for camp?"

She stared right back. "That's a lot more than you owe me."

"Yeah well, she's living in my house, and my nephew is the one who ran her into a car."

"I never say no if someone wants to help out the rescue, but it's going to be a pretty hefty vet bill. You sure?"

"Positive."

"Thank you." They were still staring at each other, and the air between them buzzed with all kinds of uncomfortable things.

"So let's go see if we can find out what happened to her then."

"Okay." She walked to Tango and let T.J. boost her onto his back.

She'd found her balance on the horse. Now it was the man himself who'd knocked her off kilter. She was awfully afraid she was going to fall, and not from Tango.

$\mathcal{C}$HAPTER NINETEEN

$\mathcal{S}$unday morning dawned early. Way too early. Merry rolled over and slapped the alarm, then smashed her face into the pillow. A variety of feet promptly landed on her back. Wet noses pushed into her hair and quickly became tangled.

"Ugh, puppies." She slid out of bed to escape them. Seriously, who had that much energy at five o'clock in the morning?

She'd sent T.J. home under the guise of a good night's sleep, but she'd also needed space to regain her footing. Lying on a blanket with him last night watching fireworks burst and pop above them, she'd felt a little too cozy, a little too comfortable.

A little too much like she didn't want this to end.

He'd be at church this morning with his family. The thought made her feel all warm and tingly. Probably just because she knew what he looked like in his Sunday best, and good gracious he was hot.

She blotted the image from her mind as she got herself ready for work, fed and walked the dogs, and gated them in the kitchen. Okay, maybe she gave herself just a moment to daydream about T.J. in the blue button-down shirt and khakis he'd worn last Sunday.

It was better than caffeine. Almost.

She made it to work a few minutes before seven, eager to check on her small patients and see who'd gone home since Tuesday, who was new, who was on the mend.

From outside the door of Room 310, she heard Jayden's high-pitched screams, and her chest caved in on itself. She pushed through the door and hurried to his crib. He'd freed his arms from the swaddle and smacked himself in the face as he wailed, his cheeks an angry red.

Merry reached for her MedLink phone, but she'd just passed Jessie in the hall on her way to give the little girl in 304 a bath. Jayden shrieked louder.

She reached into the crib and lifted him into her arms. His little body was stiff with anguish. She checked his diaper, then his digital record. He'd had his last bottle only thirty minutes ago. He was clean and full. He just needed to be held. Comforted.

Didn't everyone need that sometimes? T.J. had done it for her just yesterday. In his arms, she'd forgotten her pain. Maybe now she could do the same for Jayden.

"Shhh." She cradled the baby against her chest, rocking and soothing in a way that had once been second nature. Jayden sobbed into her scrubs, arms still flailing.

She set him on the bassinet to reswaddle him, which only fueled his meltdown. By the time she pulled him back into her arms, he was rigid, his back arched against her touch. She rocked him, shushing as she went.

Jayden screamed louder.

Merry's chest tightened. She couldn't do this. She was wasting her time. There was probably another patient out there who needed her, one that she could actually help.

Jayden's arms popped free again, his tiny fists clenched.

His piercing scream lodged deep in her soul, cracking into the tender depths of her heart.

The poor baby needed comfort, and right now she was all he had. She drew a deep breath and tucked his arms back inside the swaddle.

She kept rocking, humming the lullabies she'd once sung to Tyler. After several long, painful minutes, the baby in her arms calmed. His eyes began to droop, and he snuggled closer against her chest.

Battling tears of her own, Merry sat in the rocker and held him, rocking and humming as he slept in her arms. His little body felt so warm, so sweet, so perfect. She'd almost forgotten how it felt to cradle a sleeping infant.

She closed her eyes to absorb the moment. Something felt different, almost quiet inside her. It had been a while since she'd felt it.

Peace.

Jayden would be ready to go home soon. He'd passed the worst of the withdrawals and was close to being stabilized on his antiseizure medication.

She pictured him at home with his foster family, being loved and played with in a cheerful nursery, and it took some of the ache out of her heart. Precious babies like Jayden didn't belong here, ought never to have seen the inside of a hospital other than the labor and delivery wing.

His birth mother, Crystal, had visited him again last week. She'd been released to a halfway house and was trying to get her life in order for her son. She was clean now, and she wanted him back.

The door opened, and Lavinia Thomas, Jayden's foster mom, stepped inside. She came to visit him most mornings around this time on her way to work. Today she wore a pale pink dress with matching peep-toe heels.

Merry looked up at her and smiled. "Good morning."

"Hey, Merry." Lavinia set her purse beside the crib and came to kiss Jayden's forehead.

"You have good timing because I need to get on with my rounds, but this guy needed to be held for a little while." She stood slowly, careful not to wake him.

Lavinia held out her arms, and Merry laid Jayden into her embrace. Lavinia sat and rocked with him. Merry reached for her clipboard, fighting the empty feeling left behind.

"Any more seizures?" Lavinia asked.

Merry shook her head. "If he stays like this, he might be able to go home by the end of the week."

"Do you think he will?"

"It's hard to say. Dr. Lopez adjusted his antiseizure meds on Friday, so right now it's a game of wait and see."

Lavinia's brow creased. "I didn't really realize it could be so soon."

"Well, it's up to the doctor, of course."

"I haven't told his caseworker yet, but I'm going to have to bow out as Jayden's foster mom." Lavinia looked down at the baby in her arms, her dark eyes troubled.

Merry pressed a hand to her chest. "Oh, no. Why?"

"The seizures, they scare me. I don't think I can handle it on my own. I'm pregnant myself, eight weeks along, and I've been so exhausted and sick. He needs more care than I can give right now."

"Oh. Well, congratulations on your pregnancy."

"Thank you."

"He might be perfectly healthy, you know. There's no way of knowing how much special care he'll need long term." Merry's protective instinct was on overdrive. She wanted to beg this woman not to give up on him now, not when he needed her most. Lavinia wouldn't give up her own child if he or she was diagnosed with special needs, would she?

Maybe she would. In her time as a nurse, Merry had seen that and worse.

And while she'd never personally given up a foster dog when things got tough, she'd known many foster families who had, and sometimes she really couldn't blame them. Other family and commitments took precedence.

Merry had no one but her dogs.

"I feel terrible about it," Lavinia said. "I've never had to give up a foster child before, but it's best for me to bow out now before he gets older and forms an attachment. I'll stay on with him until DSS places him with someone new."

Merry forced a smile. "I'm sure it will all work out. I wish I could stay and talk more, but I've got to get back to my rounds. Push the button if you need me."

Lavinia nodded.

Merry stepped into the hall feeling absolutely heartsick for Jayden. She never should have held him. Now she was left with the memory of his weight in her arms, his breath against her cheek, and oh, how she wanted to protect him from the cruel realities of his life.

* * *

On Sunday afternoon, Jayden had another seizure. Merry had to watch helplessly all over again as the doctors fought to stabilize him, as his stay in the hospital grew longer.

It was heartbreaking.

And it was still on her mind as she arrived for camp on Monday morning. After spending practically every moment together from Wednesday afternoon until Saturday night, she now hadn't seen T.J. in over twenty-four hours.

It was mind-boggling how things had changed since last Monday. The things they'd done and shared. He knew about Tyler.

And she was okay with that.

Amber had gone home last night, and Merry couldn't wait to see her. She'd wanted to bring Amber back to her house to recuperate, but as she was in the middle of her work week, she'd agreed to let her come here to T.J.'s instead.

She let herself in his front door and deposited her purse in the kitchen as she always did, then went looking for man and dog. She found them in the living room.

Amber lay in her dog bed, curled around a couple of stuffed animals, her right front leg wrapped in blue vet wrap. T.J. sat on the couch, iPhone in hand. He stood and tugged Merry into his arms for a heady kiss that almost swept her right off her feet.

"Mornin'," he said.

"Good morning. How is she?"

"Still pretty sore, but I haven't had any trouble with her."

Merry slid from his arms and crouched next to Amber. The dog looked up at her with warm eyes and a shy thump of her tail. "He been taking good care of you?"

Amber licked her palm.

"Have you talked to Noah?" she asked. The last she'd heard, the boy still wasn't talking, probably traumatized by whatever had happened.

"I visited them yesterday. He's not saying a word." T.J.'s face was pinched with frustration.

"I'm sure he feels guilty." And Merry felt awful about that. Thank goodness Amber was going to be okay so Noah wouldn't have to bear the weight of a worse outcome on his small shoulders.

The front door opened, and he and Amy walked in.

"Morning," Amy said. "We wanted to see how she's doing before camp started."

"She's doing great. Come on over, Noah. She's missed you." Merry held her hand out to him, but Noah turned away.

Amber watched, her tail wagging madly as she waited for her favorite person to come greet her.

"Go on, Noah," Amy urged.

Noah stood with his back turned, his hands flailing.

Merry's heart broke for him. "You know what, I need to start setting up in the barn. Noah, could you help me?"

He nodded, then bolted out the front door.

Amy gave her a pained look. "He's been like this since Friday. I don't know what to do."

Merry touched her shoulder. "I'll see if I can talk to him about it today."

Merry looked at T.J. She saw the frustration and worry etched on his face. Then she walked out the front door, hoping against hope she could do something to help.

She found Noah in the barn, standing outside the stall where the dogs were. He'd picked the sleeves of his shirt to shreds and now stood there, hands slapping his sides, as agitated as she'd ever seen him.

She carefully extracted Ralph from the stall without letting the puppies out, then took Noah's hand and walked through the barn to the picnic tables behind.

"Wanna know a secret?" she asked.

Noah looked at her. Purple rings surrounded his eyes. The poor kid wasn't sleeping. What in the world had happened when her back was turned? Why hadn't she been keeping a closer eye on him while he walked Amber? She should have insisted on walking with him.

This was her fault, and now she had to fix it.

"Ralph is a little bit magic," she told him.

Noah's brows scrunched. "Magic isn't real."

"Sure it is. Give Ralph a big hug and close your eyes."

The boy did as he was told. Ralph rested his head over Noah's right shoulder. He closed his eyes and let out a deep sigh. Noah did the same.

"Hold on to him for a minute, just like that," she said softly, watching as Ralph worked his magic on the boy. She saw the tension leave his small frame. They stayed like that for several long minutes, both breathing slow and deep.

When Noah opened his eyes and looked up at Merry, some of the pain had dissipated from their blue depths.

"See? Magic, right?"

He nodded.

"I use his magic all the time, whenever I'm feeling upset. Works every time. So feel free to take as many magic hugs as you need during camp, okay? Ralph has an endless supply."

Indeed. Ralph had absorbed the boy's stress and banished it, looking positively blissful to have Noah's arms wrapped around him. He turned his head to kiss the boy's cheek, and Noah smiled.

"You know it wasn't your fault, right?"

Noah turned away.

"Amber loves you. She misses you. It's not your fault she got hurt."

Tears welled in his eyes.

"Maybe if you tell me what happened, I could help you sort it out."

He shook his head.

"Okay, but if you change your mind, I'm always ready to listen. I'm going to let you work with Ralph during camp today since Amber needs to rest. If you feel up to it afterward though, she'd really love if you came up and visited her at the house. She loves you, Noah."

At the mention of visiting Amber, Noah tensed up again. Ralph leaned a shoulder into him and took a deep breath, prompting Noah to do the same.

Merry had never been more proud of her dog. He truly was magic. He looked up at her with those warm, brown eyes, thrilled to be able to help Noah, and she sent him silent promises for whatever creature comforts he wanted for the rest of his life.

He was one of a kind.

"Merry?" Olivia's voice drifted from the barn.

"Out here," she answered.

Olivia walked out, Bosley at her side. "Hey, guys. How's Amber?"

"She's doing great. She's resting up at the house."

"Glad to hear it."

Merry followed her into the barn to get ready for the other kids. Noah walked behind them with Ralph at his side.

Soon the barn was filled with kids and dogs. Salsa twirled around Jules, yipping happily. Chip, who'd come leaps and bounds with his behavior, sat politely at Parker's feet, waiting for his next reward. Lucy practiced a stay with Bosley, backing her wheelchair over the hard-packed dirt while the dog waited for the command to come.

It was beautiful to watch. Merry was ridiculously proud of how far they'd all come as they began their last week of camp.

In the corner, Noah watched, his arms around Ralph. T.J. stood by the door, arms crossed over his chest, looking dark and brooding. He kept staring at Noah, but every time Noah saw him watching, he averted his eyes.

The whole thing made Merry want to cry. She had to fix this before she left.

But first things first.

"Good morning," she said. "Hope you all had a great weekend. Can everyone ask their dogs to lie down for a minute while we go over our daily schedule?"

Her anguish turned to a smile as four children gave the command to lie down and four dogs plopped onto the dirt, happily munching on their rewards. "That was perfect, you guys. Do you know how far you've come in three weeks? I am so proud of you."

"I'm proud of us too," Jules said, bouncing with excitement. Salsa leaped up to kiss her, then lay back down when Jules repeated the command.

"You should be." Merry adored that little girl and her complete, unfiltered honesty. Merry hoped she'd always be that way: sweet, happy, and one hundred percent real.

She glanced at Noah, saw him engaged in a quiet conversation with Ralph. The dog listened with undivided attention.

"Okay, guys, I do have some news. Amber had an accident on Friday. She broke her leg, and she's not going to be able to participate in camp this week."

"Oh, no!" Jules clapped her hands to her cheeks. "Poor Amber."

"The good news is she's going to be just fine. She's up at the house resting, and she'd really love if you guys could all come and see her after lunch. Sound good?"

They all nodded.

"What happened?" Lucy asked.

"Well, she got hit by a car, but—" Merry held up a hand as the kids gasped. "The vet got her all patched up. She just needs to rest and stay off that leg for a little while."

"I broke my arm once," Parker said. "It hurt like crazy."

Merry looked over and saw Noah standing with his back to them, his hands flailing at his sides. Poor kid. He felt responsible for Amber's accident. How could she help him to see that it wasn't his fault, that sometimes bad things just happened?

"I bet," she said to Parker. "The vet gave Amber some medicine to help with her pain."

T.J. crossed the barn to his nephew, talking to him in tones too low for Merry to hear. He put his hands on Noah's shoulders, then slid them down his arms, trying to help calm him, to stop the agitation causing his arms to flap uncontrollably.

The boy pulled free and ran out of the barn, flailing more wildly than ever.

"Okay, guys. I'm going to have Olivia warm you up with some leash-walking skills. I'll be around to work with each of you individually. I'm going to let you each pick one last skill or trick to teach your dog, so be thinking what you'd like it to be. Toward the end of the week, we'll fine-tune everything and get ready for the exhibition for your families after camp's over."

"Roll over!" Jules exclaimed. "I want to teach Salsa to roll over."

"Perfect, Jules." She smiled at the girl, then followed Noah and T.J. out of the barn.

T.J. stood behind him, his hands extended toward his nephew. "Stop that, buddy. You're going to hurt yourself."

Noah flailed harder, completely out of control.

"Hey, Noah, remember that magic we talked about?" she said.

Noah reached for Ralph and wrapped his arms around him. Merry walked to T.J. and rested a hand on his shoulder. Together, they watched as Noah nestled his head on the dog's shoulder, his body still and calm.

Beside her, T.J. bristled with tension.

"That's perfect, Noah." She led T.J. to the doorway of the barn, giving Noah a few moments alone to finish composing himself.

"How do you do that?" T.J. grumbled. "What magic?"

"Don't you think that's magic?" She nodded toward boy and dog. Noah sat with his arms around Ralph, his head down. Quiet. Peaceful.

T.J. turned, his dark eyes heavy on hers. "Yeah, I guess it is."

* * *

Magic.

Wasn't that the truth?

T.J. had tried everything to calm Noah and only managed to make things worse. Merry had only to invoke whatever spell she'd cast over Noah and Ralph and voilà, he was calm.

He shouldn't be jealous of her ability to communicate with Noah, but hell, he couldn't help it. More than anything, he wanted that bond with his nephew. He wanted to know what was upsetting him so much that he'd lost control of his body. Why he wouldn't tell them what had happened to Amber.

He wanted to help.

"You keep an eye on them," Merry said, then went back inside the barn.

So he stood there, helpless, watching as Noah hugged that damn dog. Why had he ever doubted that Merry was the right person for this camp?

Finally Noah stood and walked back into the barn. Ralph walked at his side, his attention completely devoted to the boy who held his leash. If Noah had asked him to jump off the roof, he probably would have done it. He was completely dedicated to helping others, especially kids. Just like the woman who owned him.

T.J. followed them into the barn. Merry stood with Jules, helping the girl teach Salsa how to roll over. She had a gift, with the kids and the dogs.

While Merry worked with the kids, he pulled them out one at a time for their riding lessons. They'd all made tremendous progress there too, thanks in no small part to Pat's expertise with equine-assisted therapy. All of them, even Lucy, could ride unassisted and complete their exercises with confidence.

Camp was a success. Except he'd failed to accomplish his goal in creating it. He hadn't helped Noah.

And that burned like hot coals in his gut.

After lunch, the kids came up to the house to visit Amber. She lay on her dog bed, tail thumping happily as they petted and comforted her. He had to admit that she'd turned out to be a pretty solid dog. Even as she lay in the street, terrified and in pain, she'd made no move to bite him or anyone else.

Noah stayed in the hall, refusing to go near her. Tomorrow he'd try to get the boy up here alone and convince him how much Amber needed to see him. Maybe Merry could help.

She hung around until the kids had all been picked up, although he knew she had to get to work.

"Bosley's getting adopted," she told him.

"Really? Wow, we're losing dogs left and right."

"He'll finish camp. They're taking him home next weekend." She chewed her bottom lip.

"That's good." He waited for her to tell him what was bothering her.

"Remember how I told you some money had gone missing from my purse?"

He tensed. "Did it happen again?"

She nodded. "It's been happening, and again today."

He couldn't believe any of those kids would steal from her. It made no sense. "Are you sure? How much?"

"Five dollars. It's always five dollars. Look, I don't have time to talk about it today, but just…keep it in mind." She gave him a lingering look full of angst and regret, then went out the front door to fetch her dogs from the barn.

What the hell was that supposed to mean?

* * *

He didn't get to ask until Wednesday. He found her sitting behind the barn, staring out at the horses grazing in the field.

"Something on your mind?" he asked as he sat beside her.

She lifted one shoulder in a halfhearted shrug. "Just thinking about a case from work."

"Anything you want to talk about?"

She shook her head. "Too depressing."

He shifted closer, so that their shoulders touched. "Try me."

She turned her head, and he saw the anguish in her hazel eyes. "It's a baby, okay? He's got long-term health problems, and his foster mom just bailed on him."

"Damn. I don't know how anyone deals with shit like that." Let alone her, who'd lost a baby of her own, watching another be abandoned.

"Life's not fair sometimes." She stood and walked to the fence.

He followed, but when she turned to him, her expression had changed. She grabbed his shirt and kissed him until he almost forgot how to breathe. He lifted her and set her on the top rung of the fence, her feet locked behind his back.

"Stay here tonight," he said, his fingers lost in the tangle of her hair, much as the rest of him seemed to be tangled up in her so that he couldn't be without her.

"I can't. I'm working a few hours tonight to cover for a coworker, but I couldn't anyway. The good news is, I'm definitely not pregnant." She winked.

He frowned at the implication of that. "You don't have to have sex with me to spend the night."

She raised an eyebrow. "Right, because we do talking so well."

"Dammit, Merry—"

"See my point? Just shut up and kiss me."

She didn't give him much choice. She dug her heels into his back, tugging him closer, and kissed him until he couldn't remember why he'd been annoyed. When she'd thoroughly hijacked his senses, she gripped his shoulders and hopped down.

"Sorry about that," she said, eyeing the front of his jeans.

"I'll live."

She stood a few feet away, arms crossed over her chest, her eyes wary. She was distancing herself from him, physically and emotionally, and he didn't like it. Didn't like it one bit. Dammit, camp ended in two days. If she thought he meant to never see her again...

"I need to tell you something before I go," she said.

"Oh yeah?"

"About the missing money."

"I wanted to talk to you about that too. Come in, let's get a cold drink." Because her tone left little doubt that he wasn't going to like what she had to say, and he needed a moment to cool off before diving into this conversation.

She nodded and followed him to the house. He poured two glasses of sweet tea and handed her one.

"Thanks." She took a long drink, distracting him with the way her throat moved as she swallowed.

He shook his head to clear it. "You have any idea who's the culprit?"

She stared at him for a long beat of silence. "I have a theory."

"All right then, let's hear it."

"They're all good kids. Whoever's doing it, I don't think they're stealing to buy candy or video games." She focused on her sweet tea.

What the hell was she getting at? "Spit it out."

"I think it's Noah."

He slammed his glass onto the table so hard tea sloshed all over the floor. "And why the hell would you think that?"

She sighed, then met his gaze straight on. "He's in trouble, T.J. We've both seen it."

His pulse thumped in his ears. "All the kids have been in here this week visiting with Amber. It could have been any of them."

"Yeah, it could have. I would love to be wrong. But why would any of them steal from me? You think sweet Jules is a thief? What about Lucy, in her wheelchair?"

"Parker, he's caused some trouble. It could be him."

She shook her head. "I don't think so. He gets worked up easily because of his sensory problems, but he's a good kid. He wears designer clothes. His mom drives a Mercedes. I can't imagine why he'd need five dollars out of my purse."

"And my nephew does? They may not be rich, but Amy provides for him. Noah is not a thief."

"I found him in here one time getting a drink from the fridge. He looked guilty as hell when I came into the kitchen. He ran from me. That was one of the days money went missing."

"Did you hear yourself? He was getting a drink."

"And my purse was right next to the fridge."

"Why didn't you tell me about this when it happened?" He heard himself yelling but could do nothing about it.

"Because I knew you'd be upset, and I was hoping I could get to the bottom of it by myself." Merry lifted her chin, not backing down. "He's in trouble. You know it. I know it. I don't want to make it worse. I just want to help."

"Help? I don't think calling him a thief helps anything, do you?"

"I want to talk to him about it and see if I can get him to open up to me."

He braced his hands on the counter. "Absolutely not. You will not accuse my nephew of stealing."

"He doesn't even know I've noticed the missing money. If I don't say anything, we'll never know what happened, or why. Don't you want to know why?"

"Yeah, I want to know why you think my nephew is a thief."

"Oh, for crying out loud!" Her temper finally spiked to meet his. "He stole a few dollars! He's not a criminal. He's a kid in trouble. If we don't find out what that trouble is and help him, it might get even worse."

"No. No way are you accusing him of this." Noah was already upset, already withdrawn. He trusted Merry. If she accused him of stealing, it would break that trust. A boy as sensitive as Noah might never get over something like that.

Worst of all, he might lose Noah's trust as well.

"Either you talk to him about it or I will," she said.

"He's my nephew, Merry. You will not have this conversation with him."

She crossed her arms over her chest. "I could talk to Amy."

"No."

She groaned in frustration. "I'm not letting this go. I can't."

He stepped closer, staring her down. "You can, and you will. I've donated a hell of a lot of money to your rescue in exchange for you completing this camp *to my satisfaction*."

She drew back as if he'd slapped her. "I didn't realize I'd traded my free will for your money. That's...that's...Go to hell."

"Leave Noah alone."

"Right. Got it. I'm glad we had this totally two-sided, rational conversation. Like I said, we do talking *so* well."

With a look that could melt steel, she stalked out of his kitchen.

CHAPTER TWENTY

Merry brushed back the annoying sting of tears. She'd expected that response from T.J. It was the main reason she'd waited so long to broach the subject.

But there was no going back now. She wasn't going to let it drop. She couldn't. Noah was in trouble. She felt it in her bones. He needed her help, and she might have to push a little to get through to him.

T.J. on the other hand? She could hardly blame him for sticking up for his nephew. But really, she didn't want to cause any trouble for Noah. She only wanted to help him. Why couldn't he see that? Why couldn't he be a reasonable, rational adult and understand her concern?

And why couldn't she be a reasonable, rational adult and get on with her day? Instead, she sat in her SUV in a McDonald's parking lot, trying to pull herself back together after what had been just one more in a string of petty, meaningless fights.

Only this one didn't feel so meaningless. Or petty.

Hurtful things had been said. Things that couldn't be taken back.

Things that made it painfully clear she'd gone too far with T.J. She'd let him worm himself in where no man ever had. In fact, judging from the ache in her chest, he'd made it all the way into her heart.

If she pushed, if she questioned Noah about the money, T.J. might break it in two, leaving her a bloody, emotional mess. If she didn't, if she let it go, she'd be failing Noah just to keep from angering his stubborn uncle.

Knowing herself, she was about to get her heart broken.

And on that note, she was going home to play with her dogs until it was time to go into work this evening. She'd been foolish to let herself get so consumed by T.J., but it wasn't as if she couldn't still fix it.

She could let him go. Hearts healed. Hers would too.

She drove the rest of the way home with her head held high. No more moping. Merry Joy Atwater did not mope. She just got on with her life.

She sat with the dogs in the living room for a few minutes to catch up on emails and rescue business. The remainder of T.J.'s donation would go toward Amber's vet bills, which left her high and dry as far as a source of income to keep TBR afloat.

Camp had sucked more time and energy than she'd expected. Between it, and work, and her relationship with T.J., she'd completely fallen behind on drumming up a new source of income. Well, it was time now. Bills kept coming, and she wasn't any closer to having the money to pay them.

Her phone pinged with a new text message.

She reached for it, then smiled.

2 more days! Can't wait! It was from Cara.

She couldn't wait for her best friend's visit either. *First stop—Red Heels*, she texted back.

I invited Liv too, Cara replied.

Perfect. I owe her a drink or two.

We have a lot to catch up on.

Yes, they did. And Merry was ready to spill it all. She needed her friend's advice, now more than ever.

* * *

T.J. spent the next two days putting himself between Merry and Noah. He didn't trust her not to bring up the money, even though he'd told her not to. Noah seemed to be avoiding her too. Maybe it was guilt over what had happened to Amber.

Maybe she'd already said something.

That thought put gravel in his gut. Noah was the sweetest, most innocent kid he knew. There was no way in hell he'd stolen from Merry, and T.J. wasn't going to sit by and watch him be falsely accused.

Merry hadn't said another word about it. She'd been business as usual ever since their argument on Wednesday. Business only. She'd gone straight home after camp yesterday, and it was driving him crazy. He needed to get her alone and work this out.

Because today was the last day of camp, and he was absolutely not ready to let Merry walk out of his life.

They were stronger than this disagreement. He knew it. But did she?

She stood in front of the group now, explaining the order of events for the exhibition on Sunday. Lucy, Jules, and Parker listened attentively, looking ridiculously proud and excited. Noah stood in the corner, one arm around Ralph's neck, looking like he wanted the ground to swallow him up.

And that overshadowed everything else.

"All right, let's practice the whole thing from the beginning," Merry said. She and Olivia stood in the center of the aisle while the kids walked in a circle around them, dogs at their sides. "Okay, everyone, now stop and ask your dog to sit."

They did. Four dog rumps hit the earth.

"Now ask your dog to lie down."

Four dogs lay on the cool dirt floor.

"And now stay."

The kids all gave the command. They took two slow steps away from their dog, then released them and lavished them with praise.

T.J. was damn proud of those kids and how hard they'd worked in camp. They were proud of themselves too, and that was the best part. The sense of accomplishment they'd achieved here. The self-confidence. The concentration and motor skills they'd honed.

If only he'd been able to draw Noah out of his shell, camp would have been a complete success.

Next, each child came to the middle of the aisle one at a time and performed a special trick with their dog. Lucy asked Bosley to shake hands. Jules asked Salsa to roll over. The puppy did a half roll, half summersault, then both puppy and girl twirled with excitement. Parker high-fived Chip. Noah, who had the advantage of a pretrained dog, held out his arm and asked Ralph to jump over it.

Everyone cheered. Merry and Olivia praised and high-fived all the kids and gave them extra cookies to reward their dogs. At the end of the hall, Pat, Savannah, and Madison whooped and clapped for them.

The last event for the dogs would be a game of "Musical Sit." The kids walked their dogs around in a circle as music played. When the music stopped, everyone asked their dog to sit. Last dog standing was out.

They practiced several times, with Noah and Ralph winning each time. Merry watched pensively, then announced that on exhibition day they'd alternate dogs so that everyone took a turn with each dog. Ralph would make sure they all had a chance to win.

After that, they put the dogs in the extra stall and got the horses ready. Parker and Jules went first on Twilight and Peaches. Pat ran them through a series of exercises they'd learned during camp with Savannah and Madison assisting and cheering them on. Next they each got to trot once all the way around the ring.

Then it was Lucy and Noah's turn.

Finally, exhausted and sweaty, they all returned to the barn. The kids helped get the horses untacked, hosed off, and turned out to the pasture. They ran back to the barn, ready to eat their last lunch together at the picnic tables.

That was when T.J. noticed two cars missing from the driveway. Olivia had left early, as she usually did to prepare for her shift at the café. But Merry had left too, without so much as saying good-bye.

Summer camp was over, and Merry was gone.

* * *

Merry could barely keep from bouncing up and down as she stood at the top of the escalator at Raleigh-Durham International Airport waiting for Cara to arrive. She felt like Jules. In fact, she envied the girl's unfiltered ability to let her excitement just pour out of her.

Several minutes later, Merry caught a glimpse of strawberry blond hair, and then Cara's smiling face came into view. As soon as she'd passed the security checkpoint, Merry threw caution to the wind and grabbed her in a bear hug.

Finally Cara pulled back, laughing. "Geez, you could at least pretend you missed me."

"Seriously, you have no idea. It's a good thing I like Matt or else I'd really hate him for taking you away from me."

They started walking toward baggage claim.

"Aww." Cara smiled. "I love Matt, and I like my new life in Massachusetts, but I missed you too. I miss North Carolina. I'm even looking forward to feeling the crazy humidity out there."

Merry scoffed at her. "Really? The humidity?"

"I know, it's crazy. Thanks again for letting me stay with you. My mom may never forgive me, but preserving my sanity will be worth it."

They stood by carousel three, waiting for the Boston luggage to arrive. Cara was looking at her a little too intently, and Merry knew she wouldn t have a choice but to confess everything. Which was a relief really. She needed to unload her problems on someone, and there was no one she trusted more than Cara.

"Here's mine." Cara snagged a pale blue suitcase off the conveyer belt, and they headed for the exit.

"Ralph's going to freak when he sees you, and you haven't even met Chip and Salsa yet."

Cara looked wistful. "Somehow I feel even more homesick now that I'm here. I forgot how much I had missed."

Merry elbowed her. "Maybe next time it won't take you so long to visit."

"You sound like my mother. Things have been hectic. I'm finally getting my photography business off the ground, and Matt's private investigation firm has been crazy busy. Trust me, this winter I'll be here as often as I can. I don't know how I'm going to survive all that cold and snow."

Merry felt a bittersweet tug in her chest. Her friend looked happy, radiantly happy. And as much as she missed Cara, Matt was the one who had given her that glow, who had convinced her to let go of her fears and start reaching for her dreams. "I'm really happy for you. You know that, right?"

Cara bumped her shoulder against Merry's. "I know. And

planes go both ways, right? Come visit us. I hear fall in New England is gorgeous."

"Okay. Count me in. I'm sure I can find someone to watch the dogs for a few days."

"Maybe that hunky cowboy of yours could do it." Cara's eyes gleamed with curiosity.

"Yeah, did I mention he's afraid of dogs? And that he's not actually *my* cowboy?"

"No, but you're going to fill me in on everything, and I do mean *everything*, this weekend."

They walked outside, and Cara turned her face toward the sun with a blissful smile.

Merry scrunched her nose. "Really? The humidity?"

Her friend nodded. "I really missed the humidity. Hopefully it'll be a brutally hot weekend that frizzes my hair and gives me a sunburn and makes me ready to go home."

"Home?" She hadn't quite expected to hear Cara call Massachusetts home, but she supposed it was true. Her friend didn't live in Dogwood anymore.

"Yeah," Cara said with a thoughtful expression. "I guess it is home now."

They chatted all the way to Merry's house, catching up on everything they'd missed in the four months since Cara had left.

Ralph nearly turned himself inside out at the sight of one of his favorite people, and the puppies were euphoric over meeting a new friend. Cara rolled her eyes at their names. She preferred human names on dogs, while Merry preferred the cutesy names that made people smile. Half the time their new owners changed them after they were adopted anyway.

When they'd calmed down, Merry handed out chewy treats so that she and Cara could sit and chat. She went to the fridge and pulled out a bottle of chardonnay. "Our own precelebration celebration?"

"I love the way you think." Cara flopped onto the couch and put her feet up. She accepted the glass of wine Merry held toward her and tapped her glass against Merry's. "To best friends."

"To best friends," Merry repeated. "You know, the last time you and I toasted, it was New Year's Eve, and I wished for a steamy new romance for you."

"And it came true." Cara smiled as she sipped her wine.

Merry sat at the other end of the couch and curled her feet under her. "And then some."

"And now, my dear, I think it's your turn."

* * *

"I'm telling you, Cara. We've got another FMH situation on our hands." Olivia tipped her martini in Merry's direction with a dramatic sweep of her eyelashes.

"If I don't get a look at this cowboy before I go home on Sunday, I'm going to be so sad." Cara made a pouty face.

"Oh, for crying out loud." Merry wanted to be annoyed— she really should be—but she was so happy to be out with Cara and Olivia that she really didn't care if they ribbed her about T.J. all night.

She would happily endure whatever they wanted to dish out.

With its soft lighting, jazzy music, and a plentiful variety of delicious martinis, Red Heels was their go-to place whenever they needed a girls' night out. Merry hadn't been here since Cara had left town, and she missed the place dearly. Her friends even more.

"What if, and I'm just thinking out loud here, but what if we all got too drunk to drive home, and we had to call T.J. to come pick us up?" Cara asked the question with wide-eyed innocence, then she and Olivia dissolved in a fit of laughter.

Of course, Cara and her sister had notoriously done just that a few months back. Cara had to call Matt, the hunky PI she'd been falling for at the time, to pick them up, and Merry wasn't sure what happened next, but it wasn't long after that Cara and Matt were hopelessly in love.

"Ha ha," Merry said. "We'll call a cab."

"Well, just FYI, Dogwood Taxi stops running at midnight." Cara took another sip from her martini. "But anyway, back to this FMH situation..."

FMH was a term Cara and Olivia had coined back in college to covertly describe a man they found to be "fuck me hot." T.J. certainly fit that bill, except Cara's FMH guy had ended up being the one who put a ring on her finger, and Merry didn't like the possible implications for her own relationship.

"Oh." Olivia's eyes brightened. "Are you coming to the exhibition on Sunday? You can meet him there."

"What exhibition?" Cara asked.

"It's an end-of-camp thing for the kids to show off for their families. You're spending Sunday with your family so I didn't mention it," Merry said.

"Well, if it's my only chance to meet T.J., then I think I have to be there."

"Oh, you need to be there," Olivia said with a nod. "Wait until you see the way these two look at each other."

"Ooh." Cara's eyes widened. "I'm intrigued."

Merry rolled her eyes. "We have chemistry, whatever. We've already been there and done that."

Olivia choked on her martini. She coughed and laughed until her eyes ran. "Oh yes, I saw all the smoldering looks. But lately it's more lovey-dovey than that."

Now it was Merry's turn to choke. "Lovey-dovey? Have your lost your mind?"

Cara just sat there, looking like a kid on Christmas

morning. Merry could practically feel the excitement radiating off her.

Olivia grinned. "When you're not bickering like an old married couple, that is."

"Oh, my God." Cara twirled on her stool. "I knew something was different about you. Are you falling for him, really?"

Falling? She'd already crash-landed. "We've had some . . . moments."

"Moments?" Olivia waggled her eyebrows, then polished off her martini.

Cara touched Merry's shoulder. "You look like I just asked if you have an STD. What's so bad about falling for a guy?"

Merry shook her head. "I don't want to get married and have kids. I don't want any of that."

"You don't have to marry him. Just relax and see where things go," Cara said.

"He doesn't even like dogs."

Olivia slapped the bar. "Are you kidding me? He may not love them the way he loves horses, but he's been great with the dogs. He even fostered Amber for you."

"Okay, he's great, whatever. Let's talk about something else." She turned to Cara. "How are wedding plans coming?"

Cara's expression softened. "Oh, it's going great. Matt's mom is a total sweetheart, and she's been a huge help. I feel like family already. I can't wait to make it official."

Merry gave her a quick hug. "Just promise my maid of honor dress won't be bubblegum pink."

"I promise. I hate hot pink."

"What about you, Liv? Anything new and exciting?" Merry asked.

Olivia shook her head. "I've been too busy to date. Between camp and work and my Facebook war against Halverson Foods, I'm pathetically boring."

Cara giggled. "I don't think anyone involved in a Facebook war could be classified as boring."

"What's the deal with that anyway?" Merry finished her martini and signaled to the bartender for another.

"We sent some undercover people in there to make a video of them abusing their chickens, but apparently it wasn't damning enough to get them shut down. They got a silly fine and promised to do better."

"That sucks." Merry stared at her empty glass. "But if anyone can make things happen, it's you, Liv."

"Speaking of Facebook, have you had any luck with TBR's page?" Olivia asked.

Merry scoffed. Her new martini arrived, and she sipped it gratefully. "It's a total waste. I get more people trying to surrender dogs than donate money."

"Are donations down?" Cara asked.

Merry stared into her drink. "Donations are practically nonexistent right now."

Cara rested a hand on her shoulder. "What's going on?"

She heaved a sigh and took a fortifying swallow from her martini. She could shout from the rooftops when the dogs needed something. Asking for help for herself? That was a lot harder. "The rescue is broke. I don't know what to do."

"Oh, my God, Merry. I had no idea! What happened?"

"I got lazy, that's what. About a year after I founded TBR, someone starting sending an anonymous thousand-dollar monthly donation."

"What? Who?" Olivia asked.

Merry shook her head. "I have no idea. But that money kept us afloat all these years, and then about seven months ago, it stopped. And I realized I had no idea how to actually raise enough money to keep the rescue going on my own."

Olivia slapped her arm. "Girl, why didn't you tell me?

Give me access to your Facebook and Twitter, and I'll get things going for you."

"It's not that easy. I've tried."

"No offense, but you probably don't know what you're doing. Let me try."

Merry shrugged. "Well, it can't hurt. Thank you."

"No problem. I'm happy to help." Olivia clinked glasses with her. "And I'd way rather manage your social media than foster for you, no offense."

They all laughed.

"Let's talk about these anonymous donations," Cara said.

Olivia swirled her martini. "Yeah, really. A thousand dollars a month? That's a lot of money. Who do you think it was?"

"I have no idea. I tried for years to figure it out. Probably it was someone who adopted from us, or maybe even someone who surrendered a dog and then felt guilty."

"How about I have Jason look into it? I'm sure he could trace the money and find out who it was," Cara offered. Jason was her fiancé's brother and a genius at cyber-sleuthing.

"Sure, if he's not too busy. It would be nice to know."

"Consider it done."

Merry took another sip from her martini and drew a deep breath. She'd opened up, and her friends had jumped in to help. "You guys are good friends, you know that?"

Olivia grinned. "Oh, we know."

They all raised their glasses and clinked them together. Maybe, just maybe, they'd even be able to help her save Triangle Boxer Rescue.

* * *

Merry and Cara made it home safely—before midnight—courtesy of Dogwood Taxi. They changed into their pajamas and settled on the couch to counteract the night's drinks with some water before bed.

"I'm getting a weird vibe from you tonight, Merry." Cara gave her a long look. "Whatever it is, spill it while you've got me here on your couch in person."

Merry took a deep breath. She and Cara had met through Triangle Boxer Rescue several years after Tyler's death, but she'd never shared her loss with any of her friends. Since opening herself up to T.J., she'd realized she had been wrong to keep Tyler's memory to herself. "There's something I should have told you a long time ago. I don't know why I never did."

Cara nodded. "Okay. So tell me now."

Instead of telling her, Merry went upstairs and got the picture of Tyler from her bedside table. She brought it downstairs and handed it to Cara. Her friend gazed at the photo and then at Merry, a look of pained understanding on her face.

That was the thing about best friends. They knew you so well that you didn't even have to explain yourself. But she did anyway. She told Cara how she'd accidentally gotten pregnant while she was in nursing school, how she'd struggled to care for a colicky baby while keeping up with her classes. How she'd fallen asleep, and her son had paid with his life.

"Oh, honey." Cara wrapped her arms around her. "I am so, so sorry for you. I can't even imagine what you've been through."

Merry dashed a runaway tear from her cheek. "I guess I thought, if I didn't talk about it, it would be easier to forget."

"You'll never forget him, sweetie. He's a part of you. He'll always be a part of you."

Merry hugged her knees. "I'm sorry I never told you."

"Don't be silly. We all grieve in different ways." Cara

stared pensively into her glass. "I have to say though, this explains a lot."

"How so?"

"I could tell there was something holding you back. You've been blaming yourself for a long time for something that wasn't your fault."

"But it *was* my fault. I fell asleep. I didn't check on him."

Cara took her hands and looked into her eyes. "He would have died even if you'd checked on him every hour. SIDS just happens."

"The nurse in me knows that, but the mom in me also knows that I failed him. Mother's intuition or whatever. Mine didn't work."

Cara shook her head. "You are such a hypocrite."

"What?"

"All those years you lectured me about being afraid to live my life when you've been doing the *exact same thing*."

She sucked in a breath. "It is not the same thing."

"Close enough. I was afraid I'd get sick again and leave behind a family. And you're afraid to start a family because you think you failed your last one. You have to let go of that guilt so that you can be happy."

$\mathcal{C}$HAPTER TWENTY-ONE

T.J. was walking from his parents' barn to the house when Merry's CR-V pulled into the driveway. His mom had invited everyone involved in the camp to Sunday brunch before the exhibition, but he hadn't been sure Merry would show after the way they'd left things.

Bless her heart, his mom had even tried to get her to come to church with them that morning. The look on her face when he'd passed along the invitation had been priceless.

Nonetheless, here she was.

And she wasn't leaving without agreeing to see him again.

She stepped out of her SUV in a knee-length pink sundress covered with little white flowers, her hair loose and wildly curly, the way he liked it best. His gaze fell to her pink-jeweled sandals. He ought to give her a hard time for wearing shoes like that to a horse farm, but she'd dressed for brunch, after all, and besides, the sandals were sexy as hell.

She was the vision of a girly-girl right now, and she'd never looked more beautiful. She lifted her eyes to his and smiled, and he forgot to breathe for several long seconds.

"Mornin'," he said when he'd finally managed to fill his lungs with air.

She fidgeted with her fingers, adorably nervous about being here. "Can't remember the last time I had Sunday brunch. I'm usually stuffing a granola bar in my mouth on the way to work." Merry had taken today off on account of the exhibition.

"Enjoying it?"

"I think I'm going to. And I can't wait to see the kids this afternoon. They're going to make me so proud."

She'd stopped a few feet away, but he closed the gap between them and took her hand. "That they are. Want a quick tour before we go inside?"

"Sure." She fell into step beside him as he led her toward the barn.

"You took off pretty quick on Friday," he said.

"Sorry about that." She looked over at the pasture to their right. "I had to pick up a friend at the airport."

"So we're okay?"

She lifted her shoulders. "If by 'okay' you mean we agree to disagree on basically all the important stuff, then sure, we're fine."

And there it was, the elephant they'd been tiptoeing around ever since their blowup over the missing money. "Look, I shouldn't have said that about you completing camp to my satisfaction. You've earned your donation, fair and square."

"Good to know." Her eyes shuttered. Yeah, he knew damn well what she wanted him to say, and there was no way he'd give his permission for her to talk to Noah about that money.

She pulled her hand from his and walked ahead of him into the barn.

"This is the broodmares' barn," he told her as they stepped inside. "Most of them are out in the pastures right now. Dad will bring them in later this afternoon to have a look at everyone, especially the ones with nursing foals. This is Comet. She came in lame last night, so they kept her in today."

The beautiful gray mare stuck her head out of the stall for a rub. She nuzzled his pockets, looking for a treat. He fed her a carrot.

"She's beautiful." Merry stroked her face.

"She sure is, but she's not the most gorgeous lady in the room." Now that they had the privacy of the barn, he drew her in for a lingering kiss. He ran his fingers over the soft linen of her dress and felt her shiver beneath his touch. "I've gotten used to you in jeans. I forgot how pretty you look in your girly dresses."

"You're looking pretty hot yourself." She tugged at the collar of his shirt.

Here she was, about to have Sunday brunch with his parents, and he had no doubt she was going to fit right in. He'd been so very wrong about her when they first met, wrong about a lot of things.

Holding her in his arms felt right. He felt truly calm for the first time all week, like he'd found his center here, with Merry. He'd thought it might be something more dramatic, like a bolt of lightning or a slap to the head, but instead it was more of a gradual awakening. Something he'd known for a while but hadn't realized what it was.

Right there, in the barn where he'd grown up, with her arms around his neck and a horse peeking over her shoulder, T.J. knew for sure that he'd fallen in love with Merry Atwater, girly shoes and all.

His arms tightened around her. "Stay with me tonight. Please."

She shook her head, her hazel eyes troubled. "I can't. My best friend is visiting from Massachusetts. She goes home tomorrow."

"Then tomorrow night." He wasn't letting her go, wasn't letting her walk out of his life after the exhibition this afternoon.

"I work a twelve-hour shift tomorrow and the next day."

"Then let me stay at your place tomorrow. I'll let you get some sleep, I promise."

"T.J. . . ." She backed out of his arms.

"I'm not letting you out of here until you agree to see me again. What about dinner at my place on Wednesday? We can sit and talk."

"Okay," she agreed, but she didn't look happy about it.

He smiled, but the victory felt hollow. He had to fix this, had to win her over. He couldn't let the woman he loved walk away.

* * *

He kept his hand in hers as they walked out of the barn toward the pastures in back. "These three pastures are for the broodmares. See the sorrel mare over there? That's Jewel. I delivered her filly, Ruby, about a month ago."

"Oh, Ruby's so cute!" Merry couldn't contain a smile at the sight of the little horse frolicking at her mother's side.

"That barn on the other side of the house is for the stallions and geldings. The stallions are in right now, while the mares are out. Come, I'll introduce you." He led her down the driveway toward the other barn.

She really should have asked him to take her up to the house because the sight of T.J. in his Sunday best amid all these gorgeous horses was seriously messing with her head. They stepped through the doorway, and she was blinded for a moment by the abrupt transition from sunlight to shadow. She heard a horse nicker and saw a long neck stretching toward T.J.

"This is Blue Sierra Diamond. He goes by Blue."

"Oh, wow." Perhaps it was a trick of the lighting, her eyes still not quite adjusted, but the horse was as white as a ghost with a long, flowing white mane. He looked at her, his eyes a bright, startling blue.

"Handsome fellow, isn't he?" T.J. patted him fondly.

"He's stunning. I've never seen a horse quite like him." She couldn't take her eyes off the ethereal creature before her. She almost expected him to sprout wings and fly.

"He's a cremello. Beautiful color, isn't it? He sired Peaches. Breed a cremello to a chestnut and you get a palomino."

Merry had no idea what that meant, but the horse sure was beautiful. "So you're Peaches's dad, huh?" She reached out to touch him, and he bobbed his head in affirmation.

"Sure is. He's sired some showstoppers. I hope to bring him out to my place someday when he retires."

"Is he deaf?" she asked.

T.J. cocked his head. "No. Why would you think that?"

"The white coat and blue eyes."

He looked at her like she was speaking nonsense.

She shook her head. "A white dog with blue eyes is usually deaf. Apparently not the same for horses."

"No, but now that you mention it, I have heard that about dogs. Come, let me show you Peppy."

She followed him down the aisle to another stall. The nameplate on this one read Peppy's Outlaw. The horse inside stuck his head out at T.J.'s approach. He was night and day to Blue. This horse was a deep espresso brown with a black mane and tail. Equally handsome with his alert, brown eyes and strong, sleek physique.

"Peppy sired Twilight," T.J. told her.

"Oh, I do see a resemblance in their coloring. And Tango?"

"Ah." T.J. stroked the horse in front of him. "King's Blue Sky, my parents' pride and joy and the farm's namesake. He passed away a few years ago."

"Oh, that's sad." She reached out to touch Peppy's neck. He glistened like spun silk in the half-light of the barn.

"You hungry?"

She nodded. Starving actually, but in no way eager to go up to the house and sit with his family for Sunday brunch. That felt way too cozy, especially after the way T.J. had looked at her a few minutes ago when he'd asked her to stay the night.

Like he wanted her to stay forever.

He looked so ridiculously handsome in his olive green button-down shirt and khaki pants. A tiny, needy part of her wanted him to hold her and never let go. Even if she was too much of a coward to marry him or give him the children he wanted.

And then there was the fact that any time they spent more than ten minutes together, they argued. Not just bickering, but things that hurt feelings and spoiled tempers. They'd likely never see eye to eye on what was best for Noah or whether dogs belonged in the house.

So she'd have dinner with him on Wednesday, but she couldn't agree to more than that, not for either of their sakes. Continuing a relationship wasn't in either of their best interest, and she'd find a way to make him see that.

He slid his arms around her waist and kissed her until she'd forgotten everything she'd just decided. Then he pulled back just enough to give her a heart-stopping grin. "Come on, let's go eat. Believe me, once you've tasted my mom's cooking, you'll be back again next Sunday."

But she knew that she wouldn't.

* * *

Sunday brunch at the Jamesons' was unlike anything Merry had ever experienced. It was loud and boisterous, and wow, his mom's cooking really was amazing. Merry had somehow managed to sit between Noah and Pat O'Day, although T.J. was giving her grumpy looks about it. Amy sat on Noah's other side. Across from them were T.J., his parents, Savannah, and Madison.

Olivia had to miss brunch to work the breakfast shift at the café, and Merry had worried it might be awkward without her. But the seating arrangement helped her feel less like T.J.'s date and more like the dog trainer from his camp, which was why she'd been invited, after all. It put her back on even ground so that she could enjoy this fabulous brunch the way she would have in any other situation that didn't involved a brooding cowboy who'd scrambled her up like his mother's eggs until she couldn't remember what to feel or why he was a bad idea.

"Call me Trace, like the country singer," his dad had said when they were introduced, with a wide smile and a vigorous handshake.

EmmyLou had pulled her in for a hug.

She'd met his parents that day at the hospital after Noah's fall, but at the time, she'd been just a nurse they'd never see again. Now she was in their home, lusting after their son and still desperately hoping to win the trust of their grandson.

She'd squandered the last few days of camp, torn between respecting T.J.'s wishes and following her own gut. And her gut was still telling her that Noah needed her help. Maybe she should mention it to Amy this morning. Or maybe she should butt out of their business and focus on her own problems.

The spread on the table included biscuits and gravy, bacon, sausage, scrambled eggs, blueberry muffins, and an assortment of fresh fruit. Even Noah smiled as he bit into one of his grandmother's biscuits.

"You get to eat like this every Sunday?" she whispered to him.

He grinned through a mouthful of biscuit and gravy.

"I am so jealous." And not just of the food. There was so

much laughter and friendly conversation as they loaded up second helpings.

Trace kept the banter lively with tales from the farm. "And then, just before I cut him loose, I realized it was a raccoon and not old Benny's barn cat."

"Trace, honey, I think you need to have your glasses checked." EmmyLou patted him on the shoulder, and the whole table erupted in laughter.

It felt good to sit around a table full of happy people, stuffing themselves on sinfully good southern food. Merry had grown up in a happy home. She and her dad had always laughed and joked with each other at mealtime. But it had only been the two of them.

At holidays, they'd go to his parents' house in Lexington, Kentucky, and enjoy meals like this, although on a smaller scale and with less amazing food. She'd looked forward to them for months in advance. The chance to enjoy something like this every Sunday must be like heaven.

When all the food had been eaten, they sat on the back porch for coffee, tea, and more conversation. Finally Merry glanced at her watch. It was past noon, and she needed to get home and walk and exercise the dogs before the exhibition started.

"Thanks so much for having me, EmmyLou. T.J.'s been telling me about your cooking, and he didn't exaggerate. It was amazing."

"Oh, thank you, honey. We're so glad you could come. You're welcome here any time."

"Thank you."

"Before you go, I put a couple of biscuits in a doggie bag for your friend from Massachusetts. Have you shown her some good southern food while she's here?" EmmyLou stood and guided Merry back into the house.

"Oh, she's a born and bred North Carolinian. She only moved north a few months ago."

The older woman went into the kitchen and picked up a brown paper bag. "Then I guess she'll appreciate some home cookin'."

"Oh, she definitely will. Thanks so much."

EmmyLou paused with the bag in her hands. "I know it's not my place, but... Well anyone with two eyes can see that you and my son are crazy about each other."

Merry drew back. "What?"

"I just wanted to give you my blessing, that's all." Emmy-Lou handed her the bag of biscuits, then gave her a quick squeeze. "I've never seen him look happier."

"Oh, well—" Merry fumbled for words.

"It's okay, sweetie. I see that you're still unsure. It took a while for Trace to win me over too. We women can be hard-headed when it comes to love."

Love? "Um—" Merry's cheeks burned.

"I've put you on the spot. My apologies. Just remember," EmmyLou called over her shoulder as she walked out of the kitchen, "you're welcome here any time."

And yet Merry knew she'd probably never be back.

* * *

The exhibition went off beautifully. The kids all looked adorable in their Camp Blue Sky T-shirts. Merry had even put a matching shirt on Salsa, just to make Jules's day. The dogs walked, sat, stayed, and performed their special tricks in front of friends and family.

Pat had brought a tent to put over the front lawn so they had a place to gather without enduring the blistering heat of the sun. Merry's chest swelled until she thought it might burst watching those kids show off their newfound skills and self-confidence.

Even Parker stayed remarkably focused and on task

despite the tent full of distractions. Chip too showed new maturity, listening attentively to Parker as he waited for his next command.

Jules wrapped her arms around Salsa, a girl in love. Last week her family had put in an application to adopt Salsa. She'd be going home with them after the exhibition. It warmed the deepest corners of Merry's heart to see that little girl with her puppy.

Merry had also approached Lucy's family about the possibility of getting her a service dog. Lucy's mother had come and observed her in camp and tearfully agreed to look into it, moved by her daughter's confidence and ability with the dogs. When she'd asked Merry if she could recommend a dog for her, she'd suggested they have Chip evaluated.

The puppy was energetic, smart, and driven to please. He and Lucy had worked well together on several occasions during camp. He was being evaluated by Carolina Therapy Dogs at the end of the month.

If it worked out, it would be another happy ending for her camp dogs. They'd all found homes except Amber.

She hadn't convinced T.J. to keep her, or helped Noah, and she wanted to change both of those things more than anything in the world. Another five dollars had been taken from her purse while she was at brunch that morning, all but confirming Noah was the one stealing from her, as none of the other kids had been there.

Merry's heart ached for him. What had happened to make him feel like this was something he had to do? And with camp over, would she ever find out the answer?

The last round of "Musical Sit" ended with a victory for Lucy and Bosley. The kids lined up with their dogs, and Merry gave them each a certificate declaring them Junior Dog Trainers. They beamed with pride as friends and family clapped and cheered their success.

Off to the side, Cara watched with a smile.

T.J. and Patrick came out of the barn leading Twilight and Peaches, groomed to perfection with ribbons in their manes. The kids handed leashes to Merry, and the crowd moved to the riding ring.

Merry walked the dogs toward the barn to get water and a cool fan going while the kids rode outside. Olivia and Cara followed her.

"They all did so amazing!" Merry knelt and pulled the dogs in for a group hug.

"They really did," Cara agreed. "They obviously had great teachers."

Olivia tossed cookies into four eager mouths. "Not that I haven't enjoyed sweating my ass off out here every day, but I'm glad to be done."

Cara laughed. "You guys did a great job. Do you think you'll do it again?"

"Again?" Merry stared blankly at her.

"Next summer?"

She shook her head. "I haven't thought about next summer yet. I had fun doing the camp, but it was a lot of work, and I had to take a lot of time off from the hospital." *And I fell for the man running the camp…*

She opened the door to the extra stall and ushered the four dogs inside.

Olivia wagged a finger at her. "Yeah, because if you start planning ahead, you might have to deal with this thing with T.J."

"Indeed," Cara said. "Now I've seen the lovey-dovey thing Liv was talking about. You're going to keep seeing him after camp's over, right?"

"We're having dinner on Wednesday, but after that? Who knows?" She shrugged.

"Who knows?" Cara smacked her arm. "He looks at you

like he wants to eat you up, but more than that, like he wants to eat you up *forever*."

Merry stared at her notoriously prudish friend, then burst out laughing. "What has Matt done to you? Girl, that's gross."

Cara's eyes rounded, and her cheeks bloomed red. "Okay, focus on the forever part, and not so much the eating you... oh, my God, I can't believe I said that."

Merry's laughter died on her lips. "Yeah, that's the problem. He wants forever, and I don't."

"Then maybe it's time to change the way you think."

* * *

Change her opinion of forever? Merry was still chewing on that the next morning at work. Her mood was already dampened by having to drop Cara off at the airport on her way in, and morning rounds didn't help to lift it.

There was a bratty ten-year-old in Room 304 recovering from surgery to repair torn ligaments in his knee after crashing his ATV down by the old quarry. His mother wore expensive perfume, even more expensive clothes, and expected the nursing staff to wait on her hand and foot.

And then there was Jayden. Now that she'd held him once, she felt compelled to do it each morning. After refilling a water pitcher for the boy in 304, she took advantage of a few quiet minutes to give Jayden a bottle, then rocked him to sleep in her arms.

Lavinia usually stopped by around eight to visit him before work. This morning she was a no-show. She was starting to detach herself from the infant, making room for her own baby. Jayden's caseworker should be in later that afternoon, and Merry was eager to hear what progress they'd made in finding him a new foster home.

He was again three days without a seizure and scoring
in the seven to eight range on his neonatal abstinence syndrome withdrawal test. If he remained stable over the next
week, he'd be ready to go home.

Merry sat a few minutes longer in the rocker, watching
him sleep. His cheeks were starting to round now that his
withdrawals had eased and his appetite kicked in. He looked
healthy and robust, like a six-week-old infant should.

Provided his seizures stayed under control, he could still
live a normal, healthy life.

She traced a finger over his cheek, then bent to kiss his
forehead.

The phone at her hip beeped, and she reached down to
silence it before he woke, although, having spent most of
his days here in the hospital, Jayden had learned to sleep
through all kinds of beeps and alarms. Hopefully that would
change for him soon.

She stood and settled him in his crib, then walked out of
his room, feeling deflated and empty. The rest of her shift
passed uneventfully. The family in 304 kept her on her toes
with constant requests and demands to see the doctor. During her one o'clock round, Jayden smiled at her, and Merry's
eyes welled with happy tears.

Despite the quiet shift, she was bone tired by the time she
got home that night. Only Ralph and Chip waited for her in
the kitchen. After the exhibition yesterday, Bosley had gone
to his new home, and Salsa had gone home with Jules.

Amber was in her crate in Merry's dining room. T.J. had
fulfilled all obligations to Triangle Boxer Rescue.

She missed him. She missed camp and those sweet kids.
Life felt a little bit empty now that it was all over. In fact,
she'd been mulling over a new idea. A canine therapy program of her own with all proceeds to benefit Triangle Boxer
Rescue. It was one of a few new ideas she'd had. She'd also

signed up for an online course on fund-raising because it
was time to learn how to do this right.

She needed help, and maybe that wasn't a bad thing. Last
night, she'd sent an email to TBR's volunteer group, and
today her in-box was full of chatter, ideas, and brainstorming
to raise money for the rescue.

Why had she thought she had to do this all on her own?

She'd been a stubborn fool.

She greeted Ralph and Chip in the kitchen with hugs and
kisses, then went to the crate in the dining room and helped
Amber out. She was still on restricted activity while her leg
healed, but she was calm enough that she was able to stay out
of the crate while someone was home with her to supervise.

All of the dogs went out back while Merry watched to
be sure Amber only walked. Then she took them in and fed
them. She opened the fridge and poked through it.

Bare.

She and Cara had eaten most everything she had over
the weekend. And in typical fashion, she'd neglected to plan
ahead for herself during the workweek.

Before she surrendered to yet another peanut butter and
jelly sandwich, she sat for a much-needed glass of water and
thumbed through messages on her phone. One from Olivia
told her to check her Facebook page and Paypal account.

Merry could hardly believe what she was seeing. Triangle
Boxer Rescue's Facebook page had gone from a hundred
and thirty-two likes to over four hundred. Olivia had sent
an email to the volunteer list asking for news and photos to
share. She'd posted several Happy Tails stories about dogs
that had been adopted, created a poll to name a new dog
just pulled from the shelter charging twenty dollars for each
vote, and set up a fund-raiser through an online pet food
delivery service.

Over two hundred dollars had been received into Triangle

Boxer Rescue's Paypal account. Two hundred new dollars to pay vet bills and save more dogs.

Olivia Bennett truly was a social media genius.

Merry called her in a haze, ready to grovel at her feet and promise her whatever she wanted for the rest of her life if she'd just keep running TBR's Facebook page. She got voice mail, left a long and rambling message, then sat in her kitchen, feeling strangely out of sorts.

If Olivia could keep her magic going, it was the start of something that might turn around her financial crisis. She couldn't support the rescue on Facebook alone, but between the ideas she was discussing with her volunteers and her plan to start a canine therapy group with local kids, she finally felt like she'd rounded the corner.

She could do this.

Then she saw the message from Cara. *Call me*.

She dialed her best friend, and she answered on the second ring.

"I have a name for you," Cara said.

"A name?" Merry rubbed her brow, drawing a total blank.

"The person who was giving you all that money?"

"Oh." Merry sat bolt upright in the chair. "Oh! Really?"

"I told you Jason's a cyber-genius. He tracked it down for you, although he says not to ask him how he did it."

"Sure thing."

"So your anonymous donor was Beverly Clarence. Ring a bell?"

Merry slid out of the chair and sat on the floor, heart pounding. "Yeah. She's my mom."

CHAPTER TWENTY-TWO

T.J.'s house felt empty, big and yawning in a way it had never felt before. He missed Merry, missed her a lot, even though it had only been twenty-four hours since he'd seen her, and he'd see her again on Wednesday.

Her absence alone couldn't explain this bout of loneliness. Loath as he was to admit it, he missed the damn dog. Amber had become somewhat of a buddy, following him quietly around the house, keeping him company without demanding much in return.

If he ever got a dog, he'd want one like Amber. Amber with a pedigree. Surely such a dog existed. But hell, even Amber the mutt wasn't half bad.

He didn't want to be alone anymore.

He stared at the corner where her dog bed had been for the last month. Having Amber around hadn't been so bad. Maybe he could ask for her back, impress Merry and cement himself for all time as Noah's favorite—albeit only—uncle.

Yeah, he could do that. He glanced at the clock. It was past eight. Merry ought to be home from work by now.

Desperate to escape his empty house, he grabbed his keys and wallet and headed out the front door.

Thirty minutes later, he rang her doorbell, armed with a loaded pizza and a six-pack of beer.

She opened it, wide-eyed in pink-striped pajama shorts and a matching tank top. "What in the world?"

"Have you eaten?" he asked.

She shook her head, gazing longingly at the pizza box in his arms.

"That's excellent news. I'm starving." His stomach rumbled, but his heart was full just standing in front of her.

"What are you doing here?" she asked, as she backed up to let him in.

He walked to the coffee table and set down the pizza and beer. Ralph and Chip clamored around him for attention, but he spotted Amber on her dog bed against the wall. She gazed up at him, and her tail started to thump the bed happily.

He walked over and rubbed her neck. She licked his cheek, tail still wagging. Then he stood and turned back to Merry. "Well, if you want to know the truth, I was a little lonely tonight so I took a chance and came over here."

"You missed her," Merry said smugly.

"A little," he admitted. "I missed you more." He pulled her in for a kiss.

"You kissed her first."

"I did not kiss the damn dog."

"Did too." She placed a teasing kiss on his lips, then pulled away. "You actually have good timing. I was about to waste away here in my barren kitchen."

She walked to the kitchen and returned with a bottle opener, plates, and napkins. She popped the cap off two beers, handed him one, and took a long drink from the other. For a moment, he thought she was going to say something else. Her expression darkened, but then she shook her head and sat on the couch.

He settled next to her as she flicked on the TV and changed the channel to baseball. The Reds were playing the Braves. They were quiet as they dug into the pizza.

"I hope it doesn't lower your opinion of me if I eat my body weight in pizza," she said between mouthfuls.

"Not at all. It might lower my opinion of you though if you didn't eat what you wanted on my account."

"Good to know." She reached for another slice.

They ate in companionable silence, demolishing the whole pizza between the two of them. Merry ate like she hadn't been fed in a week, but he knew how it was after a long day on the job. Being on your feet for twelve hours, caring for others, took a lot out of a person.

She polished off her beer, then leaned back with a satisfied sigh. She curled her feet underneath herself and rested her head on his shoulder. He put his arm around her to keep her close.

He envisioned a time when every evening was like this. And the first step toward making that happen was to ask for Amber back. Simple enough, but the words were harder to say than he'd imagined.

He looked down at Merry, saw her worrying her bottom lip the way she did when she was stewing over something. "What is it?"

Her brows furrowed. "What?"

"Your mind's spinning so fast I can hear it."

"Oh." She said nothing for a long minute. "I got some weird news tonight, that's all."

"Bad news?"

She lifted one shoulder. "No. Not bad, just . . . unexpected."

"You going to tell me about it?"

She sighed. "Right after I founded Triangle Boxer Rescue,

I started getting these monthly anonymous donations. Big donations. And then seven months ago, they stopped. I always wanted to know who was sending that money."

"And tonight you found out," he guessed.

Merry nodded, her shoulders stiff beneath his arm. "It turns out it was my mom."

"Your mom," he repeated. "The one who bailed when you were born."

She kept her eyes on the baseball game. "Yep. I looked her up once when I was a teenager, saw that she was a fashion designer out in Chicago. I guess she kept tabs on me too."

"So she was sending anonymous donations to your rescue. Why did she stop?"

"Apparently she went to jail for tax evasion. She was released a few weeks ago."

"Interesting." No wonder Merry was out of sorts tonight. This had to be awfully hard to make sense of.

"I guess neither one of us knows how to manage money."

Aha. He looked down at her. "You having money troubles?"

"The rescue, not me personally. Everything pretty much tanked after her donations stopped coming."

"What are you going to do?"

She squirmed out from under his arm. "I signed up for a fund-raising class, and I've got some new ideas to try out. Plus I let Olivia take over our Facebook page. We'll pull through."

"Good. And what about your mom?"

She smoothed her hands over her pajama shorts. "I don't know yet."

"Have you ever been in touch with her?"

She shook her head. "I've never spoken to her in my life."

"Think it's time to change that?"

* * *

Was it? That had been the question in Merry's mind ever since she'd learned her mother was behind the anonymous donations. Was it time for them to talk?

"I don't know yet," she answered T.J.'s question. "I need to think about it."

"Makes sense," he said. "No need to rush into anything."

No, there wasn't. Last year she would have said no way. Her mother gave her up, and that was that. But nothing was cut and dried anymore. She'd watched Crystal's struggle over the past month to get her life in order and become a parent to Jayden.

Sometimes people failed. Merry knew that better than anyone.

Maybe her mom deserved another chance.

Maybe.

She nudged T.J. "You're one to talk, Mr. Stuck In His Ways."

"You got me. However, I'd like to show you that even a stubborn man can change. I want Amber back."

She almost fell off the couch. "What?"

"I want her back." His dark eyes were steady and serious.

"You want to adopt her?"

A flicker of panic crossed his face. "Do I have to decide that right now?"

She was tempted to go easy on him because she knew this was a huge step for him, but she had to think of Amber too. "Yeah, you do. Amber's been bounced around a lot this summer. She's just learning to trust, so if you take her, you have to promise to keep her."

He stared at her for a long moment, then nodded. "Okay then. I'll adopt her."

Merry clapped a hand over her mouth.

He grunted in annoyance. "It's not that big of a deal."

"It *is* that big of a deal! You...you're adopting a dog, and not just any dog, but a stray."

"Yeah, I know. A friggin' mutt." But he looked at Amber with kindness and affection. T. J. Jameson was a loyal man, a man of his word. If he said he'd adopt Amber, keep her and care for her, then it was a done deal.

Amber had a home.

And if Merry'd had any hope of escaping this man with her heart intact, it was officially gone now. He'd grown. He'd overcome his fear and embraced Amber. He'd changed.

Could she do the same?

Maybe, but first she had to follow her conscience and talk to Noah. Then she'd see if there was anything left to salvage with T.J.

* * *

On Wednesday, T.J. invited Noah over for the afternoon so that he would be there when Merry arrived with Amber. Maybe seeing how well she was doing would help the boy get over his guilt about her accident and whatever else was bothering him.

Maybe it would finally give T.J. a chance to bond with his nephew.

Noah sat quietly in the corner, building with Legos. He'd created a spaceship from scratch that boggled T.J.'s mind. The kid had talent. He could be an amazing architect someday.

Later, after Noah had gone home, T.J. planned to woo Merry with a romantic, home-cooked meal and convince her that their relationship was too important to throw away. He wanted to keep seeing her. The hell with any of the rest of it.

He glanced out the front window. A storm was gathering on the horizon. Hopefully it would bring a reprieve from the heat and humidity that had left him saturated with sweat on barn calls that morning.

The storm clouds darkened, bringing to mind the afternoon he and Merry had taken that first trail ride. The storm that had chased them home, the way he'd kissed her in the pouring rain, and everything that had come after.

Maybe later tonight they could pick up where they'd left off.

Her CR-V turned into the driveway.

"She's here," he said to Noah.

Noah placed a final Lego onto his spaceship, then walked to the window. Amber's profile was visible in the back of the car, and the boy smiled.

"She's going to live here with me, but she's your dog, okay? Come play with her any time, come with me to her vet appointments. She sleeps in your room when you're here. Deal?"

Noah nodded. He fussed with his sleeve, picking at a string. T.J. shoved his hands into his pockets to resist the urge to try to stop him.

Merry walked toward the door with Amber at her side.

"Hey," she said with a warm smile when he opened it. "Looks like quite a storm brewing out there."

"Sure is. Welcome home, Amber."

Amber wagged her tail with appreciation.

"Her stuff's in the car," Merry said.

"I'll go get it." He started toward the door.

"I'll come with you. You stay here with Amber, okay, Noah?"

The boy nodded.

Merry followed T.J. to the car and opened the hatch. "More money went missing from my purse on Sunday."

He scowled at her. "It's too late for that now. Camp's over. You want me to pay you back or something?"

Her brows knitted. "Of course not. It's not about the money.

It happened at your parents' house. Unless you've been lifting fives from my wallet, Noah did."

He gripped the dog bed in her trunk. "Dammit, Merry."

"He's obviously in some kind of trouble. Maybe I can get him to open up about it to me if I tell him I know."

"Absolutely not."

She let out a sound of exasperation. "Look, I'm going to talk to him about it. I have to. And I was hoping to get your blessing."

"No way. You aren't going to accuse him of being a thief."

"I don't plan to call him a thief. I just want to find out what's wrong and try to help fix it."

She glanced at the house, and T.J. followed her gaze. Noah stood at the window, watching them. Had he over-heard any of their conversation?

"We'll talk about this later." He loaded up his arms with Amber's belongings and carried them inside.

Merry followed, uncharacteristically subdued.

"Hey, Noah, I brought you something." She held out a small, blue-wrapped box.

Noah came forward and took it, looking up at her with questioning eyes.

"Just a little something to remember the fun we had together at camp this summer."

Noah pulled the wrapping paper off carefully and set it on the table, then opened the box.

He smiled as he held up the Lego nurse figure that he and Merry had looked at together in the Lego Character Ency-clopedia that day in the hospital. In his other hand, he held a brown Lego dog. "Thank you."

"You're welcome. Now that you have a dog, you need a Lego dog, right?"

Noah ran to his Lego stash in the corner, and Merry followed.

"Wow, did you build this?" She sat on the floor beside him to look at the spaceship. Amber came and lay next to them, head on her front paws, eyes closed. Relaxed and content.

Noah showed Merry all the features he'd added to his spaceship, the rockets, the hatch, the boosters, even a bathroom for the astronauts. She sat and played Legos with him while T.J. put away Amber's stuff.

He returned the box of toys Noah had picked out at the pet store to its corner in the family room, set her bowls in the kitchen, and poured some water for her. He grabbed the extra dog bed and carried it upstairs.

His phone rang, and he lingered in the hallway outside his bedroom to take the call. Tom Hairston had a mare come in lame from the pasture today. T.J. checked the calendar on his phone to schedule an appointment.

"How does nine a.m. tomorrow work for you?" he asked.

"Great. See you then," Tom said.

T.J. started down the stairs as he ended the call. He walked back into the family room just in time to see Noah run from the room with tears streaming down his cheeks.

* * *

"What have you done?" His voice shook with anger.

Merry stood slowly. "I told him I knew about the money."

"Dammit, woman—"

She threw a hand out in front of herself. "Not now. I need to go after him."

"I'll handle it from here." He looked furious, his cheeks red, arms crossed over his chest.

"No. I need to do this." She pushed past him and ran up the stairs before he could stop her. She found Noah in the spare room down the hall. It was clearly his home away from home, decorated in basic blue with a huge bin of Legos in the back corner. The bottom drawer of the dresser peeked open to reveal child-sized sweatpants.

He sat on the bed, his back to her, his shoulders heaving with sobs. His hands flailed at his sides, flapping like a wounded bird unable to take flight.

She sat next to him and placed a hand on his shoulder. "You know I'm not mad, right? If you'd asked me for the money, I would have given it to you. I just want to talk."

Noah stifled a sob and shook his head.

"If you're in some kind of trouble, I might be able to help."

Nothing.

"Even if I can't help, it might make you feel better to talk about it."

He pressed his face against the comforter. "Go away."

"Please, Noah. Talk to me." She sat there for several minutes, coaxing, begging him to talk to her. Outwardly, she was calm, but inside she was crumbling into pieces. She'd been so sure she could get through to him.

She'd failed him, and T.J. might never forgive her for it.

She sat on the bed with him, one arm over his small shoulders until T.J. appeared in the doorway. He beckoned to her. A tight fist closed over her stomach as she followed him downstairs.

"I think you should go." His voice was quiet, but his meaning wasn't. He vibrated with anger. He couldn't even meet her eyes.

"Please—"

He looked away and shook his head. "I have to deal with this now. Go."

"Let me stay and talk to him when he comes down. Please."

"You've done enough for today. Go home, Merry."

She opened her mouth to protest, but the look in his eyes changed her mind. She swallowed over the lump in her throat and walked out the front door, leaving her dignity somewhere on his front porch.

She drove home and sat for a while on her couch, a dog on either side, just staring at the carpet. Was T.J. right? Had she been wrong to tell Noah she knew? Could it ever be right to walk away from a child in trouble without trying to help?

Maybe she should have just told Amy and let her handle it.

So many maybes.

She was startled out of her melancholy by the ringing of the telephone. T.J.'s number showed on the caller ID.

"T.J.? Is everything okay?"

"Noah's gone," he said, his voice tinged with panic. "And he's taken Amber with him."

*C*HAPTER TWENTY-THREE

*W*hat do you mean, gone?" Merry clutched the phone as her stomach took a sickening lurch.

"He's run off somewhere in this storm. He's *gone*." T.J.'s voice rose.

"Oh God. I'll be right there. I'll bring Ralph, he may be able to help us track him."

"Hurry."

The line clicked, and Merry stared at the phone for a moment in disbelief. Then she bolted down the hall to get her sneakers and Ralph's vest. He ran to her side. Chip followed, looking confused.

She threw the gate across the doorway to the kitchen and lifted the puppy behind it. "Sorry, hon. We'll be back as soon as we can."

She grabbed her purse from the table by the door, clipped Ralph's leash to his collar, and ran toward her car. Overhead, the sky roiled with dark clouds. A few raindrops splashed her windshield, and thunder rumbled in the distance.

It had grown eerily dark by the time she pulled into T.J.'s driveway. Amy's car was already there, along with several others she didn't recognize. Oh God, this was really happening, and it was all her fault. If she'd just listened to T.J. and kept her mouth shut about the money...

Now an autistic boy and his injured dog were out there somewhere in those woods, alone, with a thunderstorm looming.

T.J. came around from behind the house and stared at her CR-V.

I shouldn't even be here. She swallowed over the thought and stepped out of the car. She slipped Ralph's vest over his head and fastened it. It would help to put him in a working mind-set. He'd had no training as a search and rescue dog, but he knew Noah and he knew Amber, and maybe by instinct he could help find them.

"My parents have taken the horses down toward the stream. Amy's waiting in the house in case he comes back. If we haven't found him in the next hour, she's calling the police. You and I are going to search the woods." T.J. stared at her with cold, flat eyes.

She nodded. "Okay. Do you have something of Noah's, and something of Amber's, that I can show Ralph?"

T.J. looked down at the dog in his vest and scowled. "He's not a search and rescue dog."

"No, but we play a game of 'find it' with his toys at home. He may be able to help."

He went into the house and came back with one of Noah's shirts, the sleeves ragged from his nervous picking. He handed Merry the shirt and Amber's stuffed porcupine.

She crouched in front of Ralph and held the shirt out for him to sniff. "Ralph, go find Noah. Go find him."

Ralph sniffed the shirt and wagged his tail.

She showed him the chew toy. "Amber. Go find Amber. Go find Amber and Noah."

She let him sniff the shirt and the toy again. He barked,

excited about this new variation of the game. She unclipped his leash. "Go on. Go find Amber. Go find Noah."

Ralph dashed into the woods.

T.J. gave her an exasperated look. "What'd you take his leash off for? We can't keep up with him like that."

"Don't worry. He'll stay close by."

But he was worried, and so was she. Not about Ralph. But Noah, somewhere in those woods and possibly lost. And Amber, who'd accompanied her buddy on his journey with her leg still pinned and healing.

T.J. didn't look at her as they tromped through the trees. Her heart felt like lead, pressing into her lungs. She'd let him down. She'd failed Noah. How was she going to live with herself if anything happened to him?

The skies opened up then, pouring buckets of rain that dripped through the trees and soaked them straight through. She pulled an elastic from her pocket and tied back her hair, already heavy and sodden.

T.J. turned to glare at her. "You just couldn't let it rest."

"I'm sorry."

"I wanted—I thought—" He shook his head, apparently unable to put his disappointment into words. He didn't have to. It was all there on his face, in his voice.

"I'm sorry, T.J." Her throat burned.

Ralph came streaking back to them, barking happily, drenched with rain. He ran a circle around Merry, then nosed at the shirt and chew toy she still held. Was he looking for them or just playing? She honestly had no idea.

She paused for a moment and held them out to him again. She let him sniff each one and repeated her command. "Go find Noah. Go find Amber."

He raised his nose to sniff the air, then dashed off into the woods.

Overhead, the sky split with a flash of lightning, followed

immediately by a boom of thunder. Ralph ran back to her, ears pinned against his head. He looked up with questioning eyes, as if to ask why they were playing games in the woods during such bad weather.

He shook himself, sending a spray of water in all directions that did nothing to help dry himself off, then pressed his shoulder against her knee and whined.

"It's okay, Ralph. Go on now. Go find Noah. Go find Amber."

Ralph sniffed the shirt, then the toy, and trotted off into the trees.

"Amber's terrified of storms. What if she freaks out and hurts Noah?" T.J. asked.

"She won't. She might leave him and run off to hide by herself, but she won't hurt him."

"People and animals do strange things when they're scared or hurt." He gave her a long, dark look.

She said nothing, just kept walking in the direction Ralph had gone.

"Your damn dog had better not be leading us on a wild-goose chase," he grumbled.

"Honestly, I have no idea if he's on the right track or not. If you want to go off on your own, you can."

He kept walking beside her. It was somewhat reminiscent of that other night in the woods when Amber had slipped her collar and gone missing, when Merry had trekked out here in the middle of the night in a tank top and flip-flops. The night she'd first kissed T.J.

Maybe if she hadn't been stupid enough to kiss him that night, none of this would have happened. She could only hope Amber was as easy to find tonight as she had been that night, and that Noah was still with her.

That they were both okay. Unharmed.

Oh God, please let them be okay.

Rainwater ran down her back and soaked her jean shorts. It dripped into her eyes and squished between her toes with each step. Overhead, lightning and thunder battled in the sky.

Ralph came to them again and again, always sniffing the items she held, which were now soaking wet. His direction sometimes changed, and she feared the consequence if he had no idea what he was doing.

"The police should be here by now," T.J. said.

"That's good." Water ran like tears over her cheeks.

He stopped and stared at her. "Maybe we should go back."

"You probably should. I'm going to keep following Ralph." She hoped her instincts were right because there he came again, bounding through the trees. He barked excitedly, then took off in the opposite direction.

"I don't think your dog knows what he's doing."

"He very well might not. You can go back if you want."

They kept walking. It was getting dark now, especially here in the woods with the clouds above hiding what remained of the sun. T.J. clicked on his flashlight and panned the trees.

Ralph ran toward them. He sat in front of Merry and barked, then ran off into the woods again. This time one hundred and eighty degrees from his last trip.

"This is a waste of time." T.J. stopped and fisted his hands on his hips.

Merry looked after Ralph. When they played "find it" at home with his toys, he'd run off and find the toy, then bring it back to her. What would he do if he found what he was looking for but couldn't bring it back with him?

"Give him another minute," she said.

He'd run left and right a few times, but more often he'd run straight ahead, then returned. Maybe he'd already found them and didn't know how to tell her. Maybe he was looking for chew toys in the woods. There was no way to be sure.

She stood and watched. Ralph ran ahead through the trees until she could barely see him. He poked his nose under a bush, barked, then ran back to her and T.J. He barked again, then ran off into the woods in the opposite direction.

But then he went back to the bush. And it moved.

"T.J.," she whispered. "Watch."

Ralph ran a circle around the bush, then returned to her and T.J. He barked, sniffed the shirt, and ran off into the woods.

"That bush." She pointed. It was big and thick and quite possibly the type of place a terrified boy and his dog might take shelter during a storm.

"Wait here." He walked ahead, sloshing through the rain-soaked underbrush. He squatted and peered into the bush, then flashed her a thumbs up.

Merry's limbs went weak with relief. Ralph ran up to her, panting eagerly. "You did it. You found them. I am so proud of you. You are the best dog ever, you know that?"

He smiled up at her, tail nub wagging happily.

"You are such a good dog." She rubbed behind his ears and handed him a couple of soggy treats from her pocket. "What a good boy. You found them!"

Ralph's whole body wiggled with pride.

T.J. stood and walked back to her. "He wants to talk to you."

"Is he okay?"

"He's fine. Amber's leg may be a little worse for wear."

Merry pushed back a soggy curl. "And he wants to talk to me?"

T.J. nodded, his mouth grim. "He won't come out until he sees you."

Oh, Noah. She'd started this, she could finish it. "Hold him for me?"

She clipped Ralph's leash to his collar and passed it to

T.J., then walked ahead to the bush. She crouched down to see the boy and dog huddled beneath it.

Noah's eyes were red, his face streaked with mud and tears. Amber lay beside him, panting heavily, her eyes wide and wild. She looked at Merry, her expression that of a mother bear protecting her cub.

"What a brave girl you are, sticking by your boy." Merry held her hand out. She waited for the dog to sniff it, waited for her tail to give a wag of approval before she came closer. "Is it okay if I come under with you guys?"

Noah nodded, and Amber licked her palm.

Merry dropped to her hands and knees in the mud and crawled inside the bush. "It's kind of nice in here. You guys okay?"

Noah shook his head. His teeth chattered, despite the muggy heat of the evening. "A-A-Amber...her l-l-leg..."

Merry looked at the injured leg. It was swollen but not obviously disfigured. She probed it gently, and the dog whined. "It's nothing the vet can't fix. How about you, Noah?"

"I—I—I..." He'd become a stuttering mess. His arms flapped at his sides. His sleeves had completely unraveled. He stared into the dense branches of the bush, his eyes glassy.

"Remember that magic when you hugged Ralph? Want to try it on Amber?"

The boy wrapped his arms around her neck and sobbed. Amber licked his cheek, then stared at Merry with solemn eyes.

Noah hiccupped. "I—I—I'm going to juvie."

"Juvie?" she repeated, stupidly thinking she'd misunderstood.

"It's where boys go when they steal," he whispered.

Merry lurched upright and speared her head on a branch.

She grabbed her scalp and stifled a swear. "Juvenile detention? No. Oh, sweetie, no. I told you I didn't want to get you in trouble, not even with your mom and certainly not with the police. I just wanted to talk."

Noah closed his eyes and sobbed. "N-n-not you..."

Okay, maybe now they were getting somewhere. "Why don't you tell me what happened. Why did you take the money? I know you had a good reason for it."

"Steven. He said we'd go to juvie." Noah trembled all over. Amber pressed herself closer against his side and laid her uninjured front paw protectively across his lap.

"Who's Steven?"

"Brendan's big brother. He knows a lot about jail and stuff."

Oh lord. What had those kids gotten into? "Sweetie, you're not going to be sent to juvie. Why did Steven say that?"

"He s-said we stole his iPad. We had to pay him back for it. F-fifty bucks." Noah buried his face in Amber's fur and sobbed.

"Oh, sweetie. Oh, Noah. Come here." She lifted him against her chest and held him tight. "You didn't steal Steven's iPad, did you?"

He shook his head.

"Did Brendan steal it?"

He shook it again, even harder. "N-no. Brendan's my best friend."

"What about Steven? Is he a nice kid too?" She was pretty sure she already knew the answer to that question.

"No," he whispered, and his voice broke.

"Why didn't you tell someone what happened?"

"Because he said he'd tell the police we stole his iPad, and we'd get sent to juvie. And Brendan and I wouldn't be allowed to play together ever again. He's my b-b-best friend."

"Noah, look at me." She waited until he lifted his head. "You're not going to juvie. Brendan is not going to juvie. We're going to walk out of the woods now and tell your mom what happened, and she's going to tell Brendan's mom, and hopefully Steven will get in trouble for what he did. But you, Noah, are not in trouble. Do you understand?"

He sniffled. "I d-didn't even know what an iPad was. I had to look it up."

So that's why Amy had caught him sneaking around on her laptop. And why did a kid in low-income housing like Steven have an iPad in the first place? "I believe you."

Noah's hands fisted in Amber's fur. "I did steal from you."

"I know, sweetie. It's all right. I'm not mad."

"I'll p-p-pay you back." He hiccupped again.

"Okay." She brushed a lock of hair back from his face.

Fresh tears streaked his cheeks. "What about Brendan? Will we still be able to play together?"

"That's for your mom and his mom to decide, okay? Let's get you home now because she's worried sick about you."

"I've already called her. She knows you're safe." T.J.'s voice came from outside the bush, reminding Merry that he was listening to every word. Her heart lurched into her throat.

Noah reached out and grabbed her wrist. "I hurt Amber."

"When?" She thought she knew, but she didn't want to lead him.

"That day at Brendan's. Steven was yelling at me, and I got scared and ran. I wasn't looking where I was going. We ran right in front of that car."

"And you're lucky you didn't get hurt too. It was careless, but you're eight, Noah. You're not expected to always have good judgment. Hell, I'm twenty-eight, and I don't always have good judgment. Amber's going to be fine. It was just an accident, okay?"

Noah sobbed. "N-no. It's my fault she got hurt."

"Oh, honey." She gathered him into her arms again. Her heart broke for him, for the pain and guilt he'd carried these weeks since the accident. "It's not your fault. Sometimes bad things just happen, and they're no one's fault. You can't go on blaming yourself for it."

"I f-f-feel so bad. I hate myself every time I look at her." Noah's voice was tortured, hoarse from the tears.

"Sweetie, I promise Amber doesn't blame you. She loves you. She'd do anything for you. She is terrified of thunderstorms, and she came all the way out here with you tonight so that you wouldn't be alone. Please don't blame yourself."

"H-h-have you ever done something bad like I did?" He looked up at her with tear-filled eyes so full of desperation.

"I—" Her throat closed up, and her heart started to pound.

The branches parted in front of her to reveal T.J. crouched before them. "We all have, Noah. Everyone does things they regret. There are things we wish we could go back and change, even if they weren't our fault in the first place. It's what makes us human."

He looked at her with unspoken understanding, and her world crumbled. Floodgates opened inside her, and all the guilt, and pain, and grief just came pouring out. She pressed a hand over her eyes, desperate to hold back the tears.

T.J. pulled her against his chest, one arm around her, the other around Noah. Rain mixed with tears on her cheeks. She bit her bottom lip to stop it from shaking.

They were the same, she and Noah. Except now she had the power to help him heal, to keep him from making the same mistake she had. No guilt. No blame.

"Your uncle's right," she said, her voice as hoarse as Noah's. "Something happened a long time ago to someone I loved very much, and I blamed myself for it. I felt so guilty for so long, but...it wasn't my fault, and I can't change it. You didn't hurt Amber. It was just an accident. Blaming yourself isn't going to change what happened."

"Were they okay?" Noah asked, all wide-eyed innocence. "The person that you love?"

"No." Her voice broke, and T.J.'s arm tightened around her. "No he wasn't, but blaming myself doesn't change that either. And Amber *is* going to be fine. She loves you so much. She needs you, Noah."

"I need her too." He slid from Merry's arms to fling them around Amber. The dog closed her eyes in silent pleasure.

T.J. pulled her against him, and she pressed her face to his chest, breathing in his scent. He wrapped his arms around her and held her tight until the pain in her throat had receded, until she could draw breath without feeling like she might crumble into a million pieces.

She lifted her head, but his expression was hidden in the shadows beneath the brim of his hat. Then he slid a hand behind her neck and drew her in, his forehead pressed against hers, his stubble tickling her jaw.

"You okay?" The words were barely more than a breath, warm against her cheek.

She nodded, her hands fisted in his T-shirt, clinging to him with all her strength.

He pressed his lips against hers with a kiss so tender, so gentle that she lost a little piece of herself there in his arms, something that would never again feel whole without him.

Her heart.

Then he let her go and extended a hand to Noah. "Let's get you home now, okay, Bud?"

Noah nodded. He stood, one hand in T.J.'s, the other in Merry's. Amber followed, hopping on three legs. Ralph rushed forward to greet her, sniffing at his comrade's injured leg.

"She's hurt." Noah sounded anguished.

"I think she's just overdone it on that leg." Merry looked down at the poor dog, wondering how in the world they'd get her all the way back to the house.

T.J. bent and scooped her into his arms. "Come on, let's go."

And so they began their halting journey home. Noah's feet dragged. He was mentally and physically exhausted. The storm had calmed, but rain still fell steadily over them. T.J.'s arms must have tired, but he never put Amber down.

As she watched him carry that dog out of the woods in the pouring rain, she knew for sure she'd fallen totally and completely in love with him. She could only hope she wasn't a total fool. Because maybe she'd been wrong to confront Noah the way she did, but if T.J. had trusted her in the first place, she wouldn't have had to. Was there any getting past that?

When they got close to the farm, she saw the flashing red and blue lights. The house and yard were a blur of commotion. Family members rushed toward them, surrounding Noah and hugging him senseless.

In the melee, Merry stood at the edge of the yard, watching. Her heart ached, and her eyes stung. Would T.J. forgive her for this, for unintentionally putting Noah in danger? Would his family?

Despite her words to Noah, could she forgive herself?

Choking back a sob, she hustled Ralph to the CR-V. She needed to get him home and rested. Or that's what she told herself anyway. Not that she was running like a coward instead of sticking around to face the music and try to win back the man she loved.

CHAPTER TWENTY-FOUR

T.J. watched her run, feeling like he'd just taken a sucker punch to the gut. When the going got tough, Merry got going. Hadn't she already warned him?

Or maybe he should man up and go after her. He owed her a massive apology, after all. She'd been right about Noah all along, and maybe if he'd listened to her and backed her up, they could have avoided this fiasco. But he hadn't. And there was no way he could leave his family right now. He followed them into the house.

Everyone was crying. Amy held Noah as the tears slid over her cheeks. He sobbed in her arms, looking so much younger than eight. EmmyLou brushed tears from her cheeks. Even Trace looked suspiciously glossy-eyed.

The police finished up their paperwork and headed out, leaving the family to tend to their own. T.J. examined Amber but found no evidence her leg had rebroken. Probably, with a few days' rest, she'd be none the worse for wear. He gave her a pill to help with the pain and inflammation, toweled her off, and helped her to her dog bed.

Most of the family had gathered in the family room,

alternately crying, talking, and hugging. T.J. followed his mother into the kitchen, where she began to rummage through his cabinets.

"A family needs to eat in times of crisis," she said.

"The crisis is over, Mom."

She laughed and patted his shoulder. "Indeed, and now we're all starving. Where's Merry?"

"She went home."

"Oh, honey, you sent her home? Well, she must feel awful. Shame on you for not insisting she stay." She gave him a reproachful look.

He shoved a hand through his hair. "I wanted her to stay. She just left."

His mom was silent for a moment, then she nodded. "Well, that's for you two to sort out later then, I guess."

She turned her back to continue with dinner preparations.

T.J.'s stomach grumbled. He'd planned a romantic dinner with Merry tonight. How differently things had turned out. He felt her absence in the room like a gaping hole. They had things, so many things, to say to each other.

It felt like torture to stand here making small talk with his family when he wanted—needed—to be with her. To find out if they had a chance of fixing things.

Noah tearfully confessed everything to Amy. She held and comforted him much as Merry had, offering him the same reassurances, the same support. But nothing could top Merry's tearful confession in the woods. She'd bared her soul for him, and her words had gotten through.

T.J. saw the difference in Noah's demeanor, like a great weight had been lifted.

For a long time after his family went home, T.J. sat with Amber at his feet, looking right at home in her dog bed. He had to hand it to her; she'd stuck by Noah through thick and thin. And for that, she'd always have a place here in his home.

Finally, feeling like a man who'd lost his course, he gave up and went to bed. He tossed and turned, too restless to sleep, filled with residual adrenaline from the frantic search for Noah and tangled up in his feelings for Merry.

As dawn broke, he rose and went to the barn. He tacked up Tango and rode him to the stream. He couldn't bring himself to go down to the pool, to remember what he and Merry had shared there.

He needed to see her today. He owed her an apology, which he would have given her last night if she hadn't run out on him after Noah was found. Maybe this time, he'd give her a chance to come back on her own.

It would have to wait for now, at any rate, because he had appointments scheduled all morning. He checked on Tom Hairston's injured mare, a pregnant goat, and an elderly donkey with debilitating arthritis.

He turned into his driveway just past twelve, and his heart lurched at the sight of the silver CR-V parked by his house.

Then he caught sight of the woman leaning against it. She wore form-fitting blue jeans and a short-sleeved pink top, but that wasn't what caught his attention. Leather boots peeked from the ankles of her jeans, with pink stitching. Her wild mane of curly brown hair flowed from underneath an honest to God cowboy hat.

Merry Atwater had gone and turned herself into a cowgirl.

* * *

"Hey there, Cowboy." Merry tipped her hat at him with a wink, rewarded when T.J. nearly fell flat on his face as he walked toward her from his truck.

He stopped several feet away, his expression guarded. "You disappeared mighty quick last night."

Her bravado crumbled, and her shoulders slumped. "Hoping I can make up for that now."

He stared at her just long enough to make her squirm, then nodded. "Let's go inside."

Her knees shook as she followed him into the house. He stopped in the foyer and lifted the hat from her head. His eyes blazed into hers, scrambling her thoughts.

Toenails clattered behind them as Amber limped into the room.

"Hey, sweetie. Oh, look at you. T.J.'s been taking good care of you, hasn't he?" Merry bent to rub her head. The dog wagged happily, then limped back into the family room. "She looks much better today."

"She'll be fine." T.J. took her hand and turned her to face him. "Before you tell me why you're here dressed like that, I owe you an apology. I should have listened when you came to me about Noah, but I was too pigheaded to hear it."

Her lower lip trembled, and she clenched it between her teeth. "That's true."

"I doubted your judgment, and I shouldn't have. Amy says he's a different kid today now that the truth is out. He's grounded of course for stealing, but he's been talking up a storm all morning and asking when he can come play with Amber."

She pressed a hand over her heart. "Oh, that is amazing. I'm so glad."

"I was trying so hard to help him that I lost sight of how to do that. Forgive me?"

She choked, her eyes gone hazy with tears. "Of course. You were just looking out for him. I shouldn't have gone behind your back like I did either. Noah could have been hurt."

He shook his head. "I didn't leave you much choice. Besides, I was the one watching him when he ran away. Amy had a talk with Brendan's mother this morning. Tough neighborhood, tough kids, but his mother seemed to take it seriously, said there would be consequences for Steven. Noah can still see Brendan, but only at Amy's house for now."

"That sounds smart."

He took her hands and gripped them in his. "I had a pretty small view of my life before I met you. I thought I knew what I needed, what I wanted, but I had it all wrong."

"Okay." Her lip was shaking again, terrified of what he might say next.

"I need you, Merry Joy Atwater, girly shoes and all. I love you."

Oh, her silly heart burst right out of her chest, spilling tears over her cheeks. She flung herself into his arms, and he spun her in a circle. She clung to him, starved for him, overcome that he was hers. "I love you too. So much."

He stroked a hand over her cheek, wiping away her tears. "That's mighty good to hear."

She laughed, and more tears fell. "It really is."

He cupped her chin so that she met his eyes. "We can take this as slow as you want, but no more pretending it's not what it is, okay? Because I'd be a happy man if you'd move in here tomorrow."

"My dogs…"

He flinched, and she smacked his bicep. "Okay, okay, you *and* all of your dogs. Bring 'em. Ralph's pretty all right, and the others come and go."

"But there will always be others." She pressed her lips to his, desperate to drink him in.

"Your dogs are my dogs."

And that might be the most romantic thing a man had ever said to her.

"Speaking of others…" She pulled back. She'd been a busy woman that morning, possessed by a newfound need to grab on to everything that had eluded her over the last eight years. To make up for all the time she'd lost wallowing in her own self-pity.

To make herself a woman worthy of a kid like Noah to look up to.

First, she'd called her mother and left a message. Maybe Beverly would call her back, maybe she wouldn't. But if she did, Merry was willing to hear her out and see where things went from there.

After that, she'd gone to the Department of Social Services and filled out some paperwork.

"I have to tell you something."

"Anything." He slid his hands around her waist and pulled her close.

"I applied to become Jayden's foster mom, the baby at the hospital."

He smiled, a genuine smile that creased his eyes and warmed her heart. "That's wonderful."

"Is it? He has special needs, seizures, drug withdrawals, and who knows what else as he gets older."

He cocked his head. "You think special needs scare me?"

"No, I don't suppose they do." She went up on her toes and pressed her forehead to his. "His birth mother just got out of jail, and she wants him back. I want to help her."

"And I'm sure you will. It may seem like a selfless thing, you fostering a kid like that, but I have a feeling it's as much for your own healing as his, am I right?"

Tears flooded her eyes, and she nodded.

"Then let's heal him together, okay?"

Her heart swelled until her chest hurt to contain it. "Okay."

She remembered that night in her house, less than two months ago, when she'd prayed for help. She'd cursed God for sending a bedraggled stray instead of a financial bailout, but she'd been wrong. She hadn't needed money at all. Amber had led her to T.J., and now she'd found the very thing she'd sought for so many foster dogs over the years: a forever home.

T.J. had shown her the true meaning of love. And he was hers, for keeps.

*E*PILOGUE

*M*erry gazed at the purple storm clouds gathering on the horizon. She squeezed her heels against Twilight's sides, urging her faster. The horse responded with an easy lope. Merry leaned back in the saddle to center herself, her body moving in harmony with Twilight's steady gait.

Since she'd moved in with T.J., she'd taken to riding Twilight almost every day she didn't have to work. Horseback riding solo had intimidated her at first, but it was fun. Really fun, especially now that the heat of summer had begun to fade. September brought cooler evenings, lower humidity, and Monday Night Football, all of which made farm living even more enjoyable.

"Lookin' good up there." T.J. stood in the doorway to the barn, thumbs hooked into the front pockets of his Wranglers, effortlessly sexy in his cowboy boots and hat with a baby sling wrapped around his chest. Ralph and Amber flanked him, both fiercely protective of the newest, smallest member of their pack.

Merry brought Twilight back to a walk and headed toward them. "Thanks. Got her to lope on the first try this time."

"You're a natural." He tipped his hat.

She smiled at the baby strapped to his chest. "So are you."

Her heart swelled every time she saw him with Jayden. He'd be a kick-ass dad someday. Sometimes she pictured a baby with her curls and his dark eyes wearing itty-bitty cowboy boots.

"The munchkin enjoys helping me out in the barn." T.J. tousled Jayden's silky blond hair. "How did it go with his momma today?"

"Really well, I think." Merry had brought Jayden for his first supervised visitation with Crystal that morning. "She's really working hard to get him back. I think she can do it."

"That's great news."

"Yeah." She looked down at Jayden, snuggled so cozily against T.J. The baby smiled up at her, so robust and round-cheeked it was hard to remember how sickly he'd once been. "I think they're going to get their happily ever after."

"I talked to Amy this morning. Noah read a story to his class yesterday. She said he was still grinning ear to ear when he got off the bus."

"That's amazing. I'm so proud of him." Noah had really blossomed since starting third grade. His friendship with Brendan—and Amber—had made all the difference in his social skills and confidence with his peers.

Thunder rumbled in the distance. Twilight snorted and tossed her head. Merry reached down to pat her neck. "Easy, girl."

"Better get her cleaned up and turned out before the storm hits," T.J. said.

"Good idea."

"I'm going to take the little dude up to the house for his bath. Holler if you need me." T.J. sauntered off toward the house, baby on his chest and two dogs at his heels.

She finished cooling Twilight down, then untacked her,

rubbed her down, and turned her out with Tango and Peaches. A gusty breeze blew as Merry walked toward the house. The warm, earthy scent of the barn clung to her skin, as familiar now as the man who'd brought her here. His home, and hers.

She opened the front door, greeted by three joyous dogs, Amber, Ralph, and Tank—her newest, and somewhat over-sized, foster. From upstairs, she heard water running in the tub and Jayden's giggles.

She went into the kitchen to warm a bottle, then followed the happy sounds upstairs. She found T.J. in the guest-bedroom-turned-nursery, zipping up Jayden's footed pajamas. When he'd finished, she lifted the baby into her arms. "Hey, sweetie."

Jayden rubbed his eyes and yawned, snuggling closer against her.

"You had a busy day today." She sat in the rocker with him to give him his bottle. "Hope it makes you sleep well tonight."

T.J. kissed him goodnight, then turned out the light and left the room.

Merry sat in the semidark room, cradling Jayden as he took his bottle. She savored these last moments of the day, when he curled in her arms, all sweet and sleepy. By the time he'd finished the bottle, his eyes were drooping. She laid him in his crib and hummed him a lullaby as he drifted off to sleep.

She tiptoed out of the room and found T.J. waiting for her in the hall. Gone was the fatherly figure who'd proudly carried his foster baby while doing nightly barn chores. In his place was a sexy cowboy with a hungry gleam in his eyes.

"Thought I might help you get ready for your shower." He yanked her up against him and kissed her hard.

"You peeked," she whispered breathlessly.

"Couldn't help but notice when I boosted you up on Twilight." He cupped her ass, pressing her closer. "You know my feelings about pink lace."

She went up on her tiptoes to kiss him back. "These are new. I think you'll like them."

"Better order a lifetime supply." Then he swept her off her feet and carried her toward their bedroom.

When animal rights activist Olivia Bennett gets in trouble with the law, Deputy Pete Sampson must oversee her community service. But can he tame Olivia, or will she convince him to take a walk on the wild side?

See the next page for a preview of

Ever After

CHAPTER ONE

Red paint dripped from Olivia Bennett's fingers. She tightened her grip on the metal canister in her right hand and gave it a solid shake. Beneath her sneakers, the ladder wobbled. With a startled squeak, she sent a burst of spray paint onto her shoes.

"Sorry, Liv," Terence called from below.

"Watch it, will you?" She pressed her palm against the cool, corrugated metal of the factory wall and took a deep breath. Then she lifted her right hand and pressed the valve on the spray-paint canister, forming a brilliantly red "S" on the side of the building.

"Almost done," Kristi said.

Easy for her to say, standing safely on the ground next to Terence. At the top of the ladder, Olivia fought to keep her balance as the remnants of several margaritas sloshed in her stomach. Hell of a way to end her twenty-ninth birthday.

The beam of Kristi's flashlight cast Olivia's shadow in stark silhouette over her red-painted message. She leaned right to spray another "S." She'd have to come down and move the ladder to continue, but a muffled sound captured her attention.

Mew.

The sound was soft yet keening. A kitten? Some other baby animal? She craned her head, peering into the darkness. "Did you guys hear that?"

"Hear what?" Terence asked, his tone wary.

"It sounded like a kitten."

Kristi panned the flashlight around them, plunging Olivia into darkness. She leaned a hip against the side of the building to steady herself.

"I don't see anything," Kristi said.

"Okay, put that light back on me so I can get down."

The flashlight's beam illuminated her once more, and Olivia scrambled quickly to solid ground. "I heard some kind of little animal crying while I was up there, so keep an eye out."

"Will do." Terence moved the ladder over so that she could reach the next section of wall to be painted, and held it steady as she climbed back up.

Six letters to go, and they were out of here. Terence would drive them to his place for a post-graffiti celebration. Olivia was in no condition to drive herself anywhere tonight. Adrenaline mixed with trepidation as she stood at the top of the ladder yet again. The margarita buzz had faded enough to know she was doing a crazy, stupid thing that wasn't going to do a damn thing to help the chickens who arrived here daily, their only hope that death would be quick and merciful.

Based on what the undercover cameras had captured, that hope was slim.

Her pulse quickened. It was inhumane the way those birds were treated. Actually, it was inhumane the way most factory-farmed animals were treated, but this was happening right here in her little hometown of Dogwood, North Carolina.

Mew.

A flash of white fur caught her eye, disappearing into

the bushes behind the factory. If it was a kitten, it was tiny. Was its mother nearby? There weren't any houses for miles around. Dammit. Now she was going to have to go on a kitten hunt before she went home. She couldn't leave it out here to fend for itself.

"Hurry up, Liv," Kristi called from below her.

Olivia raised the canister and let loose another blast of red paint. She'd just started "A" when the sound of an approaching vehicle reached her. Her finger slipped, and a fresh coat of paint soaked her hands.

Kristi and Terence must have heard it too because the flashlight shut off, leaving her at the top of the ladder in pitch darkness, afraid to move. Headlights slashed through the night from Garrett Road, some two hundred feet to her left. They slowed, then tires crunched over gravel as the car turned into the factory parking lot.

Christ on a cracker.

"Get the hell down, Liv. We've got to get out of here!" Terence whispered.

A swirl of blue lights turned the night into a kaleidoscope of *oh, shit*. She pressed against the side of the building, stymied by paint-slickened fingers as she fumbled for the top of the ladder.

She was *so* not getting arrested on her birthday.

Except that she *so* was. A spotlight shone from the cruiser, illuminating her in a blaze of light so bright she could do nothing but press a hand over her eyes and count how many ways spray painting Halverson Foods' chicken processing plant had been a bad idea.

The ladder shifted beneath her, and she groped for the top rung. The combination of the spinning blue lights with the piercing glare of the spotlight was seriously disorienting.

"Hands where I can see them," a male voice boomed.

She shoved her hands into the air, managing to smack

herself in the face with the can of spray paint in the process. It fell to the ground with a muffled thump. Oh, this sucked.

"Come down from the ladder, nice and slow, and keep those hands up," the cop instructed. He sounded nice-*ish*. Maybe he'd go easy on her. Maybe...

Awkwardly, she fumbled with her right foot for the next rung of the ladder. It swayed dangerously to the side. "Terence!" she hissed, her fingernails scoring metal as she tried to steady herself.

Silence. She looked down, but the spotlight's glare blinded her, preventing her from seeing past her own paint-spattered sneakers. "Terence? Kristi?"

She managed to get her foot settled onto the rung and took a step down. No answer came from her friends. What the hell?

She lifted her left foot to take the next step, and the ladder just dropped out from beneath her. One second it was there, the next she was plummeting through space.

"Oomph," came a masculine grunt as she slammed into someone's chest, and big, strong arms closed around her.

"Terence?" Her voice was a squeak because Terence was nowhere near this strong, and he didn't smell as good either. This man smelled faintly of cinnamon, his arms solid as steel beneath her thighs, and based on the hard bulge stabbing into her kidney, he was also armed.

Oh, crap. Crap. *Crap!*

"Sorry," he answered, setting her roughly on the ground. "Not Terence."

"Oh." She staggered, still blinded by the spotlight aimed at her. Disoriented, she turned her back and blinked at her shadow on the factory's gray wall. Terence and Kristi had deserted her. *Bastards.*

"Keep those hands where I can see them," Invisible Cop said.

With a sigh, she placed them on the wall before her. Her hands glistened bloodred in the harsh light. She had been caught red-handed. *Dammit.* She'd always hated being a cliché.

* * *

Deputy Pete Sampson reached for his cuffs. When he'd taken the call about a trespasser on Halverson Foods' property, he surely hadn't expected to find a teenage girl on a ladder, covered from head to foot in red spray paint. "You want to tell me what you're doing out here tonight?"

She kept her back to him. "It's fairly obvious, right?"

He looked up. The side of the building dripped with big, red letters. It was obvious all right, but he wouldn't be surprised if she tried to talk her way out of it anyway.

"Chicken ass?" he read. What the hell was that even supposed to mean? Kids these days. He shook his head in annoyance.

She made a choking sound, squinting up at her handiwork. "I wasn't finished."

"Do tell."

"It was supposed to say 'Chicken *Assassins.*' "

"Ah. Well I suppose you know this is private property."

She nodded, her shoulders slumping.

"What's your name?" he asked.

"Olivia Bennett."

"I have some bad news, Olivia. You are under arrest for trespassing and vandalism. You have the right to remain silent." Pete snapped cuffs around her slender wrists as he read her her rights. He could spare her a pat-down because there was no way in hell she had anything concealed beneath that purple tank top or the jean shorts that hugged her willowy frame.

"It's my birthday," she mumbled.

"Sorry, kid. The law makes no exception for birthdays."

"Kid?" She turned to face him, and he saw he'd been wrong about one thing. She was no teenager pulling a back-to-school prank. This woman was midtwenties, easily, and far too beautiful to be doing what he'd just caught her doing. Her long blond hair was pulled back in a messy ponytail, and she stared at him from wounded brown eyes.

He shrugged. "Seemed a pretty juvenile thing to do."

Chicken Assassins. In retrospect, he realized he was dealing with an animal rights activist instead of a teenaged troublemaker.

"Do you have any idea what happens to the birds in there?" she asked, her eyes bright with emotion.

"They get slaughtered." He took her elbow and guided her toward his cruiser. Her breath smelled of alcohol. "You drive out here?"

She glanced over at the red Prius parked behind the building. "Um—"

"You're drunk."

"I wouldn't say drunk, exactly." She ducked her head as he tucked her into the back of the cruiser.

"Let's find out, shall we?" He took his portable Breathalyzer out of the car and crouched beside her.

Her eyes widened. "Let's not. I know my rights, deputy."

Pete stood. Great. A drunk troublemaker who knew the law. He had zero tolerance for people who drove under the influence. He'd seen firsthand the damage they inflicted on society, the lives and families torn apart.

Zach Hill had been left without a father.

Pete's gut soured. "Fine. You'll take it back at the station. Where are your keys?"

Her brows creased, and she glanced at the empty seat beside her. "I must have dropped them."

She was lying. But why? He closed the cruiser door and

walked back to the building, shining his flashlight over the gravel lot. No sign of car keys. He walked to the Prius and tried the door. Locked. No keys visible inside.

She'd been looking for someone when she fell off the ladder. Maybe she'd had an accomplice. He returned to the cruiser and opened the back door. "Who's Terence?"

"A friend." She studied her shoes.

"Was he out here with you tonight?"

She shook her head. "No, sir. Just me."

But he'd seen the flicker of truth in her eyes. She'd had an accomplice all right, probably a boyfriend, since she was protecting him. "That's unfortunate, you being out here alone and intoxicated. Judge might be inclined to think you drove drunk."

"I didn't—" She pressed her lips together and looked away.

Well, fine, if that was the way she wanted to play it. He buckled her in and slid behind the wheel. Fifteen minutes later, he marched her into the Dogwood County Detention Center. Olivia kept her chin up while she was fingerprinted and photographed. She blew a .078 on the Breathalyzer, which meant she had almost certainly been over the limit if she had driven herself out to that factory earlier tonight.

Pete wanted to know more about this Terence she was covering for. But for now, he was ready to let her sit and think over her foolish behavior for a little while.

"Judge Matthews will hear your case first thing in the morning," he told her as he led her down the hall to the holding pen. Lucky for her, she was the department's only visitor tonight. "You got someone to come bail you out?"

"What?" She eyed the cell with its steel bench, toilet, and sink, her eyes wide and horrified.

"You've been arrested, Miss Bennett. Now you need to call someone to bail you out."

"Um, right now? It's like one o'clock in the morning."

He shrugged, fighting a smile at the incredulous look on her face. "You break the law in the middle of the night, you either rouse someone from bed to bail you out or you bunk with us."

She gripped his wrist as he propelled her inside the holding cell. "Wait! Okay, yes. I need to make a phone call."

"All right." He took her by the elbow and steered her down the hall to the phone.

"Could you?" She held out her cuffed hands. "Please?"

"Fine." He uncuffed her and sat on the bench against the wall while she made her call.

She stood there, looking forlorn and vulnerable for several long seconds, then shook her head and picked up the phone. He'd expected her to dial the boyfriend she'd been looking for earlier, but instead she called someone named Merry.

"It's Olivia. I'm sorry to bother you this late, but I didn't know who else to call."

Pete tossed an arm over the back of the bench and watched her. Olivia kept her back to him, her shoulders hunched. Her friend apparently hadn't picked up, as she left a message and ended the call.

"No luck?" he asked.

She kept her back turned. "Can I try someone else?"

"Go ahead." He watched as she dialed another number, then hung up and rested her forehead against the wall. "What about your parents?"

Her shoulders stiffened. "I can't call them about this. Maybe Merry will get my message."

"All right then."

She turned those wounded eyes on him again as he led her back down the hall to the holding cell.

He slammed the cell door behind her with a solid clang for effect. "Make yourself comfortable. We'll let you know if your friend shows up to bail you out."

And with a chuckle at her expression, he left her there.

* * *

What a jerk.

Olivia adjusted her head against the metal bench. Deputy Sampson had looked downright gleeful when he'd locked her up, and that was just rude. Now she'd spent the night in jail, and oh, how it had sucked. Thank goodness she'd sweet-talked the young guy behind the desk into letting her use the ladies' room down the hall because that toilet…

She eyed it with disgust. God help her if Deputy Hot Stuff Sampson were to come back and catch her with her pants down. No way. She'd sooner wet her pants. Almost.

"Ugh," she groaned out loud. Her head throbbed and her back ached. Spray painting the Halverson Foods chicken processing plant was officially her worst idea ever. And assuming she got her ass bailed out of here before lunchtime, she was scheduled to work the afternoon shift at the Main Street Café.

Yep, she had learned her lesson. Big-time. No more breaking the law. She just needed to get out of here and find a way to put this whole thing behind her.

"Mornin', sunshine," came a low, male voice.

She squinted up at Deputy Hot Stuff himself and…ah, Jesus, her head.

"Sleep well?" he asked as the cell door clanged open.

"Just peachy." She sat up and rubbed her eyes.

He set two aspirin and a paper cup filled with water beside her.

"Oh, my God, thank you. I take back all the awful things I thought about you last night." She swallowed the aspirin and gulped the water greedily.

"Awful things, huh?" He didn't look like he'd been home—or slept—since last night either. His cheeks had darkened with stubble, and his eyes were weary.

"All forgotten." She leaned her head against the wall and looked at him. It hurt to focus her eyes, but no, her perception hadn't been altered by the margaritas. Pete Sampson was one fine-looking officer of the law.

He stood tall and strong, with olive skin, brown hair cut short and neat, and eyes as dark as coal. If he hadn't been the one to throw her in jail, she'd have definitely tried to get his number—or rather, get him to ask for hers.

He stepped back and motioned her to follow. She stifled another groan as she stood. Every bone and muscle in her body ached. And her head felt like someone was in there with an ice pick chiseling away at the backs of her eyes.

She gazed longingly at the ladies' room as he guided her down the hall, and he stopped with a sigh.

"Go on. Five minutes to freshen up. Don't make me wait."

"Thank you," she whispered, and darted inside. She made quick use of the facilities, then splashed cold water on her face and rinsed out her mouth. It wasn't much, but she felt slightly rejuvenated when she rejoined him in the hall.

He led her next door to the courthouse but stopped her outside the courtroom. He turned those ebony eyes on hers. "Let's get one thing clear before we go in there. I can't charge you with DUI since I didn't catch you behind the wheel, but unless you want to tell me who was out there with you last night, I'm left to assume you drove yourself. You ever have to walk up to someone's front door and tell them their loved one is dead? Killed by a drunk driver?"

Jesus Christ. "No."

"If I ever catch you driving under the influence, I will throw the book at you. Are we clear?"

Fall in Love with Forever Romance

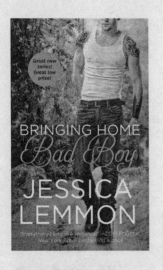

BRINGING HOME THE BAD BOY
by Jessica Lemmon

The boys are back in town! Welcome to Evergreen Cove and the first book in Jessica Lemmon's Second Chance series, sure to appeal to fans of Jaci Burton. These bad boys will leave you weak in the knees and begging for more.

HOT AND BOTHERED
by Kate Meader

Just when you thought it couldn't get any hotter! Best friends Tad and Jules have vowed not to ruin their perfect friendship with romance, but fate has other plans...Fans of Jill Shalvis won't be able to resist the attraction of Kate Meader's Hot in the Kitchen series.

Fall in Love with Forever Romance

FOR KEEPS
by Rachel Lacey

Merry Atwater would do anything to save her dog rescue—even work with the stubborn and sexy TJ Jameson. But can he turn their sparks into something more? Fans of Jill Shalvis and Kristan Higgins will fall in love with the next book in the Love to the Rescue series!

BLIND FAITH
by Rebecca Zanetti

The third book in *New York Times* bestseller Rebecca Zanetti's sexy romantic suspense series features a ruthless, genetically engineered soldier with an expiration date who's determined to save himself and his brothers. But there's only one person who can help them: the very woman who broke his heart years ago...

Fall in Love with Forever Romance

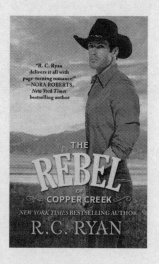

"R. C. Ryan delivers it all with page-turning romance!"
—NORA ROBERTS, *New York Times* bestselling author

THE REBEL OF COPPER CREEK
by R. C. Ryan

Fans of *New York Times* best-selling authors Linda Lael Miller and Diana Palmer will love this second book in R. C. Ryan's western trilogy about a young widow whose hands are full until she meets a sexy and rebellious cowboy. If there's anything she's learned, it's that love only leads to heartbreak, but can she resist him?

NEVER SURRENDER
TO A SCOUNDREL
by Lily Dalton

Fans of *New York Times* bestsellers Sabrina Jeffries, Nicole Jordan, and Jillian Hunter will want to check out the newest from Lily Dalton, a novel about a lady who has engaged in a reckless indiscretion leaving her with two choices: ruin her family with the scandal of the season, or marry the notorious scoundrel mistaken as her lover.